LIFE DELUXE

Also by Jens Lapidus

Easy Money

Never Screw Up

LIFE DELUXE

JENS LAPIDUS

Translated from the Swedish by Astri von Arbin Ahlander

MACMILLAN

First published in Sweden 2011 as *Livet Deluxe*
by Wahlström & Widstrand, Stockholm.

First published in English in 2014 by Pantheon Books
a division of Random House, Inc. New York

First published in the UK 2014 by Macmillan
an imprint of Pan Macmillan, a division of Macmillan Publishers Limited
Pan Macmillan, 20 New Wharf Road, London N1 9RR
Basingstoke and Oxford
Associated companies throughout the world
www.panmacmillan.com

ISBN 978-1-4472-5642-7

Translated from the Swedish by Astri von Arbin Ahlander

1 3 5 7 9 8 6 4 2

A CIP catalogue record for this book is available from the British Library.

Printed and bound by CPI Group (UK) Ltd, Croydon, CR0 4YY

For Jack and Flora

"You West Side. You musta heard of Charlie Sollers, right?"

"No."

"Goes all the way back to Franklin and Fremont. I mean all the way back to the sixties and shit."

"Sollers?"

"Sold heroin like it was water. I mean, the motherfucker made himself some money."

"I don't know who the fuck you are talking about."

"I know you don't. And the police don't. And the stick-up boys wouldn't have a fucking clue either. 'Cause Charlie Sollers just sold dope. No profile. No street rep. Just buy for a dollar, sell for two."

—PROPOSITION JOE TALKING TO STRINGER BELL
***THE WIRE*, SECOND SEASON**

LIFE DELUXE

PROLOGUE

It was the second time in my life that I visited Stockholm for a job.

The first time I was here for a wedding, as a bodyguard for one of the guests. That was seventeen years ago, and I was young then. I remember how I looked forward to the day after, when I could party in Stockholm and bed some blondes. The wedding itself was a large affair compared to the ones in my home country. They said it was considered big even for Sweden—there were maybe three hundred guests. And sure, it was grand. The newlyweds emerged from the church dressed in winter furs. They had a small child too, a pretty girl, who was also wearing a fur. The bridal couple were driven from the church in a sled pulled by four white horses. Their little girl stood with her nanny on the church steps and waved. The air was clean, the snow glittered, and the sky was clear. I remember what I thought at the time: that Sweden must be the cleanest country in the world. Then I saw the guests' faces. Some showed joy and others admiration. But they all expressed one thing: respect.

The man who was married then was the person I was here to take care of now: Radovan Kranjic. Fateful irony, to have seen the beginning of the new life that I was now going to end.

I usually don't let myself feel. No, I kill myself before every mission. I am hired, paid, independent—there is nothing personal about what I do. But to come to Stockholm this time around gave me a sense of completion, somehow.

The circle would be closed. A kind of balance would be restored.

And then something happened.

I'd been staking out in the Volvo all day. When I returned to my room, I decided to clean my handguns. I'd purchased them in Denmark, where I have connections—after the Americans' so-called war on terrorism, I don't pack heat when traveling into the EU anymore.

I had an Accuracy International L96AI—a finer-grade sniper rifle—and a Makarov gun. I took them apart and laid them on a cover on the bed, clean and gleaming. I was holding the final weapon, a revolver, in my hand.

That was when the door opened.

I realized that I'd forgotten to lock it, like I normally always do.

It was a housekeeper. I wondered what kind of crap hotel I was staying at, anyway, where the staff didn't knock before entering.

She stared at my weapons for a few seconds. Then she apologized and began to back out into the hallway.

But it was too late—she'd already seen too much. I rose, raised the revolver, and asked her to step into the room.

She looked terrified. Understandably—that was my intention, after all. I told her to pull the cleaning cart with her into the room as well, and then I closed the door behind her. I kept my weapon aimed at her the entire time. Then I had her clean my room.

It took her max ten minutes—it was obvious that she was a pro. She vacuumed the small floor area, wiped off all surfaces, and washed the sink and toilet. It was important to me that it was done thoroughly.

Meanwhile I packed my bag.

When she was finished, I asked her to look out into the hallway and see if anyone was out there. It was empty. I pushed her in front of me out into the hallway and told her to unlock the door to another room. She chose one that was two doors down.

We entered it. The room was messy. The person staying there apparently took pleasure in torturing hotel housekeepers.

I closed the door.

She looked at me.

I held up a pillow.

Then I raised the revolver and shot her through the pillow. In the eye.

PART ONE

1

The strip club on Roslagsgatan'd been rented out. Jorge eyed the place: red spotlights in the ceiling, velvet armchairs on the floor, and neon Heineken ads on the walls. Round tables with candle wax stains, beer stains—he didn't want to guess what other kinds of stains. A bar along one side of the room, a DJ in one corner, a small stage along the other side. The strip pole was still chick-free. But behind the bar: four babes flaunting more skin than clothes were pouring out bubbly. Soon they'd be boa-constricting themselves around the pole. Baring it all for the bros.

The feel of the place wasn't exactly mad deluxe. But who gave a fuck—the crowd made the mood. Jorge recognized alotta faces. Had arrived at the joint with his cousin Sergio and his buddy Javier. He saw Mahmud farther in among the armchairs—*hermano* was sipping a glass of Moët. Bonding with his own buddies: Tom Lehtimäki, Rob, Denko, Birra.

Jorge nodded at Mahmud, winked. Signaled: *I see you, bro.* They needed to talk about tomorrow. J-boy could hardly wait. Something big might be in the works. A step back into G-life. Away from M-life. M as in muffins.

Jorge'd slept like shit last night. The whole thing: like Agent Smith against Neo. Darkness squaring off against the light. The Sven life wore him down. *The dark side.* At the same time, the thing they were gonna go see about—superfly. The good side would be given the chance—if they just made it to that meeting tomorrow, everything would work out.

Maybe.

"Yo, Shawshank!"

Jorge glanced to the side.

Babak was coming toward him. Open arms—fake smile. The Iranian hugged him. Pounded him on the back. Cut him with verbal knives. "How's the café, bro? You sure the margins ain't better on kebab than coffee?"

Jorge pulled his head back. Eyed the guy from a foot's distance. Offered his gift: a bottle of Dom Pérignon 2002—apparently fancy as fuck.

Babak: Mahmud's oldest homie. Babak: Iranian dealer guru with mad pussy juju and thick project bijoux—that's how he saw himself, anyway. Babak had made the climb that Jorge'd once planned to make. Stolen the path that'd been paved for him. Started off down on the street, working corners. Learned the game. Understood the hood—how regular ghetto hustlers'd started using as much as the slickest Stureplan snobs, but with a dozen zeros added on. Figured the future. Blow today: more common with kids in their twenties than weed with the teens.

Could've been Jorge's game. His jam. But it didn't work out that way.

And today the Iranian was treating all his boys to a night out, at a club. Party with strippers, champagne, and free beer in the bar. Jorge'd been given the invite from one of Babak's underlings. Printed in Gothic lettering: CELEBRATE LIKE A REAL BANDIT! I'M TURNING 25 AND TREATING YOU TO BUBBLES, BITCHES, AND BUFFET. THE RED LIGHT CLUB ON ROSLAGSGATAN. COME AS YOU ARE.

Babak's attitude: irritating like a mosquito bite on your ass. The glitter in the Iranian's eye. His tone of voice: like being spit in the face. The little clown knew that Jorge and Mahmud slaved away every day like Romanian whores on a Saturday night. Knew they didn't flip even half as much paper in a month as he did in a week. Knew the Yugos were sucking extra cash out of them for their protection. Certain: he knew the tax man was chasing them with a blowtorch. A hundred percent: Cunt-Babak clocked that café life wasn't cutting it for J-boy.

What Jorge couldn't understand was why Mahmud didn't just break his nose and then their friendship. It was all kinds of fucked up.

But wackest of all was what Babak'd just called him: Shawshank. That name . . . honestly, Jorge couldn't take it. Shawshank—what bullshit. Babak was beating on a broken brother. Pushed the knife in further for an extra twist, sprinkled chili on his wounds.

It had been almost five years since Jorge'd broken out of the Österåker Pen. Sure, a lot of *blattes* out there'd heard his story a thousand times. A legend among the ants in the public housing hill. A story you dreamed about when the cement in the cell walls threatened to suffocate you.

But also, just like all stories: the boys out there knew how it ended. The Latino, the legend, J-boy, Shawshank—been forced to crawl back in. Like a loser. Freedom, *adiós*. It was a shitty story.

And Babak never missed a chance to remind him.

A couple of BMC guys were hanging out in the bar: leather vests like black uniforms. One percent tags, MC Sweden badges, and the Fat Mexican on their chests and backs. Tattoos on their necks, forearms, around their eyes. Jorge knew a few of those hustlers. Not exactly café owners, but nice enough. But he knew what the nine-to-fivers thought when they saw those guys. As if it were written with flashing letters on their vests—one feeling: fear.

He shook Babak.

Farther in by the side of the stage he saw the cousins and relatives. Small, downy-lipped Babak clones. For them, being at the same party as half of Bandidos MC Stockholm was like being at an ill celebrity throwdown.

One dude started walking toward Jorge. Silhouette: like a monkey. Overly broad shoulders, arms that reached far down on his thighs. The guy: Anabola-beefy, but he'd apparently forgotten about his legs—they stuck out at the bottom like two snort straws.

It was Peppe. A pen pal from Österåker.

Jorge hadn't seen him since.

Peppe was wearing a vest. On the left side of his chest: the word *Prospect*. He was obviously becoming big time.

"Yo, my brotha!" They embraced. Jorge was careful not to touch the vest with his hands. Unnecessary to mess with the rules of the one percenters.

"What's up, ma brotha? You getting pussy these days?" Peppe said.

The guy was probably a racist to the core, but still—his Million Program Swedish was tight. Jorge laughed. The dude still had the same sense of humor.

Jorge responded, "It happens, ma brotha, it happens." He pronounced *ma brotha* the same way as Peppe. And then he said, "I see you got yourself a vest."

"Fuck man, you know how much pussy I get with this thing? It's crazy, man."

"What, you keep the vest on?"

Peppe: poker face.

Jorge was about to say something. Stopped. Eyed Peppe. The guy was glaring at him.

Finally, "Don't joke about the vest."

Jorge didn't give a fuck. Some dudes took their colors too seriously.

But after ten seconds, Peppe grinned again. "Leather in the sack isn't my thing. But you tried handcuffs? Real nice, man."

They laughed together.

His Bandidos buddy changed the subject, kept letting his mouth run. Smart schemes in the construction business. Tax fraud, invoice forgeries, under-the-table pay. Jorge nodded along. It was interesting. It was important. He even thought about asking Peppe for help with the Yugos. At the same time, he knew the rules: everyone takes care of their own shit.

And the entire time: he couldn't stop thinking about tomorrow.

Tomorrow.

Jorge downed his glass of champagne.

The day after. Bag-feeling under his eyes. Hangover pounding through his head. Breath like a turd dipped in lighter fluid. Still: a kind of relaxation. With his best friend, Mahmud. On their way to Södertälje. On their way to what might be the most important meeting in J-boy's life.

It was two-thirty in the afternoon. Him and the Arab in their car. Or really: the car was owned by their café company. One of the advantages: so much shit that could be bought on the company dollar. Cell phones, computers, DVDs, 3D WiFi Full LED TVs. Like, everything—that's what they thought, anyway. But as it turned out, that's not what the tax man thought.

They were on their way to something big. The big thing at the top of the criminal hierarchy. The concrete was crawling with success stories: the Hallunda coup, the Arlanda heist, the helicopter robbery. And everyone knew that not alotta people were in the know about the planning, that only a few people were sitting on the recipes. But Jorge'd gotten an in.

And that was who they were gonna go see now. Someone who knew how it was done. A brain.

It'd started to rain, winter was losing its grip.

Mahmud turned the seat-heater off. "My balls get too hot, man. You can go sterile and shit."

"What, babydaddy, you got plans? Who you gonna knock up? Beatrice?"

Mahmud turned around. "Beatrice is good at selling lattes, but she'd probably be a worthless mom."

"Fuck, *hermano*, she ain't good at selling coffee either. We should hire someone new."

"Yeah, but no one too fine. Can't deal with that."

They drove past IKEA on their left. Jorge thought of his sister. Paola loved IKEA. She tried to decorate at home. Put up bookshelves that were impossible to figure out and took ages to screw together, nailed framed posters on the Sheetrock walls where the hooks always fell out after a few hours. Build a life. Blend in. But where did she really think it would get her? Trying to be a Sven wouldn't make her a Swede.

She was naïve. Still: Jorge loved her and Jorgito like crazy.

Mahmud was blabbering on about Babak's party the night before. Which one of the strippers'd had it poppin'. If Rob or Tom'd scored. If Babak or Peppe'd raked in the most dough. Jorge didn't have the energy to listen to him—his constant worship of the Iranian.

Outside the window: the Tumba commuter rail station. A sign hung over the road: ALBY. Mahmud turned around again. "Those are my hoods, over there. You know that."

"You fucking with me, man? You've got Alby inked over half your body. 'Course I know."

"And now we're going to Södertälje. That's almost my hood too."

"You been there before—so what?"

"What if I know this dude we're seeing?"

"I don't think so. Denny calls him the Finn. You don't know any Finns other than Tom Lehtimäki, right?"

"No, but maybe he's not a Finn. Maybe he's from south of the city. You know, alotta shit went down a few years ago. The gang war against Eddie Ljublic and his people. So if the Finn's from here, maybe he was involved. Then it's a fifty-fifty chance he was on the wrong side. With the cunts."

"What you mean, fifty-fifty? The risk is much lower than that."

"Yeah, but still not. Either he was with the cunts or he wasn't—there are two alternatives. It's one or the other, that's fifty-fifty. So I think you can say it's fifty percent chance."

Jorge grinned. "*Eres loco, hermano.*"

At the same time, the questions were piling up in his head. Who was it they were gonna go see? How did they know he wasn't some pig infiltrator? Were they gonna make a deal with him? And if not, what were they gonna do about the tax man and the Yugos? The Swedish government and the underworld's government were about to gang-bang the shit out of the café.

The car's heat vents were spurting sound. The windshield wipers were squeaking.

Maybe: on their way to the biggest gig ever.

Maybe: on their way to a fresh start.

Twenty minutes later. Södertälje. More like a suburb to Stockholm than like a city in its own right. The two of them took turns going there every other morning. The place where left-wing extremists burned down grocery stores, housing project teens shot at the police station with assault rifles, the X-team warred against the Syrian brotherhood, and the industrial bakeries baked the fluffiest ciabatta north of Italy. The city from which Suryoyo TV and Suryoyo Sat broadcast all over the world, the place that was actually called Little Baghdad.

Södertälje: where it was rumored that over half of all CIT robberies in Sweden were planned.

They parked in a parking garage behind the pedestrian street in the center of town.

Mahmud pulled out a steering wheel lock.

"What're you doing?" Jorge asked.

"This is Södertälje, man. Every other kid born here is a soccer pro, and the rest are car thieves."

"Yeah, but we go here every day."

"But not *here* here. Not downtown."

Jorge grinned. "I think you're a little jumpy, buddy. We're in a parking garage."

They got out. Walked down to Storgatan. The weather still sucked. All around: mostly old people, kids, and mustachioed men drinking tea in the cafés.

Mahmud pointed at the old men. "That's what my dad looks like."

Jorge nodded. Knew: if Mahmud got going, he could talk for hours about how Sven Sweden'd betrayed his old man. How Beshar first hadn't gotten a job, lived on welfare, then got a job—a job that fucked up his back so bad, he had to go on disability for the rest of his life. His buddy was right, but Jorge didn't have the energy to listen.

They veered onto a side street off Storgatan.

Jorge's phone rang.

Paola: "It's me. *Que haces, hermano?*"

Jorge thought: *Should I tell her the truth?*

He said, "I'm in Södertälje."

"At a bakery?"

Paola: J-boy loved her. Still, he couldn't take it.

He said, "Yeah, yeah, 'course I'm at a bakery. But we gotta talk later—I got my hands full of muffins here."

They hung up.

Mahmud glanced at him.

Up ahead, the place where they were going: Gabbe's Pizzeria.

A bell rang when they opened the door. A dank pizza place. One wall was exposed brick; the other had a poster tacked to it: NEW: MEXICAN TACO PIZZAS. Jorge thought: *Yeah right, real new. That ad must've been there since the nineties.*

There were old ladies' magazines and tabloids on the tables. It was four o'clock. The place was completely empty.

A man emerged from the kitchen. Flour-stained apron, T-shirt with red lettering: GABBE'S DOES IT BETTER. Two fat gold link chains hung from his neck.

Jorge winked at the pizza baker. "Vadúr sent me."

The dude stared at them. Mahmud squirmed anxiously behind Jorge. The pizza baker disappeared back into the room behind the counter. Spoke quietly with someone, or into a phone. Came back out. Nodded.

They walked out the back of the store. A black Opel. Jorge quickly sized up the car: the passenger seat and the backseat were filled with pizza boxes. The pizza guy climbed in behind the wheel. Jorge and Mahmud had to squeeze in with the cardboard in the back. They rolled away from downtown. Past the mall, the district court, the parking lots. Outside the city: the Million Program high-rises coiled like mountain ranges—same scenery as his home turf.

So far the pizza baker hadn't said a word to them.

Mahmud leaned close to Jorge, whispered in his ear: "That player's gonna drown. Look how much he weighs."

Jorge whispered back, "What, why?"

"The gold he's got 'round his neck's gotta weigh more than a bowling ball. If homeboy doesn't watch himself next time he's cooking up red sauce, he'll fall in and never come back up."

Jorge almost laughed. The fact that Mahmud was joking felt good, cut the stiff air a little. Really, there wasn't anything to be afraid of today. If it worked, it worked. That's all there was to it.

They got out by a high-rise.

The pizza baker pressed the button for the elevator. They waited. The metal doors squeaked. Carvings with tags, telephone numbers to alleged hookers, Arabic curses.

They rode up. Jorge almost got that dropping sensation in his stomach, like you get in very fast elevators. The sixth floor. They stepped out. The guy fished out a set of keys. Unlocked a door. Jorge managed to glimpse the name on the mail slot: EDEN. It felt like a sign.

The apartment looked empty. No clothes, no hangers, no shoes or shoe racks. No carpets, mirrors, dressers. Just a single bare bulb suspended from the ceiling in the entranceway. The pizza baker gestured: *I have to frisk you.*

Jorge looked at Mahmud. *Hombre* didn't look so jokisimo anymore. Now they just had to go with the flow.

Rapid, light movements: a pro.

The pizza guy gestured again: *You can go in.*

Jorge walked first. Short, silent steps. A hallway. Gray walls. Bad lighting. They reached a larger room. Three chairs were set up inside.

The dude left them alone. Another man entered the room.

He was wearing black jeans, a dark hoodie, and a ski mask pulled down over his face.

The man said, "Welcome, have a seat."

The chairs creaked. Jorge took a deep breath.

The man spoke perfect Swedish.

"You can call me the Finn. And you, Jorge Salinas Barrio, did time with my buddy Denny Vadúr. So I've got reason to trust you. Vadúr and me, we go way back."

"Denny's an all-star," Jorge said.

The dude was silent for a moment. Then he said, "Yes, he's nice. But he isn't an all-star—those are your words. He talks too much. And he made a fool of himself last time. Well, you know where you met him. He tried to do his own thing. That's what happens when you try to fly solo. But with me, it's different."

It sounded like the Finn was eating something—he kept smacking his mouth at the end of every sentence.

Jorge waited for more.

"You've sought me out because you want a recipe," the Finn said.

"Yes."

"That's not the kind of thing I just give away. You understand that, right?"

"Of course, it costs."

"That's right, it costs. But that's not all. It's about the right feeling too. I have to trust everyone involved one hundred percent. Let me put it this way: I deal in planning. I sell designs. Recipes. But no design works, no matter how good, if the right people aren't involved. It's a whole, the sum of many parts. Do you understand?"

Jorge nodded, but didn't say anything. Unsure if he was understanding fully.

"You might be right for this. You could be the parts that make up the whole."

Jorge and Mahmud didn't dare interrupt.

The dude kept smacking with his mouth. "I want you to get five guys you trust. And they can't be idiots. I want a list of their names and personal identification numbers. Handwritten."

Jorge waited to see if the guy had more to say. The Finn was silent.

Finally Jorge said, "No problem, we got that."

"And that's not all. Do you know what else you need?"

Silence again. Jorge didn't know what to say. This whole situation: shady. This wasn't how he'd thought it would go down. He'd expected a guy like him, a couple years older maybe: some concrete hustler who was livin' large. A self-made G. A man who'd leaned back—let others do the dirty work. But this whole deal with the ski mask and the fancy talk—fine, maybe people wanted to hide their identities, but this seemed more Hollywood than reality.

At the same time, Jorge knew: it was real. He'd heard stories in the pen, in Sollentuna, from his homies, and from his homies' homies: the guys who sat on the recipes were serious. Meticulous. Cautious in the extreme.

Mahmud glared at Jorge. He had to say something now.

"There's a lot we need," he responded. "We need good planning. We need good organization."

The Finn played the ball right back to him. "That's correct. But listen and learn. Here is my first piece of advice. No big-scale gig has ever succeeded without someone on the inside. You need an insider—that is the founding principle of any heist. Someone who's in the know about—and preferably has access to—the CIT in question. I've planted people like that for years now."

Jorge could muster only one word: "Damn."

"You might say that. The one I've been in touch with for the longest time has worked for over seven years in the security guard industry. He's entrusted with all kinds of assignments. So if we're gonna do something, we're gonna go big."

Jorge couldn't stop smiling inside. This was so huge. This was the beginning of the end of his time as a café owner. The beginning of the end as a blackmailed pauper. *El grande* muffin massacre.

He saw images in his mind. Ski masks. Dark security bags. Stacks of five-hundred kronor bills.

He saw easy money.

2

Deputy Inspector Martin Hägerström drove Sturegatan down toward Stureplan. The suit-people on the streets were on their way to their banks and law firms. They were correctly dressed, well combed, appropriately stressed out. Some were leaning forward slightly, as though they were chasing something in life and needed to reach to get there. At the same time, Hägerström was aware of the fact that he was generalizing—he knew too many suit-suckers personally to actually believe that their lives were only about chasing money. His brother Carl, who was three years younger, worked around three hundred feet from here. His future brother-in-law worked here. Many of his old friends hung out in this neighborhood.

But the morning was no time for deeper reflection, so Hägerström allowed himself to simplify reality.

It wasn't difficult to succumb to bad thoughts at this time of day. And it wasn't difficult to predict which two tracks his bad thoughts would take.

Four months had passed since his father Göran's funeral, and seven months had passed since he fell ill.

And it had been one year, three months, and fourteen days since Pravat was taken from him. He counted every hour like an atomic clock. The images in his head were as clear as if it had happened yesterday. The way Anna had slammed the door and walked away with Pravat in hand. How furious Hägerström had been, but how he hadn't wanted Pravat to see him lose control. How she had been completely calm.

Now, in retrospect, it was almost scary to think how structured Anna's actions had been. He had waited in the apartment for two hours, calmed down a little. Then he started calling. But she didn't pick up, and she didn't come back. He had called the day-care center and her sister. He had called her friends in Saltjöbaden. But he couldn't find out where she had gone. Where she had taken Pravat. Then, almost a week later, he was able to get some information. Pravat was in an apartment on Lidingö. Anna had signed a lease on it in secret two months ago. Pravat was going to eat his snacks on Lidingö, sleep in his little bed on Lidingö, had apparently gotten a spot at a day-care on fucking Lidingö.

One year, three months, fourteen days.

They said he only had himself to blame. In the beginning, he had begged and pleaded: "Come back, come home, please." She ignored him. Hung up when he called, didn't respond to his texts, e-mails, or Facebook messages. It took another week before she chose to respond. At that point, she had already started getting Pravat used to the new day-care center.

The paper war took over. Lawyers, mediation meetings, court documents. Meaningless attempts to try to make her understand. You can't just separate a child from his father without *a reason*. A child needs both his parents. She didn't care—there *were* reasons, that's what her lawyer claimed in writing. There were people who were not suited to be parents. People who never should have been allowed to adopt a child. According to the lawyer, Hägerström had acted extremely irresponsibly when he had taken part in a police operation with Pravat in the backseat. Hägerström knew that it had been an idiotic thing to do. But he was still a good father. And his son should be allowed to see him more than a few measly days a month.

He drove up to the police building on Kungsholmen. The area outside the main entrance was crowded with motorcycles. Men with bikes were definitely overrepresented among Stockholm's finest.

Kronoberg: Stockholm police headquarters. A large building—so many hallways, interrogation rooms, and coffee break nooks that he didn't even know about half of them. He nodded to the guard in the main entranceway while he slid his key card through the reader and followed the automatic turnstile inside. His office was on the fifth floor.

It was eight o'clock. He looked at himself in the mirror on the elevator ride up. His side part was a little tousled and his face was pale. He thought the wrinkles on his cheeks had deepened since yesterday.

Room 547: his world. Messy as usual, but for Hägerström there was an internal order that was invisible to others. His former colleague, Thomas Andrén, used to say that you could hide a motorcycle in there, and not even the technicians from the forensic lab would be able to find it. Maybe there was something to it. Not a motorcycle but possibly a mountain bike. Hägerström grinned to himself—the strange thing was that, at home, an anal, German style of order ruled.

Along one wall was a bookshelf filled with books, newspapers, and above all, binders. Next to the bookshelf were piles of bursting file folders. The rest of the floor was covered in preliminary investigations, incident reports, seizure reports, informational material, and reconnaissance reports, with or without plastic sleeves. The desk was cluttered with similar stuff. It was also covered in coffee mugs, half-drunk bottles of mineral water, and Post-it notes. There were thirty-odd pens in a pile right in front of the computer screen. There was a framed photo of Pravat in the middle of the chaos, and up against it Hägerström had recently propped another photograph. It was a photo of Father wearing a summer shirt, linen pants, and loafers without socks, taken ten years ago out at Avesjö.

The pens and the photos—the pillars on which his work rested. He needed his pens—going through things over and over again was his method. He marked up the material, underlined, drew arrows, and scribbled notes in the margins. Fit one piece of the puzzle to the next.

And the photographs: he thought about Pravat all the time. The photo gave him strength. He thought about Father alarmingly seldom. Maybe the photograph would serve to remind him to do so more often.

Fika, the ceaseless coffee break his Swedish countrymen so loved, was going on in the *fika* room. Hägerström could hear his colleagues' voices from a distance. Micke was making gay jokes as usual. Isak was laughing too loudly as usual. He remembered what Father used to say about the coffee breaks: "*Fika*—that's what they call it in the public sector, right? You *fika* more than you work, don't you?"

His father had always been an inveterate enemy of what he called the "Titanic sector." But not even Father thought the police force ought to be privatized. And what's more, Hägerström was convinced that there would be just as much *fika*-time if some venture capitalist bought the whole mess. Cops have coffee pumping through their veins—it's in their genes.

But maybe he was more affected by Father's attitude than he wanted to be, because he usually skipped the coffee breaks. There was hardly enough time to get everything done as it was.

A knock at his door.

Cecilia Lennartsdotter poked her head in.

"Martin, why don't you come have a cup of coffee?"

Hägerström looked up at her. She was wearing her holster and service weapon even though she was here, inside. And she had even strapped an extra magazine to her belt. For the hundredth time, he wondered if Cecilia really thought things were going to escalate up here on the fifth floor—maybe one of the secretaries would get it into her mind to rob the fridge?

There were always colleagues who overdid it. But then, maybe everyone here overdid it. He had nothing against Lennartsdotter. Actually, he liked her.

"No, unfortunately, I don't have time today," he said.

"As usual, then? You work while the rest of us have a good time."

"Yes, as usual."

She winked at him.

Hägerström turned back to his keyboard. Pretended that he didn't understand that she was joking.

The hours ticked on. Hägerström was working on a preliminary investigation regarding a serious narcotics case. Amphetamines had been smuggled in from Estonia in the double-welded floors of minivans. Seven suspects had been detained for five months. Been interrogated a total of four hundred hours. There were thousands of pages to go through. Some of the suspects were mules, some of them were dealers, and one was the brain behind the smuggling operation. Now they just had to determine who was who.

His phone rang. A phone number that Hägerström didn't recognize.

"Good morning. This is Inspector Lennart Torsfjäll."

Hägerström reacted immediately when he heard the name. Detective Inspector Torsfjäll was a hotshot. A supercop. A legend in the force, known from several massive operations. But according to certain rumors, Torsfjäll's work methods weren't always completely kosher. Apparently, he had been transferred due to differences of opinion with the county police chief regarding certain operations. The inspector hadn't just given orders as to where and how his troops were to make the hit—he'd also commanded how much violence they were to use.

And in most cases, the orders had been clear enough: collar suspects as quickly and as roughly as possible.

He was working on something else nowadays. Hägerström didn't know what exactly.

An hour later he was standing outside the door to Torsfjäll's office. The inspector had asked him to come immediately.

Torsfjäll didn't have his office on Polhemsgatan, where all the other hotshots were. He also wasn't to be found at one of the other ordinary police stations in the district. The office was situated in a much more humble space—Torsfjäll carried on in the building reserved for the department in charge of the service of process. Serving defendants their processes: after the seizure department, it was probably the dullest, least sexy thing a cop could do. But Hägerström suspected that he was actually involved in more sophisticated business.

He had no idea what Torsfjäll wanted from him. But asking him to come here had not been a question. It had been an order.

He knocked on the door and stepped inside.

Inspector Torsfjäll's room looked like a museum. Or rather, more like a kitschy art gallery. He had framed and hung every single diploma and every single course certificate and credential he had ever received. There was a diploma from the Police Academy, anno 1980, a certificate from a shooting test, a coat of arms from the Norrmalm's SWAT team dated 1988, a certificate for a number of courses in criminology taken at Stockholm University, courses in DNA-search and wiretapping techniques, leadership distinctions, the public prosecutor's police courses parts one to five, certificates attesting to collaborations with Interpol, the State Police Department in Texas, and different police units within the EU.

Hägerström could come up with only one word to describe the room: *unpolicelike*. He wondered how Torsfjäll had had time to work these last twenty-five years. What's more, the inspector had hung up so many photos of children and grandchildren that you might get the idea that he was a Mormon.

Torsfjäll interrupted his staring. "Welcome. Please, have a seat. Aren't they cute?"

"Absolutely. How many are there?" Hägerström asked, even though he had already figured it out.

"Seven. And I've babysat them all."

"That's nice."

Hägerström sat down. The chair frame creaked when he leaned back.

Torsfjäll's desk was bare except for a file lying in front of him. Rays of sun were streaming in from the window. Not a single speck of dust gleamed in the light, Hägerström noted.

Torsfjäll opened the file in front of him on the desk. "I don't know how familiar you are with developments within organized crime in the Stockholm area today, so I thought I would go over some of the background information."

Hägerström looked him in the eyes. Still didn't understand where this was all going. But he didn't ask. Let Torsfjäll say what he wanted to say first.

The inspector began describing the reality in the city. He counted off numbers, statistics, theoretical truths. They'd made thirty hits against the new designer drug mephedrone just this winter. New gangs were being created in the projects faster than you could say *integration policy*. Internet fraud had risen 300 percent since the New Year alone.

Suddenly he fell silent. Hägerström waited for him to continue.

Torsfjäll smiled. Then he leaned forward over the desk and brushed Hägerström's arm. "Let me give you some more background information."

Hägerström felt his arm twitch, but he shut the feeling off so that it wouldn't show.

"Five years ago we made one of the biggest cocaine hits ever in Swedish history. Operation Snowstorm. Over two hundred and twenty pounds. Do you know how they'd smuggled that shit in?"

"Yes, I remember. They grew the drugs into vegetables."

"Good, good. You're familiar with the case. We pinched a couple of the guys who were involved. One is Mrado Slovovic, infamous hit man and midlevel boss in the so-called Yugo mafia, which is controlled by Radovan Kranjic. Another is Nenad Korhan, who was also part of Kranjic's network and active within the narcotics section of the operation. The third is named Abdulkarim Haij, an Arab who sold for the Yugoslavs. And then there was a strange bird too."

Hägerström interrupted him, "Johan Westlund, JW, the guy from up north who lived a double life. He was spared the murder charge, was convicted on aggravated drug charges."

Torsfjäll smiled his broadest smile yet. Hägerström thought it must be impossible for a human being to smile broader than that.

"You *are* good, Hägerström. How come you know these details?"

"The case interested me."

"Excellent. There's obviously nothing wrong with your memory either. So Johan Westlund was a very different kind of character. Maybe that's why he only got eight years. Considering the enormous amount of cocaine involved, he should've gotten fourteen, if you ask me. But the courts in this country are pussies. In reality, since he'll probably get released early, he won't end up with more than five years. He's being released on parole soon. At present, JW is serving his final months in the Salberga Penitentiary."

Hägerström tried to analyze what Torsfjäll was talking about, but he still didn't see how it was all connected to him.

Maybe Torsfjäll could tell what he was thinking by looking at him. He said, "Don't worry—soon you come in." He glanced down at the file on the desk.

"Hägerström, you are simply made for the operation I've been planning. I've looked through your history and your career. Let me explain. You grew up in a grand forty-three-thousand-square-foot apartment on swanky Östermalm. Your father was the CEO of Svenska Skogs AB, a successful company on the commodities market. Your mother was a physical therapist but comes from a wealthy background. Old money, as it's called. Landowning money, as I like to say. You have a brother who's a lawyer and a sister who's a real estate broker, but you chose a health care focus in high school at Östra Real. A solid family with predictable career choices, to put it simply. Except for yours."

Hägerström put one hand over the other. "I don't recall you saying this was a Stasi review."

Torsfjäll chortled. This time it seemed more genuine. "I understand if this seems strange. But there is a point, I promise. When you were a senior in high school, you were evaluated for your military service. You were in good shape already, after years of tennis training at the Royal Tennis Academy. But even with your background, your results were extraordinary. It was easy for you to be admitted as a coastal ranger in Vaxholm—you would've gotten in anywhere."

This run-through was feeling stranger and stranger. So far everything was true, even if it wasn't exactly like this stuff was confidential or anything. Though Hägerström was flattered, he wanted to know where this was going.

"You finished after two years with top marks," Torsfjäll continued. "In your final certificate I note the following statement, for instance."

The inspector flipped through the file. "'Martin Hägerström belongs to a small group of trained rangers who can be trusted with any kind of assignment, no matter the external circumstances or level of difficulty.'"

He grinned. "If I were you, I'd hang a recommendation like that on my wall."

Hägerström refrained from commenting.

Torsfjäll kept talking, "But then, you did something that wasn't exactly comme il faut in your family's circles. You applied to the Police Academy. Or rather, you were headhunted by the police. That was good for us. And now everyone says you will be made inspector any day. Not bad."

Torsfjäll obviously wanted to recruit him for something, since he was showering him with flattery. The inspector already seemed to know everything, even Martin's family's attitude toward the police profession.

"And in this context, there is one more thing about you that I'd like to mention. You have, I am sorry to say, gotten a divorce. And lost custody of your son. I am really very sorry. Some women are cunts."

Hägerström didn't know what to say. This entire conversation was strange: a summary of his life that mostly resembled a tribute. And now this stuff about Anna. Sure, she'd taken his son away from him, and that was unforgivable. But no one was going to call her a cunt.

Torsfjäll regarded Hägerström. "I may have used an inappropriate word. I apologize for that. But now I'm finally getting to the heart of things, so to speak. You are perfect for a job I have in mind. A special kind of operation, with permission from the feds."

"I suspected that you were going to say something like that."

Torsfjäll was sitting completely still now. Only a faint smile danced on his lips. His eyes did not radiate a speck of life—only his voice was human.

"I wonder if you want to become a UC operative."

Silence.

"Perhaps you can guess who it is I want you to approach?"

Hägerström waited. Sure, he had taken a course for undercover operatives, but only one. He had no idea whom Torsfjäll wanted him to approach. Then he thought about Torsfjäll's lengthy run-through. The way cocaine and amphetamines were routed into Sweden. The Yugo network, Radovan Kranjic—the godfather of godfathers. Hägerström didn't speak Serbian and wasn't well versed in their culture. Other names popped into his mind. Operation Snowstorm: one of the biggest hits in Swedish police history. Mrado Slovovic. Nenad Korhan. Abdulkarim Haij. The odd man out: Johan "JW" Westlund.

The pieces fell into place.

"You want me to approach JW," he said.

"Exactly. I want you to gather information from Johan Westlund and his circles."

"I understand. You think I'd be good for the job because JW played the part of a Stockholmer, even though he was actually from up north. You think I'd be good because my background conforms to JW's striving to rise among Stureplan's party crowd. You think he'll look up to me and that I'll be able to get under his skin. I just have one question: why exactly do you need an infiltrator?"

"It's not just any old infiltration operation," Torsfjäll responded. "We want you to start working in JW's unit as a corrections officer. The feds suspect that he's currently using one of the screws there, Christer Starre, as a mule somehow."

"You've given this some thought, I see."

"I give everything thought, always," the inspector responded, missing the irony in Hägerström's comment. "There is one more circumstance that makes you perfect."

"What's that?"

"You don't have any children—you're alone."

"That's incorrect. I have Pravat."

"I know. Of course you have Pravat, your adopted son. But not on paper. You don't have custody anymore. As far as the outside world is concerned, it appears as though you're single, without kids."

Torsfjäll fell silent. Hägerström wondered if he expected an answer right away.

The inspector crossed one leg over the other. "There's a war out there."

"No, there's no war."

For the first time during their conversation, Torsfjäll stopped smiling. "Why not?"

"Because war has an end," Hägerström said.

"You're absolutely right," Torsfjäll spoke slowly. "And that is exactly why you're perfect. No one is going to try to go after your son in the unlikely event that something goes wrong. No one can see that you have a son. We can't find anyone better than you. There is no one better than you."

3

Natalie was waiting with mixed emotions. Viktor was meeting Mom and Dad for the first time tonight. That was a big deal in and of itself—but almost the bigger deal was the fact that he was coming over to their house. To sit on their leather couches, look at the moldings in the ceiling and the busts that Dad'd had made of himself and Mom. He was going to sip their tea and probably be served *rakia*. He would eye Mom's potted plants and laugh at her framed picture of the king that was hanging in the guest bathroom, where the smell of air fresheners was so dense that you could hardly breathe.

But above all: the biggest deal was that Viktor was going to meet Dad.

Dad.

Natalie'd come home from Paris a few weeks before. She'd been there for six months. Studied French two days a week, and the rest of the time she'd worked in a restaurant that was owned by a friend of Dad's—working there had been better for her French than being in school. She felt more at home in a restaurant than in most other places. Dad'd been bringing her along to his joints since she was little. And at fifteen, she'd started working at different restaurants in Stockholm—not because she needed the money but because Dad thought it was important that she did right for herself. In the beginning, she waitressed mostly. But later she worked the bar and ran the cash register at the entrance to clubs. During the final years, she'd been head of the weekend staff at Clara's Kitchen & Bar. She knew that industry inside and out. But she didn't plan on staying in it forever.

She'd met Viktor a few months before she left for Paris. He was a good guy who knew half the city and had the right attitude about life. And he was hot. Sure, maybe he wasn't the love of her life—but this was the first time a boyfriend would be permitted to come for an audience. It was important that Dad and Mom learn that she could keep company.

Natalie walked out and met Viktor by the gate. He almost looked like a dwarf in the front seat of his X6. Just as he rolled up the driveway, a green Volvo crawled up behind him. For a brief second, she thought Viktor'd been stupid enough to bring a friend. But then the car disappeared off into the darkness of the street.

Parked in the garage were Dad's two cars, Mom's Renault Clio, and Natalie's own Golf that'd been a present on her eighteenth birthday. Viktor had to park outside in the driveway. The wheels crunched on the gravel. He lifted one hand from the wheel and waved to her.

Mom met them in the entranceway. She was dressed in a pair of black slacks and a sheer blouse from Dries Van Noten that was almost completely see-through. Her belt was from Gucci with a G-shaped buckle.

She approached Viktor. Put on her happiest face. Her broadest smile. Purred in her Serbian accent.

"Hi there, Viktor. It is nice to meet you. We hear soooo much about you."

She leaned forward. Her face against Viktor's face. Her mouth by Viktor's cheek. He hesitated for a second too long, unfamiliar with the greeting ceremony. But he got it at last. Almost kissed Mom the right way—it should've been two kisses on the right cheek, but it'd have to do.

They went into Dad's library.

Radovan was sitting in his leather armchair as usual. Dark blue blazer. Light corduroy pants. Gold cufflinks with the family's symbol on them—Dad'd designed it himself—a curlicue K with three royal crowns above it. Their family crest now.

There was dark wallpaper in the library. Bookshelves along the walls. On the walls, above the shelves: framed maps, paintings, and icons. Europe and the Balkans. The lovely blue Danube. The battle at Kosovo Polje. The Federal Republic of Yugoslavia. History's heroes. A portrait of Karađorđe. The holy Sava. Most of all—maps of Serbia and Montenegro.

Mom almost pushed Natalie into the room, one hand on her lower back. Dad rose when he saw Viktor.

"So, you're my daughter's boyfriend?" Dad shook his hand.

"Sweet library," Viktor said.

Radovan sat down in his armchair again. Didn't respond. Just picked up the bottle that was placed on the side table and poured out two glasses. *Rakia*—as expected.

"Have a seat. It'll be a little while before dinner is ready."

That was Dad's way of saying that Mom could go back out into the kitchen and continue prepping.

Viktor sat down in the other armchair. Straight-backed, almost leaning forward slightly. He looked attentive, ready.

Natalie turned around. Closed her eyes briefly.

Walked out.

Dad liked good food. He and Mom'd visited her in Paris over a long weekend. On Saturday they'd rented a car and driven to the Champagne district. In the afternoon they checked into a hotel in a small village with an authentic feel to it. A wooden reception desk, an old hotel porter in a white shirt and black vest with a broad moustache. The rooms were small with red wall-to-wall carpeting and creaky beds. The view: miles and miles of vineyards stretched out.

Dad'd knocked on the door and poked his head in. Said in Serbian, "Froggy. We're eating. I made a reservation eight weeks ago. The food is pretty good, I hear."

"Eight weeks ago? That sounds totally crazy."

"Hold that thought until you try the food." Dad smiled and winked at her.

Afterward Natalie looked up the restaurant. She found it in the *Guide Michelin*—it had three stars and was ranked as the best place in all of Champagne. Louise, who she shared an apartment with in Paris, just shrieked when she heard about it. "Oh my god! That's, like, so cool! Next time you just have to let me come."

Mom finished preparing the food. The meze dishes were served on square platters. *Burek*, *pečena*, sausage, the smoked, air-dried beef. The *kajmac*-cheese in a glass bowl. It smelled like *ajvar* and *vegeta* seasoning, but that was always the way Mom's food smelled. Natalie'd missed her cooking. In Paris, she hard-lined the LCHF diet—low carb high fat, which, in France, mostly meant *chèvre chaud* and lamb cutlets. It's not like Mom always cooked according to traditional recipes. She often used recipes from *The Naked Chef* or some health food cookbook. But when Dad ate with them, he wanted food that he was certain he would like.

Mom sent Natalie out to the dining room with napkins. White, pressed, with the family crest embroidered on them. They were to be folded like cones and placed in the crystal glasses, which also had the family crest engraved on them. She could do it blindfolded.

She went back into the kitchen.

"I'm so happy you're home again," Mom said.

"I know. You say that every day."

"Yes, but I feel it today especially, when we're cooking this kind of food and eating in the dining room and everything."

Natalie sat down on a stool. It had hinges in its middle so that it could be folded up to become a short ladder.

"Is he a good guy?" Mom asked.

"Viktor?"

"Yes, of course."

"He's okay. But we're not getting married or anything. And anyway, we can't talk about him now when he's here."

"He doesn't understand Serbian, does he? And you know we just want the best for you."

The door opened. Dad and Viktor walked into the kitchen.

Natalie tried to read Viktor's face.

A half an hour later. The meze plates'd been carried out. Natalie was helping Mom in the kitchen. The first half'd gone well. Viktor'd told them a little about himself: about his business with cars and boats. His plans for the future. It felt okay: Dad wasn't interrogating him Guantánamo style, took it easy instead. Mom mostly asked about his parents and siblings.

Viktor was a good talker. Natalie was usually impressed by him. That was one of the things she liked about Viktor—he could talk to anyone. It helped him in his business. And it helped him when he ended up in trouble. And it didn't hurt that he looked good—he was a beefier version of Bradley Cooper, one of her fave actors. She and he were suited for each other. They shared views on a lot of things: the need for a plush financial situation, an appropriate attitude toward strangers and the State, the right social circle. Viktor seemed like a guy on the rise—she hoped.

He prattled on. Fired off sharp comments about his business—stuff that, with any luck, would impress Dad. He tried to ask counterquestions, acted interested in Mom and Dad's newly remodeled kitchen, their summer home in Serbia, the nice silver cutlery with the family crest engraved on it—maybe he'd prepared.

The main course was served. Pork belly, onions, *sremska*, fried potatoes.

Radovan raised his wineglass. "Viktor, my friend. Do you know what the difference is between a Swedish and a Serbian pork belly?"

Viktor shook his head, tried to look genuinely interested.

"We don't put beer in our food."

"All right, but it looks good all the same."

"I can promise you that is it is. Because that's the way it is with us Serbs. We don't have anything against taking a shot or drinking fine alcohol. But we don't *need* it. It's not something we have to dump into every dish in order for it to taste good. Do you understand?"

Viktor kept his wineglass raised. "Sounds interesting."

Dad didn't say anything, but he kept holding his wineglass in his hand.

Natalie waited. Microseconds as long as minutes. She looked down at the pork belly.

Dad's voice broke the gridlock, "All right then, cheers. And once again, welcome to our home."

An hour and a half later. Dinner was over. The dessert: *baklava*, *schlag*, and cake'd been eaten. Coffee'd been drunk. The cognac, Hennessy XO: drained from the glasses.

It was time. Viktor's smile muscles were probably sore by now.

Natalie wanted to go out tonight. Maybe sleep over at Viktor's place after. Or rather: she would be allowed to leave with Viktor only if Dad was satisfied.

They rose from the table. Natalie eyed Dad the whole time. His dinosaur movements. Slow and goal-oriented, the head living a life of its own: it swung back and forth—right, left, left, right—even though the rest of the body was still. She tried to meet his eyes. Get a pleased expression. A wink. A nod.

Nothing. Why did he have to play this game?

They were standing in the hall, ready to put their jackets on. Their coats were hanging behind some drapery.

Natalie didn't plan on folding. If Dad didn't want her to go with Viktor, he'd have to say it straight out. Viktor's jacket rustled, a black North Face, so thick and downy that it could probably handle fifty below. Natalie slipped her feet into her Uggs. Then she put on her rabbit fur vest—it was warm, but probably not half as warm as Viktor's Michelin coat.

Mom prattled on: about what road was best for them to drive, when they were going to see each other tomorrow, how nice it'd been to meet Viktor.

Dad remained silent. He stood, just watching them. Waiting.

Viktor opened the door. Cold air blew in.

A car rolled past out on the street—it may have been the same green Volvo that she'd seen earlier.

They took a step out through the door. She was standing with her side to the door. Half her body in the light from home and the other half outside. She saw Dad out of the corner of her eye. She turned around. Looked at him head on.

"See you tomorrow," Mom said.

"I'll call. Love you," Natalie said.

Radovan took a step forward. He leaned out through the door. His torso out in the cold. A thin cloud of steam rose from his mouth.

"Viktor."

Viktor turned to him.

"Drive carefully," Dad said.

Natalie smiled inside. They walked toward Viktor's car.

The street was quiet.

4

Jorge was sitting in an armchair. Eyeing the place—his own digs. His café—*his*.

Him: a dude who ran this place.

Him: a dude who *owned* something.

At the same time: still shadyish.

Dig it. J-boy: Chillentuna's ghetto Latino *numero uno*, ex-coke king with a reputation—was sitting on an ordinary fucking business. Worked an ordinary fucking gig. Paid a protection fee like an ordinary fucking bar Sven.

He saw his face reflected in the windows facing out toward the street. The closely cropped, curly hair was smoothed back. The five o'clock shadow looked good. Dark, sharp, well-plucked eyebrows, but above them: wrinkles. He must've gotten those in the pen. Or else it was the sun in Thailand that'd carved the lines into his forehead.

He remembered what he'd looked like during the year after his prison break. The memory still made him grin. The escape with a capital E: a magical attack on the Swedish corrections machine, a *blatte* display with class, a clear signal to all the brothas on the inside: *Yes, we can.* Jorge Royale: the *blatte* who fucked the screws straight up the dirty, salsa-style. The homebody who busted out of Österåker with the help of a few bed sheets and a hook made from a basketball hoop. The *blatte* who'd disappeared without a trace. Slam dunk—took his bow and split. *Hasta luego*, Big Brother.

Back then: the man, the myth. The legend.

Nowadays: that was all a long time ago. He'd lived on the lam. Sweden's Most Wanted, like a fucking murderer. Remade himself. Rocked a new look—*el zambo macanudo*. Nigga Jorge in the free world. Tricked his old homeboys, tricked the pigs, tricked a whole bunch of family. But hadn't tricked the Yugos. Mrado Slovovic, Mr. R's piece-of-shit slugger, had found him, pounded him real good. But they didn't win. Jorge rose from the ashes and shook Stockholm like a storm.

And then: he'd jumped ship, gone to Thailand to get away from it all. But in the end, he came home again—he didn't really know why. Maybe it just got too boring.

The authorities collared him. What'd he expected? To live on the lam for the rest of his life? Only white-collar criminals and old Nazis who'd changed their names and bought houses in Buenos Aires did shit like that.

He checked into Kumla. A heavy penitentiary for bros with a taste for tunneling. Release on temporary license: forget about it. Release on parole: nope. Unsupervised visits: don't kid. Still: he'd patted himself on the back—it'd been worth it. More than a year and a half on the run. He'd had time to whip up some thick shit, including a bunch of fruity Thai parasol drinks.

And now: the new project was simmering.

The café was closed for the day. He was waiting for Tom Lehtimäki. Was gonna ask him if he wanted in on the CIT gig. His first recruitment attempt, other than Mahmud. Important. At the same time: dangerous. What if the dude didn't want in? What if he started yappin' about how Jorge was spinning a web?

Tom: an old friend of Mahmud's to begin with. Jorge knew him from the café—Tom'd helped them with their bookkeeping. Lehtimäki: an economic fraud guru, like those dudes in the construction business that Peppe'd talked about. Lehtimäki: a street-smart motherfucker you could trust. The dude: like a mini-lawyer-slash-accountant at the same time. Tricked the tricks, fixed the fixes that had to be fixed.

Clear: Tom would be an asset.

Jorge'd texted him. Short and sweet, hadn't mentioned what it was about. Just: *Wanna meet me at the café after closing. It's important.*

Jorge leaned his head back. Waited for Tom. Reminisced. How he'd talked to Mahmud the first time. A tougher talk than the one he was gonna have now. Mahmud: his right-hand man, his homie, his *hombre.*

Jorge'd been anxious. Maybe the Arab would understand. Maybe he'd get pissed off. It didn't matter. J-boy had to change his situation.

After Jorge'd caged out, he'd bought himself into the *fika* joint with Mahmud. The Arab thanked Jorge for wanting to be his partner. Mahmud'd decided to make his papa proud: abandon the G-life. Become responsible. Almost become a Sven wannabe. Jorge planned on copying his style—try not to bounce back in, try to earn steady money, try to avoid sticking out.

They worked their connects to get the place in order. Bought café gear from some Syrians that Mahmud knew through Babak. Got armchairs and sweet tables with mosaic in the wooden surfaces from a dealer in Alby. Bought mugs, plates, spoons, and shit like that online. Tom helped them with wholesalers for buns, pies, and pastries. The coffee retailer and the sandwich wholesaler were dudes Mahmud'd met when they bought love from the whores he used to poon-nanny.

They even hired people. Three of Mahmud's buddies' little sisters were paid an hourly wage. They were young, but the idea was simple: pretty girls put people in the mood, especially for coffee.

Summa summarum: tip-top feel. A 100 percent feel. After a few weeks: the place rolled like a Maserati on an autobahn.

They poured their souls into the place. Worked twenty-four seven. Jorge almost quit blazing to keep his energy up. The Arab lifted weights only twice a week in order to have enough time for it all. Jorge saw it as an investment. Café security—no more chasing after easy money. Plus: he needed something to do. He used his last savings: from blow sales and other gigs during his year in freedom. Became Mahmud's partner in the calm, easy, honest life.

Months passed. The trend was unmistakable: everyone seemed to love to *fika*.

They rolled muffin dough out and green dough rolled in. The days flew by at Matrix-karate-speed. They worked like maniacs. Got up at five every single morning to receive milk orders at the café or drive to the megabakeries outside the city. During the rest of the morning, they prepped breakfast chow. Prepped lunch salads pre-noon, flipped the same greens like idiots during the lunch rush. Rocked cappuccinos, caffè lattes, caffè macchiatos, caffè-whatever during the rest of the day, until nine o'clock at night.

Mom grew prouder and prouder. His sister, Paola, looked at him with new eyes. She could honestly tell her son: Jorge *es un tío bueno*.

It ought to feel awesome.

Ought to feel phat as hell.

Still: felt shady.

Honestly: felt mad shady.

Him: Government-grown, institution-infected, slammer-soaked. Had skidded through life like a ricochet. Dealt with prejudiced teachers, deadbeat counselors, whiny-feminist welfare hags. Tricked pretend-understanding parole boards, brutal screws, even more brutal cops. Stretched his arm out, roared, and gave society's quasi-racist bullshit the middle finger. Sven Sweden's rules weren't for him.

Plus: everything wasn't rolling that smoothly anymore. The tax man didn't like their bookkeeping. Racketeering cunts'd started showing up. The suppliers whined about advances.

But still: he was basically straight. At least as honest as a *blatte* like him could get.

But the deal: instead of feeling fly, it felt faggy.

Instead of being peaceful, it was dangerous.

Ideas were spinning in his head. Kept scratching his bandit-itch. The same thoughts every day. It was too early to get benched. Throw in the towel, blow off the game. It wasn't time to give up, not yet. Not time to roll over and die.

Jorge'd heard Mahmud's feet on the stairs. When the Arab finally did ring the doorbell, J-boy was jumpy as hell. His bro: rollin' like one chill hombre. Superthick puffy, gray sweats, and Sparco shoes. Not as beefy as before, but still double J-boy's size. To most people: the Arab had authority. His calm way of walking—hands in the top jacket pockets, swaying back and forth with every step—sent clear signals: *Take it easy. You don't want to test this.* But Jorge knew: in Mahmud al-Askori's chest pumped a heart bigger than, like, Melinda Gates and his own mama's combined.

Mahmud met Jorge's gaze, lowered his eyes—almost like he was shy. It was really true—his buddy was soft somehow.

They shook hands, not like regular Svens do: a weak handshake and a quick meeting of the eyes. No, they swung their arms before they slapped their palms together, letting their thumbs meet in a massive grip. Like the concrete. Like the Million Program. Like real friends.

They ate and shot the shit. Ran through the city's latest gossip. About who was really behind the massive heist—fifty millions for bootleg booze and smuggled cigarettes. And how things were going for Babak and the rest of Mahmud's buddies—boys who still played the game. Jumped pussies who played tough, pushed product, boosted electronics from the chain stores' huge warehouses, and flipped the same shit fourteen times retail online.

All afternoon: Jorge'd tried to calculate how to present it. How to begin. Explain what it was he wanted to say. How he would make the Arab understand.

Okay, they were having trouble with profitability. They were having trouble with the Yugos. But still: Mahmud could go apeshit. It might even make him weepy.

Jorge put his hand in his pocket and fished out a Red Line Baggie. Held the bag in the palm of his hand.

"Look what I got."

Mahmud shook his head. "Not for me. Not tonight. It's my turn to go to Södertälje tomorrow morning at five."

Jorge slapped the bag against his other palm. "Stop sulking. Check it, we ate good, you pumped some iron, we feel good. Weed's not gonna give you a hangover."

Jorge poured the weed out and mixed tobacco into it. OCB in a roll—nice to roll and extra thin. The roach would smolder slower.

They took deep hits.

Mahmud leaned back. "This is some good shit."

"Mahmud, I've gotta talk to you about something serious," Jorge said.

Mahmud didn't even look up, just kept that crooked grin plastered on his face, the one he always had when he was high. "Sure, is it business?"

"I've done this thing with you for six months," Jorge said. "The café's a good gig, pretty honest, we fork over alotta taxes, we got insurance and shit, we're even saving for retirement, like real Svens, man. I dig you, Mahmud, we've got a sweet deal together."

He put the joint down. "But it's just that it's, like, not working for me, *hombre*."

Mahmud eyed him. Looked like the guy didn't even blink.

"I mean, it's not that it's not working with you. You're my brother. But this life, you know?"

Mahmud's eyes narrowed. Jorge waited. Maybe the Arab would freak out now? Start cursing. Steam up, boil over.

Jorge rose. Started pacing back and forth. Tried to make the same words he had in his head come out of his mouth.

"That last turn, you know, that I had to take at Kumla. I was in with a real old-timer, maybe you know him. His name is Denny. Denny Vadúr, from Södertälje."

Mahmud didn't say anything. Just waited to see where Jorge was going with this.

"My first long stint, I learned a lot about blow. Swallowed information like Jenna Jameson swallows cock. But there's other stuff that's better. That demands a real lotta brain."

Jorge paused. Gave Mahmud the chance to guess.

The Arab stared at him. "What?"

"You've read about it in the papers a thousand times. We've talked about it tons of times. The latest helicopter heist on the roof of the G4S. I'm talking CIT, man. And you don't even know how much cash we're talking about. When the papers write five million's missing, the real take's four times that. But the banks and the armored car companies don't wanna admit how much they actually lose—then they'd get picked over more. And the people would be even more pissed off. You know the Spånga robbery—remember that?"

"Yeah."

"Those guys are from Södertälje. They hit the armored car with a fucking steamroller. The papers said they got hold of four million. It was actually twenty-two million. You follow? Twenty-two million. This guy Denny Vadúr might have to sit out a few years, but when he gates out, he'll laugh all the way to the ditch in the woods where he buried the cash."

"They're kings."

"Exactly, *huevon*. They're kings. One hit, and you can be set financially for the rest of your life. Not have to rot in a café. And you know what the thing is? You know what's big?"

"No."

"I saved Denny's life in there. A couple players with fire extinguisher and Denny alone in the Ping-Pong room. They tried to break open his skull with the sprayer, but little J-boy got in the way. You with me? What Vadúr owes me can't be paid back in cash. So he's put me in touch with the guy who's sitting on the recipes for CIT heists in Södertälje. He's gonna get me in there. I've got a chance to do something dope."

Jorge took a final hit on the spliff. The ash almost burned his fingers.

Back to the present. Tom rolled in, an hour late. Time for the next talk.

Jorge fixed him a latte. They went into the office.

It was a small room behind the kitchen. No windows. Two folding chairs. A table that was so mini that it hardly fit two coffee saucers. A poster on the wall: a fog-covered bridge over some river in New York City.

Jorge folded out a chair, sat down. Tom sat down. Drank his latte. Got white foam on his upper lip.

"Tom, glad you could come so soon."

"No prob."

"Did you know we started cutting our barista milk with speed?" Jorge looked dead serious.

Tom looked like a cartoon smiley face. "Yeah, right."

"Is that why you're trying to save it all on your upper lip instead of drinking it?" Jorge grinned.

Tom laughed. Ran his tongue carefully over his lips.

Jorge got right down to it. Tom Lehtimäki was the kind of guy you were straight with. An honest man.

"Yo, I wanna talk business with you."

"Don't you do that every day?"

"Yeah, but this has nothing to do with the café. This shit is a million times bigger."

Tom downed the last drops of coffee. Waited for Jorge to go on.

"Mahmud and me, we got an in to a CIT."

"Fuck, man. Hope it's as good as the helicopter robbery, except without all the badges watching."

Jorge kept talking. The basic ideas—the little info the Finn'd given him so far. Like: how many bodies they needed to be, what kinds of sums they were talking about, where they should strike. He didn't say anything about the Finn, but Tom wasn't stupid—he understood that J-boy hadn't come up with all of it on his own.

"So we're not talking some small shit," Jorge said. "This is gonna be historic. The heli-robbers were smart, but not smart enough. We're gonna break all records. Based on what we've heard, we're talkin' at least forty million. You follow? This is not a game, man."

Jorge fixed his gaze on the homeboy across from him.

Tom blinked.

J-boy popped the question. "Tom, I gotta know, you want in?"

5

Hägerström was familiar with the police's undercover routines. But the UC course he had taken on the subject hadn't really given him much. It was just like everything else within the police force—you learned to do the work in real time, in the field.

Torsfjäll had given the operation the name Operation Tide. It was supposed to focus on laundry, he said. Money laundering on a high level. For Hägerström, the work would be different from regular undercover work. First of all, it was for a limited period of time—the plan wasn't that he infiltrate and live like a criminal for several years or that he even hit up some corner and pretend to be a user for a few weeks before switching corners a few weeks later. He would take on the role as a corrections officer and make a connection with someone in the underworld—JW—who, in turn, would hopefully lead him to the people who used JW's services. Torsfjäll said it was unique for a police officer to go in and assume the role of a screw.

Actually, the inspector claimed, it was the first operation of its kind in Sweden. It was important that his colleagues didn't run into him as a CO and wonder if he was working extra or was just being weird. So Hägerström had to be fired officially from the police force, preferably with a certain amount of publicity involved. Only one person in a special unit within the Department of Corrections was informed about the project—all to minimize the risk of leaks. But Torsfjäll said the only people who actually knew that the operation involved Martin Hägerström specifically were his direct superior at the Stockholm County Police, Superintendent Leif Hammarskiöld, and himself.

The advantage of the setup was that since Hägerström would be playing a corrections officer, there was less risk of suspicion. It would've been another thing entirely if his mission had been to play a criminal. Few criminals would trust a former cop who suddenly tried to be like them—but things were different with a screw. Torsfjäll also didn't want to give him a new identity—it would be too easy to bust. All it would take was for a police colleague to come to the penitentiary and recognize Hägerström.

Some might think it strange that a fired police officer would choose to become a corrections officer. But honestly, there weren't that many other potential jobs for a former cop.

It ought to be watertight.

Torsfjäll and Hägerström had met once more after their meeting last week. Hägerström wanted additional information in order to make up his mind.

Torsfjäll explained the motives behind the operation. JW was very likely one of those responsible for a huge money-laundering system. Several hundred Swedes might be involved. But unfortunately, the police didn't know much more than that. JW apparently ran a smooth operation.

Torsfjäll went over how Hägerström would be prepped for the assignment: what he had to research and study, who else worked on the staff at the penitentiary, how he should play the game, how the dismissal would take place. The latter: the fact that Hägerström had been fired had to be known widely enough that JW learned about it.

Hägerström wondered if he wanted to do this thing at all. It was exciting. It was definitely a challenge. But it was undoubtedly very risky. Torsfjäll had been clear during their previous meeting: the fact that it wasn't listed anywhere that Hägerström had a child was a good thing. Still: to get away from the Police Department for a bit was enormously tempting. What was more, he was certain that he would do well as a double agent.

Torsfjäll finished his run-through. "Just so you know: You are not a police officer anymore. You are a corrections officer with an assignment. You have to act on your own without immunity. Is there anything about that that doesn't feel right to you?"

Hägerström thought it over briefly. He would still be a cop, after all, but in secret, and Torsfjäll promised that he wouldn't take a hit financially. He went over the different challenges that might come up. It would probably be a matter of smuggling in a cell phone or two and bringing out information. Maybe bringing in a few ounces of weed or a few grams of amphetamines. Hopefully, it wouldn't be a matter of bringing weapons in.

"I assume that's part of the standard procedure?"

Torsfjäll smiled. His teeth were unnaturally white. "The standard procedure? There isn't any such thing for this situation, I'm afraid. But I want you to start tomorrow. You have to learn everything there is to know about this JW guy."

Once again the big question: Should he really do this? Hägerström thought it over. He had wanted to be a police officer his entire life. Had even chosen the health care track in high school because it was the focus that was best suited for becoming a cop afterward. His mother, Lottie, and Father were already upset by that, even if Mother never really showed that kind of thing. His results in the army evaluation and the military, however—they were nothing but positive about that. Especially Mother, who thought, "Maybe you can become an officer in the reserves like Gucke. Wouldn't that be great? And anyway, wearing a uniform when everyone else is in white tie looks so good." Gucke's name was actually Gustaf, and he was Hägerström's cousin on his mother's side—the men in her family had gone through officer training for generations. It's what the landowning gentry did. But Hägerström had enrolled in the Police Academy instead. Mother's dismay was so great that she never mentioned the officer thing again.

"Martin, aren't you wasting your talent this way?" Father asked.

"Martin, aren't there more interesting jobs out there for you?" Carl said.

"Martin, isn't it dangerous?" his sister, Tin-Tin, said.

Dangerous.

He had worked on patrol, on the streets, for the first few years. It was physically demanding—it was not uncommon that you were forced to get a little rough sometimes, maybe had to take a hit or two. You ran into boozehounds who spat in your face, indignant citizens who thought the police didn't do their job, and young punks who wanted to be superman and tried MMA grips, even though they always had to taste the tarmac in the end. But dangerous? He had never really felt at risk. Always had good support from his colleagues.

But Operation Tide was dangerous.

And he could just imagine what Mother would say when she found out that he had been fired from the police.

Maybe he should decline after all. Keep doing what he was good at: investigating crime, arresting suspects, building investigations. Now was his last chance to blow this off.

*

I needed a new handgun. I wrapped the one I'd used on the cleaning lady in a plastic bag and threw it into the Baltic. The new hotel I was staying at was near the water.

Fortunately, I got the contacts I needed from my employer, who I suspect is from Sweden. A bar in an area in central Stockholm: the Black & White Inn.

I went there. The pub was closed, it said, but the front door was open. I stepped inside and looked around. The woman was standing behind the bar drying glasses. I handed her a slip of paper with a name on it. She looked down, then looked up. Maybe she recognized me, but she didn't give anything away.

She gestured for me to follow her. We walked back behind the kitchen. It smelled faintly of cleaning detergent. The wall paint in the hallways was peeling, and a fluorescent light hung crookedly from the ceiling. It could have been anywhere in Europe. The feeling was familiar, the dankness the same. The woman was silent, but she straightened up as soon as she'd understood what I was here to get. She was pretty, and her mouse-colored hair was pulled back in a ponytail. She reminded me of my first—and only—wife.

She opened a door and told me to stand still—in my own language. I extended my arms, and she patted me down along my back, arms, and sides. She felt around my shoes and in my pockets. Finally she brought her hands up along my legs and groin. I felt a tickling sensation down there. Just for a microsecond. Then I turned myself off. She nodded. I was clean. She must have known that before.

The woman opened a sheet-metal cabinet and brought out two metal bags. She set them on the table, turned the coded locks, and opened them. I saw dark-colored foam rubber and cutouts where objects rested, wrapped in fabric. Four in one bag and five in the other. She unwrapped the fabric. Laid the weapons down on the table.

I weighed them, inspected them, made sure they had the right feel to them. Finally, I bought a Glock 17, second generation. It is reliable, can take most kinds of ammunition. And then she had a Stechkin APS with a Makarov magazine. Not everyone would choose that weapon, but I know it better than I know my own cock. The fact is that I got a little nostalgic in a way that suited the mission.

I would finish the job when the opportunity arose. I knew that it could take weeks, but now I was prepared materially once again. And I wasn't planning on taking more risks like the one with the cleaning lady.

In my business, we don't think like other people. We act according to our own set of rules. I think that's how we're made. We are solitary authorities. We can't change. That is our strength. Like Alexander Solonik—may he rest in peace—used to say, "Eto vasja sudba"—"*It is your fate.*"

I was ready now.

I would eliminate Radovan Kranjic.

6

Natalie was sitting in the passenger seat next to Stefanovic. New car smell, tan seats in luxury leather, built-in media system in the middle console, and a crucifix dangling in the rearview mirror.

Dad was riding in a different car. That's how he wanted it. Dad's business didn't always exactly conform to Swedish government regulations. And sometimes he was forced to get tough with people who tried to pull a fast one on him—so there were people out there who didn't like him at all. But all this about riding in different cars seemed over the top.

Stefanovic was driving in a relaxed manner, one hand in his lap and the other resting lightly on the steering wheel. Natalie and Stefanovic used to sit the opposite way—her behind the wheel and him beside her. Stefanovic'd been one of the people who taught her to drive a year and a half ago, when she'd slaved away to get her license. Total: more than seventy classes at the driving school, and probably more than a hundred with Stefanovic. Lollo laughed her ass off every time they talked about it. But then Natalie passed the test on her first try—Louise had to try four times before she nailed it.

They were on their way to an MMA gala at the Globe Arena: Extreme Affliction Heroes. Natalie'd been to a few other K1 and boxing events, but never MMA.

"Before, everyone talked about K1, but now the UFC hysteria's hit Sweden," Stefanovic said. "We're in on twenty-five percent of this gala and twenty-five percent of one of the gyms. There are UFC-signed fighters here today. But our guys kick ass."

It was hilarious when Stefanovic tried to use expressions that he thought were young and hip. Like *kick ass*—seriously, it sounded just as funny as when Mom said her new Chloé shoes were "to die for."

"It's the first time," he went on, "that Extreme Affliction Heroes are up in an arena as big as the Globe. It's the next big sport in this country."

They drove over the bridge from Södermalm to Gullmarsplan. Natalie gazed out the window. The water looked like gray sheet metal. It was raining. Again. A spring almost entirely without sun.

Natalie's rabbit fur vest was in the backseat. She was wearing a Swarovski necklace and a white ruffled shirt from Marc Jacobs that she'd borrowed from Louise. She was wearing jeans that she'd bought at Artilleri2, a pair of Victoria Beckham Wide Leg in dark indigo blue. She was relaxed enough to fit in at the gala. Her dark hair was pulled back in a ponytail. She examined herself in the rearview mirror—met her own brown eyes and long lashes.

The Globe Arena was glowing in the distance—purple and blue spotlights were supposed to make it nicer than it actually was. Natalie remembered the outdoor lighting in Paris. The French knew how to illuminate a city at night—spotlights aimed at majestic facades.

They drew closer, looked for the parking signs. Drove in under the Globe. A massive parking garage. A green Volvo pulled in after them. A common color these days?

Viktor'd wanted to come along to the gala. But Dad'd deemed it not appropriate. That was all right with Natalie.

The gala was crawling with men. The atmosphere in the air: excitement mixed with expectation mixed with insanely high testosterone levels.

They stepped in through entrance A. The arena opened up below them. A dark sea of people and, in the middle, a thirty-foot high metal frame with spotlights in different colors. The spectators, the TV cameras, the spotlights—all with the same focus: the ring. On one side, where the stage was usually built when they had concerts here, giant flags from the competing countries were suspended from the wall. Sweden, USA, the Netherlands, Russia, Japan, Romania, Germany, Morocco, Serbia. On the other side hung a huge banderol, the official flag: Extreme Affliction Heroes.

Stefanovic shook hands right and left. Greeted acquaintances who threw themselves in his path, shook his hand, were given a gentle nod.

Farthest down: the ring, covered in netting, just thirty feet ahead of her. Natalie fixed her gaze on something far away in the distance and did not make eye contact with anyone. Did not look around. Rocked a completely disinterested expression.

She glimpsed a group of silicone chicks with bleached-blond hair, vulgar cleavage, and skirts that were too short. They were supposed to hold up the match signs and stuff like that during breaks. She took note of shaved gym guys with cauliflower ears. She saw suit-clad men who sat calmly, almost pissed-off looking, just staring straight ahead. Dad was probably sitting there somewhere. They looked like his people.

She made her way around the edge of the ring.

Someone beside her rose.

It was Dad.

"*Dragi*, how wonderful that you came!"

There was an empty seat next to him. Natalie sat down. Goran was sitting on her other side.

The spotlights caught every new fighter who entered. The speakers called out the guys' names, their clubs, and nationality. Electric guitars screeched on max volume between the matches. The silicone chicks put on tight T-shirts with ads on them and held up signs with the number of the next round. Natalie thought: *So, this is how they make their living when dreams of magazine centerfolds don't pan out.*

True, Louise'd had her tits done last year, but she hadn't gotten all exaggerated like that.

Dad chatted with Natalie between the rounds. Talked about the fights and that she had to enroll at the university as soon as possible. He thought she should study law or economics.

Natalie thought about that morning. Viktor'd come over to her house while she was still in bed, even though it was eleven-thirty.

She heard him exchange a few words with Mom. Then he came into her room with a breakfast tray in his hands. Tropicana orange juice California style, espresso coffee, a boiled egg, and bread from the Kringlan bakery on Linnégatan. Even if she didn't eat bread because of her diet: he was a nice guy, after all.

Viktor sat down on the edge of her bed and set the breakfast tray down carefully on the comforter. She sipped the coffee. Cracked the egg's shell.

After breakfast, they downloaded a flick with Adam Sandler in the lead—they always watched rom-coms when they were together.

"There's something I want to talk about," Viktor said.

"Okay."

"You know what I do for work, right?"

"Yeah, yeah, of course. Cars and boats and stuff."

"But you know, things're pretty shitty right now. First that nasty fucking recession made people stop buying cars and Jet Skis like they used to. So I took on some loans to keep the business afloat during the tough months. And now I've got problems."

He continued to talk about how his competitors sold shit at lower prices. That his landlord'd raised the rent. Natalie was only half-listening—deep down, she was interested in business, but Viktor's stuff felt banal somehow.

And anyway, she was beginning to sense where he was going with this.

"I have to pay off the loans. It's not exactly an ordinary bank that I owe the money to. And then I've got some other debt here and there. Taxes too. Things're tight, actually. You know, at first I was thinking of just lighting the whole shit on fire and pulling an insurance scam."

"I don't believe that."

"No, not me either, really. An insurance scam would've been dumb—the insurance companies are like hawks. So I don't know what to do. Quit? If I can't pay the rent, I could end up in bankruptcy and shit like that. Do you know what that means? If I can't pay the taxes, I might end up in personal bankruptcy too. And if I can't pay my debt, I might really end up in trouble. It's not good, baby. Really, it isn't."

She looked at him. Obviously she knew what bankruptcy was. At least five of the companies Dad owned'd folded. And to not repay debt to the wrong people—she wasn't stupid, of course she understood.

Viktor could look so sad. While she knew what he was getting at with this conversation, she regretted not having made her stance clear about ten minutes ago. She didn't want to mix worlds—she wanted to keep Viktor out of Dad's sphere. And above all: the other way around.

She got up. Made sure to end the conversation before it went any further.

"I have to deal with my college applications now."

It was true.

Three hours with the online application to the law program. Really, you didn't need high school transcripts or standardized tests—anyone who succeeded in filling out these forms correctly was obviously intelligent enough.

She thought about Louise again: she was already in her second year at the university. It seemed pretty chill: Louise updated her Facebook status, like, twenty times every morning. They were mostly about all her constant coffee breaks.

It was almost time for the heavyweight match. Dad said that it was the one everyone had come to see. And the thing was that a Serb was going up in the ring: Lazar Tomic from Belgrade, a real UFC fighter. He was facing off against a guy from Sweden: Reza Yunis.

When Serbia was competing, it was serious stuff.

The emcee introduced the fighters.

When the Swede's name was called out, the arena really exploded. At least ten thousand male voices roared. Support. Strength. Supremacy.

The gong sounded, the first round began. Dad delivered a stream of commentary about what was happening into Natalie's ear. Yunis was apparently pushing hard and rocking a high tempo against Tomic. Only a few seconds into the fight, he was flat on the ring floor after the Swede swept him down. Yunis jumped on top of him. Fed punches at the Serb's face. Tomic tried to protect himself, block as much as he could. The seconds kept on ticking. He succeeded in wrapping his legs around the Swede. They rolled around. Made it back up on their feet. Danced around each other and kicked at hip height.

The round ended.

Extreme Affliction Heroes: MMA in its finest form. Everything was allowed except for head-butting, biting, poking in the eyes, or hitting the back of the head or groin.

Dad asked if she wanted something to drink. He sent Goran during the break. He returned with mineral water for her right before the second round was about to begin.

Dad kept talking. "Tomic has competed a lot in the U.S. He is good at feinting and uneven shifts in tempo. He likes to take it slow for a while before he comes back strong. We'll see."

Natalie was getting bored. They were fighting like crazy up there. Kicks to the shins, jabs to the body, different grips when they were down on the mat. Knees in ribs, jabs to the head, punch after punch to the face. The people around her were howling. The fighters up in the ring panted, wrestled, and circled around and around, like dudes in a bar who are about to launch a pick-up ambush on a girl.

She played with her iPhone. Played Bubble Ball. Checked the hours at the gym. Navigated Facebook—Louise's status: "Home again after a sweet afternoon with the girls at Foam café."

Well, compared to that, Extreme Affliction Heroes was damn exciting.

Something wet. Drops of sweat from Tomic landed on Natalie's forehead.

Goran looked at her.

"Nice," she said.

Third round. They continued their war. Tomic, Dad's hero, was dominating more and more. Natalie was only half-watching. Now and then she glanced down at her phone.

Stefanovic, Goran, and one more of Dad's cronies, Milorad, had stood up. Were so into the fight that, when Tomic took a hit, it almost looked like they were getting whipped too.

Natalie tried to concentrate during the last seconds of the fight.

Tomic used his knees well, but so did Yunis. Tomic jabbed and tried to sweep. Yunis got up close and threw punches at Tomic's kidneys. Tomic tore free and attacked with hard jabs to the Swede's head. But, unexpected: Tomic's swings didn't bite, Yunis shadowed him so that Tomic ended up on the mat instead. The Swede threw himself over him. Pressed Tomic's arms down with his knees. Showered punches over his face. Tomic tried to twist out of his grasp. But he was stuck. Natalie saw how Yunis's fists pounded into Tomic's nose, landed on his chin, cheeks. Tomic almost seemed to give up.

But then he made a swift move. They rolled around and ended up next to each other. Suddenly the Serb was fast. He gripped Yunis's head between his thighs. Pushed. Pressed. Yunis's face grew redder and redder. Tomic continued to squeeze his thighs together. The Swede was being suffocated. The referee nudged Tomic. The Serb ignored him, continued to strangle the Swede.

The referee nudged him again. Yunis's face was growing blue.

The referee pushed Tomic aside—he stood up.

Everyone waited.

Yunis didn't move.

Joy rushed through Natalie. She stood up. She pumped her fist in the air. "Yes!"

The Swede remained where he was. The referee counted off.

"One.

"Two.

"Three."

Emergency medical personnel rushed up into the ring. Natalie sat back down.

Dad was still standing up. Screaming, "*Ostani.* Stay where you are! Keep lying there. Don't get up, *pićko*, you pussy!"

"Four.

"Five.

"Six."

The arena was in uproar. Was the Swede even alive? The EMT guy bent down, yelled into Yunis's ear.

"Seven.

"Eight."

Yunis stirred where he was on the mat. Sucked after air.

The referee was holding nine fingers in the air.

"Nine."

It was over.

When they left, Goran walked first. Divided the swaths of people the way Stefanovic'd done on the way in. Kind of like a president with bodyguards—all fans and photographers: step aside. Except now it wasn't as easily done as when they'd arrived. The crowd pushed. Stefanovic walked behind Natalie and Dad at an angle and made sure the space around them widened. Milorad was walking behind her.

It felt good. High spirits. Lazar Tomic—a hero. Extreme Affliction Heroes, a success. They talked about the fight, laughed, recounted over and over again: Tomic's thigh muscles, Yunis's bluish-purple face.

It was a good day. They were going to go eat at Clara's Kitchen & Bar, all of them together. Still, Natalie felt strange. An uneasy feeling in the pit of her stomach. Something unpleasant.

They reached the parking garage. People were streaming out of the elevators. The cars were queuing up, on their way out into the Stockholm night.

Stefanovic was going to drive Natalie. Dad was going to ride with Goran and Milorad. She saw his Lexus over there. He turned around to hug her, said, "See you soon." Kissed her on the forehead like he always did.

That's when she heard something.

Sharp sounds. Bangs.

Like fireworks.

Natalie saw Dad in front of her. His movements were choppy. As if she were seeing what was happening image by image in a video-editing program. As if she were watching the frames in an animated movie. Small changes like jerky breaks in the flow. She saw everything: shifts in people's gestures, expressions, ways of breathing.

Another bang echoed through the parking garage.

And again.

The movement around her stopped.

Dad screamed, "I've been shot!"

After that everything happened so quickly. Stefanovic threw himself over him. Pressed Dad down onto the ground. A second later she was lying with Goran on top of her. She saw Milorad waving a gun around. Yelling at people to stay back.

Everyone was screaming.

She could feel Goran pulling her. The parking garage looked so small.

She saw Dad underneath Stefanovic.

She saw a puddle of blood, spreading.

She saw his hand, still on the concrete floor.

No.

NO.

7

The first real recruit—Tom Lehtimäki said yes, of course. The dude was smart. Two, three million in cash, straight up. Or whatever his cut would be. RIP—right in pocket. Not even he could swing that much in such short time, no matter how many number-juggling tricks he had up his sleeve.

In the days that followed, Jorge spoke with Sergio, Robert Progat, and Javier—in that order.

They were all of the same opinion: Your Royal Highness Jorge Bernadotte, you're Jesus, man. Obviously everyone wanted in.

OBVIOUSLY.

The team was taking shape. The group was growing. The pieces were falling into place.

Heat, *Reservoir Dogs*, *Ocean's Eleven*—this time it was for real.

At the same time: Stockholm'd just been hit with the scoop of the decade.

The news of the century. The highlight of the fucking millennium—someone'd tried to pop Radovan. The Yugo boss, to Jorge: his hate was so deep, it dug a ditch inside him. He'd attacked Mr. R's interests before: the hit to Smådalarö, the shots in the brothel in Hallonbergen. And in his dreams: over and over again. One sweet day J-boy would crush the Yugo king for good. In other words: the attempt on Radovan's life was big. Not just for Jorge. For the entire underworld. Everyone was gossiping, ruminating, speculating. Offering their opinions. A transfer of power was in the works, a new king was on his way up the hill. An opening for more players to take over the territory.

But still: he couldn't focus on that right now. The smartest CIT in history, that's what counted now. Jorge imagined the newspaper headlines he wanted to read after the fact: *No more cash in Stockholm's ATMs—the robbers got their hands on a record sum. The coup that outdid all previous coups. The biggest CIT heist ever.*

The latest recruits: two Svens.

That was the Finn's original order: "You need a few real Swedes too. To get tools, vehicles, and things like that. People who have more connections in the construction business than you do."

Jorge didn't protest. Tom Lehtimäki suggested names. They discussed back and forth. Who you could trust. Who was 100 percent.

Jorge had individual meetings with the two guys Tom suggested.

One of the dudes was named Jimmy. Tiler who reported zero but hauled in cash through off-the-books gigs and flipped construction machinery online. The guy: overly positive, super into it, totally on board.

The other dude: more calm. Talked like he already knew all there was to know. Still, gave off a good vibe—the guy didn't seem dumb. Ran his own business. Worked with cars and boats. Drove a BMW X6. His name was Viktor.

Tom said Viktor was desperate for cash. The guy's business was apparently sinking, even if he claimed the opposite. And he was loaded with private debt all the way up to his plucked eyebrows. Jorge saw possibilities: a dude who oughta be prepared to take care of the dirty work.

Jorge thanked Tom for the tips—these guys would be assets.

Jorge and Mahmud met the Finn one more time.

This time: somewhere completely different. The dude: nasty smart—if they'd been snitches, they wouldn't have been able to tell the five-oh where they were meeting.

Jorge and Mahmud made up different names for him. The Architect, the Planner, the Brain.

They drove the Södra länken highway, the tunnel, straight out toward Nacka.

The regular car, the pickup. But Mahmud'd hung up some green thing with a Muslim text on it in the rearview mirror. He pointed. "It means luck."

Jorge grinned. "You people believe so much weird shit, *amigo*."

"What's weird about it?"

Jorge slapped his finger on the little piece of plastic with the text on it. It swung back and forth. "What's this thing supposed to do for our luck? Can you even read it?"

"Quit it. You don't know shit. That's the creed. The most important thing we got in our religion. Honest man, it's the most important thing in the world for everyone. *Walla*."

"Okay yeah . . . sure . . ." Jorge rocked an ironic style. Mahmud talked a bunch of smack: the dude wasn't more pious than a Sven.

Mahmud kept his eyes on the road.

"Answer me. Can you read it?"

Outside: heavy rain. The windshield wipers were moving steadily back and forth. The Arab didn't say anything.

"So, can you or can't you?"

Continued silence.

Finally, Mahmud: "None of your business."

The parking lot above the beach was completely empty. Farther off: a shuttered snack stand. A deserted jungle gym. Behind the snack stand: a parked Ford Focus. Was it the Finn's? What a lame car.

Mahmud parked next to the Ford even though there were tons of empty spots all around.

He switched off the engine. They didn't say anything. A microsecond: the feeling of a little, little bit of stress. A little, little stomachache. Sort of like something was moving in there.

Jorge opened the passenger door. Winked at Mahmud. "Come on, *amigo*, let's go for a swim."

They walked down to the lake. Spring this year was ice cold. Jorge was too lightly dressed. Track pants and a hoodie. On top of that, a thin red jacket with Formula 1 logos on the back and arms. He pulled the hood of his sweatshirt up over his head and tightened it. Then he flipped the collar on the jacket up all the way so it formed a kind of tube around his neck. Only his eyes and nose were visible.

The sand was crusted over but still wet. It made squelching sounds.

Mahmud'd wrapped a scarf high up around his neck. Looked like he belonged in Tahrir Square. He pointed out over the lake. "Can you believe there are Svens who go swimming this time of year?"

Jorge shook his head. "Learn one thing, comrade, you're never gonna understand *los Suecos*. They're not from this planet."

They glimpsed someone, three hundred feet in the distance.

Jorge understood: the meeting spot was perfect. Completely shielded from view. No one could see them from the lake because of the trees. And the dunes were high enough on the other side so that no one could see them from the road either.

The Finn came closer.

Today he was wearing sunglasses despite the weather. A hat and a scarf.

"Where did you park your car?" he asked.

"Next to a Ford Focus," Jorge said. "Yours?"

The Finn didn't respond, just said, "Did anyone else drive into the parking lot?"

"No. It was completely empty, except for the Ford."

"Good. You have to understand that this is like a house of cards. You have to build it the right way, plan the job from the ground up, begin at the beginning. Every single piece has to be perfect. All it takes is one crooked card in the bottom row for the whole shit to come falling down. Do you understand what I'm saying? All it takes is that you stop paying attention for just one second."

Jorge and Mahmud mmm'ed. Kept their cool.

"Over the past few years," the Finn went on, "all the hits've gotten more complex. You know that. Ten years ago, it was like stepping into a day-care center and juxing the kiddies for their shovels and buckets. You only needed to follow the CIT companies' routines for a week, and then one more week. After that you knew exactly how they drove, where they drove, and the security they kept around the transports. It doesn't work that way anymore. The helicopter robbery was incredibly well planned. And it still went to hell. The pigs woke up."

They talked for a while. Went over Jorge's recruits. What topped their to-do list. The Finn wouldn't give up the whole recipe at once. Instead: piece by piece. They'd have to pick up information at spots designated by him. What a cunt.

He continued to preach. "The thing is, you gotta do the right things the right way. You gotta do the right things, and they've gotta be done in the right way."

The dude talked routines. Never talk about the hit on the phone. Never even have a phone on when you're talking about it. Switch phone plans as often as possible. Don't talk with anyone on the outside, not even wives, bros, hos.

“Can we meet the insider?” Jorge asked.

“No, of course not,” the Finn said. “That’s not how things work in this business.”

Jorge thought: the Finn was a cocky fucker. Okay, the dude had an insider in his pocket. He had ideas. But who would be taking all the risks? Who would be doing the dirty work?

In J-boy’s head: a pitch-perfect idea. A thought was taking shape. A plan of his own. He was going to make sure he got paid extra for this gig. This CIT had to benefit him more than the Finn.

He was gonna pinch more for himself. Rip the Finn off.

Somehow.

8

Torsfjäll had sent Hägerström to pick up insider information from a former Serbian hit man. They had mentioned him before, Mrado Slovovic. Sentenced to fourteen years in prison for one of the biggest cocaine-smuggling heists during the 00s.

Mrado wanted his DNA, mug shot, and fingerprint entries erased from the police's registries at his release. He wanted fifty thousand Swedish kronor in cash, ten thousand euros in an account in Beogradska Bank in Serbia, and the same amount in Universal Savings Bank on Cyprus. He wanted a house with a garden outside Čačak. And there had to be a plum tree in that garden. Apparently the hit man's daughter liked fruit.

Torsfjäll claimed that he had promised him half the money and the house if only he spoke with Hägerström. He hadn't promised him any plum trees.

Mrado was valuable. Hägerström met him twice in the visiting room at the Hall prison. He offered up some general information about his former organization's hierarchy and structure. Dropped names of restaurants, bars, companies. Above all, he name-dropped men. Everything revolved around the king, *il padre*: Radovan Kranjic.

The Yugos were not like the MC gangs or the gangs from the housing projects. No colors or vests. No stupid names or tattoos.

"All the papers write about the MC guys like they're some kind of mafia," Mrado said. "But look what happens when they hit a rough patch. The Bandidos, the Hells Angels, it doesn't matter. There're a lot of people who won't back down, and then they go crawling back."

The Yugos' solidity was built on more intimate connections than that. They shared sentiments about Serbia, about honor and glory. They all spoke the same language, liked the same *slivovitz* and *schlag*.

They were close to one another, were sometimes family, in-laws, had houses in the same vacation resorts by the coast or in the Čačak region. They all respected Mr. R. Everyone's *kum*, as Mrado put it. Everyone's godfather.

The man whom Mrado apparently hated. But also: the man who had built Mrado up into what he had been. And now: the man someone had tried to assassinate in a parking garage under the Globe Arena.

Hägerström and Torsfjäll tried to see a pattern. Connections between companies and actual owners: the ones who controlled the finances behind the front men's registered names. Video rental stores, tanning salons, and bars: laundromats. MB Accounting Consultant AB took care of the paperwork. They got lists of restaurants and cafés that paid so-called street insurance to Radovan's boys. The deductible that had to be paid to the real insurance companies if something happened was higher than what the Yugos demanded for their protection anyway, so most people chose the street variety. Now a few other gangs had joined the competition, but they would get whipped soon enough. The Yugos' business empire was broad. The bodegas that bought smuggled cigarettes from Russia, the restaurateurs who sold moonshine poured into Absolut Vodka bottles, the coat checks at those same bars that didn't want to report their income. The potentates who needed protection when they came to Sweden for half-shady business, business leaders and union hotshots who wanted women at their representational parties. And more: lots of business in the gray zone who were involved one way or another. Needed help collecting when Intrum Justitia failed. When the financial crisis hit. Needed protection when they had duped some whiny client.

A lot of what Mrado told him was old news—he had been locked up for more than five years, after all. And when it came to JW, there was even less meat on the bone. Mrado hadn't seen the guy during the entire time he had been locked up. But he had kept an eye on that little puppy, as he put it.

According to Mrado, the guy was a financial genius who could have amounted to something big in the legal world. But it had gone to hell.

It was ten past eleven. Martin Hägerström unlocked the front door. He peered in through the barred inner gate to the doormat. It was specially made by Liz Alpert Fay and existed in only one copy—this one.

Resting on the Alpert Fay doormat were three envelopes and one plastic-covered magazine.

He unlocked the barred gate. It squeaked.

He liked his apartment on Banérgatan.

He took his shoes off.

He draped his jacket over the stool that stood against one wall and slipped on his velvet slippers—he didn't traipse around in just his socks, never. Around twenty years ago, when he had been given his first flat, Father had come over and said, "All foyers need a stool."

And then he had set out a wooden stool from the classic design store Svenskt Tenn, with a seat covered in iconic Josef Frank fabric—a more potent seal of class than wearing a gold signet ring. It was timeless, and it was still standing in Hägerström's hallway.

The idea was that guests—and the person who lived in the place too, certainly—would have a chance to sit down when they took their outdoor shoes on and off. No one should be forced to bend down in an undignified manner just because they were changing into indoor shoes. According to Father, the presence of a stool simplified the hallway's most important function. But Hägerström never sat on it. Instead, he threw his sweaters, gloves, bags, and jackets onto it. So his father had been a little bit right, after all—it simplified the life of the hallway, but not in the way Father had intended.

On the wall was a ten-foot-square concert photograph of David Bowie, bought at last year's Sotheby's auction. Milwaukee Arena, 1974. Bowie was holding the mike, his grip almost looking cramped. He had balled his other hand into a fist, hard. He looked cool.

There was a kilim rug on the floor in the hallway. Inherited crystal sconces hung on the walls. He liked his personal mix of old and new. Hägerström had been interested in decorating for a long time. It wasn't something he had started getting into since the TV personality Martin Timell conquered the Swedish populace's homes. Do-it-yourselfers, at-home tinkerers, pretend decorators, and so-called design experts had invaded all the TV channels but had failed to inform the people what good taste actually was. Everyone thought it was about the same old hackneyed Scandinavian design: Myran chairs, Super Ellipse tables, and AJ Pendulums. People were nervous; that much was obvious from how everyone thought everything had to look the same.

He sat down with the mail in the kitchen. A vase with flowers stood on the sideboard. That was one of the cleaning lady's additional duties—to always make sure there were fresh-cut flowers in the house. A portrait of Count Gustaf Cronhielm af Hakunge hung over the kitchen table. The painting was more than a hundred years old, and small cracks in the paint were visible in the light from the directional spotlights.

He tore the letters open with his finger. One electricity bill. One invoice from his lawyer. If it weren't for his inherited money, he wouldn't have been able to pay it—his entire police officer's salary wouldn't have been enough to cover the lawyer's fee.

The door to Pravat's room was open. He always left it that way—he wanted to be able to see the boy's toys and bed.

The final letter was junk mail about a lottery. Crap.

He picked up the magazine. *Vanity Fair*. Flipped through it listlessly.

The clock on the microwave read eleven-thirty. A long day at work. But maybe he worked fifteen hours a day in order to forget. Water down his anxiety about not being allowed to see Pravat more often. Move on without having to feel too much.

He had eaten at the speciality hot dog place on Nybrogatan. Bruno was the owner's name, the old German guy who had more than thirty kinds of sausages in a sixty-five-square-foot space. Hungarian *kabanos*, German *Zwiebelwurst*, Tunisian *merguez*, Argentinian *chorizo*—say what you wanted, and Bruno'd have it. And best of them all: *Zigeunerwurst*—Gypsy sausage. Hägerström ordered two in Bruno's special French bread. Walked home in the gray weather. Chewed every bite with pleasure.

Mother Lottie tried to joke about the divorce. "Anna was from Norrland, after all," she said. "And up in the north, everyone is named -ström something, so that's probably why she thought you two belonged together."

Well, if that was the case, then these days Mother belonged up there too. She had been named Hägerström longer than he had, after all. Actually, she had never really gotten over the fact that she had gained a plebeian Sven name. Her maiden name was Cronhielm af Hakunge—Count Gustaf hanging on the wall was her grandfather. Mom was from a noble family, but according to the Swedish laws of nobility, her children were demoted. She had to live with the fact that they would always belong to the lower castes of society. Except for Tin-Tin, of course. She was going to marry back into the right caste.

Mother's father came from Idlingstad Manor outside of Linköping but had moved to Stockholm in the 1930s. Lottie herself was born on Narvavägen. She had moved between three addresses in her life: her childhood home, her first flat with Father on Kommendörsgatan, and then the current flat on Ulrikagatan. A journey through life of less than two thousand feet. So Kommendörsgatan was maybe the closest she had ever gotten to the North.

Hägerström thought about what Mrado had told him.

For a man like Mrado, it hurt, it was fucking nasty to be sentenced to fourteen years in prison—but it was nothing to be ashamed of. It was nothing he hadn't calculated might happen. A stint in the pen was something that everyone in his world counted on, though perhaps not quite that long. But for JW, his entire life had come crashing down. Or rather: both his lives.

First the ordinary, normal Swedish world that he actually came from. His mother couldn't understand. His old high school friends up in Robertsfors had been shocked. His father couldn't forgive.

And then his new world, the upper-class life. None of his friends had visited him during those years—at least that's what the Department of Corrections claimed. None of those he had done everything to resemble had even so much as sent him a letter. No one. So much for true friendship. But then again, the Department of Corrections didn't know who had called him over the past few years. They didn't keep a record of that kind of thing.

Hägerström didn't like it when Mrado said "upper class." He knew what that meant—people who used that expression wanted to divide Sweden and label his family as different. And what was more, Anna used to say it when she ran out of things to attack him with.

But he didn't let it get to him. His family *was* different. A little bit, anyway.

Mrado had told him that during the first months after the sentencing, JW had been completely lethargic. But then he had come back slowly. With a plan, evidently. He had accepted his fate. Started making new friends. New connections. JW had apparently succeeded in hiding away some money that he was able to control from the pen. He started lending people small sums. The Department of Corrections had granted him permission to take university classes at a distance—but that was just on paper. According to Mrado, he actually spent his time managing his money and thinking up smart ways to help others with the same needs.

Mrado knew people who had been helped by the guy. Robbery

money, drug money, whore money, blackmail money: everything could be laundered, as long as you were meticulous and patient enough.

But Mrado refused to name names. That was a setback.

Torsfjäll said that he could have pretty much figured out what Mrado had told them on his own. JW was clearly helping people on the outside with money laundering. The question was what the scope of the operation was. How did he bring information in and out? And above all: Who were his customers?

Torsfjäll was aware of another detail too: JW was carrying around a secret story. A tragic mystery that had taken place a few years before he was convicted. Camilla Westlund, his sister, had been in Stockholm. Fraternized with the wrong crowd. Hung out at the wrong places. But something had gone wrong. JW's sister had disappeared, and no one seemed to know what had happened to her—but everyone knew that it was something bad. JW had hunted, researched, searched for her.

Torsfjäll didn't know what he had found out. But it was something.

Hägerström looked down at the *Vanity Fair* magazine. He tried to summarize the information. He had to get a grip on JW. He had to get to know this man from a distance. Understand him. Burrow his way under his skin, like a shrink.

He opened his computer. Apple's tune sounded when it started up. What he should really do was go to bed—he was finished thinking for tonight. But he was going to do one thing first.

A while later: twenty or so images that he had found on different Web sites were open on the screen. Different camera angles: from above, from the side, from below. Uncomfortable positions. Cold light. Close-ups that seethed with frustration.

He skipped between the images. He zoomed in. He zoomed out.

Sometimes it felt like Count Gustaf was staring at him from the wall.

Fifteen minutes later, he was lying in bed. Cock wiped off. Teeth brushed. Pitch black in the room. He wasn't thinking about anything at all. He shut his eyes.

He had to stop living like this.

Father was dead now.

Anna and Pravat didn't live here anymore.

His life needed a boost.

***

POLICE OFFICER DISMISSED AFTER ASSAULT

A police officer in Stockholm has been dismissed after being accused of assault. He is the fifth person within the police force to be fired so far this year.

The disciplinary board was not unanimous in its decision to dismiss the officer. Three members of the jury wanted to write the case off.

The man, who worked as a deputy inspector, had visited a hot dog vendor on Nybrogatan in Stockholm while off duty. He claims that he witnessed two other customers accosting a younger woman. After trying to talk to one of the other customers several times, the police officer punched him in the face so that he fell to the ground.

But the customer and his friend give a different account.

"This man punched me completely unprovoked, and I have no idea why. It's fucking crazy for police officers to run around and do this kind of thing in their free time. And he was drunk too."

Witnesses whom reporters spoke with confirm the customer's account.

TT

9

Wet pillows, crumpled sheets. Cold in the room, even though Mom'd turned the thermostat up to seventy-three degrees. Constantly: static thoughts, cyclical sorrow, anxious memories.

Natalie didn't leave the house. She was *not allowed* to leave the house. Mostly she sat in the kitchen with Mom, talked to Viktor on the phone now and then, and watched YouTube clips to push the thoughts away. Most of all she lay in her bed and studied the structure of the ceiling.

She drank a cup of tea in the morning and tried to eat a fried egg for lunch. That was all. Mom nagged at her, telling her she had to eat more—made salads and ordered in healthy food. But Natalie couldn't do it. As soon as she looked down at the tomatoes, it felt like the lunch egg in her stomach was on its way up again.

At night the same scene came back to her, over and over again. The parking garage: the puddle of blood growing under Dad. The movements around him. The people throwing themselves on the ground, running toward the exits, cowering behind big cars. She heard the screams and the cries. Stefanovic yelling orders in Serbian. Goran roaring. After a few seconds, everything became calm around her. She knew what it was called: the eye of the storm.

Goran pushed her into a car. Shoved her onto the floor in the backseat.

Natalie wanted out. Goran held her down.

"No, Natalie. More shots could go off out there. You have to stay, for your father's sake."

She howled. Screamed. "Is he alive? Goran? Answer me."

But Goran couldn't answer. He just held her. A firm grip around her torso and arms. She tried to look up at him. See into his eyes. They were wide open. Staring. And now, after the fact, she knew that she'd felt something else: Goran's arms and hands'd been shaking. Trembling, somehow.

They waited. One minute. Maybe two. Natalie pulled herself up. She managed to peer out through the car window.

Stefanovic was on his knees next to Dad. It looked like he was trying to examine something. He leaned down. The wounds. His hands, bloody. Dad was lying still, like a doll.

Two minutes.

Time was all they had. Why was it standing still right now? Why was no one coming to help?

She threw herself against the car door again. Goran's arms were steadier now. She struggled to break free. He pulled her back.

She had to go to him.

Finally an ambulance pulled into the parking garage.

Two EMTs jumped out and started working. They put Dad on a gurney.

Goran relaxed his grip. Natalie tore open the car door and rushed out. Dad on the gurney. An orange blanket over his body. His face, unscathed. It looked clean. Peaceful.

She raised the blanket. Blood everywhere. She searched for his hand. Found it. Goran was close behind her, his hand on her shoulder.

She leaned over. Dad's stubble against her cheek. She listened. Heard his breathing. Faint. Wheezing. Irregular.

He was alive.

Dad was alive.

She'd been told that he was at a hospital somewhere in Stockholm. But she and Mom were not allowed to visit him. Stefanovic said that the person or persons who were out to get Radovan might be keeping their eye on them too. So it was best that they didn't know where he was being cared for. Stefanovic used the same words over and over again: *delicate situation*, *a new time for the organization*, *aggressive competitors*. But no details—he never explained what he meant. Mom just nodded, seemed to accept everything. And Natalie didn't want to let her herself ask the obvious question: What was actually happening?

According to Stefanovic, a bullet'd been caught in Dad's bulletproof vest. Thank God he wore it. The second bullet'd passed right through his thigh. The third one'd busted his knee, not trashed it completely but enough to make him limp for a few weeks. The fourth bullet was the worst—it'd hit him in the shoulder, right on the seam, between the area of his chest that was protected by the vest and the unprotected outer part. Ligaments, muscles, and nerve fibers'd been destroyed. The doctor didn't know how long the arm would be out of function. But Stefanovic said the doctor promised he'd be fine in the end.

She was sitting in bed with her iPhone. Checking out some news app.

She'd propped up her back with a couple of small pillows that usually belonged in the armchair. She was wearing her pink velour Juicy Couture tracksuit. She didn't bother with Facebook today. Didn't want to be forced into some chat with so-called friends she'd never even wanted to have on there. Didn't want to see other people's status updates—small deceitful brag blogs with one sole purpose: to show off a happy, pleasant, nasty little life. She didn't want to have to see any more party photos from Louise and Tove's latest dinner or night out. She wanted to avoid all the pathetic wall threads.

But her worry was beginning to transform into something else, thoughts that burned in her mind. Whoever it was who'd shot Dad, they had to find him. Whoever it was, he had to be punished. When she thought about the shots in the parking garage, Natalie could think of only one word: *revenge*.

Mom appeared to be in a trance. She was stressed out, said there was so much that had to be taken care of. Natalie wondered whether Mom was feeling what she was feeling.

Stefanovic'd been there. During the day, he ordered workers around who were installing new alarm systems, switched out the regular glass panes in the windows for more durable materials, built new barred gates inside the front doors, and set up new surveillance cameras outside the gravel driveway, in the garage, under the roof along each long end of the house, and above the front and kitchen entrances. They'd even set up cameras on small poles out on the front lawn. Afterward Stefanovic'd walked around and inspected the work that'd been done over the past few days. He personally set up a portable alarm box in every room—like little remote controls for safety. He checked the motion sensors on the windows, the outdoor and indoor alarms that were connected directly to different security companies. And to him. The police couldn't be trusted in this racist Sweden Democrat country.

To put it simply: Stefanovic was everywhere, all at once. Always with some important thing to do.

He even slept at the office, which was to say in Dad's study. A foldout cot and a bag with clothes and stuff was the only thing he'd brought. For all eventualities, as he said.

The aim was to make them feel safe. But after a few days, new workers showed up and started building a room. The rec room was sectioned off with a wall, put up in a metal frame—and they installed large beams both in the ceiling and along the walls. They put in new water pipes, did the electrical wiring, dealt with safety features, and installed metal panels on the walls and floor.

"This is a safe room," Stefanovic explained to Natalie and Mom. "We've reinforced the windows and the doors in the whole house so that help will have time to make it here. But if someone really wants to hurt us, if the windows don't hold, then you need to go into this new room. It can handle a lot. It's better than a tank."

The fact that they were building a safe room in their house was crazy in and of itself. But there was something else: he'd said "us"—as if he were part of the family. As if he'd stepped in as the new dad.

After a few days, Stefanovic moved out and a new guy named Patrik moved in. Natalie'd met him a few times before. Patrik wasn't a Serb—he was an ultra Sven, looked liked an oversized soccer hooligan: faded tattoos with Viking motifs and runic writing that wound its way up along his throat and neck. Patrik wore T-shirts that said HACKETT and FRED PERRY on them, Adidas sneakers, chinos, and a side part.

Normally: Natalie wouldn't have trusted a racist pig like that for a second. But Patrik'd worked in Dad's company and had done time in prison for him. She'd even been with Dad at the guy's gate-out party three years ago.

Stefanovic said Patrik would live with them on a more permanent basis than he'd been doing himself. He moved into the guest room instead of the study. They set up a weapons locker and a proper wardrobe where Patrik hung up his polo shirts. He put a little flag in the window: the soccer team AIK's emblem on one side and an image of a rat on the other, dressed in an AIK jersey.

"Patrik will be good for you," Stefanovic said. "Until things've calmed down. He's a pretty fun guy. I think you're going to like him."

A few days later. The builders, fitters, installers, security consultants'd stopped swarming their house. Now they were surrounded by electronics and reinforced glass. They'd had a home alarm system for as long as Natalie could remember, so that wasn't new. But all the new codes, voice recognition readers, and cameras irritated her. It was like Stefanovic'd built them into a bunker.

But she was back online for real, on Facebook. Couldn't avoid the place forever.

In a way, it was nice to be back: everything was the same. Louise with as many pics of herself with a champagne glass in hand as usual. Tove with as many idiotic status updates as usual.

Louise wrote to her in the chat, *Natalie! Haven't seen you here in ages!*

Natalie responded in a more tempered way, *You know how it is.*

Yes :-(but how are you doing?

Better.

Louise wrote, *You're invited to a party at Jet Set Carl's ;-) Did you know?*

Natalie couldn't really take it all in. Sometimes Louise seemed to think everything was just like normal.

Later that night Patrik strode into the kitchen and positioned himself in the doorway. Natalie'd had a smoothie that she'd made herself—her appetite was better now.

Patrik waited for her to look up. "Viktor's coming. He's parking his car on the street."

Natalie nodded. Thought: Stefanovic's cameras were obviously working as they should. Except Natalie already knew that Viktor was on his way. He'd texted her and asked if he could come.

She got up, walked out into the hall. A framed map of Europe was hanging on the wall. It looked old. The borders were different than today, from, like, before the First World War.

The front door was new, made of metal. Before, they'd had one with a square window in it. Now there was a flat monitor beside the door. On it, she could see Viktor opening the gate farther off. She'd texted him the code for the gate. He walked up the path. Dressed in his Italian sweater and patched jeans. He stopped for a few seconds. Straightened up. Stared straight ahead. Rang the doorbell.

The new locks were difficult. She opened the door.

They hugged. Viktor kissed her on the mouth. He asked how she was doing. Then he stopped. Natalie looked at him. His gaze floated past her, in toward the house.

Natalie turned around.

Patrik was standing farther back in the hall. Watching. Controlling. Guarding.

"Don't mind him," Natalie said. "He lives here now. You know, after what happened."

Later. They'd watched *The Blind Side*, which Viktor had on his iPad. Basic gist: Sandra Bullock was nice and helped build up an American football hero. A cute movie, of course—that's what real life was like. Not.

They were lying in Natalie's full-size bed. Was cramped compared to Viktor's king-size one. It felt weird, sleeping together at her house.

Usually they hung out at his place, in his rented one-bedroom on Östermalm. He'd paid a lot of money for an off-the-books rental contract, but couldn't afford to buy anything of his own.

Viktor, bare-chested. It was nice. When the movie was over, he stood in front of the mirror and inspected his own tattoos. He had some tribal motif over his right biceps and shoulder—long, pointy black flames that wound into one another and up onto his neck. On his left forearm in curlicue lettering: 850524-0371—his own personal identification number—and two all-black five-pointed stars. And on the other side, written along his entire forearm in Gothic gangsta lettering: BORN TO BE KING—like on a Latino gangster from South L.A. That's what Viktor thought, anyway.

She looked at him. Viktor's tattoos were so silly compared to the ones that decorated the forearms of Dad's business contacts and friends. Goran's half-faded tattoo: the double eagle and the four Cyrillic letters CCCC—the Serbian Republic of Krajina's national coat of arms. Milorad's Indian feathers: ugly, 1980s-looking, monochrome. Or Stefanovic, walking past her bare-chested once at a pool when she was a little girl. She'd never forget the tattoo that covered his chest over his heart: a crucifix with a snake wrapped around it. She liked Viktor. But was he right for her?

The velvet reading chair that'd belonged to Grandma in Belgrade was standing in one corner of her room. Dad'd had it delivered when Natalie was born. Hanging from the ceiling was a white lamp with tulle around it. Along one wall was a bookshelf with some books in it: Camilla Läckberg mysteries, Marian Keyes paperbacks, Zadie Smith's novels, and two books by that lawyer writer. The bookshelf also held framed photos from language trips to France and England: Louise's gleaming smile, platinum-blond hair, and abnormal tits. Tove's sunburned arms holding up a bottle of Moët & Chandon. Several pictures of Natalie herself at different places in Paris: the bar at La Société, the dance floor at Batofar. Two photos of Richie, Natalie's Chihuahua that'd died three years ago.

She'd brought out some favorite pairs of shoes from her walk-in closet and put them in the bottom of the bookshelf—it was almost like an installation. Black pumps from Jimmy Choo made completely in leather netting, a pair of red patent-leather Guccis, a pair of crazy Blahniks with feathers at the ankle strap. Shoes for thousands of euros. Daddy's money was good to have.

She liked her room. Still: she could feel it clearly—it was time to move away from home, soon.

They turned the lights off. Almost pitch black. Viktor was playing with his watch. Held it up to their faces. It glowed in the dark.

"I bought a new one. What do you think?"

Natalie squinted. "I can't actually see that much."

"No, but you can see how crazy glow-in-the-dark it is—check out the twelve and the six. They're the strongest. It's a Panerai Luminor Regatta. Really sick, if I say so myself. Almost an inch thick. The Italian air force used to wear these."

He put his arm around her.

"I think I'm going to be admitted to law school after the summer," she said.

"Cool. And what're you gonna do until then?"

"It's summer soon, so I'm just gonna chill. You know the situation right now."

"Yeah, I understand. But do you like my new watch?"

Natalie wondered how he could afford to buy that new watch. But maybe he was going to get money soon—that's what he said anyway. Viktor'd seemed distant lately, only cared about himself and his job. Talked about how he was going to make some massive deal happen any day now, that he was going to hit the big time.

Maybe it wasn't time just to move away from home. Maybe it was time to dump this guy too.

Natalie realized she was awake. She turned over on her side. The pillow was cool. She squeezed her toes together. Threw her arm out. Searched for Viktor.

She couldn't reach him. No Viktor. She opened her eyes.

He wasn't in bed.

Natalie raised her head. He was not in the room.

Her cell phone read: eight forty-five. She wondered where he'd gone.

She set her feet down on the carpet: a green-grass-colored shag. Like a lawn in her room, a sense of summer year round.

Natalie put on the white silk robe that Mom'd given her before she left for Paris. She tied the belt around her waist.

Past the guest room. Patrik wasn't there. Then through the hallway. There he was, Patrik. Waiting, watching. She walked past the TV room. She peered down the stars into the rec and safe rooms. Goran was standing at a window, looking out.

She walked toward the kitchen. Wanted to talk to Mom. Wanted to drink a cup of tea. Wanted to find out where Viktor'd disappeared to.

She opened the door. Stefanovic was sitting in there, talking to a man she'd seen before. Big build, mouse-colored hair, Swedish. According to Dad, he was a former cop. The man got up, offered her his hand.

"Good morning, Natalie. Do you recognize me? My name is Thomas Andrén. I'm sorry that we had to drive your boyfriend home."

His grip was firm—but not in that exaggerated way that many of Dad's employees used.

"What's going on?" she asked. "I thought there'd been enough people in this house lately." The comment was directed at Stefanovic.

Thomas Andrén smiled. Said, "Your dad is coming home in an hour."

*

Those who are best in my domain are the ones who are able to discern patterns the quickest. I thought I was one of them.

Humans are creatures of habit. A creature that functions in accordance with structures. Every person's way of moving and living their life becomes a pattern, a structure that must be dissected and analyzed.

It was a failure. I acted like an amateur, a rookie, a B-player who tried to go through with the attack without proper insight. I didn't even get in touch with my employer. I was ashamed, like a child who gets his knuckles rapped.

I tried to reconstruct the sequence of events in the days that followed. Why did things end up the way they did? I went through my notes. Looked at my surveillance photos, cleaned and checked my weapons. Reached the same conclusion over and over again. First of all: I know that he almost always wears a protective vest. Still, I chose a distance that demanded shots to the body. Second of all: I know he usually has a bodyguard. Still, I chose a location where it was easy to protect him.

What's more, when he'd exited the elevator and was about to step into the line of fire, Radovan'd veered to the right instead of to the left, where his car was parked. He'd arrived in one car but decided to leave in another. I should have aborted the mission at that point.

I thought about the hit that I executed against Puljev in 2004, at that discothèque in St. Petersburg. I made my way past four bodyguards and shot him at a distance of sixteen feet. I knew he wore a bulletproof vest. One shot to the forehead was all it took, I could handle it at that distance.

But Radovan wasn't stupid.

I admit to myself that I underestimated him. I thought that little Serb would be more naïve and less vigilant than his peers out in Europe just because he was the king of peaceful Sweden. But I was the one who was naïve. I was the one who was unvigilant.

My client obviously knew that I'd failed. The Swedish newspapers apparently loved to hate Radovan Kranjic. I saw pictures on news bills, understood fragments of headlines, flipped through page-long special features.

But I knew an opening would arise somewhere.

All I had to do was wait. In the end, my client would get what he wanted.

10

Jorge was sitting at one of the surf computers at a 7-Eleven.

7-Eleven: colorful signs about special deals. Coffee and a bun for only fifteen kronor—these were the kinds of places that seriously tripped up real café owners. J-boy drank a Red Bull instead.

His duffel bag was at his feet. In the duffel: a gat. Walther PPK. The police's old model. Plus four full magazines. The thought that was burning in his head: *What if something happened?* At the same time: nothing could happen. He was just sitting here, surfing—chill, nothing suspicious. Drop the paranoia, *huevon*.

He needed to concentrate. Repeated one of the Finn's rules to himself: no surfing on your own computer. Always left a trail. IP addresses, stuff on the computer's hard drive. Jorge was no hacker, but he understood this much: the five-oh always managed to dig shit up, even if you deleted it. So 7-Eleven was perfect—he could do his surfing on public waves.

The research for the day: places on the Web that sold jammers.

The Finn'd given him a few addresses he thought would work. Jorge was even prepared to head to Poland and pick up a jammer on the spot.

He gulped some Red Bull. A sweet artificial taste. Still good.

He needed the energy. The past couple of days: he'd worked 110 percent with the CIT plan. Never dropped the hit. Endless planning and shit to take care of. Constantly on his mind. The café had to run itself for a while—they gave Beatrice more responsibility.

He glanced away from the computer. The evening papers were screaming out the latest global headline: YOUR COUGH COULD BE A FATAL ILLNESS. That was standard news in those shit papers. Some headlines Jorge'd seen over the past few years: HEADACHES: A LETHAL AFFLICTION. STOMACHACHES ARE EXTREMELY SERIOUS. STUBBLE CAN BE AN INDICATION OF DEATH. According to those rags: Jorge should've been deader than Michael Jackson and 2Pac combined ten years ago at least.

Still: today was the first day they weren't going on about the attempted murder of Radovan the Cock Kranjic. Too bad—Jorge liked the fact that someone'd tried to pop that fucker.

Back to the plan. The keys to a successful hit, according to the Finn: advance planning, serious preparation, tight players. Jorge called it his *mandamientos*. Every part: a commandment. A foundation. A pillar. Every *mandamiento*: a law that CIT kings followed.

Detailed breakdown: advance planning, necessary for any pro. The Finn never let up about that: it was truer than all Scorsese films combined. Didn't matter how ill your plans were—if you started scheming too short before the hit, you were gonna run into trouble. Without good lead time, the pigs'd be able to trace your tracks back in time. They were like fighting dogs: once their jaws clamped down, they didn't release their grip. Cracked your excuses like an egg against a frying pan.

Jorge knew even more. Buddies who'd been busted told stories you couldn't trust. They were always *soo* smart. But J-boy was smarter. He read up on things on his own. Got help from Tom Lehtimäki to order a bunch of court records. Courts all over Sweden sent fat stacks of paper to a P.O. box he'd rigged under a false name. The heli-robbery, the Akalla robbery, the Hallunda robbery. Jorge studied hard, sat with paper and pen in hand. Learned the mistakes others'd made. The clowns who'd fucked up—hadn't had tight alibis, babbled like bitches in the police interrogations, hadn't clocked that the cops might've had wiretaps, lived it up like billionaires in the days immediately following their hits. He understood how the police traced the steps you'd taken. How they questioned you on the spot when you were picked up. Pressured you in interrogations at the police station. Pulled fast ones on you in the courtrooms.

"We can see here that all of you put new SIM cards in your phones on the day before the event."

"It has come to light that you purchased two magazines for an assault rifle two days before the event."

"There is evidence that you were ten people in a studio apartment the week before the robbery. Why?"

Why? That question should never even come up.

Planning: The Finn's second rule. Honestly: most of the people who attempted hits weren't exactly the sharpest tools in the shed. Classic: boys with top-shelf confidence overestimated themselves more than the Svens overestimated the national soccer team in the World Cup. The jackpot every *hombre* thought would come rattling in at some point in their lives. Flip the script and make Sweden shake. Seemed so easy to do something so hard. Tightly packed dollar bills in briefcases. No, that was a *fugazy*.

Actually: planning meant mad research. Above all: a fat headache. Jorge never would've been able to do it without the Finn, and it was still gonna be tough. But all the same: in the end, the responsibility rested on his shoulders—a heavy burden to bear. How the fuck would it work? The answer was clear. Spelled p-l-a-n-n-i-n-g.

And last but not the runt, the most important rule. The rule that you must never forget. The Finn's third pillar. Repeated again and again.

Team members who were 100 percent.

The Finn nagged: "Are your bros trustworthy?"

J-boy understood.

One single rat—and it could all go to hell. Some cunt couldn't take the pressure, caved to the cops' promises about reduced sentences, personal protection, a new identity, money, a house in the country somewhere, a discount on their punishment. Slippery interrogators played nice. Cop swine served pizza in the jail cell and brought a porno over at night. One single canary sang, and that was it. One single cunt's cowardly confession. It could be enough for a prosecution. Worse: it could be enough for a conviction.

And that was why you had to know that you were surrounding yourself with ass-tight bros. Not just ones that wouldn't ordinarily snitch—no one did that. They had to be built to handle more pressure than that. Had any of them ever collaborated with an authority? Had any of them been in jail for months with full restrictions? Max one hour per day outside in fifty-square-foot rec cages—the only time in the day you could smoke. No contact with other inmates, no TV. No phone calls or letters to the outside world, not to their *amigos* or to their mama. Just by themselves. Alone.

How had they acted? Talked? Handled the five-oh?

He thought of the forms that the Red & White Crew and other gangs had their prospects fill out—like a fucking application to continuing ed or something. Maybe Jorge should do that too.

But he knew Mahmud, Javier, and Sergio inside out. Tom was 100 percent. Mahmud swore on Robert. Tom swore on Jimmy and Viktor.

They were tighter than the gangs with their vests and made-up regulations—the heaviest hitters never rocked idiot shit like that: that was like attracting the cops' attention on purpose. The heaviest hitters operated without being seen.

Still: the third pillar—if you compromised with that, you deserved to do time.

He thought about the progress he'd been making over the past few weeks.

He'd searched on Google Earth like a freak. Satellite photos over Tomteboda: mad *Enemy of the State* shit. You could see everything: cars, fences, the control booths by the entrances, the train tracks, the loading docks. You could even angle the images in 3D. Move back and forth like in a computer game. Jesus—it was so awesome. He tried to order blueprints of the reloading facility—got shot down. Apparently classified. He wondered why WikiLeaks only released documents for terrorists but nothing for robbers.

The Finn got hold of hand-drawn blueprints instead. Jorge studied them as if he'd just been admitted into a program for security room architecture. The Finn drew lines on the paper: *This is how we get out.*

He lifted a digital camera from Media Markt. A small piece: Sony, three hundred grams. He and Mahmud let an old drunk rent a car for them and headed out to Tomteboda. Drove around half the afternoon. Ill espionage setup. Learned the roads. Got acquainted with the signs, the roundabouts, the number of lanes. Got closer, bit by bit. Taped the camera to the instrument panel with duct tape. Wrapped a T-shirt around it. Boom: hidden recording device.

Spring for real now: small white flowers in the lawns, leftover sand on the roads, defrosted dog shit on the sidewalks.

Tomteboda glimpsed in the distance. A huge building: two thousand feet long. Outer shell of sheet metal. Glassed-in rooms that jutted out, pillars and elevator shafts on the outsides of the walls. Thick pipes, air-conditioning ducts, awnings, drainpipes, chimneys, and lots of shit everywhere. The place looked like a spaceship.

Unfortunately, they couldn't get too close. The best view they got was from a little hill about three hundred yards away, on the other side of the train tracks. According to the Finn: Wednesday was the day in the week when the CITs were driven. But the cash in transit companies apparently changed their routines a lot; it was impossible to know the exact time. They'd figure it out—the Finn's insider would have to deliver.

Jorge fished out a pair of binoculars. Aimed, scouted. Spun the focus. Perfect view. Gravel and pavement around the building. The sun was glittering in the warehouse's metal coating. The loading docks in a row, numbered: twenty-two of them. Yellow trucks with the Postal Service's logo on them were driving in and out. Backing up. Postal workers in blue shirts were pushing carts with blue crates on them. Rolled the carts, one by one. It was regular mail—uninteresting, really. But could be good to see anyway.

They waited. Jorge unwrapped the plastic-covered sandwiches he'd bought at a deli.

They ate.

Kept their eyes open.

Drank orange soda.

At one o'clock, two black trucks drove in through the southern entrance. But J-boy already knew which loading docks they would stop at if they were carrying the right cargo, the ones that were blocked off: numbers twenty-one and twenty-two.

The point of the Finn's plan: they wanted to pluck the delivery when it was being unloaded. Not up on the road or when the valuable cargo was in the depot. That way they'd avoid having to force the armored cars or the depot's security system.

They kept scouting.

Jorge played with the camera, tried to film—they were too far away. The image quality sucked.

People climbed out of the trucks. Green uniforms, dark baseball caps. A few of them: with cell phones or walkie-talkies. A couple of batons. They worked quickly—pushed big steel carts with bars on the sides. The color of the bags with the large handles in the carts was clearly visible.

The Finn's insider knew what he was talking about, that little snake.

That's the way the security bags were supposed to look. Big handles. One and a half foot high. Black.

Shit. Bull's-eye.

Jorgelito vs. the Postal Service's assets in transit: one, zero.

Back at the 7-Eleven. He thought of the stack of bills at home in his apartment. At least eight large. Collected from the group. Mahmud had an identical stack at his house. One hundred and sixty-five hundred kronor bills wrapped with a rubber band. Stuffed into a plastic bag and hidden in the water tank of the toilet.

Jorge. Mahmud. Tom. Sergio. Javier. Robert. And the Svens: Jimmy and Viktor. Solid soldiers. Mahmud kept nagging: *We should bring Babak on board too.*

Hombre could forget about it.

It was almost time for a big group meeting. Jorge'd gone over everything with the Finn. He was gonna present the plan to the boys. Bring them up to lightning speed: this shit was on a whole other level.

Jorge deleted the history in Internet Explorer. Closed down the browser. Got up.

In his hand: the duffel with the gat.

Mahmud was waiting outside in a Range Rover Vogue that he'd borrowed from that Babak fag. On paper, some forty-year-old homeless guy was registered for the SUV. Babak: a douchebag, but no dummy.

On their way to the storage facility. They were gonna drop off the Walther. Another of the Finn's rules: never keep weapons at home.

More difficult that you might think. Jorge and Mahmud: loved to flash heat. Show off at parties. Just let the gun hang nonchalantly in the lining of their pants. Pose for their bros, take pictures, and text them back and forth. Test-shoot in the woods like real g-boys.

None of that now. Every last piece had to be put in storage.

Jorge turned to Mahmud. The Arab was wearing a fanny pack today. What did his bro have in that, anyway? J-boy considered asking if it was his makeup pouch but let it go.

Mahmud turned off the stereo. Said, "I came up with a math thing for the perfect crime."

"Whattya mean, math thing?"

"Check it, man. You can count coins. Turn coins into bills. Fix and sell shit for years. You can pressure people, do little hits here and there, whatever. But this is the deal: the more dough, the better. The less time you risk sitting, the better. Right?"

"Obviously."

"Right, so. If you take what you make and divide it by how much time you could get slammed with, you get a number. You with me?"

"*Hermano*, I passed motherfuckin' math."

"Right. So, for example, if you can get five million and risk five years in the pen or can get eight million and risk ten years in the pen. What do you do?"

"It depends."

"But think about it like this, five million divided by five is one million. Eight million divided by ten is only eight hundred large. So you should do the first gig. More kronor per year. That's how the HA think. They started doing a bunch of white-collar shit 'cause you get no time for it."

"Okay, I follow. But you might want eight million instead of five, right? Maybe you wanna drive a Ferrari instead of a BMW."

Fifteen minutes later. They rolled onto Malmvägen. Jorge's childhood. The Million Program's ten-story high-rises with peeling concrete. The place where he'd become who he was: J-boy, the C-Señor, the chain-buster, the café owner. Where his mama'd done the best she could. She still lived nearby, in Kista.

He wondered what people were saying about the car. The Range Rover: fucking enormous. Bus feel to it.

He thought: Malmvägen was a country within the country. A Sweden within Sweden. Its own nation where people like him knew the laws. That's what Sven Sweden would never understand—'cause they'd gotten used to divorced moms, half-siblings, plastic papas, fourteen-year-old chicks who got raped when they were boozed out, old people put in homes, broken A-teamers with cirrhosis stretched out on park benches with families who didn't give a shit. Far from perfect. So the projects had to protect themselves. Build their own system within the Swedish system. Preserve their thing. Most things in the hood were better than in their Sweden. People cared about each other. Life actually meant something. Friendship, love, hate—the feelings weren't just fake.

He looked up. The basement storage unit was in building number forty-five.

Behind them: a sound. A light.

He turned around.

An undercover cruiser. Flashing lights on the roof. Jorge couldn't believe he'd missed it. A Saab 9-5 with dark windows in back and a weird amount of radio antennae—the bucket screamed UC *pacos*.

He looked down at the duffel on the floor between Mahmud's feet.

He stopped the car. "We're fucked."

Jorge turned around again. A civvie stepped out. It looked like there was one left sitting in the car.

He saw drops of sweat on Mahmud's forehead.

A headache descended like an ambush. Fat jabs against the inside of his skull.

His stomachache churned faster, the gags pushed upward.

Fucked. Royally fucked.

The cop approached. A chick. She was tall, blond. Hands tucked into her belt: fake relaxed. Jorge glimpsed a holster.

Mierda.

The chick walked up to the driver's side. Knocked on the window. Jorge rolled it down. How slowly could a car window be rolled down, anyway?

He stared straight ahead.

His thoughts, in chaos.

No point in playing the pig. No point in even thinking the thought.

At the same time: he was still fast. He was called Shawshank for a reason.

He saw Malmvägen's weather-beaten walls outside the car. The entrances to the buildings—all the same. Only the graffiti was different. The culverts under the houses, the inner courtyards, the basements.

He knew his way around here.

He knew his way around better than Michael Scofield'd know his way around in *Prison Break*.

The cop chick poked her head in. "Would you please step out of the car?"

Jorge reacted. He slammed his foot on the gas. The car skipped forward. The V8 roared. Three hundred horsepower in full gallop.

The cop chick screamed something. Jorge didn't care.

Mahmud yelled, "Drive, man! Drive!"

Jorge swung to the right, tugged at the wheel. His body almost slammed into the inside of the door.

He saw the cop car switch its lights on. Heard the sirens.

More pressure on the gas.

Malmvägen, fifty-five miles an hour. The cop car, a hundred yards behind them.

He was thinking with supersonic speed. Wanted to turn into one of the pedestrian walkways. At the same time: if they were able to dump the weapon, the cop fuckers would still try to nail them for reckless driving.

He kept pushing straight ahead. Drove all in.

Screeching right turn onto Bagarbyvägen. Didn't pick up more speed than necessary.

Mahmud was yelling a bunch of mixed-up shit: "I'm gonna toss the piece!"

Jorge told him no.

They made another turn. An area with one-family homes. Jorge'd nicked so many apples here as a kid, he could've started a cider factory. He knew these roads. He knew his way better than Andy Dufresne. That's right, Shawshank.

A little farther ahead: two side streets that turned. Perfect. If they took one of them, the cops wouldn't have any idea which one. They shouldn't be able to see him—as long as he made it around the bend. All they needed to do: stop and dump the duffel with the gat.

They had to get rid of this heat.

No way it could be game over already.

11

In the pen since a few weeks back. As a screw.

Officially, Hägerström had been fired from the police force.

Unofficially, he was an infiltrator.

Officially, he had a job as a corrections officer at the Salberga Penitentiary. Unofficially, his new assignment spelled: UC agent in the field.

His mom, Lottie, didn't say much, but he knew that she worried about the fact that he wasn't working as a police officer anymore.

Martin Hägerström already knew a lot about life on the inside. He had read reports and investigations about institutional life in Sweden, the analyses the Department of Corrections made about the inmates' circumstances and problems, Torsfjäll's own memos with insider information. But the real thing was different. The theories and the learned methods melted away in the reality of everyday life. The security routines appeared stiff and marginal. Even the information he had gotten from Mrado Slovovic seemed insubstantial.

What was important were the people; every single person was a challenge he had to tackle. Every single situation was a little theater show. But Hägerström knew he was a pro at that. He was always playing a part—that's what it felt like, anyway.

A CO colleague took him under her wing. Esmeralda—the girl had at least ten earrings in each ear and arms that were more pumped than Madonna's—explained the lay of the land. During every coffee break she prattled on about what she thought and what he ought to know. The rumors that were going around. The pecking order among the inmates. What actually happened when the cell doors were closed, who was considered hard, who was considered soft. She was a talker and used more soccer terminology than a sports commentator during live coverage. The prison staff had to read the game, she'd played an away-game all weekend, some of the female screws were really offside, and so on. Esmeralda was a soccer fanatic and a prison fetishist. Hägerström appreciated the excess of information. There was a lot to learn.

The Salberga Penitentiary was relatively new and therefore in pretty good condition. But that didn't make it any less hard on the inside—even if wasn't one of the country's supermaxes. The security system was carefully developed and fine-tuned. The contrast between the facade and the business going on behind it only reinforced one single truth: life behind bars couldn't be changed by a fresh paint job and electronic supercameras. Certain things were just an indelible part of the prison institution.

There was no rec yard. The inmates were allowed out five at a time for one hour a day in a fenced-in quad. They could choose whom they walked out with. The division happened naturally: ethnic belonging, gang membership, type of crime. Some guys could go anywhere: bikers, Swedish robbers, drug kingpins. Certain guys went out on their own or in pairs: the ones who were convicted of sex-related crimes or domestic violence. And some stayed in their cells around the clock, no one even wanted to look at them: the snitches. They truly lived dangerously.

When a new inmate arrived, the same routine every time: someone on a block ordered the court papers. Everyone got to read, pronounce, denounce. Play the judge. The snitches had to drink piss out of plastic cups three times a day, got feces in their lunchboxes, were beaten bloody with billiard balls stuffed into socks. The snitches: the ones who requested to switch blocks after less than twenty-four hours and to transfer out after forty-eight. Once a rat, always a rat, they said. Hägerström thought about his assignment. If he succeeded but was found out, he might as well leave Sweden for good.

He learned the unwritten rules on the inside. How you handled provocations that would have made any regular cop on the beat pound the person in question black and blue. How you handled people who drank a gallon of water a day—to water down their urine so the drug tests wouldn't come back positive—or who cut themselves and mixed the blood in their piss, another way to hide what you had been taking. He became an expert at controlling the inmates' cells. They glued Red Line Baggies with hash into their TVs with the help of dried toothpaste. He screwed apart computers: the inmates were allowed to have laptops of their own but no Internet. They were perfect hiding places for shivs of the smallest size. He learned to frisk the inmates in the smoothest way possible—it wasn't the same as on the street; there was nothing to threaten them with if they made a fuss. Cell phones were often hidden inside their boxers. Esmeralda just laughed. "Sweaty, hairy crotches are my favorite."

After a few days, he realized what was really important in here. The routines. That the commissary cart rolled in at the same time every day, that the rec hours didn't change, that mealtimes remained intact. These boys didn't need any more chaos in their lives. And many of the inmates thought the time inside was good for the first six months or so. If you had spent many months in jail pretrial, prison life was liberating. You were allowed to eat together, play games, had a proper schedule with things to do.

If they wanted to, they could make nine kronor an hour working. Fold envelopes, build clothes hangers or birdhouses. Some of them saved their weekly pay in the prison's accounts, others blew their whole load on tobacco and soda. A few sent every krona home to their families in South America, Romania, or small-town Sweden. One inmate demanded that his savings—around four thousand kronor—be transferred into another inmate's account. The prison administration suspected a gambling debt and forbade the transaction. The guy went crazy, refused to come out of his cell for two weeks. In the third week, he started to smear feces on the walls. Desperation took the upper hand sometimes. An unpaid poker debt could be worse than all the shit in the world.

The vast majority didn't bother working. Would rather hang out in the block all day. Played cards or video games. Lay in their cells and watched TV. Played Ping-Pong in the Ping-Pong room.

Sometimes the entire block walked through the culverts to the prison's gymnasium. Played floor hockey or basketball. But it almost always ended in upheaval. People wouldn't take any injustices on the court. But at least it was better that they took care of it there than with a sharpened toothbrush in the shower.

Hägerström's mission was to become a well-liked screw, a foul screw, a friend. The fact that the inmates knew he had been a cop didn't make it any easier. A canned cop, sure—but still. FTP, ACAB. The graffiti in the cells spoke its own, clear language: FUCK THE POLICE. ALL COPS ARE BASTARDS. He had to gain the boys' trust. Become someone known for being crooked—just enough. Never call for the riot squad unnecessarily. Always give an extra half an hour in the visiting room with the ethnic woman that everyone but the prison administration understood was a whore. Not argue even if the cell doors were open after eight at night. Not do overly thorough room searches. Make sure to neglect checking the space between the bed and the wall or the cracked sole in the prison-issue slippers.

One night, when he was about to try to have a talk with JW, Hägerström heard sounds. A closed cell door, number seven. He opened the hatch and peered inside. At least five inmates were crowded in there. Loud. Trashed. Happy. He knocked before he stepped inside. Wanted to show respect. They fell silent. He opened the door. They had gotten hold of yeast and raisins and made pruno in a mop bucket. Hägerström tried to be cool with the guys. Reason with them and make them understand: *This isn't a good idea. I can let it slide without a warning, but leave right now.*

He could only guess what the other screws were thinking. Laziness wasn't a point of pride. But among the inmates, the incident raised his status immediately. He could feel it as soon as no other screws were around. They had started to dig him.

But—there was a but. Time was running out. In a few months, this window would be closing. He had to set things in motion with JW before then.

They had spoken many times. JW rocked a polite, accommodating style. No fuss. No backtalk. No long harangues about why he should get another serving at dinner, had the right to stay in someone else's room, or anything else that was constantly being discussed, asked, demanded. He was easygoing, articulate, positive. A few of the screws thought he was slippery like lube, but in general they liked the fact that he was calm and well behaved.

In a cautious way, Hägerström tried to ask around about whether anyone on the staff had a good relationship with JW, if there was someone he spoke more with. If someone had got closer to him, beyond that overt polite facade. The answer was clear: no one working now had any such relationship to JW. But Esmeralda confirmed Torsfjäll's claim, the entire reason Hägerström was here: "I guess Christer Starre did, but he doesn't work here anymore. Did you meet him before he left?"

Sometimes Hägerström thought the suspicions directed at JW appeared weak. Why would someone use an inmate to help with a complex white-collar crime? At the same time, if it was as Torsfjäll believed, it was genius. No one would suspect that a federal penitentiary was the planning hub for a money-laundering scheme.

Hägerström did what he could, every day. At the same time, he didn't want to appear too forward. JW wasn't stupid. Hägerström and Torsfjäll already knew that he was quasi-paranoid, and with every right too. And there was no real reason for JW to bond with a new screw just because the screw was nice. It would take something more than that. Hägerström thought he knew what.

Most of the inmates sat in the dining hall during lunch. The two halls of cells on level three had a shared kitchen, where those who were interested in cooking could prepare their own lunch and dinner.

JW always sat at one of the middle tables. He was blond with four-inch-long hair. He wasn't broadly built, but still in good shape. Hägerström had figured out his routines. JW ran six miles on the treadmill at the gym three times a week. What was interesting was that no matter who was using the treadmill, when JW came into the gym, that person stepped off and gave JW the spot. It was obvious that the guy's standing in here was out of the ordinary.

The screws ate at the same time as the inmates. The prison administration's idea was that it would create a friendly feeling of camaraderie. That was mostly on the surface. All the screws sat at their own table. But today Hägerström was planning on trying something out.

JW was eating with three other inmates. Hägerström knew who they were too. Torsfjäll's memos covered all the details. To JW's left was a fifty-year-old Yugo called the Tube, but whose real name was Zlatko Rovic. Twenty years ago he had been beaten up so severely he lost the hearing in his right ear. But the doctors had put in some kind of equipment, a tube, in his ear canal, and the Tube could use his ear again. He was a former hit man who had changed gears and worked with invoice fraud and other white-collar crimes these days. On the other side of the table was a younger talent nicknamed Crazy Tim. His real name was Tim Bredenberg McCarthy. The guy was thirty-three years old, a former soccer hooligan and leading rabble-rouser in the 1990s. These days he did white-collar stuff, but on a smaller scale. The last man at the table was Charlie Nowak. A different category altogether: 100 percent violent criminal. Convicted of aggravated assault and blackmail. He was twenty-two years old. He must fit into the gang in some way other than through white-collar-crime contacts, but that didn't surprise Hägerström. Unholy alliances of this kind were normal these days. The raw knuckles joined the brains in the pen, as Torsfjäll put it.

Hägerström asked if they minded if he sat down.

The Tube put his silverware down. Crazy Tim froze. Charlie Nowak stopped chewing.

Screws and inmates didn't share tables. Like oil and water, unmixable. In other words, unthinkable.

JW continued to eat, unperturbed. Kept on talking to the others. Didn't even look up.

Enough of a signal. It was okay with JW.

The others relaxed.

Hägerström sat down. The Tube didn't drop his gaze for a second.

JW continued to cut his pieces of stroganoff. Held the knife far down on the shaft, meticulously. He cut every piece of sausage in three parts. Mixed with rice. Pushed one of the pieces that he had chosen onto his fork. In Hägerström's eyes, his manners belonged to a food-obsessed teenager.

He couldn't even remember how young he had been the first time Mother had said, "Hold your knife and fork high up. So people don't think you're putting your fingers in your food."

In other words: not the way JW was holding his.

JW opened his mouth. "How long have you been here now, Martin?"

An opening. He said, "Not long enough to know my way around all the blocks yet."

JW laughed politely.

"But I like it better every day," Hägerström said.

"Easy for you to say," the Tube muttered. "You don't have three more years until you get to go home."

"I know, maybe it sounds weird to say I like it here. But the atmosphere in this unit is pretty cool."

"You're probably right," JW said. "I've seen a lot worse. This place is chill. The only thing I miss is better workout facilities."

Crazy Tim grinned. "Doing time's good for you, man. Freshens you up. No booze and shit. Good in the head, I mean. But you get fucking fat too. Too little training and too little fucking."

Everyone around the table laughed. Hägerström laughed too. Crazy

Tim, Mensa candidate. And his sex jokes were similar to some of Hägerström's cop colleagues' bro'y lingo.

He was trying to come up with a clever retort, but his brain had apparently checked out for now. He didn't come up with anything. He felt stupid.

The Tube, Crazy Tim, and JW kept chatting. Hägerström's presence didn't seem to bother them. A step in the right direction. But it didn't bring him any closer to JW, not really.

He knew it would take time.

After ten minutes, they got up. JW rose first. The others followed him like kids toddling after their day-care teacher. Hägerström remained seated. He was thinking about his next move. Too many of his talks with JW had ended up like this—pleasant, accepting, and simple. But no trust. No opening.

He had to break into JW-land soon.

He had discussed several different strategies with Torsfjäll.

Soon Hägerström would kick his operation into full gear.

He had a plan.

12

Louise said it was, without a doubt, the party to beat all parties—the year's most expensive, exclusive, elite private throwdown. Natalie's attitude was more balanced. She was geared up to go. She was always let in to the clubs around Stureplan—if you'd worked the bar circuit, looked okay, had her legs and above all her dad, things usually worked out. But still: the fact that they were invited to Jet Set Carl's housewarming party along with two hundred other special guests—that was seriously VIP.

At the same time: she didn't feel all that great about the night ahead—what'd happened to Dad was scary.

Carl Malmer—alias Jet Set Carl, alias the Prince of Stureplan—had gut-renovated his penthouse on Skeppargatan and was celebrating with a big, bad blowout bash. More than three thousand square feet on posh Östermalm, Stockholm's Upper East Side: that was some sky-high class. Jet Set Carl'd bought the neighboring apartment a year ago, torn down the walls, made the place like a loft—lots of open space. Not because he really needed more space but because he didn't want to have neighbors who complained when he partied. It sounded like an exaggeration. But it's what Louise said, anyway.

Louise'd kept Natalie up to speed in the days leading up to the party. Scribbled her Facebook wall full. The hottest guys were coming. The brats from the best families. She got herself more and more worked up. *Keep your cell phone camera on—there are gonna be crazy photo ops, promise.* Sometimes Natalie thought Louise wasn't just a little bit of a bimbo, she was almost a hazard to herself. What did she imagine Jet Set Carl would think if he saw her posts?

The tabloids were amping up the mood too. Jet Set Carl: romance rumors with Hollywood starlets and European princesses. Jet Set Carl's company: bigger turnover than the entire Stureplan Group. Jet Set Carl: ranked as the most powerful person within the Swedish entertainment industry by the gossip site Stureplan.se.

Louise seemed to think that they'd been invited because of her. Normally, that might've been true: she went out every weekend and was treated to bubbly by dudes with their shirts unbuttoned who just wanted to get off and get gone. But Natalie knew why they'd actually been invited.

Louise had a tendency to place herself at the center of attention a bit too often. She was a serious germophobe, never touched her mouth to the bottle when she drank, pulled her sleeves down to touch a door handle, never touched anything in a bathroom without disinfecting her hands afterward with her little tube of DAX Alcogel. And yet she would suck anyone off for a few hours of validation. But Jet Set Carl was friendly with Dad. If it wasn't for that, Natalie and Louise wouldn't even have been let into the afterparty.

Dad wasn't happy about the fact that Natalie planned on going. She understood, that's how it had to be. Her parents hadn't exactly been Sweden's most liberal before the assassination attempt, but they also didn't want to treat her like a child anymore. Now they were trying to rein her in. And she understood them: the entire family had to be careful.

And what's more: they didn't just need to be careful. They had to avenge what'd happened.

Louise whined about Natalie being wishy-washy. "You've gotta come. You need it. Or I'll go with Tove instead."

Natalie wanted to go, but she didn't have the energy to comment on Louise's childish attempt to play her against Tove. Plus: Louise should know better than to nag at her—she knew what'd happened.

But two days before the party, Mom was actually the one who brought up the question. They were sitting in the den watching *Grey's Anatomy*. Not Natalie's favorite show, but she was okay watching it 'cause Mom liked it. Mom said that she'd talked things over with Dad, that they couldn't keep her locked up forever. That Natalie must to be allowed to go out, live her life. They wanted her to have fun. Like before.

But when they'd discussed the matter again, Dad'd been kind of short: "You're sleeping here, at home."

"Okay," Natalie said. "But maybe Viktor can pick me up and drive me home?"

"Isn't he going to the party?" Dad wondered.

"No, he's not invited." Natalie was actually kind of relieved about that. Viktor worked around the clock these days. But not with his car showroom in Hjorthagen. Instead he said things like "I'm out on a job," and "Soon, soon the money will start flowing." She thought the whole thing was a bore.

Dad didn't comment. He ended the discussion instead. "Since you'll be sleeping here, me, Patrik, or Stefanovic'll drive you home. Where and when do you want to be picked up?"

Back at Jet Set Carl's enormous pad. Overflowing clothes hangers and a huge guy with a shaved head and unmistakable appearance: dark jeans, black leather jacket, and a turtleneck that fit snugly over a bulletproof vest. Bouncer, to the millionth power.

He checked his list. Natalie didn't know if she and Louise were on it.

Louise tried to flirt. Pouted her lips. "Will you be inside at the party later? I want to get a picture of us together. I've never seen such a cool bouncer before."

Louise smelled too strongly of J'Adore—and she was acting like someone who wears too much perfume too.

The bouncer didn't even glance up. His fingers stopped at a point on the page. He looked at Louise, then at Natalie.

"You're Kranjic, right?"

She nodded.

"Welcome."

They took their jackets off. Louise asked Natalie if she thought she'd put too much self-tanner on her face.

Natalie was wearing a dress she'd found at a vintage place in the Marais. Diane von Furstenberg—smashing, if she did say so herself. She was carrying a purse from Louis Vuitton. Stuffed with her iPhone, wallet, two packs of Marlboro Menthol, keys, a blush, YSL's classic gold mascara, at least five Lancôme Juicy Tubes, and the new portable emergency alarm.

Louise was wearing a short, ruffled skirt and a tight tank top that she'd bought at the Marc Jacobs sale in Paris. Her push-up bra pressed her boobs up more ridiculously than usual. She would've needed a push-down instead.

The heat, the din from the party, and the smell of expectation in the air rose up like a wall of wonder. They pushed through. Inside: blond babes, B-list boob models with D-cups, and blazer boyz abounded.

The goal was to quickly find someone they knew or to be hit on by someone. They wanted to avoid having to stand around like losers, waiting for something to happen. To look alone was totally taboo.

They went into the kitchen—an enormous room, probably a thousand square feet. A bar'd been built in one half of the room. Smirnoff ads covered the walls: Jet Set Carl knew his product placement. Bartenders who'd been hired from the biggest club downtown bubbled up a steady golden stream of Taittinger and mixed drinks with the advertised booze as the main ingredient. In the corners: huge speakers were pumping out Eurovision-style music—appropriately ironic. The ceiling was covered in spotlights. Suspended from it were two crystal chandeliers the size of motorcycles. The light was reflecting in them like in the disco balls at the clubs Jet Set Cal usually controlled.

Natalie stared straight ahead. All her friends rocked that look all the time: the dead gaze. On the street: determined steps, head still, don't turn it for anything except possibly avoiding being run over. At bars: stand and wait for your friend outside the ladies' room and never meet anyone's eyes—showing that you cared about others was a weakness.

A mix of B- and C-list celebs were milling about. She eyed the makeup of people: the model Rebecka Simonsson, the writer Björn af Kleen, one of the many Skarsgård brothers, Blondinbella and a dozen other boobie bloggers, the actor Henrik Lundström, and the fashionista Sofi Fahrman paraded past.

Smack in the middle was that cheesy writer who'd been in the tabloids recently for appearing on TV with a spray tan and his shirt unbuttoned to his navel.

Natalie missed Paris. She missed the time before everything'd started happening with her dad.

Louise had Lady Gaga eyes, without even having done a line yet. Did her best to maintain the bored, dead-gaze expression. It was obvious: she didn't want to show how impressed she was.

The host was standing a bit farther in the room. He was dressed in a pink tux.

Louise pinched Natalie on the arm as discreetly as possible. "D'you see? Over there, that's Jet Set Carl. Damn, he's so hot."

Natalie didn't bother responding. The host'd obviously seen her. He made his way toward them. A look in his eye that seemed genuine enough. A broad smile that looked gross.

"Natalie, I'm so glad you could make it. How is everything, really?"

"It's fine. How are you?"

"I'm great. So fantastic to have this done, finally. It took almost a year and a half. But it ended up pretty sweet, right?"

Then he sounded more serious. "But I understand your situation. It must be very scary. That's why I'm so glad you could come tonight."

Natalie didn't know what to say. Her father'd been subjected to an assassination attempt, and here she was, partying. She felt like an idiot.

"It's fine." She turned to Louise. "This is my friend, Louise Guldhake."

Louise's smile wasn't a real smile, more of a grimace that she thought looked like a smile. But it seemed to work on Jet Set Carl. He kissed her on the cheek.

"Hi, Louise. Wonderful to see you here. You're having a good time, I hope?"

Then he leaned over and whispered something in Louise's ear. Natalie thought, *This might be a memorable moment for Louise Guldhake.*

Later. She walked out into the foyer, found her shearling coat, smiled at the bouncer, and took the stairs up.

The terrace looked like a forest of metal mushrooms—gas-powered heaters to temper the cool May air. Jet Set Carl didn't take any risks—a third of the terrace was covered in a party tent filled with infrared heaters. But it was okay out. The guests were crowding in. Enormous speakers were blazoning out Rihanna's latest hit.

The same ads for Smirnoff everywhere.

She eyed the people. The same mix as downstairs in the apartment. The same meaningless expressions on everyone's faces. Except for the ones who were too high to conceal their fascination with the celebs.

Natalie glanced down over the railing. The sky was dark blue. Light rose from the city. She glimpsed the dome and spire of the Hedvig Eleonora Church. Farther off, she saw the tower above Saluhallen, the large luxury food market. Dim silhouettes in the spring night. She remembered the conversation she'd had with Dad when he came home from the hospital.

"Natalie, I want to exchange a few words with you," he'd said. Always that complicated Serbian, even though he knew Natalie preferred to speak Swedish.

They'd gone into the library.

Stefanovic had been sitting at the desk, Goran in one of the armchairs, Milorad in another. All three of them'd been down in the parking garage at the time of the assassination attempt. Dad sat down in his armchair, the one he always sat in. One of his arms was dangling in a sling.

Natalie greeted the men. They kissed her on the cheeks: right, left, right. She knew them all. They'd been part of her family's inner circle for as long as she could remember. Still, she didn't know them at all. She got the feeling that they were meeting as adults now. For the first time.

Dad poured out a glass of whiskey.

He let the liquid spin around a few times in the glass before he tasted it.

"Natalie, my daughter, I think it's important that you take part in some of the conversations we are having in here. Would you like some?"

Natalie looked at him. He was holding the whiskey bottle and a tumbler in his hands. Johnnie Walker Blue Label. It was the first time in her life that he offered her whiskey.

She accepted the glass. Dad poured.

He turned to the others in the room. "This here is my daughter, do you see? She doesn't turn down a drink. A true Kranjic."

Stefanovic nodded over in his corner. The men in the room liked her, she could feel it—Dad's associates. The only people outside the family whom she could trust right now.

Dad began to speak again, "We are at a crossroads."

Natalie took a sip of whiskey. It burned pleasantly in her throat.

"I want you to be here, to understand what is happening. The demolition firm, the alcohol and cigarette importing business, the gambling machines, the coat checks—you know what I do, Natalie. We do some other business too. But we don't have to talk about that right now."

He swirled the whiskey in his glass again.

Natalie was aware of more things than what Dad was mentioning now. His business sprawled in all directions. A lot of what he did wasn't considered kosher by people like Louise—but that was the immigrant's lot in life. And was it really that much better to make your money as a venture capitalist who slaughtered companies and fired workers, then created smart solutions so that you didn't pay a cent in taxes, like Louise's dad did?

Radovan'd come far, considering that he'd started out as a twenty-year-old at the Scania factories in Södertälje. He'd worked himself up from nothing, against all odds. Most of the businesses he ran today weren't illegal, but he would still always be considered a criminal in the eyes of Swedish society. So the Svens could go fuck themselves—if you never gave someone a chance to do honest work, you had to accept that that person sometimes played outside the rules. The land of the Sweden Democrats was only going to get worse.

"Stockholm has been our unthreatened market for many years," Dad continued. "We've faced challenges, of course. Kum Jokso was killed. Mrado Slovovic tried to trick us. Those fuckers who blew shit up out at Smådalarö wanted to break us once again. But, and you know this, no one breaks a Kranjic. Right, Natalie?"

Natalie imitated Dad, spun the whiskey around in her glass. Smiled.

"And now someone tried to rub me out in a fucking parking garage. This is a new time we're living in. We've been following this development for a few years. More and more players want a piece of the pie. You know who I'm talking about: HA, Bandidos, Original Gangsters, the Syrians, the Albanians—they've been around for a long time. But they've done their business, and we've done ours. And really, it's only HA who've been playing in our league. But the newbies: the Gambians, Dark Snakes, Born to Be Hated—I mean, it's like the damn *Jungle Book*. Before, people used to accept us, knew it was best for everyone not to attack us. But these new little monkeys haven't understood that we've had a stabilizing effect on Stockholm's gray zones. They lack history, they haven't understood that everyone appreciates order, even the cops. HA, Bandidos, and the older factions make good money in their own fields. The higher-ups in the hierarchy hire illegal workers and manufacture invoice frauds in the construction industry. The ones lower down on the rungs do their racketeering and dope. But all the new tadpoles want is chaos, as long as they're kings of their own fucking ghettos. So maybe there are some people who think they've got something to gain by getting rid of me."

He took a deep breath.

"But—the guy in the parking garage was no amateur, that's for sure. So you can rule out some of those greenhorns right away—they only deal with *un*organized crime. Someone is making a serious attempt to get rid of me. I don't know who it is, but it means that someone is trying to get rid of *all of us*."

Natalie listened. She agreed with her father. Someone was trying to get rid of him, that much was clear. And this someone hadn't just started a war against Dad. It was a war against her entire family and everyone sitting in the study right now. That could not be tolerated. It was humiliation.

She regarded the men in the room.

Dad was wearing a cuffed shirt and chinos. He looked grave.

Stefanovic was nicely dressed. Well-ironed, striped shirt with French cuffs and silver cufflinks that had GUCCI written on them. He wore his hair in a sharp side part, had well-trimmed stubble, and a tight silver bracelet around one wrist. Stefanovic was the only one who cared about his appearance like that.

Goran was wearing a black tracksuit, as usual. Always Adidas. Worn-looking running shoes, Nike Air—all the time. Funny to think that Goran, the most untrendy Serb in northern Europe, had purchased a pair of retro-hip shoes. Or else he'd just worn the same shoes since 1987—actually, that was not entirely impossible.

Milorad rocked jeans and a polo shirt—a pink Lacoste. He was tan and looked really fit too. Saint-Tropez here I come, or whatever. Milorad tried to look young, but in Natalie's world, he'd been around for as long as Dad had.

She wondered who these men really were. If they would protect Dad. If they were capable.

And then a final thought shot through her mind. A thought that burned: Could they really be trusted?

Dad kept talking about new ways of working. About diversifying the business more. Switching their routines. Not repeating the same methods too many times. Recruiting new staff, increasing security checks, cleaning up among those who were not doing a good job.

The men were sitting in silence. Listening. Interjected something now and then.

Constantly on their faces: respect.

Then she looked at Stefanovic. She glanced again. She was certain: his eyes were gleaming.

Louise was chatting with some guy with a pink handkerchief in his breast pocket and a watch on his wrist that looked like Viktor's.

Natalie'd called Dad to pick her up.

She'd talked to Louise, with some other girls she usually met out at clubs, had exchanged a few words with Jet Set Carl again, nonsense-talked with someone named Nippe, grinned at a six-foot dude who was high like Burj Al Arab and pronounced the word *turquoise* in an incredibly funny way. There was nothing wrong with the night per se, but she wanted to go home now.

Dad called. Said he was parked down on the street. She could come down.

She took the elevator.

The entranceway to the building was Östermalm-style on steroids: old-fashioned moldings and Nordic frescos decorated the ceiling. A real Oriental rug on the floor as a welcome mat. Through the glass-paned doors she could see a dark blue BMW parked out on the street. It was Dad's car.

She walked out.

The BMW was parked twenty or so yards farther down the street.

Someone strolled past the car. Disappeared around the corner onto Storgatan.

She couldn't see who was sitting in the car.

One of the windows was rolled down a few inches.

She heard a voice. "It's me."

A hand waved. Dad was calling to her.

Natalie walked toward the car. Saw Dad in the driver's seat.

He started the engine.

Ten yards left.

Then: a sound. Something exploding.

Natalie's body was thrown back, up into the air.

She didn't understand anything.

She heard a monotone sound.

A ringing in her ears that wouldn't stop.

The BMW.

She tried to get up. She was on all fours.

Smoke was billowing out from the car.

13

Outside, rain. A low, spattering sound. As if there was a tap running somewhere in the house.

J-boy was peering outside. Massive trees. Bushes. Long leaves of grass. A little cottage that Jimmy called a tool shed. Three parked cars.

The *drip-drop* sound kept steadily on.

Spring was slow going this year.

He looked up. Beams in the ceiling. Looked weird: why build a house without finished ceilings? Had to be a Sven thing. But at least they were dry. So that's not where the dripping sound was coming from.

He looked farther. Wallpaper with a faggy pattern: blue and pink flowers. Wood-colored bookcases, thin curtains, a fat moose horn over one of the doors. A bouquet of dried flowers above the other door. On the floor: a rug, a basket with firewood, electrical heaters that made ticking sounds.

The place was way out in the boondocks: they'd driven there on a winding road. All around: farmhouses, barns, and worn-down tractors parked in sheds that looked like they were about to cave in. Outside Strängnäs, or "inland," as Jimmy put it.

The house: a so-called vacation home. One of those little red houses with a chimney that every single Sven seemed to own.

But why would you want one, anyway? Poor insulation, no dishwasher, no finished ceilings. Shit, they didn't even have a DVD player or an Internet hookup out here. Jorge didn't get what the deal was with this house.

Flashing thoughts. Images. He thought about the car chase in Sollentuna.

The tires'd screeched. The seat belt'd dug into his shoulder. The cell phone that'd been nestled behind the gearshift'd flown around the car like in a pinball machine.

He'd turned into one of the streets in the residential area. Drove like a maniac as soon as they were out of the cop's sight. Roared at Mahmud to turn around.

"Do you see them? Do you see them?"

Mahmud didn't see them. The cops didn't seem to have turned onto the same street. Jorge slammed the brakes. Tore up the duffel bag with the gat. Threw open the door. Jumped out of the car. Looked over his shoulder. Black licorice marks all over the pavement behind the car. Fuck. But no cop car, not that he could see anyway.

To Mahmud, "Take my seat. Drive outa here. I'll catch you later."

Jorge sprinted—like a rerun of his break from the Österåker Pen. Over a hedge. Onto someone's lawn. Over a sandbox. He panted. Breathed. Rushed.

Away, away from the street. Away with the piece.

Into the residential area.

Into the protected world of the one-family homes.

He sprinted faster than Usain Bolt over the gardens, away toward downtown Sollentuna.

He looked around. Ran down to the train station. Jumped onto a train.

He talked to Mahmud later. After a minute or so, a cruiser'd appeared from a different direction and stopped the Arab. The cops hadn't found much. A cell phone charger, a hoodie that belonged to Babak, and a pack of cigarettes. But no weapons. They said they'd seen Jorge in the car, but who the fuck cared. They couldn't prove that they'd driven like lunatics in the residential area. Clean.

Still: an embarrassing story.

Jorge told Mahmud not to say anything to Babak.

Back in the cottage. Jorge turned around. Behind him: two tripods. A whiteboard. A projection screen.

That *drip-drip* sound again. There must be a leak somewhere.

In front of him: seven soldiers.

Mahmud was sitting closest to him, on a wooden chair. Dressed in a tracksuit, as usual. The Adidas stripes were like gang colors for him. Bags under his eyes—he and Jorge'd been up half the night.

On the couch: Sergio, Robert, and Javier. They looked interested. Talked among themselves. Big gooey pile of cozy.

Jimmy was sitting in the other armchair. Hunched down low, naturally calm.

Tom and Viktor were sitting on the two plastic sun chairs from the garden. The Viktor dude looked jumpy. Tom was in a good mood—pulled joke after joke: so old he must've heard them on a radio. "What do you see when you a look a blonde in the eye—the inside of the back of her head."

Still, the jokes lightened the mood.

Jorge took note: the group was gathered.

And now: the first general assembly was coming to order—so boner-inducing, it made his cock hurt.

They'd borrowed the cottage from Jimmy's mom. Apparently the dude'd sat off his entire summer vacations here as a kid. Jorge thought: What the fuck'd he done all summer? There was nothing here. And the only weed around was what the cows chewed.

Still, Jimmy said he'd been livin' *la vida*, said he had it all out here. "It's only a couple hundred yards to the beach, you know."

Jorge recalled his own summers as a kid. Mom'd packed a blanket and a plastic bottle with Kool-Aid. Picnic in the park behind the Sollentuna Mall. Mom, Paola. And the asshole he wanted to wipe from his memory: Rodriguez.

"*Tierra virgen,*" Mom said. As if a couple-hundred-square-foot park were a nature reserve.

In his head, Jorge ran through what'd been taken care of already. One of the Finn's main principles: no written lists—could become lethal evidence for the cops after the fact. But J-boy had a good memory. This stuff filled his head during the days.

Last week: Tom Lehtimäki'd gotten eight shiny new phones from two different stores, through some boozehound. Chosen stores that didn't have camera surveillance. Tom slipped the drunk five hundred kronor and a handle of whiskey for his trouble.

What's more: Tom'd gotten walkie-talkies. Maybe they'd need gear that couldn't be tracked through the telephone networks. Tom pulled the same trick: asked some drunk to shell out so that no one saw him touch the equipment. Tossed the receipts into a storm drain.

The other guys: been rocking out on a swiping spree. Buckets, crowbars, axes, gas cans, screwdrivers, trestles, spray adhesive, and other shit they were gonna need.

Jorge bought thirty rolls of aluminum foil at the grocery store in the

Sollentuna Mall. The cashier asked if he was gonna wallpaper with foil. She didn't know how right she was.

Jorge stood up like a fucking homeroom teacher. Was planning on waiting until everyone shut up. Wasn't gonna clear his throat. None of that "Hey, I was gonna start now" bullshit. Just wait. Him: the leader.

A few seconds: they got the hint. Settled down. Leaned back. Fixed their eyes on him.

Jorge said, "*Hermanos*. Today is our day. This is the first time we're all getting together. So I thought I would explain this thing to everyone. Not every detail and whatever, but most of it. I want you to understand the basic way we're thinking about this hit. If something happens, if one of you disappears or whatever, the rest of you need to be able to step in and do his job. *Entiendes?*"

Jorge'd prepared his spiel. Had to show the boys he was a pro.

"We might need to meet up like this more times. We're gonna need to work together on shit. We can handle it, no problem."

He heard the Finn's words coming out of his own mouth.

"I'm gonna start by writing down a few rules on this whiteboard. Things we all gotta think about. Rules we gotta follow. Believe me, we do something wrong, and it's gonna turn into the world's biggest fucking fuck-up, all of it."

Jorge started writing on the board while he explained.

"Everyone's gotta stop doing their own usual shit. And I know you know what I mean."

He didn't need to say more. Everyone knew: Javier dealt weed and chased after whores four nights a week. Robert ran some racketeering now and then. That Viktor dude reregistered boosted German luxury buckets and sold them through his company.

"All business that isn't *blanco* stops now. If I catch any of you doing some side shit, you're gonna have to answer to me."

He continued to write down rules.

No heavy drinking.

No tripping.

"That's obvious. When you're drunk or high, you start talking. Leak worse than the American army. That's always how it is."

Always park legally.

"If you park somewhere wrong—pay the ticket, and after you pay it, don't forget to toss it somewhere other than where you live. Or else the cops can find that ticket and figure out where you've been, after. Always let someone else drive ahead of you if you're packing heat in the car."

He thought about the chase in Sollentuna again. If they'd had a lead car, like Jorge was pushing for now, that probably never would've happened.

He continued listing rules:

No written reminders.

No texts.

Don't touch anything important without gloves.

Most important of all: no talking with anyone about this. Not even girlfriends/homies/bros.

No one.

"You got that?"

Jorge glared at them. One after the other. These weren't guys who took shit. These were guys who, normally, would've skull-crushed anyone who ordered them around. Still: this was it. The big time. If they weren't planning on following the rules, they could get the fuck outa here.

After a while: Jorge opened his bag. Picked up a black case, as big as a DVD player. Unzipped the zipper. A projector. He tinkered with the video camera. Connected the cords. Played with the buttons. Technology wasn't really his thing—but he'd double-checked the equipment at home first.

An image appeared on the projector screen. A shaky road through a car window.

"What you see here is the road leading to Tomteboda."

The film rolled. Jorge: gave running commentary. He knew this area now. The fence around the building and the loading docks like little toys far in the background. Zoomed. Closer to the fence around the buildings, the surveillance cameras, the train tracks, the access roads, the control booths.

Zoomed: the massive sliding gate. Motorized.

"Me and my contact are working on how we're gonna get in. Either we cut the fence somewhere, but that might be too slow going. Or we blow our way in. Or we force the gate somehow. We'll figure it out."

They saw trucks pulling in and out. Employees walking through gates where they flashed key cards in order to be admitted.

Zoomed: the guards in the control booths. Suspicious. Vigilant.

"They're gonna unload the valuables at the loading dock here. But there's a vault too. If we get into that, it'll be like double jeopardy. The biggest question right now is how we're gonna do that."

Later: a few minutes into the film. Roundabouts, roads, exits. Signs that hung over the rode: STOCKHOLM DOWNTOWN, SOLNA, SUNDBYBERG. Finally: images of the police stations. Solna. Kronoberg. Södermalm. Above all: long shots of the exits to the garages. Jorge paused the film. Let the image freeze at the final one: the exit to the Västberga police station.

He tried not to sound cocky, "You see, this heist is special. They don't think anyone can make a hit against the central depot for cash in transit because it's so close to downtown. And that's where we come in. We're gonna floor the five-oh like bowling pins."

Jorge paused dramatically. Gauged the guys' reactions. Did they get it? They were gonna eliminate the *pacos*—like true cash terrorists.

Sergio opened his mouth first. "I don't get it, man. How we gonna wipe out the five-oh in Stockholm? They everywhere."

Jorge knew that they could see his crooked smile. The crescendo. The Finn's ideas. The coup that divided real Gs from wannabes—what would give them legend status.

"You saw the pictures of the cop stations and their garages, right? We're not gonna use helicopters or whatever to get into Tomteboda—you know what happens when you try to be too flashy. No, we're gonna slaughter the pigs instead. We're gonna secure our escape."

Another dramatic pause. Jorge looked around.

The dudes were sitting in silence.

Once again Jorge thought about all the unanswered questions. How were they gonna break through that fence? How were they gonna get into the vault? Then he zoomed in on his own big question: How would he gyp the Finn? He hadn't even said anything to Mahmud about that.

He had to forget the question marks now. Said, "We're gonna trash the cops' possibilities. Light fires in the right places. We're gonna knock this whole city out."

A few of the guys grinned. Tom looked like he was thinking. Viktor shook his head.

"What, Viktor? You don't follow?" Jorge said.

"Yeah, I follow. But I don't follow what's so fantastic when you don't even know how we're gonna get into that vault. And is torching shit really that smart? You know what they're gonna call it? Terrorism and shit."

Jorge didn't respond. Just glared.

Thought: Why was Viktor peacocking? Why didn't he just shut up? The dude acted like a little Babak, like a little *culo*.

Jorge wondered if this dude would really be able to handle the pressure.

14

Hägerström thought about how things had gone with JW so far: nowhere. A couple conversations in the chow hall. Some shooting the shit in the hallway.

He had even sat in the guy's cell and tried to talk about his noble family. Same reaction every time. Polite response. Nice enough attitude. But no progress. JW was obviously interested in Hägerström's life in Stockholm—he loved when he talked about restaurants and bars downtown or the summer people in resort towns like Torekov and Båstad—but not in talking about the other stuff. Hägerström assumed that JW wanted to see some tangible evidence before he let his guard down.

It would probably work out in the end. Hägerström was putting his plan into action today.

A sly path to JW's confidence.

An ugly path, some might say.

But in this case, the ends justified the means. And besides, Torsfjäll had greenlighted it.

Hägerström was feeling fresh even though it was only seven o'clock in the morning. He was on his way to the penitentiary in his Jaguar XK. That alone was pure pleasure. The XK's 400-horsepower V8 motor sounded like it was powering a racing car. But what had made him buy it was the design. The lines of the XK were drawn perfectly. Some said that Jaguar had even one-upped its E-type with the XK.

Any other car, and this kind of luxury would have felt flashy. Expensive cars could easily signal new money, in the same way that exaggerated home movie theaters could. What's more, Hägerström was trying to keep a low profile among his colleagues. But when it came to the Jaguar, he just couldn't help himself. It was simply classic. Let his colleagues talk.

He almost thought of the penitentiary as a normal place of work. That was a strong point. The more at home he felt, the better he played the game.

In the beginning, he commuted from the city, but since it took over two hours there and two hours back, not including traffic, his days weren't spent efficiently. After three weeks he got an apartment in Sala, which was less than two miles from the penitentiary.

Sometimes he went home on the weekends, mostly to see Pravat. He was discreet about it. If the other screws found out he had a place in Stockholm, they would begin to wonder. How could he afford two apartments? Wasn't the Jag enough? In that case, why didn't he work in the Stockholm area? But if they thought he just visited someone in the big city once in a while, that was okay. They knew he had been fired from the police force in the capital, after all.

Hägerström parked the car in the staff parking lot outside the prison. It stood out, as usual. Most people here drove semi-run-down Volvo V50s or Passats. Esmeralda drove a BMW from the 3 series, sure, but it was a few years old and could be compared to a Jaguar XK in about the same way that a Certina watch could be compared to a Patek Philippe.

Hägerström walked up to the outer fence. Slid his key card through the slot. Pressed the button. He didn't need to say anything, they buzzed him in.

He walked up the gravel path. Fence on all sides, except in front of him—that's where the wall towered up. He repeated the same procedure. Slid the card through the slot. Pressed a button, looked up at the surveillance camera, and smiled.

A general state of confusion prevailed among the inmates. What had happened to Radovan Kranjic—the Yugo godfather, alias the mafia king, Mr. R—was creating waves on the water. Rumors were cropping up faster than all the conspiracy theories about 9/11. The questions lumped together like institutional mashed potatoes: Who was behind the assassination attempt? How would the police respond?

Hägerström thought about the operation. He had been focusing on a newly admitted inmate named Omar Abdi Husseini. Sentenced to five years in prison for incitement to commit aggravated robbery against two Swedbank offices in Norrköping. Omar Abdi Husseini had that dense, bored look that you only rock if you haven't gotten enough sleep or if you want to show how much you don't give a shit about anyone or anything. He walked slowly, talked slowly, even picked his nose slowly.

The dude reeked of authority, for miles. Or else one might think he just reeked of unstable freaking psychopath. Not clear which was worse, really.

Hägerström had asked Torsfjäll to look the guy up.

After a few days, he was given a copy of a so-called multisearch, a search that was run through all the police's accessible databases at once: the criminal records, the records over potential suspects, the customs investigation's databases, the tax authority's databases, and so on. As well as a printout of a section of a report from the Stockholm County Police, a few articles from Swedish newspapers, a memo written by the Special Gang Unit with information from the SGU's own informers, undercover agents, and canaries.

A clearer image of the man started to take shape when Hägerström studied the SGU's insider information and the general reconnaissance register, which contained all reconnaissance observations that had been made over the years, regardless of whether there was actual suspicion of crime.

It was strange: the social worker ladies always blamed broken relationships, absent fathers, addict parents for creating the juvenile delinquents who, a few years later, were living the gangster life or were doing time at one of the supermaxes. But guys like Omar Abdi Husseini—and Hägerström had seen this kind of thing before—were not led astray by the fact that their families had fallen apart and were unable to set boundaries. Abdi Husseini had a good family, his dad wasn't a total deadbeat, and his mom wasn't a crack addict. It was something else.

The thing about Omar Abdi Husseini was that all unofficial information led to the same conclusion: the dude was president of Born to Be Hated.

And BTBH was Stockholm's fastest-growing gang. The gang had come from Denmark to Malmö to Stockholm and truly understood the potential of the young, angry kids from Stockholm's ghettos. They recruited riot boys who torched cars and garbage chutes and then peppered the firemen who came to put out the fires with rocks. They weren't like the Yugos or the Syrians, who kept to their own ethnic brethren. Not like the HA or the Bandidos, who mostly recruited among maladjusted Svens or relatively well-integrated second-generation immigrants. And not like the Fittja Boys or Angered's Tigers either, who were based around only one particular geographical area. The Born to Be Hated skipped the touchy-feely loyalty bull and the motorcycles.

They didn't care about the media or even try to run legal front businesses. They didn't try to glamorize any particular ghetto. They had a president and a vice president but didn't give a shit about complicated rules or venues to meet up in. The prisons, the gyms, the pizzerias, and the rec rooms in their parents' homes—that's where they gathered. They recruited the craziest *blatte* boys from the entire region. And they were on the rise.

Omar Abdi Husseini was perfect for what Hägerström had in mind.

Hägerström made his first overture one week after Omar came to the Salberga pen. The BTBH president was lying under the bench press machine in the workout room. Huffing and pressing. Making small noises with every lift. They didn't keep the free weights locked up here, as they did at a lot of other prisons.

Hägerström positioned himself next to him. Helped the guy on the last lifts, which he wouldn't have been able to do otherwise. The president was huge. Not just tall and wide—everything about him was big. It looked like his fingers could have popped a soccer ball, his head was double the size of Hägerström's, and his biceps were comic book outlandish—he must have taken juice before he was locked up. The tattoos on his neck were clearly visible: BTBH and ACAB. He had Arab writing and eagles tattooed into his arm. Crocs on his feet.

Omar looked up. "You want something?"

Hägerström tried to look relaxed. He had to meet Abdi Husseini with respect. Not be too forward.

"I just wanted to check what's up," he said. "Everything good?"

"You go ahead and keep checking."

"So how was Kumla?" The classic question put to a newbie who'd been sentenced to a longer prison term. They all passed through the Kumla Supermax, sat off at least three months there in order to be evaluated and placed. The risk classification that had been attached to Abdi Husseini had been good reason to keep him at Kumla, but he didn't have any previous convictions, so the Department of Corrections was forced to him move out of there.

Omar responded, "Just fine, man."

The president sat up on the bench. Wiped his face with a towel that was draped around his neck. He looked away. But Hägerström knew how to relax the giant.

"I just wanted to say that I've heard a lot of good things about you."

"From who?"

"Gürhan Ilnaz. I used to work at Hall." Gürhan Ilnaz was the former VP of the same gang as Omar. Hägerström had actually never met the guy, but it would take time for the truth to circle its way back to Abdi Husseini.

Omar flashed him a broad smile: a bolt of satisfaction in his enormous face.

"Cool. Gürhan's solid, man."

Omar got up. Wiped his forehead again, then he wiped down the bench's vinyl cover.

Walked back to his cellblock.

Two days later it was time again. Omar was talking with another inmate outside his cell door. The inmate was supposedly a former member of the Werewolf Legion. Hägerström approached them. Made some small talk. The weather, the chow, the new treadmill at the gym, a little of this and a little of that. He could do that kind of thing. He was known as a cool screw.

After five minutes, the Werewolf Legion dude walked away.

Omar remained. Still monosyllabic, but he also didn't seem to have anything against shooting the shit.

After a few minutes, Hägerström changed the subject. Started talking about other inmates instead. He told him how much gossip was going around. He brought up all the bullshit. He didn't mention JW, but he could see that Omar was listening.

The message was expressed: people were talking.

The message was impressed: there was some shit going around.

The message was stressed: there were those who were spreading rumors about Omar.

Hägerström walked in through the central guard area. Greeted the guards on duty. Continued into the locker room. Fished out his cell phone. Hung his clothes in the locker. Put his work clothes on: dark blue chinos, a sturdy leather belt, and a dark blue button-down shirt with the Department of Corrections logo on it. He passed through the metal detectors, hauled his keys up onto the conveyor belt. He greeted the screw on guard duty. He didn't set off the alarm signal. He never did.

He walked through the corridor toward his unit, still high on the rush of joy from the weekend.

Saw images in his mind's eye. He had picked Pravat up at day care on Thursday. They had gone to Grandma's house. Lottie still lived in the flat, even if it was probably a bit lonely since Father passed away.

He should really talk to Mother about certain things. But he couldn't do it now, not when Pravat was with him. And what was more, she was probably worrying too much about how he had been fired from the police. How would she ever understand what he was really doing?

It was a beautiful residence—actually appropriate to use the word *residence* rather than *apartment*. Grandma Lottie called all apartments residences, though. She didn't use the word *apartment* at all. All apartments, even Hägerström's first studio that'd only been 250 square feet, were residences. He smiled to himself.

Lottie opened the door. It smelled the way it had always smelled when you walked into that foyer. A mix of Mother's perfume—Madame Rochas—old furniture, and cleaning solution. It wasn't an unpleasant smell, but it also didn't smell of sterile cleanliness. For Hägerström, that smell would always be *home*.

Pravat ran straight into her arms. Lottie was dressed in well-pressed camel-colored pants and a pale blue shirt with a silk scarf tied around her neck, from Hermès or Louis Vuitton but probably the former. "After Hermès," Lottie liked to say, "comes nothing, then comes nothing, then comes nothing. Then maybe comes YSL."

She shouted to Pravat, "Hello, my little golden nugget!" It was almost surreal to hear Lottie shout like that. Something she would normally consider highly vulgar.

Pravat took his coat off. Lottie helped him change into a pair of indoor shoes that she had bought for him.

They walked into the inner hall. Josef Frank's classic chrysanthemum-patterned wallpaper on the walls. Hägerström could hear how she was bringing out his old bandy clubs.

He began walking around the apartment. The parlor, the dining room, the library, the gentlemen's salon, Father's old office, the guest room, the nanny's room that was now a den, his brother's old bedroom, which Father had remade into a showcase for his hunting trophies, and his sister's old room, which was now a laundry room.

He could see himself on a scooter flying through the four largest rooms that were all in a row. The parlor, the dining room, the gentlemen's salon, and the library. Probably a hundred feet of genuine Persian carpet: a perfect racetrack for an eight-year-old. When the nanny was there, he could ride as much as he wanted. But Mother always came in when he was reaching his top speed and stopped him. Not angrily but determinedly. As always. She never lost control, but she knew what she wanted.

Cronhielm af Hakunge paintings hung everywhere. The count, the count's siblings, Mother's father. Wood paneling along the walls. Crystal chandeliers over the tables.

Hägerström kept going, past Mother and Father's bedroom. His own bedroom was almost untouched. His old Danish wood-frame bed was where it had always been, but it had been given a new coverlet. Same with the nightstand, the narrow desk, and the wooden chair. His three paintings hung in the exact same spots as they had always hung. He looked at the one by Andy Warhol. A colored, treated photograph of Michael Jackson. It had also been used as a cover for *Time* magazine in 1984. Hägerström had been given it by his father that same year. He had turned twelve, and the King of Pop was his greatest idol.

Two paintings by the Swedish turn-of-the-century painter J. A. G. Acke were hanging on the other wall. One was of a burly man who looked like he was stretching his muscles; the left leg was stretched back. There was a wolf in the background. The man was bare-chested and had covered his lower body with a loincloth. The other was even stranger: an ocean with blue waves splashing up against the observer. On a cliff sticking up in the middle of the water stood three naked men. Pale, young, thin, but still athletic. They were not covering themselves.

Hägerström had chosen both of the paintings from Father's art collection when he turned eighteen. He stood still. Observing the men on the cliff. Their white, sinewy bodies. Their short hair that was blowing in the wind. The foam on the crest of the waves. The men's cocks that were hanging, unabashedly, down toward the cliff.

Maybe they were just posing, showing off their naked bodies and taking pleasure in being observed. Hägerström awoke from his reverie. Heard Pravat's voice behind him, "Daddy, aren't you gonna eat with us?"

He looked down at Pravat. The boy was also staring at the paintings.

Hägerström took his hand and left the room.

Mother had set the table in the kitchen, not in the dining room, which he took as a healthy sign. Things should be relaxed and familial when Martin and Pravat came to visit.

"Pravat, we don't say 'gonna.' We say 'going to,'" she said.

Pravat laughed. "I love your grub, Grandma."

Lottie said, "We don't say 'grub,' darling. We say 'food.'"

Hägerström was still running the same race at the pen. Worked the Born to Be Hated president. Acted chummy. Accommodating. Open. Brownnosed like crazy. Repeated the mad positive talk that was going around about him at the Hall pen.

And at the same time: Hägerström kept hinting about the negative talk that was going around about him here. That other inmates had opinions about him, mentioned him, looked down on him.

And in other conversations: Hägerström talked to the Werewolf Legion guy and other inmates in the unit that he knew weren't close with JW—spread the word. JW didn't like Abdi Husseini. JW had opinions about Omar. JW was shitting on the BTBH president.

What's more: Hägerström made sure that Esmeralda confiscated the cell phone that JW kept hidden under the Tube's pillow. He asked another screw to destroy a bunch of printouts that JW stored with Crazy Tim. All to soften him up for the overture.

Hägerström counted on the machinery of the gossip circuit to do the rest. Enough to create the myth of a schism. Omar would have to put the pieces of the puzzle together on his own.

There was no mistaking the overall impression. The Born to Be Hated's leader wasn't worth much in the eyes of Johan Westlund.

The strategy seemed to succeed after a few days. Hägerström heard from different factions that the soup he'd cooked up was starting to boil. By talking to other screws, he learned that the rumors had taken root. He heard directly from Omar that the Born to Be Hated president had heard the same things from the Werewolf Legion guy and others. That JW cunt apparently had a bunch of opinions. The dude thought too much. Talked too much.

Hägerström continued to spread misinformation.

He knew that Omar's conclusion would be as simple as a rule of nature: JW had to get burned.

At seven-thirty one night before lockup, the fuse blew. Hägerström observed the entire situation from a safe distance, without intervening. This wasn't a game any longer. Omar didn't take shit.

JW was sitting with his cell door ajar, studying—that's what he called it, anyway.

Omar pushed the door open without a sound and stepped inside. Then he cracked his knuckles with a loud sound: *pop-pop-pop*.

JW looked up. "Hey, you want something?"

Omar didn't say anything. Just met JW's perplexed eyes. There was another guy behind Omar, called Decke, who was standing with his arms crossed.

Silence in the cell.

The Tube and Crazy Tim's voices could be heard outside: a tough round of Hold 'Em was being played at the communal table on the block.

Omar leaned down. Next to him, against the wall, he set down a metal chair leg.

JW stared straight at him. Never drop your gaze—that was one of the pen's golden rules.

"You talk too much," Omar said.

JW glared at him.

"That's not how things work in here," Omar said. "That's not how things work anywhere. But I'm in a good mood today, buddy. Thirty large, and I'll forget everything. We'll pretend nothing happened."

JW continued to stare at the huge guy and his friend standing there in the doorway. "What are you talking about? I hardly know who you are, Omar."

"You deaf, little boy? Now you owe me fifty large. And if you say one more thing about me, I'll break you. *Walla.*"

Omar picked the chair leg up in one hand. Decke took a step forward, rolled up his sleeves.

"Who do you think you are?" JW asked. "Get out of here before I really tire of you."

Omar's long legs: two steps. Reached JW. Landed a blow across his back. JW fell off his chair. Screamed aloud.

Omar hit him again, across the legs.

JW tried to roll in under the bed while shielding himself with his hands.

The cell door flew open. The Tube and Crazy Tim rushed in. The Tube grabbed hold of Omar's raised arm. Decke pushed him aside. Crazy Tim bounced right back. He jumped up, took a half-step across JW's bed: gained height. Aimed a knee at Omar's head. But the president had already reacted. Took the knee with a ready neck, muscles tensed. Decke pushed Crazy Tim one more time, hard this time. Omar turned around. Struck the Tube with full force. The fattest fist in the iron pen, right into the Yugo's stomach. The Tube gasped for air. Wheezed. Lost his grip. Fell backward. Crazy Tim struck Decke with a right jab. The guy blocked. Shoved him again. Omar slammed the chair leg with full force over Crazy Tim's hand. Then one more time. Crazy Tim's fingers cracked. Blood sprayed on JW's sheets.

Decke held the Tube back.

Omar bent down. Thrust the chair leg under the bed where JW was cowering. He beat as hard as he could.

The Tube screamed.

Crazy Tim screamed.

JW screamed worst of all.

Omar struck again and again.

When he retracted it, the chair leg was covered in blood.

Decke walked out of the cell.

The president himself turned in the door.

He bent down, yelled in the direction of the bed, "You little cunt. Next time, you're dead."

Curtain.

* * *

AFTONBLADET, EVENING NEWSPAPER

BOMB AIMED AT THE LEADER OF ORGANIZED CRIME

Radovan Kranjic, 49, whom the police have suspected of being one of the leaders of Stockholm's organized crime scene for many years, has been the victim of a bomb attack. At 3:05 a.m. residents of the area around Skeppargatan in Östermalm in Stockholm were awakened by a loud explosion. A car had exploded down on the street. Radovan Kranjic was in the driver's seat. Another man, in his thirties, was also sitting in the car.

"I was on my way home and saw a huge explosion a hundred feet farther up the street," a witness said. "The pressure wave threw me to the ground. A bunch of windows were blown out in the surrounding cars and apartments. It's some fucking suicide bomber again, that's what I thought."

Apparently Radovan Kranjic was in the car in order to pick up his 21-year-old daughter, who had been at a party at the home of the famous Stureplan personality and party planner Carl Malmer, alias Jet Set Carl.

Malmer, who lives on Skeppargatan, told *Aftonbladet,* "There were a lot of people at my house, and we were playing music. But suddenly we heard an explosion that overpowered the music and made everything tremble. I thought it was an earthquake."

Police were on the scene within minutes. Sections of the street were cordoned off, and the party at Malmer's home was shut down. Kranjic was brought to a waiting ambulance on a gurney. His daughter remained by his side the entire time.

When he arrived at the Karolinska University Hospital, it was determined that Kranjic was in critical condition. The 35-year-old passenger was also brought to the hospital. No suspects have been detained, but Kranjic was the victim of a shooting only a few weeks ago, in conjunction with a martial arts gala at the Globe Arena. That time he made it out alive thanks to the bulletproof vest he was wearing, although he sustained severe injuries to his shoulder.

As of this morning, the police had no certain theories as to the motive behind the attack.

"We've suspected that Radovan Kranjic has played a significant role, which we have been unable to prove, in the world of organized crime," said Claes Cassel, the police press secretary. Since he has been subjected to a previous assassination attempt, the bombing did not come as a complete surprise.

The police now have around twenty witnesses to question in regard to the incident.

Anders Eriksson

Lotta Klüft

* * *

***AFTONBLADET*, EVENING NEWSPAPER**

THE KING OF THE UNDERWORLD IS DEAD

Radovan Kranjic, 49, has died, according to reports from the Karolinska University Hospital. "Kranjic had sustained serious burn and shrapnel injuries and extensive injuries to his inner organs," the responsible doctor in the ER said.

Radovan Kranjic's car was blown up last night on Skeppargatan in Stockholm. Kranjic was at the address to pick up his daughter, who had been to a party at the home of the Stureplan personality Carl Malmer, alias Jet Set Carl. A 35-year-old passenger was also in the car at the time of the explosion and is still being cared for in the intensive care unit of the Karolinska University Hospital.

Witnesses recount that a strong explosion shook the car. A number of windows in parked cars and in nearby apartment buildings were blown out. The sound of the explosion could be heard all the way to the southern part of the city.

Both men in the car were brought by ambulance to the Karolinska University Hospital.

"Since he arrived at the unit, our teams have tried to save Kranjic's life," said the chief ER doctor. "But we did not succeed. At 11:14 we concluded that there was nothing more we could do."

A source with the police told *Aftonbladet* that the police are still investigating a number of leads but do not yet have a prime suspect.

Anders Eriksson

Lotta Klüft

* * *

***AFTONBLADET*, EVENING NEWSPAPER**

THE GODFATHER'S LAST REST

Radovan Kranjic was alleged by many to be the godfather of organized crime. He will be buried tomorrow. The police are dispatching extra security.

Radovan Kranjic has been pointed out as one of the major leaders of the underworld, by both the media and the Stockholm police. Many people believed that he ruled parts of Stockholm's illegal businesses, as he knew.

"I know they call me the Yugo Boss and a lot of other crap," he said in an interview with *Aftonbladet* four years ago.

More than six feet tall, fit, and weighing 220 pounds, he felt invincible. No one would be able to break him.

"I'm just a normal kid, but I've been working out for thirty years," he said, and laughed.

Radovan Kranjic came to Sweden from the former Yugoslavia more than thirty years ago. According to multiple sources, he knew the art of being exceedingly charming and spreading money around. Horse racing was among his interests, and he owned three horses. He also liked martial arts and personally sponsored many fighters.

But Kranjic also served time in prison for, among other things, attempted assualt, assault, illegal weapons possession, and tax fraud. Since 1990, however, his record has remained clean.

"Those were youthful sins. I don't do that stuff anymore," he told *Aftonbladet*.

He had close friends in the Serbian nationalist movement in Serbia, among them Zeljko Raznatovic, better known as Arkan, who led the private paramilitary army the White Tigers. It is believed that Kranjic himself participated in the war in the former Yugoslavia during 1993–95, when he was absent from Sweden for long periods of time.

Kranjic began work as a bouncer at different clubs in Stockholm. He was a good friend pf Dragan Joksovic, better known as Jokso, a leader in Stockholm's organized crime world until his murder at the Solvalla Racetrack in 1998. Many see Kranjic's death as a replay of Jokso's fate.

Kranjic built up his business empire over the years. He ran a security guard company and did various businesses in the real estate and construction industries. The police suspect that, parallel to that, he built up a cigarette and alcohol smuggling empire. Sources within the police have told *Aftonbladet* that Kranjic is also suspected of running brothel and racketeering businesses in the Stockholm region.

One person associated with Kranjic told *Aftonbladet*, "Radovan Kranjic lived a hard life, but to many of us, he was a hero. Tomorrow, he will be buried in peace and quiet. A king will finally be able to rest."

The police, however, are of a different opinion and are dispatching special security personnel for the funeral.

Anders Eriksson

Lotta Klüft

15

Choir singing. Harmonies. Sacral atmosphere. Then the bishop sang a solo for a few minutes.

The choir again. Church Slavic. Kyrillos holy texts.

The air was filled with smoke and myrrh. Natalie tried to listen to the words even though she couldn't understand them.

Mom crossed herself. Natalie felt as if she were lost, not there.

Lit de parade. Natalie was standing closest to the open casket. There were mountains of flower wreaths all around it. She tried to pin her gaze to the wooden cross behind the casket, but she couldn't tear her eyes from Dad. He looked so alone even though the chapel was packed with people. Dressed in a black suit. Combed side part. Arms crossed over his chest. An icon with his *svetac*, Saint George, in his hands. He looked small. And he was still.

So still.

The previous day Natalie and Mom'd talked to the bishop. Gone over the way in which they wanted the ceremony and the rituals to be done. Every Serbian Orthodox family has its own saint, a *svetac*. The Kranjic clan'd had Saint George as its saint for over a hundred years. And according to the legend, Saint George was the one who'd slain the dragon. He was a warrior. That suited Dad better than any other.

The night'd been long. According to tradition, the body should have been in the ground within twenty-four hours. But there hadn't been time to assemble all the guests on such short notice. Plus, the police wanted to do an autopsy. So they'd decided to wait for a few days. But over a week would have been scandalous. They spoke with the Swedish-Serbian priest from Södertälje about paying his employees in the church to watch over the body and read the Book of Psalms. It was important: no one would be able to say that the Kranjic family hadn't done everything according to the rules. Mom drove out to the chapel every day and checked on them. Dad was to be treated like the hero he had been.

Natalie was wearing a black, long-sleeved dress from Givenchy with a round neckline. Nothing made it obvious how fancy it actually was. That wouldn't do. The bishop'd been clear about that. No showing off, no high heels or skirts that were too Swedish.

Mom was even more conservatively dressed, in a black suit with a skirt that went down to mid-calf. She was wearing a hat with a dark veil.

It was warm—probably two hundred people in the chapel. But Natalie knew that at least another three hundred were shoving elbows outside. And then the dispatched police on top of that, for some reason.

Mom and she'd arrived two hours earlier. Seen the casket carried in, feet first. They accepted condolences, flowers, kisses on their cheeks. More than five hundred faces to greet. She didn't know a tenth of them.

She shut out the choir, the faces, the soft flames from the wax candles. She saw Dad in front of her. On Skeppargatan. On the gurney. Under a yellow blanket. Under tightened straps. Dirty. Bloody. Her ears were still ringing from the explosion. Still: Dad was without sound.

The ringing in her ears. Dad.

The chaos.

She was running next to him.

They'd had to tear her from the ambulance.

After the car bomb went off, she'd sat in a cramped room in the hospital for ten hours. No flowers, no boxes of chocolate. Just machines with digital numbers on their displays. At first, they hadn't wanted to say where they were caring for Dad, but this time Natalie demanded that they bring her there. The bed's metal frame gleamed in the rays of sun that found their way in through the blinds. Half his face was covered in bandages, and there were tubes going up his nose and arms.

Mom sat at the foot of the bed, sniffling. Natalie and Goran sat in chairs. Stefanovic ought to have been there—but they said he was also being cared for in the ICU. There was a policeman on guard outside the room. The police feared more violence.

After a while, a nurse came into the room. "You have to go now. He is going into surgery one more time."

Mom stopped crying. "What are you going to do?"

"You'll have to ask the doctor."

"Is it as serious as the last operation?"

"I'm sorry, I don't know."

Mom and Goran rose. Natalie didn't want to leave. She wanted to stay here. She wanted to sit next to Dad for the rest of her life.

"Come, honey," Mom said in Serbian. "It's time."

Natalie rose, leaned over to kiss Dad on the forehead.

Then: his hand trembled.

Natalie looked down. Put her hand over his. It was more than a tremor. He was moving his fingers.

"Mom, wait. He's moving."

Mom hurried forward. Goran also leaned down. Dad raised his hand from the mattress.

Natalie thought it almost seemed as though he wanted to say something. She leaned in even closer.

Heard a breath.

Felt Mom, close behind her.

Another breath.

Then, a weak voice. Dad whispered in Serbian, "Little frog."

Natalie squeezed his hand.

"What is he saying?" Goran asked.

"Quiet," Natalie hissed, without turning around.

Goran leaned in closer, tried to listen.

Dad's voice again. "Little frog. You will take over."

Natalie looked at him. She couldn't see his lips moving. It was deathly quiet in the room.

Dad spoke again, "You will take over everything."

The bishop held his speech. He was dressed in something that looked like a cross between a black dress with gold decorations and a magician's cloak. Natalie'd been to Serbian Orthodox mass perhaps seven times total in her life, always on Easter. But the priest today wasn't just anyone. The bishop was a hotshot on the holy circuit. Bishop Milomir: bishop of Great Britain and Scandinavia. Normally he lived in London, but he'd flown in for this right away.

The bishop droned on. About how Dad'd come to Sweden in 1981, looking for work. Started working at Scania in Södertälje. How he'd advanced, started companies, created businesses. Become a wealthy man, a successful man, a respected citizen. How he continued to attend mass regularly, donated money to philanthropic causes and to the building of the church in Enskede Gård. Above all: how he always stood up for the Serbian people and the Serbian faith. He'd clearly heard some things from others, or else he'd made them up. Like all that about Dad going to mass all the time—that was about as real as the Easter Bunny.

The choir began singing again. The bishop swung an oil lamp over the floor. Everyone sang together: the informal national anthem about Saint George—it'd never been more fitting. The candles that everyone was holding in their hands were burning low. The flames were flickering slowly. For over an hour now.

The bishop began to read in Church Slavic. He poured oil over Dad's body. Drops on Dad's pale forehead.

The smell of myrrh. The monotonous drone of the mass.

It was over now.

The Swedish priest from Södertälje announced that it was time for the last kiss. Mom started moving. It had to happen in a particular order, and you had to walk counterclockwise back to your spot.

Natalie held her hand tightly.

They approached Dad.

His sand-colored hair looked lighter than usual. His jaw, which ordinarily looked so wide when he smiled at Natalie, appeared thin. His neck usually looked broad, strong. Now: fragile as a bird's.

Mom bent down and kissed Dad lightly on the forehead.

Natalie stood above the casket. It felt as though everyone in the chapel stopped to look at her. Waited to see what she would do.

She looked down. Dad's face. His closed eyes. Shiny eyelashes.

She bent down. Stopped with her lips a few millimeters above Dad's forehead. She didn't cry. Didn't think. Didn't mourn.

She only had one thought in her head: *Dad, I am going to make you proud of me. Whoever did this to you will regret it.*

Then she kissed him.

The crowd was beginning to thin out. There were maybe a hundred people left in the graveyard. Even the cops were beginning to drive away.

Natalie walked toward a taxi that she'd called over fifteen minutes ago. That alone irritated her—to have to wait more than fifteen minutes when there ought to be cabs around the corner.

Viktor was walking a few paces behind her. Mom'd been clear: "You're not married yet, so unfortunately, he can't stand with us in the chapel."

Viktor hadn't seemed to care about that. Honestly, he hardly seemed to care about anything lately.

Farther off, by the fence, Goran was walking toward them.

Head angled slightly down. Goran had shitty posture.

He stopped when he reached her.

Right, left, right. Even though he'd already kissed her cheeks before the funeral. "Natalie," he said. "I'm sorry."

She wondered why he was repeating this routine.

He extended his hand. Took Natalie's hand in his. Held it for a few seconds. Squeezed it. His gray eyes bored straight into hers. His look was not pitying, like the those of the others. It was determined. Sharp.

He released her hand. Continued walking toward the graveyard where Mom and a few others were still standing.

Natalie remained where she was. Looked down at her hand.

A scrunched piece of paper.

She unfolded it—messy handwriting, in pencil; two words and a time: *Stefanovic. Tomorrow. 1800.*

Viktor caught up with her.

"What was that all about?"

Natalie folded her fingers over the note.

"Nothing."

The taxi was waiting outside the gates. She saw a cop climb into a car farther up the street.

"Nothing at all."

16

Jorge was on his way to visit Paola. And Jorge Jr. reined himself in, tried to keep to the speed limit. After that car chase business—even less room for risk taking.

His head was spinning with details. The plan was now fully set in motion. After weeks of planning, it was almost time.

Shiiiit—so dope.

The pieces were in place: Javier'd stolen Taurus pistols from a hardware store. Copies of Parabellum, a Brazilian cop piece. Black, heavy enough. Realistic as shit. Crazy when he thought about it: the Swedish government wanted control over weapons—so why could any motherfucker get a perfect copy in a matter of minutes?

The Finn's idea: they were gonna dump the fake guns at the crime scene—so they couldn't get slammed with aggravated robbery if things got fucked.

Robert and Sergio'd boosted cars in Norway and parked them out at Jimmy's vacation cottage—the Finn's idea. They'd cleaned them, no fingerprints. Covered them with tarps.

The Finn delivered mad connections with Syrian weapons dealers en masse. At least one Kalashnikov plus an ill brand gun'd been promised. Jorge hadn't decided who was gonna have the AK yet—but it should probably be him. Heaviest heat for the heaviest *hombre.*

Jorge drove around the city every day. Checked the police stations, the area around Tomteboda, flight routes. Kept an eye on the boys. Bounced ideas off the Finn. Talked to Tom about getting a sublet somewhere.

Things were falling into place. But two things were still eating away at him: How would they force the fence? And above all: How would they get into the vault?

You could cut the fence with bolt cutters in several places. But that wouldn't be enough. They had to get in and out of the area by car. And the only place where there was a paved road was through the front gate. So that's where they had to do it—the gate was what they had to break through—and it was thick as fuck. The Finn informed him: it was an industry-grade gate, security-class issue. A bolt cutter would never be enough, but the Finn said it'd work with sharp angle grinders. The problem: there wouldn't be time to jump out of a vehicle to cut the gate. They had to find another way. The question was: how?

Same deal with the vault. They'd have to blow their way in. Alternately, the insider might be able to get someone who could unlock it from the inside, but fat chance that would happen. So: they needed dynamite.

The Finn was loud and clear: "In order for this to work, you need real blueprints for the place. Or else you can't have someone calculate how much dynamite you need and stuff. You with me?"

Jorge followed: no blueprints, no vault.

Jorge really wanted to come up with his own solutions. But it was the Brain who was the brain in all this. What's more: the Finn *should* have to work a little too. The way it was now: Jorge was working his ass off, while the Finn just gave orders and philosophized. Made claims. Commanded. Controlled. But in the end, it would be different. Reversed roles. Jorge and Mahmud'd planned their little side gig by now.

Another problem was on the rise: Viktor. Like all his backtalk at the meeting wasn't enough—the guy dragged his feet, was slow doing what Jorge asked him to do. He was supposed to've gotten work gloves, overalls, and other shit. Instead, he whined every time Jorge got hold of him. Said the whole thing was getting out of hand. That it was too dangerous, too crazy. The potential prison sentences were too long.

Often he didn't even call back.

After a few days: the dude pretty much vanished off the grid. Jorge called two, three times. But the Sven fucker didn't bother calling him back. Jorge talked to Tom. Asked him to deal with his buddy—make Viktor understand. Jorge's patience was like a bomb with a fuse two millimeters long set to blow up in this clown's face.

The days passed. *Nada*.

Jorge climbed out of the car. Robbery thoughts interrupted. Looked up at Paola's apartment. Fifth floor. Hägerstensvägen. Örnsberg. Paola: had moved as far away from Sollentuna—their home turf—as she could. She was making a point—wanted to show that she made her own decisions. But Jorge wondered if she'd forgotten about Mom. Okay, she probably saw her more often than he did. But at least Jorge lived closer.

He rang the doorbell.

Heard sounds from inside. Saw something dark in front of the peephole in the door.

Two seconds later: she opened.

"Come in," she said.

He took his shoes off. Walked into the apartment. There were Legos and Playmobil parts on the floor.

Jorgito came running. "Hi, hi, hi. Come look!"

Jorge picked the boy up and threw him into the air, kissed him on both cheeks.

Said the same things in Spanish that his Mom'd always said to him: "*Caramba, cómo has crecido!*"

They walked into Junior's room. Blue wallpaper with animals on it. A rug on the floor covered with the image of streets and houses. Plastic toys everywhere.

Paola's shuffling footsteps in the background.

He set Jorgito down again. Looked at Paola. "What's wrong?"

"What?"

"Paola, don't even try. You may not know me, but I know you. What's wrong?"

Paola bent down. Took Jorgito's hand. "Come on, let's go to the kitchen."

Her face was stiff.

He positioned himself in front of her, blocking her path. She brushed past him to the sink. Poured a glass of Kool-Aid for Junior.

Jorge positioned himself in front of her again. Took her face in his hands.

"Paola, what *is* it?"

"I got fired today."

Paola looked crushed. On the verge of tears. She released her son's hand. She probably didn't want him to see if she started crying.

The little guy looked up at Jorge. "Did you bring me an airplane today?"

Jorge tried to smile. The last time he was here, he'd brought a Playmobil airplane. This time, he'd brought another gift.

Fuck—he didn't have time for family problems right now. The CIT planning was taking all his time. Still: he knew how happy Paola'd been about her job in the accounting department of an IT company. What's more: he knew how tough she thought it was to be a single mom.

He gave Jorgito the present, a Lego set. Totally crazy, if you thought about it: "Lego Racer 8199—Cash-in-transit robbery." He read the text on the back of the box: *The armored car has been stopped due to road construction when the green truck, which wants to take the money, rams into it.*

He tried to ask Paola what'd happened. Why she'd been the one let go.

They talked for a while. Sat down. The wooden table had round stains on it from hot tea mugs.

"I'm not the only one who was laid off. They're making cuts everywhere. There are rules for this kind of thing."

"But what about in the accounting department?"

"There were only three of us there, and I was the most recent hire. Last in, first out. That's what it's called, the rule. If I don't get another job in ninety days, it's gonna be tough."

Jorge felt bad for her. At the same time: guaranteed unemployment for ninety days sounded pretty sweet. She'd been a nine-to-fiver. Part of the system. And soon he would be financially independent—would be able to help her with anything she needed.

He put his arm around her. Saw images in his head. Him and Paola together. Mama's stereo turned on. CD cases all over the floor. Paola was digging through the CDs. Reading jacket texts. Trying to explain to Jorge why Janet Jackson and Mariah Carey were the best of all. She played songs, sang along to the lyrics: "*Oooooh, I'm gonna take you there, that's the way love goes.*"

But to Jorge: she was his biggest idol. Honest: the only idol he'd ever had.

Jorgito came back into the kitchen. Looked at Paola. "I've built the robbery now."

"You gotta show me, little man," Jorge said.

Paola looked at him. "What did you say, Jorgito?"

"I built the Lego now. A really nice robbery. The truck hits the car with the money in it."

Paola turned to Jorge. Sighed. "That is not okay."

Jorge tried to grin.

"You have to go now," Paola said. "We can talk more later."

"Don't be like that, he likes Legos. And I promise it's all gonna work out. You don't gotta worry, *hermana*."

"No, you can go. And I don't want your money. I don't want dirty money here."

Jorge stopped. "What you mean? Don't pull that old shit again. I thought we'd gotten past that."

Paola was on her way out to Jorgito's room. "You can't afford to support me on your café. I know that. So if you're talking about doing something for me, I know you're talking about dirty money. And we don't want that here. *No lo entiendes?*"

Normally: Jorge was a king. J-boy the man—the dude with whip-fast comebacks and mad flow. Now: stumped. Blank like a busted phone display. Pathetic like a beat-up brat on a bar floor.

He walked out into the hallway. Glanced quickly into Jorgito's room. Thoughts were bouncing around his head: If Paola didn't want his help, then she could quit whining. If she didn't want his cash, Jorgito wouldn't have it either. If his dough was dirty, then the Lego set was filthy too. Right? He should go in there and take the Legos from Junior's room with him.

He took a step into the kid's room. The boy was sitting with his Lego project. Waiting for him and Paola to come look at what he'd built.

His curly hair, his smiling, slitted eyes. An unspoiled human being.

Jorge walked out again. Into the hall.

Opened the door.

Closed it. As hard as he could.

As he was leaving: a fat knot in his stomach. He turned the radio to *The Voice*. Robyn—as usual on every single station.

His cell phone rang. He thought it would be Paola, calling to apologize.

It was Tom Lehtimäki. A brief conversation, without mentioning names or details. According to Jorge's rules.

"We've got a problem."

"What?"

"A bunch of shit, actually."

"Can we meet up?"

"I'm home."

"Okay, I'll be right over."

Jorge'd had a feeling this was coming. That Viktor fag was cracking. That Viktor dude tried to hitch a free ride on the rest of their backs.

It was time to have a talk with that guy.

The next day they were sitting at Jimmy's mom's summer shack again. The chairs were in place. The tripod with the whiteboard was set up. The sun outside was strong—summer was here. It was gonna be a long summer filled with fields of clover.

But everything had to fall into place. Everything had to fly.

The end was drawing near. A lot'd been taken care of over the past week. Some little Viktor cunt wasn't gonna fucking free-ride on this. No way in hell.

But there were still a few major things left to do. The fence. The vault. The secret side plan he and Mahmud were cooking up.

He eyed the guys in the shack.

Mahmud: Brother in coffee. Brother in planning. Brother in arms. Those sad, dark eyes with their long lashes: like upside-down crescent moons. The Arab looked tired.

Sergio: his own cousin. Javier: Latino. Both: *hermanos*—but they might love weed more than they loved the plan. Last time he'd spoken with Javier, the guy was so high, his dandruff was snowing on the moon. J-boy himself'd been a blazer once. But for him, that was over now. Still, he let it go—needed those guys. Plus: Javier wasn't just anyone—he knew half of Alby.

Robert: quiet. Got his shit done. But didn't take any initiative on his own. Actually: kind of a relief.

Jimmy: was handling himself okay too. The only downside with that Sven: the guy was buds with Viktor.

Tom: a talent with a sense of humor. A technician with intuition. So far he'd handled himself perfectly. At the same time: he demanded *mucho*. Wanted a hand in everything, every detail. Get his say. Liked the sound of his own voice. But Jorge thought: Hombre *can do whatever he wants—as long as he delivers.*

Viktor on the other hand: the freeloader who should've apologized long ago.

Jorge started into his spiel. Briefly went over everything they'd already done. He talked about the plan, the equipment, the weapons.

He went through dates, times, hours. Cash-out envelopes from the entire Stockholm region were emptied into the bank's service boxes, collected, picked up by guards and CITs, and ended up at Tomteboda's cash conversion depot. The money that was being delivered the following day was also stored there.

What's more: the remainders were stored in the vault, the stuff that might not've been sent out, things left over from last week. Fat stacks of extra cash.

The guys looked pleased even though Jorge said he still didn't know how they were going to get through the fence or into the vault.

"But we have another problem too," he continued, "a real bad problem. I'm gonna keep it real. One of us isn't doing what he should be doing. One of us is totally blowing this gig off. Only thinking of himself. Like a cunt."

The guys stared at him. Only Tom and Mahmud knew who Jorge was talking about.

Jorge's head: boiling over.

"One of us wants everyone else to do the work, and he just wants to reap the benefits. Hitch a free ride, like jumping stiles in the subway. Except this time he apparently wants to cash in too."

Jorge's eyes: on Viktor. The dude was starting to catch on.

Might as well drop the bomb.

"I'm talking about you, Viktor. You're not doing a fucking thing. You don't even pick up your fucking phone. Do you understand the risks the rest of us are taking for you?"

The other guys turned to Viktor.

Exhaled—relieved that Jorge wasn't talking about them. At the same time: quizzical expressions. Was it true that Viktor was just trying to use them?

Between Jorge's temples: bongo drums. Spit went flying.

His thoughts were exploding: Who did this little Sven *puta* think he was? Who did that Viktor faggot think he was tricking?

Jorge stood up. Raised his voice.

Kept stoking the fire: attitude problems, nonchalant fairy style. Viktor: shit attitude to the hit. Crap approach to the team.

Viktor just stared back at him. Jorge tried to understand. The guy's eyes were full of fear. And still he was bugging out. What the fuck was his problem?

After a few seconds: Jorge paused to breathe. Stared. Was still standing up. Locked on Viktor's eyes.

"Are you done?" Viktor asked. "'Cause I'm starting to get really fucking tired of you."

"Say that again."

"I said, you're such a fucking bore. You're so full of shit that it's coming out of your ears."

Jorge's temper: went totally ballistic. He roared. Took a step toward Viktor. "*No me jodas*, you motherfuckin' cocksucker!"

Viktor: dropped some cocky comment like a grenade. Stood up.

Everyone's trouble scale: on deep red alert.

Mahmud also stood up. "Cool it, Viktor."

Viktor screamed, "Come on, you fucking clown, come on!"

Tom stood up. "Viktor, sit down. Chill out, dammit."

Too late.

Jorge threw himself the final feet. If this fucker wanted to get beat, let him have it.

Everything was bubbling up inside him: Paola's shitty gratitude, Viktor's attitude, the difficulties they were having with the gate and the vault.

He shoved Viktor in the chest with full force.

The guy went tumbling backward. Hit the couch.

Jorge: over him.

Bitchslapped that *zorra*. Smack, smack.

Viktor tried to wave off Jorge's arms. Flailed his arms like a chick.

Tried to get up.

Jorge fed punches: hit the jerk-off with a few half-ass jabs.

Then it ended. Javier and Mahmud were restraining him. Took a grip around his waist. His arms.

Viktor's cheeks were as red as Jimmy's mother's shack—the dude was spitting dirty words. Then he turned around.

Ran out of the house.

Ten minutes later. Jorge'd calmed down. Was sitting in the kitchen with Mahmud and Tom. In one corner: an old stove—like a hundred years old or something. Black iron, initials carved onto the front, lots of curlicues on the handles. Jorge didn't understand why you'd save a piece of junk like that.

The others were still sitting in the living room.

Tom was speaking to Jorge in a low voice: "I think Viktor's really fucking scared."

"So why the fuck'd you drag him into this?"

"My bad, I'll take that. But honest, he's scared for real."

"'Cause we're gonna torch some cars?"

"No. Don't you know who Viktor is?"

"Yeah, a vagina."

Tom drummed his fingers on the table.

"What is it?" Jorge said.

Tom stopped drumming. Waited a couple of microseconds. "Viktor is dating Radovan Kranjic's daughter."

Jorge stared at him.

Tom said, "The dude's got bad financial problems. The guy's scared our operation's gonna go to hell. But most of all, he's scared for his life. He's wound up in a family that's dangerous for real."

17

Early summer was rolling in with full force, even at the penitentiary. The cells were brighter, there was birdsong from the outer walls, a warm breeze swept over the rec yard. You could usually tell by the inmates, Esmeralda said. Better morning moods, physical restlessness, and more broad jokes. You know, warm-up before game time.

But now: the atmosphere was at rock bottom. The reason, according to Esmeralda: there were too few fans in the stands and shitty team spirit on the field.

A cold conflict in the cage, which could break out into full-fledged war at any moment. Again. The fight in JW's cell: Omar plus sidekick had jumped the Tube. The president had given Crazy Tim a real whipping. And JW had taken so many hits with the chair leg that he'd had to fix a tooth, get two stitches in his eyebrow and eight in his thigh, and be cared for in the infirmary for four days.

Hägerström was pleased with the results of his plan. Torsfjäll was even more pleased. He pulled some strings so that the Tube and Crazy Tim were transferred out. That was par for the course. If serious conflicts arose, you split up the troublemakers. Someone got bus therapy, someone might have to go into the box for a few weeks. Or else you punished them in other ways. Guarded parole could be revoked, or the worst threat of all: strike their EPRD—they wouldn't be released after two-thirds of their time. For JW, that would mean up to two more years behind bars.

But the linchpin was that Omar Abdi Husseini was staying, he wasn't going to switch prison or unit. And JW would stay put as well. Two cocky cocks in one chicken coop.

In other words, JW was left alone with his new nemesis. He would have to squirm. He would have to worry. What's more, he was probably missing his paperwork and his phone.

Now there was something he wanted from Hägerström.

The days passed. Hägerström worked like a maniac, picked up every shift he could get. He wanted to be at the prison all the time.

JW kept to himself even more than before the conflict. Mostly sat in his cell. During lunch, he walked with the younger guy, Charlie Nowak, near him at all times. But the feeling was different than before. Charlie Nowak tried to take command. Play JW's bodyguard, control the situation. But without the Tube and Crazy Tim, there was no patent power, no heavy names.

Fear of more attacks hung heavy in the air, even if no one wanted to show it.

At night, Hägerström tried to come up with things to say. Jotted down different scripts. Tried to get inside JW's head. They knew he had used the CO Christer Starre before. But the question was, how?

Hägerström would know soon. Hopefully.

He got another weekend with Pravat. They ate lunch at Grandma Lottie's again. Homemade meatballs with macaroni for Pravat and veal filet with roasted potatoes for Martin and Grandma. They ate in the dining room. A checked oilcloth tablecloth on the table. A cloth napkin in Pravat's little lap.

Grandma pointed at the tablecloth. "I bought that yesterday for the little nugget's sake."

Hägerström laughed, "Really? For Pravat's sake?"

Lottie set down her knife and fork and carefully wiped her mouth with the cloth napkin. Martin could tell that she was about to come out and say something.

"To what do we owe your new lack of coiffure?"

Martin had shaved off all his hair a few weeks ago. As far as he could remember, no one in their family had ever had a buzz cut.

"It's easier this way."

Mother looked at him. Changed the subject. "Martin, why did you come over so rarely when Father was alive?"

The question came as a surprise. Martin Hägerström's mother usually acted according to a golden rule: never start uncomfortable discussions in the family. She had tolerated a lot from Father in her day. Working around the clock several days a week, insane tantrums, and possibly extramarital affairs. But she didn't fight in public. He'd never even heard her argue with Father. That trouble would descend over her family because of her? Over Lottie Hägerström's dead body.

According to Mother, uncomfortable questions had no place in the Hägerström family. But what she'd just said was different. Maybe it was because Father was gone. That it was just her and Martin.

Martin didn't even know what to respond. He should probably just tell her the truth. How difficult it had been to see Father after his divorce from Pravat's mom. How Father had looked at him in a strange way.

Divorces just didn't happen among Mother and Father's friends. Hägerström knew that one of Carl's friends had gotten divorced, but right now he couldn't remember who. At the same time, Mother must understand that he was happier without Anna, though not without Pravat.

Hägerström and Anna's life had been so filled by the adopt-a-child project that they hadn't been able to see how little else they had in common. And their sex life was a joke. It had been from the very beginning.

But now, in front of Pravat—he couldn't do it.

Some of the finest paintings from Father's collection were hanging on the walls in the dining room. There was a Miró and a Paul Klee. The latter showed a number of viaducts that had begun to move. They marched, paraded, colorful, leggy. Buildings that moved—it was a bizarre protest. The bridge revolution, the stable viaducts' revolt. Maybe that was the way Mother was feeling right now. A solid structure that had stood still its entire life, immobile in its concrete foundation—that finally took a step.

He drove Pravat straight to day care on Monday morning. Hägerström had the rest of the day off. The prison administration had forced him to take a day off since he had worked so much recently. He had lunch with his brother at the upscale downtown staple, Prinsen. He bought two shirts and a pair of jeans at the NK department store.

That night he settled into the couch in the living room. Switched the TV on. Zapped between channels. The news. *CSI: Miami.* Some talent show: *Idol, Top Model, Let's Dance*, every starry-eyed-nobody-who-wanted-to-be-somebody. He wasn't familiar with the shows, but he knew that he didn't want to watch them. He paused at a documentary about Russia: old KGB soldiers in death squads who executed dissident journalists.

He went out into the kitchen. Put a capsule into his Nespresso machine. Livanto, intense coffee with a roasted flavor. He listened to the buzz from the machine. Brought the coffee back to the TV.

The documentary made him think about his own military service. The coastal rangers were supposed to defend the country's borders but, above all, carry out guerrilla operations if the country was invaded. That was back in the days when the Russians were seriously considered a threat to Sweden.

He had finished the coffee. And three glasses of Bordeaux too. Hägerström wasn't used to all this free time.

He wondered what he should do. In one way, sitting at home without even finding something decent to watch on TV was a waste now that he was finally back in the city. He could watch a movie. He could look at pictures of Pravat and let himself drift off into daydreams. He could go to bed and try to sleep. Or else he could call someone, go out, and have something more to drink. But who? He was thirty-eight years old, and it wasn't even a weekend. All his friends were either married with kids or divorced—but still with kids. What were the chances that they would be able to grab a spontaneous beer? He knew the deal. If you wanted to see one of them, you had to plan it, often weeks in advance. The only one he could think of who might be willing to throw himself out into the Stockholm night to see him was Thomas Andrén, his former colleague. He had a kid too these days—also an adopted son—but he usually never said no. On the other hand, they hadn't seen each other in over two years. And what was more, rumor had it that he had crossed over to the other side. Hägerström didn't feel like seeing him tonight.

An hour later: he was sitting alone at Half Way Inn by Mariatorget—his favorite haunt.

In the beginning of his career, he'd worked at the police station near here. A few of his colleagues used to grab a beer or two after work, mostly on Fridays, but sometimes on other days of the week too. It wasn't Hägerström's kind of place. But still: a beer or a glass at Half Way Inn, and his head felt better after a day at work.

And there was one more thing. Half Way Inn was in Södermalm, the southern part of the city. For Hägerström, that was radical. When he graduated from the Police Academy in the mid-1990s, he had even moved here. A small apartment near Hornstull. He could still see his mother's, father's, and brother's faces when they found out where it was. "Södermalm—but *why*?"

Nowadays Hägerström had calmed down. He still preferred to go out in Södermalm, but he lived in Östermalm. He was over making a point of things. He just chose what worked best, and Östermalm was home, after all.

The place was a classic British pub with an aquatic theme. An old-fashioned sign hung over the door: HARDY & CO. FISHING RODS. A plastic swordfish in the ceiling. A brass railing along the length of the bar. Green Scottish plaid wallpaper on the walls, and photos of the Highlands, bagpipers, and ships. There was nasty old wall-to-wall carpeting on the floor, soaked in years' worth of spilled beer.

In the bar: Samuel Adams, Guinness, Kilkenny. And—despite the fact that French usually didn't jibe with this kind of style—Pelforth in all flavors: dark, blond, *ambrée*.

There was a mixed clientele. In the corner to the left of the door, facing the window, was where the old guys always sat—whiskered, half fat, fully sloshed. Södermalm's native population. Before the gentrification. At the tables in the middle, in front of the bar, were ordinary moms and dads, friends and work colleagues. Grabbing a beer, chilling out, talking about life. And farthest in, near the digital jukebox, that's where the trendy, hipster crowd sat. Hägerström had seen them change their clothing style over the years, but they never varied in relation to one another. Beige chinos, white sneakers, and full beards on the guys. Hats and tattoos on the girls. Fashion could apparently only have one look at a time in Södermalm. Same story with his own brother and friends—they were clones too, but of a very different variety.

Two hours later, he left.

Spinning house facades. Red teeth. Wine taste in his palate. It was twelve-thirty at night.

The bartender was in the process of chaining the outdoor café furniture together in order to close up. He pushed the pub's fake plants toward the wall and turned to Hägerström. "Should I call you a cab?"

Hägerström shook his head. He wasn't planning on going home. He wanted to fuck.

The Side Track Bar was right next to the Half Way Inn.

There was no line outside.

A bouncer nodded, let him in.

The upstairs was minimal. He took the stairs down. A rainbow flag was pinned above the staircase leading down. Hägerström held the banister in a tight grip. Leaned back, tried to maintain his balance. The stairs turned, and Hägerström turned with them. One step at a time.

A large room. Crystal chandeliers suspended from the ceiling, and lit candles on the tables. Loud, with lots of tables with checked tablecloths and diners. No one took note of him.

He continued farther in.

The lighting got dimmer down there. A bar stretched out in front of him.

They were playing ABBA.

The ceilings were pretty low here. A crystal disco ball was rotating slowly above the bar. Red spotlights were reflected in thousands of small red diamonds of light all over the room. Farther in was yet another room and a dance floor with black-painted walls.

Straight ahead: clusters of men. Men in tank tops. Men in blue jeans and jewelry. Hägerström lowered his eyes. The floor was made up of porcelain mosaic. He looked down at his feet. The mosaic was the color of the rainbow. Someone touched his shoulder. He looked up. Was met by a set of pale blue eyes.

"Are you nearsighted?" The guy smiled.

Hägerström smiled back. "No, I just wanted to get some attention."

"It worked."

The guy's head was shaved, but he had a beard. He put his arm around Hägerström. Led him farther into the venue.

Hägerström's spine was shooting out signals. Strong synapses. Sending tickling sensations all throughout his body.

They were playing Lou Reed. "*Said, hey baby. Take a walk on the wild side. And the colored girls go doo do doo do dooo do do dooo.*"

Hägerström followed the man with the beard out onto the dance floor.

The crystal ball rotated slowly.

Doo do doo do doo do do dooo.

It was two-thirty in the morning. Hägerström and the man with the beard stumbled out onto the street.

Hägerström heard a voice. "Hi?"

He turned around. Focused his gaze.

It was one of his brother's closest friends, Fredric Adlercreutz, who was standing there on the street, dressed in a dark coat with a tux underneath.

Hägerström returned the greeting. "What are *you* doing here?" He parroted his brother's tone of voice whenever they talked about Södermalm.

"What do you mean?" Fredric asked.

"I mean, in Södermalm. What else would I mean?"

"I was at a gentlemen's dinner." Fredric looked away. He probably didn't know how to handle the fact that he had just seen Hägerström hand in hand with another man. Polite as ever.

A taxi pulled up. Hägerström took his chance. Grabbed hold of the man with the beard and jumped into the car. He couldn't drop Fredric's expression. It wasn't the first time someone had seen him like this, but it still always felt kind of shitty.

Then he thought: a gentlemen's dinner in Södermalm? Maybe Fredric Adlercreutz had actually been on his way into the same place that Hägerström had just stumbled out of. But if so, why had he chosen to greet him at all?

They drove to the man's apartment on Torsgatan. His name was Mats. They started making out as soon as they got into the foyer.

Tore each other's clothes off. Caressed each other's arms, chests, necks.

Mats smelled musky, of perfume that had been worn all day.

They fell into his bedroom. The bed was unmade. He had pictures of his kids on one wall and a smoking jacket on a hook on the other.

Mats was a PR guy, he said.

Mats took Hägerström in his mouth on the edge of the bed.

Mats saw his kids every other weekend.

Mats brought out lube. Put his finger up Hägerström's ass.

Mats said he had seen Hägerström at the Side Track Bar before.

Mats put his cock inside Hägerström.

They both groaned.

It felt unbelievably good.

Back at the prison. One morning after breakfast, Hägerström knocked on JW's cell door. The guy barricaded himself in there, but you couldn't exactly lock out a CO.

Hägerström eyed JW. The stitches over his eyebrow were still visible. The blond hair wasn't as slicked back as usual—it was hanging more in wisps around his ears. Still, he looked pretty calm. Considering.

According to plan. Exactly the way Hägerström wanted it.

He had a seat on the edge of JW's cot.

"So how are you doing? Really."

JW was sitting on his chair, the laptop open in front of him on the table. "You're pretty new in here, Hägerström, but you know what happened. It's part of life on the inside, but that doesn't make it fun."

"I understand. And your boys have been transferred."

Hägerström had devised his word choice carefully: *your boys.* A signal referring to the basic premise of prison life. You had your boys, your camaraderie—in JW's case: your protectors.

"Yeah, bus therapy. Too bad—they were good people."

The way he breathed when he spoke: Hägerström thought he could hear his suppressed northern dialect.

"I have a proposition," he said.

He rose, walked over to JW's cell door. Carefully pushed it shut. Sat back down on the edge of the bed.

"Abdi Husseini is still here. His people are still here. You're left here, alone. That's not a good combination, to put it simply. Like a cat and a mouse. But I could make sure he gets transferred."

JW closed his computer. Slowly, attentively. Hägerström could tell: JW was listening, closely.

"You don't know me," Hägerström continued, "but I've got good connections. Good feel for the Department of Corrections. A few phone calls, and it's a done deal. Abdi Husseini disappears from here, and you don't have to worry anymore. How many months do you have left?"

"Less than three."

"Okay, almost three months with Omar. Or three relaxed months without that lunatic."

"The second option sounds nicer."

"So what do you say?"

JW smiled. A crooked smile. A business smile. He understood—in the end, it all comes down to price. That was his basic outlook in life too.

"What do you want?"

Hägerström bounced back like a ricochet: "Fifteen thousand."

JW played the ball right back to him: "Ten thousand. And how fast can you make him disappear?"

Hägerström could hear his own victory cry ringing through his head. "In max four days, I think. But in that case I want fifteen."

JW chuckled. His teeth were as white and shiny as Torsfjäll's. "We have a deal."

Hägerström thought, *I've got you on my hook.*

Now all I have to do is reel you in.

18

The day after the funeral: Natalie was sitting in the armchair in her room. Gazing at her reflection in the switched-off television set.

Dad'd given her the television.

Really, what she should do was go into the city and meet up with a friend. Take a walk with Mom. Work out. Or download a movie. Do something.

But nothing worked.

She was supposed to meet Stefanovic this afternoon. The note Goran'd given her after the funeral: not a question—an order. But he wasn't in a position to command Natalie to do anything. She wasn't at anyone's beck and call. No one made decisions for her—Dad's employees were only supposed to shut up and obey. But still: she actually did want to see Stefanovic right now. See how he was doing, hear what he had to say.

She remained sitting in the armchair. The same reflection in the television's black screen. The same meaninglessness.

On the wall: the photo of Dad when he was young.

On the dresser: the diamond earrings from Tiffany's that Dad'd given her.

Dad.

She saw the same images flicker past in her mind over and over again.

The dark blue BMW across the street. Dad's voice from the car. The flames. The smell of burned leather and human flesh.

Then she heard a sound. An irritating, penetrating indoor sound. It was the warning signal from the gate. Someone was making their way up to the house. Someone who'd chosen not to announce themselves through the intercom. Neither Mom nor Patrik seemed to hear it. The signal continued to blare out. It was only ten o'clock in the morning.

For a brief moment, she considered running to the safe room. But that seemed a little over the top. She should check the monitors to see who it was.

The doorbell rang. Whoever it was, he was apparently standing outside the door, wanting to get in.

She rose. She'd owned the T-shirt she was wearing now since she was fourteen. It'd been washed so many times that it was soft as silk.

She walked out into the hall. Looked at the security monitor. Standing outside the door were three men she didn't recognize. They didn't look like murderers.

"Can you see who it is?"

Natalie turned around. Patrik was standing behind her.

"No, no idea. There are three of them. Should I ask?"

"No. I'll take care of it. Get out of the hall, Natalie, until I've checked who they are."

Natalie walked into the kitchen.

She heard Patrik's voice: "Who are you?"

That canned sound from the speaker by the door: "This is the police."

At least it wasn't someone who was out to hurt them on a physical level.

She heard Patrik open the door.

Natalie was about to go out and greet them. She hesitated for a second before walking back out into the hall. A feeling coursed through her body—might be good to take it a little easy.

She heard their voices.

"We're from the Economic Crimes Bureau."

"Okay, and who are you looking for?"

"We're not looking for anyone. May I ask your name?"

"My name is Patrik Sjöquist."

"Please identify yourself."

A rustling sound. Natalie was tense like a rubber band about to spring. It didn't seem like these cops were here to talk to her, not to solve Dad's murder. There was something else they wanted.

She heard one of them say, "We are here to go over Radovan Kranjic's papers. Accounting, that sort of thing. So if you would be so kind as to show us where he kept that kind of material, we'll take it from there."

Patrik wasn't going to match their game of pretend politesse. "You're in the wrong place. We don't keep paperwork here. It's all kept in the offices of the businesses themselves or with the accounting firm.

You'll have to go there. This is where the family lives. And they are in mourning."

Natalie tried to evaluate the situation quickly. She didn't know if Dad kept bookkeeping and stuff like that at home. But she knew that whatever they wanted to get at, she didn't want them to succeed.

She could hear Patrik continue to talk back out in the hall.

Finally, a cocky cop voice said, "Listen, buddy, calm down. We're the ones who'll decide if there's something for us to find or not. And if you don't quit it, we're going to have to call for backup."

Natalie'd heard enough. She left the kitchen. In the hall outside: she listened for the cops' voices. She was several rooms away from them now.

She walked past Mom and Dad's bedroom. It was empty. A six-foot-high headboard—like a canopy bed but without the canopy. The king-size bed was bedecked with a purple satin coverlet with the large Kranjic coat of arms embroidered on it.

The wall-to-wall carpeting muted her footsteps.

She walked past Mom's bathroom, the den, her own bedroom. A bend. She walked past the guest room where Patrik was staying. The door to the library and Dad's office was three yards away.

Now she could hear Patrik's angry voice at a distance. Good—he was still arguing with the cops.

She opened the door to the office. The solid oak desk was covered in a large leather pad. On top of that was a pile of papers and a paperweight with the Kranjic coat of arms on it, a closed laptop, and a pencil stand—several of the pens had the Kranjic coat of arms on them. There was a real Persian carpet on the floor and decorative vases all around. On the bookshelf: books on finance, piles of paper, binders.

There was no time to be picky. Natalie moved toward her goal like a well-trained dog: the bookshelf. She grabbed as many binders as she could carry. Opened the door with her foot. Glanced back into the office one last time. There was one more thing she wanted to bring with her—an open binder on the desk. Dad must've been looking at it before he died.

She set down one of the binders she was carrying. Grabbed the binder on the desk. Total: she was able to carry seven binders if she balanced them on both arms at once. If there was time, she would come back and grab more.

She left the office. Walked down the hall.

She heard voices.

Cop voices.

Jerk voices.

Natalie opened the kitchen door. Walked out the back way to her car. Hoped that the cop fuckers didn't see her.

She drove into the city. Called Louise to ask if she could stop by. Louise wasn't home. She called Tove. Drove to her house with the binders.

She was back in her car again. She'd had a nap. Talked to Patrik, who guaranteed that there was nothing to worry about. He said all the important stuff was kept with Dad's accountant, Mischa Bladman, at the offices of MB Accounting Consultant AB.

The cops'd cleared out Dad's office. Natalie didn't say anything about the binders she'd managed to take with her.

Now she was on her way to Södersjukhuset, the hospital that Stefanovic'd been moved to. It was conversation time.

She had plenty of time. Drove through the city. In by Norrtull. The Vanadis roundabout with lots of annoying pedestrian crosswalks where people ran straight out into the street. The city hadn't been washed over with that familiar summer lull yet.

She drove Karlbergsvägen. Glanced down St. Eriksgatan. You could see all the way over the bridge to Kungsholmen, almost all the way to Fleminggatan. An unusually long view in her line of vision. A slice through the city. An artery that pumped life into Stockholm. Dad's territory. Her territory.

She parked the Golf in a visitors' parking lot below the hospital. Almost forgot to lock the car. Pressed the button on the key when she was twenty yards away. She heard the lock click.

The main entrance was large. She eyed the people. Old men with walkers, seven-year-olds with casts and their moms in tow, Somalian women draped in layers upon layers of fabric despite the sun that was shining outside. Natalie had no idea how she was going to get to the unit where Stefanovic was being cared for. She was afraid of getting lost.

But that wasn't all. She was also afraid that she wasn't going to be able to handle this. The meeting with Stefanovic wasn't all. Stuff was happening constantly. The day before yesterday: she'd been called in for questioning with the police regarding the murder. They wanted to know what she'd seen on the street when the bomb exploded. Yesterday: the funeral. Today: the panicked binder-rescue mission right under the cop fuckers' noses. And every day since Dad'd been murdered: terrierlike journalists who wanted her to comment on the events. What the fuck did they think—that she was going to open up about her feelings to *them*?

Unit 43.

She walked slowly down the corridor. A guy who looked to be around twenty-five was sitting outside one of the rooms. Natalie didn't recognize him, but she recognized the style—track pants, a zippered sweater that said BUDO NORD on it, plus-size muscles, and distrustful eyes. He had to be one of Dad's employees.

She nodded at the guy. He rose and opened the door for her. Natalie stepped inside.

A bright room. Windows looking out over the water, Årstaviken. Flower print curtains and furniture in light colors. Textured wallpaper, linoleum floor, and one hundred percent hospital feeling.

Stefanovic was sitting propped up by pillows in the bed that stood against one of the walls.

Goran, Marko, Milorad, Bogdan were sitting in chairs. One chair was empty.

Stefanovic's face looked pale. Other than that, she couldn't see any traces from the explosion. She almost couldn't look at him—everything reminded her too much of Dad.

"*Dobrodošao.*"

Stefanovic remained where he was. The other men rose, kissing her on the cheeks, one by one.

Natalie sat down in the empty seat.

Stefanovic propped himself up even taller against the pillows and said, in Serbian, "Good, everyone's here. We can begin."

He turned to Natalie. "It'd be good if you'd turn off your cell phone."

Natalie met his pale eyes. "It hasn't been on for a long time. The journalist assholes, you know."

"I understand."

He looked dead serious.

"I appreciate that we could all get together so soon. First of all, I want to say that I've heard from many sources that yesterday was very dignified. An important manifestation for us. Many powerful people were present. Dmitrij Kostic, Ivan Hasdic, Nemanja Ravic. Magnus Berthold, Joakim Sjöström, and Diddi Korkis, to name a few. I am happy for your sake, Natalie."

Stefanovic's spiel was weird—he was talking more about the guests than the actual ceremony. But Natalie didn't say anything. Let him finish.

"And now we have to deal with the reality at hand. Two things. First of all, we have to save Kum's assets. The Economic Crimes Bureau has visited the Kranjic family at home and also demanded the bookkeeping material from the accounting firm. If it wasn't for my condition, I would've dealt with the binders days ago, but it's too late now. The companies are probably going to be getting some pretty unfortunate letters from the tax man pretty soon. Natalie, I want to tell you that you should expect to get the same demands directed at the estate. There are accounts in several countries that we have to look into and secure. I have a suggestion for an estate manager for you.

"We are getting into formation," Stefanovic went on, "readying ourselves to face every mommyfucker who thinks we're down for the count. I promise you, the little punks out there think we're going to lie down and die just because Kum Rado is gone. I'm assuming you've all already been called in for questioning with the police. They've been here anyway, and I got the distinct sense that they don't want to investigate this properly. You know, the cops aren't doing shit. They don't want to find the murderer. No—they're happy that Kum is gone and see their interrogations as a way to press us for information. And they want a war to break out in this city in order to make us all weaker."

Natalie was listening. The men discussed the issues that Stefanovic'd raised. Goran and the others offered their opinions. Discussed plans. Talked alliances. Analyzed: who was a friend and who was an enemy.

And throughout, Natalie couldn't help but note: Stefanovic was laying down the law like a little mini-boss there in his bed. Seemed like he thought he was the new Dad.

They name-dropped gangs, ghettos, prisons. They talked about deliveries of amphetamines, bouncer companies, and foreign weapons dealers. They discussed the companies briefly. Delegated tasks. Hoped that Mischa Bladman'd managed to save as much material as possible. She still didn't say anything about the binders she'd hidden away.

Natalie was familiar with most of what they were talking about. But some things were news to her. She let the men talk. Played ignorant. Listened.

Learned.

They ended the meeting an hour later.

She felt tired. Dizzy. Confused. That she'd even been invited to participate in this meeting—a new feeling. At the same time: Stefanovic's attitude was strange.

Goran followed her down to the car.

He spoke Swedish now. "How are you, honey?"

"Fine," she lied. "It was good that I was allowed to be here for this."

"I was the one who thought that was best."

"Thank you. I'm being questioned by the police again soon."

"Okay. In that case, I want you to think about a few things."

"What?"

Goran told her how he thought she should behave. Not answer unnecessary questions. Not speculate with any theories of her own. "You can't help them find Kum's killer anyway."

Then he suggested that she record all the interrogations on her iPhone from now on.

Natalie thought that sounded strange.

Goran said. "No, it's not strange. If they don't do their job and find your father's murderer, we might have to take this into our own hands."

She promised to think it over.

"It was important that you were there today," Goran said. "You're the daughter."

"What do you mean?"

"You're Rado's daughter. You're the heiress. I heard what Kum said in the hospital. Do you understand? I heard."

"Yes. We'll have to talk about that some other time."

"Absolutely. And hey, you should get another cell phone number. And when you've done that, could you please inform me of the number? Do it through Patrik. Don't call."

"I understand. I won't call."

"And one more thing."

Natalie wondered what he would say next. She was so tired right now.

"Do you and your mom have a good sense of the estate's assets?"

"I don't really have such a good sense of it, but I heard what Stefanovic said. I haven't had the energy to deal with it. But we're going to hire a lawyer who can deal with the tax authorities."

"I don't just mean because of the tax authorities. There are a lot of other sticky fingers out there."

Goran walked toward her. His gray temples almost looked white in the sunlight.

He kissed her on both cheeks.

"Try to find out what's in the estate. That's my advice to you."

Natalie nodded. Was too tired to wonder what he meant. All she wanted to do was go home and sleep.

"So, is everything okay?"

Natalie didn't know what to say.

19

Today: the most important preparation of all. Or really: the time of preparations'd passed—it was starting now.

Two days ago: Jorge'd been given the time by the Finn, who'd been given it by the insider.

Plus: Jorge had his own plan. There were pro opportunities out there. Soon one of his bros was gating out: JW. A *vato* in the know. Had continued working his business inside the walls. Advanced shit. Money transferring, dough kneading, zillion-zero-adding. To put it simply: laundry. JW would be able to take their booty and make magic happen. Total makeover: instead of paper—digits in accounts. Tied to the finest credit cards. Miles from the Finn's dank Södertälje hideouts.

A new life. For real.

Obsessed with the daydream: the delivery of the year. Summer paychecks plus bonuses, the extra withdrawals from the ATMs before the citywide vacation month kicked in, the tourist invasion of the city—everyone needed cash. And cash had to be transported to Stockholm's ATM machines. What's more: the insider'd given the Finn new leads: they had a new unloading routine, they had new GPS transmitters, they might have additional flow from the vault. The dude seemed like he was the fucking CEO of the security company or something.

It was starting now.

Like, shit, IT WAS STARTING NOW.

Jorge, Mahmud, Tom, Sergio: on their way out to the helicopter base.

Tom: a star—he'd done ill research, *à la* Al Qaeda preproduction.

Three questions.

The fence: Tom'd done some math. Asked around. Read up on other robberies. The Finn was right: an angle grinder was a bad idea. But according to Tom: they'd be able to bust through the gate if they had a vehicle that was big and heavy enough. Suggestion: wheel loader, dumper, or motor grader. Tom'd even test-driven through a gate at a construction site with a wheel loader. It wasn't as hefty as the sliding gate at Tomteboda, but still. It oughta work.

They made up their minds. Jorge informed the Finn. The dude agreed, it was a good suggestion. The only hitch: they probably wouldn't be able to bring the vehicle back with them after—risk of DNA traces was a big no-no. Jorge thought: *Tom'll probably come up with something.*

Second of all: the helicopter thing. When Jorge thought about it: surprising. There were only six ghetto birds in all of Swedeland. Eurocopter EC135—their model. Parked in helicopter airports around the country. What was Sven Sweden thinking, exactly? Only six pig choppers in an entire country—*loco*. And they really should've learned their lesson after the helicopter robbery a few years ago. But the Swedish State had only themselves to blame: CIT *capo*, Jorge—the heist guru—would school them. Without blades in the air—no hunt. Without blades in the air—a cakewalk. The Finn'd thought the whole thing through. And Jorge'd figured out his own version of it all.

Three questions. Two solved.

The final one: the vault.

The Finn still hadn't been able to get his hands on blueprints or other information about what it looked like. How the walls were constructed. The lock mechanisms in the vault doors or how thick they were.

He was clear: "I need to know more in order to blow that shit up. But the insider claims he can't get anything."

Probable: they wouldn't be able to get into the vault.

Question: Should he put Tom on this too?

The BIG question: How would he keep as much as possible from the Finn?

A night out in the bush: cottages, farms, and animals in half-light. Trees, fields, and more trees. The concrete inverted: the real Sweden for the kind of people Jorge didn't know.

The feeling: tense. His stomach: in knots. Irritated that the familiar anxiety was sneaking up on him right now. Mahmud on the other hand: seemed mad chill. Was playing Arab music as usual. Haifa Wehbe, Ragheb Alama—authentic Middle Eastern groove, as he said. Soundtrack for the scene outside the window where the blue sky cut across the yellow fields: the Swedish national anthem.

The feeling: shit, this is it. It was go time. Couldn't go belly up. Couldn't blow this thing. Never fuck up—a motto to live by.

'Cause some people fucked up: that Viktor fag'd messed shit up with his fagginess. They needed to be at least eight people. But Jorge was never gonna let that V-fag be in on this after he'd fagged out at Jimmy's mom's place. Started messing around, making a scene. So: only seven men left. Wouldn't be enough.

Fucking fag.

Tom said the guy was yellow. That he was in the shit, couldn't take the pressure. Was apparently anxious over everything that could happen since Radovan was bumped off. But what the fuck—why couldn't he get it together? But now it was over, the guy was off the squad.

And the snitch risk? Zero. Jorge let Javier and Sergio have a little talk with Viktor. Explain in detail how it'd feel to get a pipe shoved up the anus, then plug the end up after a rat was put inside it. The rat only had one way out.

Mahmud'd brought it up one night when they were sitting at the café. Beatrice'd gone home for the day—she ran the place herself now, like a fucking business executive.

Mahmud'd lost weight over the past few months. Usually: the Arab worked out often. Not like before their café days—back then he was a juice junkie—but still a lot. Now: he was only training for the job—that was what you called a professional criminal.

Jorge tried to think of replacements. Kept a running list in his head. Old homies: Märsta *muchachos*, prison pals, coke criminals. Eddie'd been locked up. Elliot and his brothers, who Jorge used to run Sunny Sunday with'd been kicked out of Swedeland—residency permits were apparently not their strong suit. Vadim and Ashur—buds from way back—couldn't be trusted: they'd gone from safe blow to trashy amphetamine. From ghetto classy to basement ashy.

He thought of other boys from Chillentuna. There were a few that he thought could handle it—but they were hard-asses: would demand too large a cut.

He thought of Rolando: the *blatte* from the Österåker pen who'd taught him more about blow than a gaucho knows about horseshit. Nowadays: the C-Latino'd straightened out. Gotten a family. Bought a row house. Sold insurance over the phone. Lived like a Ken doll without a cock between his legs.

The Finn was at him: "Get someone else. You need to be eight."

Jorge had to find another guy.

The Arab brought up the issue. "So, whatta we do about that Viktor guy?"

"He's out. Plus, Radovan was offed."

"Yeah, that's huge, man. Honest, it means a lot, that the Yugo boss is gone. Maybe we should stay in Sweden after the gig?"

"Who's taking over, who's taking over. That's all anyone ever talks about."

"But who we gonna bring on instead of Viktor? We need somebody else."

"Yeah, that's what the Finn says too. One of the pig pens's got too many garage exits. Two people can't pull it off. Trust me, I've tried to think of someone."

Jorge was drinking coffee. Mahmud was drinking juice.

He held up the bottle. "It says this shit is a hundred percent fruit. But this juice tastes like apples. Not oranges. Then you look who made it—the Coca-Cola Company, man. *Click*—aha! Those Jews are always pulling a fast one on you."

"What're you talking about? Coca-Cola ain't Jews, and we've got to solve this Viktor shit now."

Mahmud took another sip of the juice. "I've asked Babak."

Jorge slammed his mug down. Black coffee all over the table. Drops over the table edge.

Mahmud pushed his chair back. "What the fuck's wrong with you?"

Jorge tried to say something.

Nothing came out.

It was so obvious: Babak—Mahmud's best bro. 'Course the Arab'd asked that fucker. For Mahmud, it was a simple, obvious thing to do. But Jorge didn't want the Iranian in on this—that *blatte* was on J-boy's back like a bully in grade school.

At the same time: he understood why Mahmud'd asked. Babak was deep in the coke game. Definitely not a snitch. Someone to trust, Jorge couldn't deny that.

Fuck.

All he felt like doing was screaming. Still, he kept his mouth shut.

Finally he said, "What the fuck's *your* problem. Why didn't you ask me first?"

Mahmud slurped up the last of the juice in the bottle. "What? We can trust Babak. He's solid."

"You know the rules, bro. Don't talk to outsiders. No matter what."

"Listen. To me, Babak is no outsider."

Mahmud's mouth: a straight line.

Jorge's mouth: a grimace.

Felt like shit.

Back in the bush. In front of them: Myttinge landing strip. Tom and Sergio'd gotten out of their car. Were waiting in the twilight.

The stars were hardly visible—the sky was summer bright. Jorge and Mahmud parked next to Tom's car. Got out.

Farther off, the helicopter hangar towered. Like a round, gray mountain in the middle of the field. A short distance behind the hangar were blue lights that indicated the placement of the helipads.

They approached Tom and Sergio.

"Nice. So far so good. Sergio, you can take Tom's car back."

Sergio nodded. Everyone knew what had to get done.

"Tom," Jorge continued, "you go down to the water and get things tied up there."

Tom half-jogged down the road. Disappeared into the darkness.

Sergio climbed into the first car. Started the engine. Pulled out slowly.

Drove back to the city.

Jorge and Mahmud were the only ones left. They walked back to the boosted car. Both of them were wearing overalls. They popped the trunk.

Everything was calm. The woods around them were silent like a sleeping rock. Jorge thought about the times in his life he'd been in the woods. During field trips with school—he was sent home. As an adult—that's when he'd been worked over by the Yugos. To him: woods equaled bad vibes. Woods belonged to another world. A scary jungle for someone who hadn't been there before. For someone who wasn't born to be comfortable in the woods. But now Jorge was confident: he'd finally navigated correctly. The forest was his friend today. He was finally close to getting his ultimate break.

His stomachache released its grip. Now it was just full speed ahead.

They put their gloves on. Got two black garbage bags from the trunk of the car. Unrolled them. A Kalashnikov each. Mahmud also pulled out a bag, put the rifle in it. Jorge kept his in his hand. Inspected it: AK-47. Dark metal that looked black. The handle, the piston, the grip under the pipe felt cool—the wooden parts matched his skin. They'd gotten hold of two of them, as luck would have it.

A real gangsta gun. A gun for a ghetto boss.

The adrenaline started pumping, but J-boy still felt calm. He thought: *For Svens, adrenaline equals stress. But people like me—we grow calm.*

They crossed the road. High grass. Damp against their thighs.

The fence was hardly seven feet high. They'd been here last week and done some reconnaissance. Knew everything already. Mahmud got out the bolt cutter. Jorge held the flashlight.

Chop, chop. The Arab cut the fence as if it were his toenails.

They climbed in through the hole.

Maybe an alarm'd gone off somewhere already, but so far they didn't hear anything.

Sixty-five feet to the hangar.

Cameras: two of them placed in every corner, each pointing in a different direction. No one could approach the outer walls without showing up on the surveillance tapes. The hangar manufacturer's logo was visible on the wall: DeBeur. Sounded Dutch.

They pulled their ski masks down.

Thirty more feet.

Still deathly silent all around.

Ten feet.

Then: spotlights switched on. Illuminated the grass in a thirty-foot radius around the hangar.

That was to be expected. The surveillance cameras needed light.

What was unexpected: Jorge heard sounds. Yapping, growling sounds.

Two German shepherds came bounding toward them. Jorge barely turned around in time. Stared straight into drool and lunging jaws. Six feet away.

Barking monsters.

He hated dogs.

Mahmud screamed, "Shoot the fuckers!"

Jorge took a step back. Raised the AK-47.

Tried to aim.

Bam-bam-bam. The beast of a *perro* made a whinnying sound. Collapsed on the ground.

Jorge turned to Mahmud. He was running. Fifty or so feet farther off. The other dog was chasing him. Jorge sprinted in that direction.

He couldn't shoot in the dark.

"Mahmud!" he yelled. "Come here!"

He heard Mahmud. He heard the dog.

Then: the Arab with panic in his eyes. Running in a circle. Getting closer to Jorge. To the light.

The dog was three feet behind him. Jorge raised the gun. Followed the pooch in his sight.

Aimed. The sight. The groove. The fucking dog's open jaws.

Poof. It howled.

Poof again.

Game over.

Mahmud was panting. Leaned over, hands on his knees.

Jorge laughed, "You were pretty scared, huh?"

Mahmud looked up. Spit in the grass. "*Kaleb*, I hate dogs. They're unclean animals."

They didn't have time to talk, they had to keep going now. Ran over to the hangar. Not many seconds left to do this.

Mahmud rummaged through the bag. Was holding something in his hand. Gripped it like a tennis ball. Jorge didn't need to use the flashlight. The spotlights by the surveillance cameras were doing the job for him now.

He knew what Mahmud was holding. A real apple: grenade, M52 P3. Mahmud rolled it in under the metal that jutted out at the very base of the wall. A quick motion with his hand. Jorge'd moved away a good distance. Mahmud took long steps backward. Thirty feet.

BANG.

A pressure wave from the explosion. Ringing in their ears.

Abbou—what an explosion!

The metal of the wall was torn open three feet to the side.

They rushed forward. Crazy adrenaline now.

Jorge used the flashlight to shine inside the opening. He glimpsed two helicopters in the dark of the hangar. The rotor blades were as long as the wings on an insect.

They poked the AK-47s through the hole. Set to automatic.

Ra-ta-ta-ta-ta. Jorge was a pro now—had practiced on the dogs.

The smattering echoed through the hangar. Sounded different than it had outside.

The magazine was empty.

Mahmud dug through the bag. Two apples in each hand.

He pulled out the pins. Rolled them in toward the helicopters.

They ran back toward the hole in the fence.

The sky was dark blue. The day after tomorrow they were gonna be multimillionaires.

They heard the explosions almost immediately.

Boom.

Boom.

20

Hägerström was on his way to see Inspector Lennart Torsfjäll. To brief him about the latest developments in the case. The road from Sala to Stockholm was backed up all the way to Enköping. He had left late enough to escape the worst of the traffic on the E18 highway, but so far none of the slower summer pace appeared to have kicked in yet. Still, he liked this road. The landscape all around was very rustic. Tender potato plants were poking up in rows, the grain fields were a light green color, harvest was still a long ways away. Hägerström wasn't a country kind of guy, but he wasn't totally clueless either. Mother Lottie loved the countryside. If it weren't for the fact that Idlingstad Manor operated under the rules of primogeniture, she would have loved to take it over from her parents. And these days Carl lived year-round at Avesjö, the place on Värmdö Island that Mother and Father had bought in 1972. Hägerström had spent his summers there as a child, had seen the tenant farmer's cows plod around in the pastures, had come with the same farmer to see the chickens slaughtered and help Mother with the rhubarb plants in the vegetable garden. One day maybe he would want to buy a house somewhere too. The only question was who he would share the pleasure with.

He thought of the guy he had met at the Side Track Bar a few days ago. Mats. But no, that was a regular old one-night stand. Mats didn't awaken any dreams of a quiet life in the country.

The apartment was on Surbrunnsgatan. Probably belonged to Torsfjäll's unit in the force somehow. The last time, they had met in an apartment on Gärdet, across town. According to the police chief, the force had access to a number of apartments in different parts of the city to use for informants, infiltrators, witnesses, and other loose pieces of different puzzles who needed to live in undisclosed locations for a while. Since there was a constant rotation, they always kept a few apartments empty in case they would need them. They were good meeting places.

Hägerström was standing in front of the door to the apartment. It said JANSSON on the mail slot. That was Sweden's most common last name, according to some statistic Hägerström had read at some point. He rang the doorbell.

Torsfjäll opened.

The inspector was dressed in light brown chinos and, as usual, an impeccably ironed shirt. Today he was also wearing a tie in a loud purple paisley. It didn't look like it was of particularly good quality—it didn't shine in a way that suggested 100 percent silk. Hägerström knew you could never be certain if a tie was nice, but you could always tell when it wasn't nice. What's more, ties that were too loud were ridiculous, at least on police inspectors.

Torsfjäll smiled. His teeth were even whiter than the last time they had seen each other. He must use some sort of bleaching system.

The apartment was sparsely furnished, just like the other places where they had met. Actually, the apartments all pretty much had the same decorating job—they must've gotten a bulk discount at IKEA. A forty-six-inch superflat flat-screen TV was hanging on the wall. Hägerström was surprised that the police had splurged on such an expensive piece of equipment, but he assumed it was often the person living here's best friend. If you had snitched, you probably wanted to stay indoors all day.

Torsfjäll asked him about his drive and commented on the death of the Yugo boss. Radovan Kranjic had been blown to pieces in the middle of Östermalm—according to Torsfjäll, the incident could lead to more violence in the criminal underworld.

Hägerström wanted to get right to the point.

"He's starting to open up."

The inspector smiled and squinted. It was doubtful if Torsfjäll was able to see anything at all when he laughed.

"Tell me," he said. "I'm on the edge of my seat."

Hägerström smiled back. *A quiet, relaxed smile*, he thought. At least he had made some headway in the operation.

"He's starting to use me."

"Good, very good. So it worked."

"Exactly. You already know what he did in order for me to get Abdi Husseini transferred. We agreed on fifteen thousand. I asked how I would be paid. JW said that was part of the deal, that I'd have to take care of the payment myself."

Torsfjäll was beaming. Hägerström had already told him parts of this, but the inspector seemed to like hearing it told more than once.

"He gave me an e-mail address and an eight-digit code. The following day I sent an e-mail with the number combination and my bank account information in Sweden. The address was gs@nwci-management.com. I got a reply an hour later, saying that money would be transferred from an account with Arner Bank & Trust in the Bahamas, via another account with the Liechtensteinische Landesbank. And abracadabra, four days later, there was fifteen thousand kronor in my SEB account."

"Whose was the Bahamas account? Did you get any info on that?"

"Unfortunately, no. But in my account statement it said, 'Furniture.'"

"Which means?"

"JW said it was in case I was asked questions about it. I was to say that I'd sold a piece of furniture to a private buyer through an ad online."

"Who?"

"I was supposed to say that I didn't know the buyer's name. That it was just someone who saw my ad and came to my house and picked up a couch. Apparently he has ads ready in case there's any hassle."

Hägerström didn't need to consult his notes. He remembered all the dates and times like a robot. Omar Abdi Husseini had been transferred to Tidaholm a few days later. On top of that, Hägerström had made sure to smuggle in a new cell phone to JW—tapped, yes, but he didn't know that. JW was pleased. Even other COs had come up to Hägerström and pointed out how the guy had gotten noticeably sunnier.

Torsfjäll said, "You're his new mule now—good. But the phone didn't end up as we'd intended, right? He must've switched it out, maybe for another phone. All we're getting is calls from some other inmate right now. Someone running cocaine deals outside the walls, sure. But if we grab him in a sloppy way, JW will understand that the phone is tapped."

Hägerström nodded. It was a shame that it hadn't worked.

He detailed how JW had approached him in the chow hall a few days ago. He had kept it all very discreet. No big gestures or strong words, just a wink. Then he had asked if Hägerström wanted to stop by later.

He dropped by JW's cell that afternoon. JW was sitting with his laptop open and the schoolbooks in front of him, as usual. The other inmates called him the bookworm—it was clear why. JW pushed the door shut when Hägerström came in.

Hägerström paused dramatically in his tale. The inspector was sitting stock still, eyes glued on Hägerström.

"First we shot the shit for a while. He likes clothes and shoes, especially British shoes, Crockett & Jones, Church, and stuff like that. So we talked leather soles."

Torsfjäll opened his mouth. "He likes clothes? Isn't that a little . . ."

The inspector looked meaningfully at Hägerström, eyes glittering. Hägerström knew how that sentence was meant to be finished. He glared at the inspector.

Torsfjäll just grinned.

Hägerström continued his story. He had continued to talk about his family and background. JW was obviously impressed. But what was more important was that Hägerström had made JW understand that he was ready to run errands for him. When they finished making small talk, JW had asked him for a favor. He needed to deliver certain information to a certain person. Nothing complicated. JW wanted to go about it in a new way this time, and he would give Hägerström two thousand for his trouble.

Hägerström asked what it was about. "Numbers," JW said. "Just a lot of numbers."

"So he asked me what kind of cell phone I had. I described the model and stuff. We leave our private cell phones in the locker room. But he asked me to bring a SIM card the following day. You know, there is just a tiny bit of metal in those cards, and according to my analyses, they don't set off the metal detectors. I bought a new SIM card and put it in my wallet, just to be on the safe side. You always take that out before you go through the metal detectors anyway."

Hägerström could see the situation in front of him while he was telling the story. The guard CO's happy face when they greeted each other. His name was Magnus and he probably wanted to become a cop, like so many others in the Department of Corrections. Hägerström experienced a slight sting of nervousness when he passed through the metal detector. Sure, the worst thing that could happen was that he got fired from the job.

Hägerström continued the story.

"The entire system is based on a certain trust for the staff, so it takes a lot for them to do some kind of in-depth check-up on someone. I was able to bring the SIM card in, and at one point when I was alone on the block, I went to JW's cell. He inserted it into his computer, which has a special reader for memory cards and SIM cards. Ten seconds later he gave the card back to me and explained what I was supposed to do."

Hägerström took a deep breath. That was how it had begun. And that was how he began to understand how JW had worked with the previous mule, Christer Starre.

Hägerström asked JW how it was possible for him to have all his information on the computer—didn't anyone check it or ask questions? JW laughed and said, "Let's put it this way, the COs don't have the sharpest computer skills. They don't even understand the difference between Word and Excel, so how are they supposed to understand the difference between school documents and real documents? I'm studying economics at a distance, remember."

"So that's how that trickster does it," Torsfjäll said. "It's a mystery to me that the Department of Corrections permits inmates to have computers at all. But that they also allow computers with those memory card readers is just completely incomprehensible."

"Yes, you might say that. But it still takes a crooked screw for it to work. Visits are monitored much more closely with handheld metal detectors and, sometimes, body searches. And he can get only certain information this way. I think he conveys most of it through simple verbal communication to the visitors he has. We've looked them up."

"I assume you're making copies of everything?" Torsfjäll asked.

Now it was Hägerström's turn to make a joke, "Is the pope Catholic? But there are problems. The information is encrypted."

The inspector chuckled. "Okay. You can send it to me for analysis. The national forensic lab knows how to handle that kind of thing. And worst case scenario, we'll have to send it to the Brits."

Hägerström nodded.

"I was asked to deliver the actual memory card to a person at the Central Station. A man in his thirties. He said I would get it back the next day. I followed him, of course."

"Exemplary."

"He led me to an accounting firm on Södermalm. MB Accounting Consultant AB, formerly a division of Rusta Finances, Inc. The company is controlled by a man named Mischa Bladman. The accounting firm has a number of midsize companies as clients. Including Building Plus AB, KÅFAB, and Claes Svensson AB. But also the Demolition

Experts in Nälsta AB and Saturday's AB, which previously owned Clara's Kitchen & Bar and Diamond Catering. Does that ring any bells?"

Torsfjäll's smile grew wider and wider with every company name Hägerström listed. Hägerström almost had to cover his eyes in order not to be blinded.

"Of course it rings bells. The last companies you named are in some way connected with the deceased Mr. Radovan Kranjic. Not completely unexpected, but still very interesting."

"Exactly. And the fact that he was just murdered doesn't make it any less interesting."

"We've got to put a tail on Bladman."

"And we ought to get permission to put a wiretap in the visiting room."

"Get permission? We don't need to do that. I've already put ears on that, just so you know."

Hägerström balked: Why hadn't he mentioned that earlier?

"And now," Torsfjäll continued, "I'm going to plant hidden recording devices on that accounting firm too. What you've told me is probably enough to get permission."

Hägerström noticed how Torsfjäll phrased it: "is *probably* enough."

There was something to the rumors about the inspector. Torsfjäll didn't hesitate to get creative with the rules.

21

Since Dad's murder: the worst hours she'd ever had to suffer through. The most unbearable, sorrowful, worst seconds she'd ever been forced to breathe. There'd already been too many seconds of desperate longing.

And it wouldn't end.

She was going in for another round of questioning at the police station later today.

Right now she was just sitting in her room. Thinking about the meeting at the hospital. Stefanovic's attitude was bothering her. He was trying to lay down the law and seize control. That was wrong.

Who could she trust now? The cops she'd met didn't give a shit about her. And even less about Dad. The last time she'd been there, it'd felt like a comedy—they'd acted like real pigs. She was planning on taking Goran's advice, recording the interrogations from now on. And the economic crime suits who'd come to their house only wanted to raze Dad's business empire.

Certain people in Sweden couldn't deal with the fact that someone had succeeded the way Dad had. It was okay for people who were born outside Scandinavia to become fantastic soccer players or track runners. To run pizza places, successful dry cleaning businesses, max a restaurant chain—that was also expected. To sing well and break through on *Swedish Idol*—that was tolerable. But that someone owned companies of the magnitude that Dad'd done—that wasn't even on the map. Some things were simply not acceptable. But it was sick that society couldn't even show a deceased family man some respect. Natalie remembered what Dad always used to say: "*There is no justice. So we have to create our own.*"

It was true—there was no justice. The police ought to be supporting the family. Searching for the murderer, protecting Natalie and Mom. Instead: society was pissing on everything that resembled honor. Justice, you had to take care of that on your own.

Just like Dad'd always said.

She'd picked up the binders that she'd hidden at Tove's house the night before—and not slept a wink since. Just read what was in the binders, page by page, pen in one hand and a notepad in the other. Highlighted everything that seemed interesting, stuck on page markers. Jotted down questions that she had to ask. She didn't know whom to ask. The lawyer they'd hired to deal with the estate seemed nice enough, but he wasn't suited for this kind of thing. Maybe Goran would know.

The binders were in front of her on the floor: seven of them, black, thick. The Kranjic coat of arms on the spines. There'd probably been hundreds of them at the accounting firm. At least fifty of them in Dad's office. And the cops'd confiscated every single one except for these.

First she'd flipped through them at random. Then she'd sat down and looked closer. She found something that made her stop.

This was an opportunity to learn more about Dad. Above all: to try to find leads to figure out what'd happened. Who'd carried out the attack.

WHO?

She tried to wrap her head around the material. Create some semblance of order. Find a structure. Prioritize what might be important and what was patently uninteresting.

Two of the binders were full of receipts and copies of receipts. Five years of Dad's life—in consumption. He seemed to have saved receipts no matter if it was for a dinner at Broncos or a luxury car for 150 euros at Autoropa. There were Levi's jeans from the NK department store, a pair of handmade shoes every year, cufflinks from Götrich—that men's store near Biblioteksgatan where he always liked to shop—probably two hundred dinners out, many cell phones, Bluetooth gadgets, computers, lampshades, Hugo for Men perfume, face lotions, plane tickets to England, Belgrade, and Marbella, furniture, and even a few meals at McDonald's.

Four of the binders were divided into sections. Within the sections were documents for different companies. There were annual reports for the recent few years and other things: accounting paperwork, correspondence with accountants. In total: twenty-one tabs—in other words: twenty-one companies. Natalie wrote their names down on a slip of paper, as well as what their turnover was during the years that she'd found the income statements for.

Honestly: she knew she had a head for numbers. Kranjic Holding AB and Kranjic Holding Ltd., the Demolition Experts in Nälsta AB, Clara's Kitchen & Bar, Diamond Catering AB, Dolphin Finance AB, Roaming GI AB, and so on. She recognized some of the names: Kranjic Holding AB was Dad's parent company. Well, she hadn't known that there was a foreign company too, but she wasn't surprised. Dad'd run Clara's for ages, same with the catering firm, and Goran and the others often talked about the Demolition Experts. But it wasn't really the fact that there were companies she didn't know about that surprised her—it was the sheer quantity of them. More than twenty companies. Four of them'd reported zero turnover over the last few years. Five had over twenty million in turnaround each. She knew that Dad was good at business—but this: he was *big*, for real.

But it was what she found in the last binder that made her react. Minutes from AGMs, prospectus, purchasing contracts, and a few documents about keys and alarm systems. Everything was about one and the same thing: an apartment on Björngårdsgatan on Södermalm.

She read the apartment prospectus over and over again. It was a loft apartment, top floor, 893 square feet. Open floor plan. Luxury renovations with solid materials: floors made of limestone from Gotland, walnut wood paneling, kitchen from Poggenpohl. Apparently someone named Peter Johansson'd bought it for 5.3 million.

In the margin, next to a heading in one of the minutes from the co-op board meetings, there was a handwritten note: *Dangerous.*

DANGEROUS.

The thing about the note: it was written in Dad's handwriting.

The heading in the minutes was about how the apartment on the top floor wasn't inhabited by the person listed as a member of the housing co-op.

Despite the name of the owner, Natalie was certain this apartment had something to do with Dad. Dad had some sort of connection to an apartment in Stockholm that he hadn't told them anything about at home. And it'd been dangerous in some way.

She had to find out more. She wondered again who she could talk to.

There was only one person.

She called Goran. "I've got binders here that the cops want."

"What binders?"

"Company stuff, binders that were at our house. They were here yesterday, the economic crimes guys, but I managed to get hold of some material."

"Hide them in a safe place. We'll look at them together."

"I've already gone over them. I almost know them by heart."

She didn't say anything about the note in the minutes for the apartment.

"Okay," he said. "Just hide them. We'll have to talk about them as soon as possible."

"Yes."

"And one more thing, Natalie. Don't do anything that you'll regret. You have to understand something: your father's life was not always easy. Some say he chose the easy path, but one thing is certain—not many walked that path with him. There were a lot of people who hated him, do you understand that? So now you have to choose your own path—remember that. And doing bad things won't make it any easier."

For a second, Natalie considered asking what he meant. But she decided not to—he was right. Dad's path hadn't been easy. And she didn't know what she wanted for herself right now.

She was going in for questioning at the police station soon. She knew what she was going to do before then. Mom'd put Dad's jackets in the office. They hadn't even talked about it—what they were going to do with all his things: cell phones, watches, pens, computers, clothes. But Mom didn't want the jackets hanging in the hall. Natalie agreed—no one wanted to be reminded needlessly right now.

She walked into the room. A glimmer of hope in her mind. A goal.

She gathered the jackets and his overcoat. They'd been hanging out in the hall up until the day before yesterday. A trench coat from Corneliani that must've cost a fortune. A Helly Hansen sailing jacket that seemed too young for him. A no-brand leather jacket—that felt the most like normal Dad.

She went through them. The outer pockets, the inner pockets, the breast pockets. The sailing jacket had at least ten pockets.

She didn't find anything.

She did the same thing one more time.

Nothing.

She sat down on the floor in her room. The binders were spread out around her. Thought: *Where might Dad's key chain be?* Maybe the police'd found it and taken it with them.

Then it struck her. Of course he must've had it on him the night he was killed. So it couldn't have been in one of the jackets that he left hanging at home. But he hadn't been buried in it, she knew that. Either Mom must've got it back from the police and put it somewhere or else it was still with the police.

She made a lap around the house. Mom was sitting in the den. Natalie continued on to her and Dad's bedroom. She approached the closet where Dad used to keep his clothes. Opened it. They were still there.

A wave of pain washed over her body.

She almost couldn't look. Dad's pants, sweaters, and shirts in the part of the color spectrum that stretched from white to pale blue to dark blue. His belts: on three hangers on the inside of the closet door. His ties: on four retractable tie hangers on the other closet door—the family crest on several of them. His jackets and suits, organized by color.

His smell.

Natalie wanted to turn and leave. Run into her room again. Stretch out on the bed and cry away the afternoon. At the same time, what she was feeling now: she knew what she wanted—she wanted to find the keys. She wanted to get somewhere.

She took a deep breath.

Pulled out a drawer in the dresser. A humidor. A small dial on the outside displayed the humidity. She opened it—Cohiba for thousands of kronor. No keys.

She pulled out another drawer in the dresser. Cufflinks and tie clips with the K-emblem on them, lots of silk scarves, three empty wallets, a money clip with the Kranjic coat of arms on it again, four watches that probably weren't expensive enough to be kept in the little safe by the bed: Seiko, Tissot, Certina, Calvin Klein.

And: a key chain.

She picked it up.

Maybe.

22

They began early today. Jorge'd been awake since five a.m. Opened his eyes without an alarm, like a baby who can't fall back asleep. Had been thinking only about the hit.

He made coffee. Walked around, in just his boxers. Drank water. Pissed over and over again.

Jorge could feel his stomach. That damn anxiety: the curse of all G-boys.

Today: the outbreak of war—D-day. Super Bowl Sunday. The CIT day.

To conclude: the day when J-boy would become the most loaded Latino north of the Medellín cartel. Still: the worry was creeping around inside his body worse than during a bad trip.

It was time. And they were all showing it.

Robert and Javier'd called a bunch of times during the night to ask stuff, even though it was against the rules.

Jimmy and Tom'd sent texts about planning stuff, even though they already knew the answers. He had to remind them to toss their SIM cards and phones.

Mahmud and Sergio'd rung his doorbell at seven a.m., even though they'd agreed on eight o'clock.

Even the Babak clown'd called at two in the morning to ask something. The Iranian who, otherwise, always knew best. That's what he thought—who was the genius now, huh?

Tension in the air so thick, you could cut it with a knife.

In four hours, it would be time. An insanely packed schedule till then.

They'd taken a boat from Värmdö, from the bombed hellies. Tom'd been prepared: had boosted a little motorboat the night before—easy peasy. It had been tied to some Sven's summer dock, just locked with a padlock on a chain.

A boat. Again: not something for Million Programmers. Honest—Jorge'd never sat in a dinghy before. Serious thoughts: boats, vacation homes, oceans, cows—for pureblood Svens, that was all probably as natural as taking a shit. For Jorge: as unnatural as forking over a pile of dough in taxes.

The boat rocked. The water was dark. Close. If he were to stretch his arm out, he could touch the surface of the water. He tried to look down. Couldn't see anything but a shimmer. The motor roared. Cut through the water like a machete. They rode past two other motorboats. A small red lamp on the left side, and a small green lamp on the right. Other than that, they were alone on the water.

But there oughta be full-throttle response over at the helipad base by now. Except they wouldn't find jack shit, just two dead dogs and two totaled choppers. Sergio'd driven the honest wheels out to the ferry dock and pushed it in.

Back from his mind trip. Mahmud and Sergio were sitting on Jorge's couch. Sergio *hablando.* Joked, messed around. Buzzed about the helicopter massacre.

"Did you read *Expressen*? They wrote that now they won't be able to use the choppers to blast the mosquitoes full of poison."

"Is that true? Fuck, man. That's terrible. Don't they have rescue choppers?"

"Yeah, but they can't use those for the mosquitoes. You get how we fucked the Swedish people—they're gonna get bit. *Dios mio!*"

Jorge grinned. Ran through his mental lists. The coveralls, the robbery phones, the SIM cards, the cars, the blockades, synching their watches. He thought about his and Mahmud's own scheme for cashing in—the bonus that was for the two of them alone.

He and Mahmud inspected the weapons. An airsoft gun and the two AK-47s. They worked, at least they knew that by now. The rest of the gear was already with Tom and the others.

They checked their phones. They'd used a separate set of phones for the helicopter bombing. Once they were in their given positions, before the hit, they were gonna turn on new phones. The reason: no way the cops could track the phones to towers near their apartments.

Eight o'clock rolled around. Jorge got a text from Tom. *One zero.* That was the code: Tom was up and ready to go. *Magnífico.*

Sergio and Mahmud studied the maps one final time before they went to burn them down in the garbage room.

Lists scrolled past on the inside of his eyelids. The jammers, the aluminum foil, the walkie-talkies, the angle grinder, spike strips, the wheel loader. The last thing on the list: Jimmy'd gotten hold of one of those—it would crush the Tomteboda gate easier than the Lego set J-boy'd given Jorgito.

Still: Would the guys pull this off?

At eight-thirty, Jorge's cell started blowing up: four texts: *Four zero, Three zero, Five zero, Two zero.* The G's were awake and ready to go. He responded with the code: *Good results.* They'd understand: he, Mahmud, and Sergio were in position.

They went down to the street. People on their way to work, to day care with their kids. Stressed, speedy steps, stiff stares. Screaming babies. Whiny bosses. Bus drivers who shut the doors in the face of retirees who hadn't quite made it to the stop in time. A life that Jorge never wanted to live.

The van was parked four blocks away so no one would see it near Jorge's building. He squinted at it. A Mercedes. Boosted this week, with one plate switched out and the other torn off. If they were stopped and asked why they were driving with a stolen plate, they could say that they were the ones who'd reported it stolen. Point to the torn-off plate. "Look, we're missing one." That'd been Mahmud's idea. Real smart, actually.

Sergio opened the back doors. They squeaked. Jorge climbed in.

Inside the storage area in the back: silver wallpaper. As decided—Sergio'd dressed the inside of the back of the van with three layers of aluminum foil. They closed the doors. Lit a flashlight.

Sergio pointed to the walls. "It took a whole day, man. And that spray glue, man, it was better than ten grams of hash."

Jorge's finger on the foil. "This oughta be good. But like we said, we're not taking any risks. Is that the jammer?" He pointed to a black garbage bag.

Sergio nodded. He bent down. Pulled the garbage bag off.

The jammer.

Jorge grinned. "Fuck, *cabrón*, that's so ill."

They played with the apparatus for half an hour. Turned it on and off, set it to different frequencies, checked that it was working against their own phones.

Nine-thirty: Tom swung by and picked up Mahmud and Jorge's cell phones. They checked the walkie-talkies, the police radio. In an hour: their robber cells would be switched on. Jorge eyed Tom—for the first time, *hombre* seemed stressed: was talking fast, playing with his walkie-talkie. Looked wiped—dark circles under his eyes, like he'd been punched in the face. Jorge could feel it too. Constantly: that slow churning in his stomach.

Fifteen minutes: him, Mahmud, and Sergio in the van. Driving toward the city. On their way to pick up the wheel loader.

They were driving in silence. Sergio'd quit his punning. Jorge was leaning his head back, looking up at the roof of the car. Mahmud was holding the wheel, concentrating on not driving too fast. The wheel loader: the key to their success. According to the Finn: the wheel loader made this hit invincible.

Then Jorge thought: *The Finn can hit the showers*. Jorge and Tom were the ones who came up with the wheel loader idea—*not* the Finn. J-boy and the boys were the ones taking all the risks. And what's more: the vault—a story in itself.

Past Frösunda, Brunnsviken's water on their left. Mahmud turned off the highway half a mile from their destination. Exit: Haga Norra. A sharp exit from the highway down toward the park: the Haga Park. The trees were green: looked like a rain forest. They drove up to the gates. A small parking lot. *Vato* stopped the car.

Jorge reached for his backpack in the backseat. Picked up one of the new cell phones. Inserted a SIM card. Then he picked up a walkie-talkie: MOTOTLKR T7—Motorola's hottest model. Over a six-mile range.

He turned it on. Pressed the talk button. "Hello?"

Crackling on the other end.

He waited a while. Met Mahmud's eyes. Every step of the way had to click now.

He held it up again. "Hello?"

Still just crackling.

A third time: "Hello, can you hear me?"

Crackling, buzzing, hissing sounds.

Finally Tom's voice. "Yo, man. I hear you. And I'm here. Ready to rock and roll. Over."

Jorge did thumbs-up for Mahmud and Sergio. "And the others? Over."

The idea: no calls would go to Jorge's robbery phone. Instead: everyone reported to Tom, who was keeping track of everything and keeping Jorge informed over the walkie-talkie. Cop-block: no cell phone calls could be connected to the place where the actual hit would take place.

Tom responded. He was using real names; the pigs couldn't pick up radio waves after the fact.

"Babak and Robert are in position by the big cop station downtown. Jimmy's at Stora Essingen, ready to drive north on the Essinge highway. Javier is in position at Kungsholmen. Everyone's ready. Over."

The entire time he was talking, Jorge was looking at Mahmud. Sergio was sitting in the backseat. The mood in the van: concentrated like in an ebola research lab.

The clock struck ten-fifteen. Almost time now. Very soon.

Jorge held the walkie-talkie up to his mouth. "Okay, let's roll. Keep reporting to me the whole time. Over and out."

Tom's voice sounded happy. The stress Jorge'd seen in him this morning was gone. He bellowed, "Yes, sir!"

Jorge turned to Mahmud and Sergio. "We'll check everything one last time."

They nodded. Mahmud climbed out—checked that the jammer in the back was still working. Sergio checked that he had the keys to the wheel loader. They checked the arsenal, the ski masks, the keys, and all the rest. One last time.

The last time.

The walkie-talkie on the instrument panel vibrated. Tom's voice again: "Everyone's driven up to their positions. We're ready to roll. Just give us the word, boss. Over."

Jorge tried to grin even though he knew it looked forced. "Fire away," he said.

Mahmud started the van. Jorge was sitting with the walkie-talkie tightly pressed to his ear. Following every step of Tom's ongoing reports.

Tom was driving a boosted car. He'd parked a clean car on the street outside the pig station in Solna the night before.

Mahmud was driving calmly. They were approaching the spot where the wheel loader was supposed to be parked. Ten minutes till strike down.

Tom was describing what he was doing over the walkie-talkie: "I'm standing outside the car. I've busted the instrument panel. Torn out all the shit I can. They're not going to get this bucket moving for hours. Not even the best booster in Alby could do this now. The only way is to get a tow truck. I swear. Over."

"Good, Tom. You heard from the others?"

"Yep. Javier's driving slow like a grandpa on the highway by Klarastrand. And Jimmy's driving as slow as his mama on the Essinge highway. Over."

"A'ight, dope."

Tom kept doing what he was doing outside his police station. "All the tanks of gas and the car tires were already crammed in. This'll be easy."

Jorge heard how he slammed a car door shut. Tom sounded out of breath. Jorge knew what the dude was carrying: one of the bomb bags.

Mahmud and Tom'd built the bombs. Ones like it'd been used for Swedish CIT heists before. But it didn't matter, according to the Finn—the cops could never be careful enough. They'd lifted six cabin bags from a department store storage site where one of Sergio's friends worked and let them in. Tom'd shoved old car batteries into the bags, hooked up starter cables. Mixed nine pounds of all-purpose flour with water, divided the dough into six plastic bags. Wrapped a couple turns of black electrical tape around the whole package. Tom spray-painted the word BOMB with white text on the bags. Fucking ill terrorist workshop. Al Qaeda would've been proud. Hamas would've been jealous. ETA would've scowled in the corner and wanted in on it all: you're such bomb-building pros.

Honest: they looked mad real.

And now: Tom was panting like a marathon runner. "I've set down the fake bomb, in the middle of the street, and turned it so the text is visible. They won't be able to drive past here with any cop cars. Now I'm walking toward the clean car. In thirty seconds, the gas car will go BOOM. Over."

"Sick. And the others? Over."

"Just got a text from Babak and Robert. They're about to torch their cars by the Kronoberg station. Over."

"That leaves six minutes to go."

Mahmud drove the van toward Haga Södra. There were cars parked outside the restaurant, or whatever it was. Jimmy and Robert'd parked the wheel loader behind the building the night before. There were four tennis courts next to the restaurant—people were playing like crazy. Jorge slipped on a pair of shades.

He heard a sharp *bang*. Then Tom's voice in the talkie: "*Abbou!* Fuck what a boom, man!"

Then: car doors opening. Tom must've sealed the deal: set out the bomb contraption, torched the burn car.

The five-oh would have a hard time getting out of the station. The bomb squad would take their time. Stupid idiots.

"You should've seen it!" Tom howled.

Jorge tried to laugh along with him. "Drive away from there right away. Step on it! And brief me about the others."

He set down the walkie-talkie. The guys so far: band of brothers, so tight.

Jorge jumped out of the van with Sergio. They walked toward the restaurant. Jimmy'd described the wheel loader: a yellow nineteen-ton Volvo Construction Equipment. Massive like a concrete mountain. The dude'd succeeded: talked to contacts of contacts in the construction biz who'd helped him take it off a guy selling construction equipment in Skogås for thirty large, cash. Still cheap for a monster.

The massive vehicle couldn't be missed.

Sergio turned to Jorge. He looked pale.

"*Hombre*, if this goes to hell, what lawyer you want?"

Pessimist question. Still, important. The last time Jorge was convicted, he'd had some tired-ass public defender appointed by the court. That was a long time ago. Before he became a Gangsta with a capital G. Before he was crowned the Coke King of the concrete. Before he'd lived in Thailand.

Jorge answered Sergio, "I don't know, man. Not the same suit as last time. Maybe Martin Thomasson, or that guy Jörn Burtig. I heard they're supposed to be ill. Then there's that new star child. That tall guy. I think his name is Lars Arstedt."

Sergio was silent.

"But what the fuck, *hermano. Calma te.* We're not gonna blow it."

They walked behind the building. Large windows facing out toward the water. Brown-painted wood.

A small parking lot. Three cars: a Volvo, an Audi, another Volvo. Three empty spots.

No wheel loader.

"It was supposed to be here, right?" Sergio asked. His voice sounded high and pinched.

Jorge looked around. He didn't see anything that so much as resembled a wheel loader.

He called Tom. "Check with Jimmy or Robert where the wheel loader is."

How was it possible?

Jorge couldn't believe it. Like his head'd been beaten in.

No wheel loader.

NO FUCKING WHEEL LOADER.

A thousand thoughts at once.

Like bombs going off inside his skull.

He screamed.

His stomach exploded.

One thought beat out all others: *It's all going to hell.*

He threw up everywhere.

23

Hägerström would soon be back in the city. There was a particular reason he was on his way to Stockholm. JW was going on day parole—twenty-four hours—and Hägerström was the one transporting him into Stockholm. The paroles were more frequent these days since he needed to get adjusted to life outside the prison walls.

He and JW had ridden in the prison's transport car. An interesting drive: they had spoken a great deal. Hägerström was on his way now. On his way into JW's world. And Torsfjäll was cued in too—if something interesting were to happen today, he was available.

He lived undercover on two fronts. It was one too many.

The weeks inside the prison. The weeks of advances, of kissing ass and trying to win JW's trust. Maybe he was close to a breakthrough.

But JW was still overly careful. More paranoid than an American ambassador post WikiLeaks. Thought the cops were tapping his phone conversations and his visits. And he was right about that. What's more, Hägerström had done his best to encourage that line of thinking—the more cautious JW was, the more he would let Hägerström do.

It worked. JW had started asking Hägerström to do him favors more and more. Call in a message to X or Y. Send a text to this number with the following number combination. Print this letter and send it to the bank man there and there.

JW was constantly buying new calling cards for the pay phone—spoke on the phone for at least forty minutes a day. The other inmates started complaining. Some called him the Jew instead of the bookworm—the dude was occupying the phone booth like Israel occupies the Middle East. Mischa Bladman paid him a visit once a week. The fact was that all of his visiting hours were used up by that accounting guy. Torsfjäll bugged the visiting room, but it didn't give jack shit: either JW and Bladman were whispering, or they were speaking in code.

JW could've asked Hägerström to smuggle in another cell phone or an Internet hookup for his computer. But Hägerström made sure the other COs became more watchful about those kinds of things. The unit increased the number of shakedowns and searches. They found other inmates' porn stashes rolled inside clothes hangers, amphetamine on the drawings given to them by their three-year-old daughters, cell phones in crevices carved into the walls. JW became even more cautious. Refrained from unnecessary risks.

Needed Hägerström even more.

At night, he tried to analyze what was actually happening. The information he had smuggled out. The number combinations, the banks he had called, the e-mails he had sent. A pattern was beginning to crystallize. Some kind of move was in the works. Companies were being liquidated, relationships with banks were being ended, accounts were being closed, and funds were being transferred. Liechtenstein, the Virgin Islands, and the Cayman Islands. Meanwhile other companies were being created, new bank relationships were being made, accounts were being opened, and funds were being transferred to other jurisdictions: Dubai, Liberia, Lithuania, Bahamas, Panama. Credit cards were being ordered, bank guarantees were being proffered, account slips were being sent. Maybe it had to do with changing secrecy laws in certain countries.

But there were never any Swedish names. Always foreign companies and behind them: foreign lawyers, accountants, or other front men.

Torsfjäll raved about terrorist activities. Meanwhile he complained that nothing of significance had been revealed through the wiretapping. He went on and on about how they had to hack into JW's computer somehow. But Hägerström had other ideas.

Torsfjäll said that he had let an economic crimes specialist go through all of it. That those fucking nigger countries had stronger secrecy regulations than the Swedish Security Service. That the specialist had concluded that it must be a matter of complex money laundering, but that they wouldn't get any help from any of the nations where the bank accounts were based.

One problem was that they hardly saw any sums actually move from companies or accounts in Sweden. If they had discovered large cash flows, then perhaps they could have traced them from the source. That kind of thing was easier nowadays.

JW and his people must be bringing the money out of the country in cash. Couriers. Or else they had help from some money management service in Sweden: a bank, an exchange office, a credit institution, or something like that.

The question was how it could be proven that what was going on was illegal.

Back in the transport car. First they had talked about the usual stuff. The chow at the prison, other inmates, new routines. JW didn't say much about what he was going to do on his parole.

Hägerström pushed the conversation in a different direction. Started name-dropping. Old high school friends and buddies of his brother. Financiers, lawyers, industry magnates, heirs, friends of the royal family. Men born into a world that they now owned. Men who lived with their families in townhouses in Östermalm. Men who had owned land in the Uppsala region for generations. Men who had been JW's role models five years ago, before he was locked up.

Hägerström continued to name-drop from his sister's friend group. Same story there. Tin-Tin's friends had been the queens of Stureplan five years ago. When JW had been the number-one wannabe. He ought to recognize most of the names, maybe wonder what they were doing today, if they had boyfriends, where they lived.

Hägerström pronounced all the names correctly, once again proved who was in the know. Wachtmeister with a *k* and an *e*, Douglas with a short *u*-sound in the first syllable. And the most difficult of all: du Rietz, which ought to be pronounced *Dyrrye*. Noble names, aristocratic families with blue bloodlines.

Hägerström knew he'd hit a bull's-eye. It clicked. JW's penchant for the fancy life: the upper crust, the crème de la crème. The guy's desire to be part of a world he didn't belong to. But that was the world Hägerström was raised in.

Earlier, before Hägerström became JW's messenger boy, he might not have really listened. But now JW was soaking it up. Hägerström told him about the invitation to his brother's wedding. Each guest had been sent a large box, delivered by messenger. A bottle of Lanson pink, suntan lotions and skin care products from Lancôme, and a specially made DVD. One of Sweden's most famous comics, Robert Gustafsson, guided through the Bérard family home—heckling, joking, poking fun at everyone and everything. A small card invited the guests to the actual wedding: UNDISCLOSED LOCATION. THREE DAYS. LEAVE YOUR KIDS AT HOME. LEAVE YOUR CREDIT CARD AT HOME. BRING YOUR PASSPORT.

But soon Hägerström wanted to get into hotter territory. And JW seemed to understand.

Only the two of them in the car. That was probably against the rules, but Torsfjäll had pulled some strings. A two-hour journey. Hägerström said that he was the one who had arranged so that they were alone in the car. JW seemed to be softening up. There was no reason not to cut right to the chase.

But JW beat him to it. "Do you know where I actually come from?" he asked.

Hägerström knew.

"No idea, but you don't really seem the prison type, to be completely honest with you."

"I'm from Västerbotten. Can't you tell?"

"Not at all. You sound like a Östermalmer, born and bred, actually. No, more toward the Lindingö area maybe. You pronounce your *I*'s that way."

JW chuckled. Obviously pleased with Hägerström's response.

"You know, I've had quite a ride."

Hägerström's brain tingled. Now he was being invited onto private property, no trespassing. To have had the kind of class ride that JW was referring to wasn't necessarily something to blazon out in the world Hägerström came from, where it was best to be born into your position. The fact that JW told him that meant he was opening up.

"I went to the Stockholm School of Economics," JW continued. "But they didn't let me finish my degree there because I was a convicted felon, so now I study at the university in Örebro instead. I'm basically done, I just need to have my thesis evaluated."

Hägerström turned to him. Grinned. Winked. "Studying?"

JW smiled weakly.

"If you want," Hägerström said. "I would be happy to introduce you to some business contacts when you're out."

"That sounds interesting. What kind of contacts?"

"You know, people who need help with their money. The tax policies in this country force people to think in new ways, even if we've had a better government lately—thank God."

"Yeah, no one could agree more. You hunt people down who've been successful and made money, but you let the murderers and rapists go free. But you know that—you've been both a cop and a CO."

This was deep water. Even if he felt safe with the fact that JW had started to trust him, there were rules for how you talked about crimes, even among criminals. The custom was to not open up any which way. You didn't trust anyone. You had to avoid getting dragged into something. Hot information could become a burden.

Hägerström kept his eyes on the road. "Exactly. So people need help knowing what to do with the money later, to avoid the Swedish State's sticky fingers and a lot of unnecessary chitchat."

JW scratched his head mindlessly for a while. Almost looked uninterested. He was a good actor.

Then he said, "Okay, let's talk . . ." He paused.

Hägerström had time to think: *Jackpot.*

Then JW went on, ". . . when I've gated out."

Shit. This would take a while.

But maybe it was still a victory: JW had understood. And accepted.

They drove to Djursholm. JW asked to be dropped off on a street called Henrik Palmes Allé. Hägerström had him on missile lock. He saw JW walking down the street and turning onto Sveavägen. He stopped the car. Jumped out. Jogged to the intersection. He saw JW 160 yards farther up the street. He turned again, to the left.

Hägerström ran like hell. To the next intersection. He had to see where JW disappeared to.

Right on time. JW was standing outside the door of a large house a hundred yards away.

Someone opened the door for him. JW stepped into the house.

JW in a villa in Djursholm. This wasn't just any old residential suburb. This is where the largest homes in Stockholm could be found. The heftiest properties in any of the major Swedish cities. This was top shelf for real—Greenwich, Connecticut, Sweden edition. And this was where JW had chosen to go on his parole.

Hägerström Googled the address. No one was registered as living there. He called the tax authorities. Was informed that a British company owned the house: Housekeep Ltd. Shady as hell.

He called Torsfjäll and asked him to do some more research on who lived in the house.

Then he hid behind some hazel bushes. Eyes fixed on the house that JW had disappeared into. Didn't drop it with his eyes.

The house had yellow stone walls. It was two stories, perhaps a total of 3,300 square feet. The garden looked well tended.

He saw someone moving around in there. He thought about calling Torsfjäll again and asking him to send an undercover cop who could get closer than he could himself. But he changed his mind, wanting to handle this on his own.

He remained where he was, waiting. JW couldn't stay in that house all day, could he?

An hour later. A taxi pulled up to the house.

The door opened. JW was standing in the open doorway. Another man followed him out. Closed the door, locked it.

The man had light-colored hair, was portly with hangdog cheeks. He was wearing red chinos and a green jacket. Maybe fifty years old. Hägerström focused his eyes to try to see better. He tried to snap pictures with his cell phone. It was pointless. JW and the man were too far away.

They got into the cab. Taxi Stockholm, the city's biggest taxi company. The car rolled off.

Hägerström called Torsfjäll again.

"JW is leaving now with a man in a cab with the registration number NOD four eight nine. Can you get Taxi Stockholm to save the film from the cab's surveillance camera?"

"Of course. Brilliant idea. I love our Big Brother society. And I can inform you that I just received an e-mail with the name of the person who's using the house. Someone named Gustaf Hansén used to be registered at that address. He was CEO and branch head of a bank office for Danske Bank before he was fired. According to the registries, he's been a resident of Liechtenstein for four years. There's so much white-collar stink around this that I have to cover my nose."

Hägerström looked at the house. "What do you think I should do?" he asked. "I can't exactly trail the cab in one of the Department of Corrections's painted transport vehicles."

"No, you can't. But you can break into the house. You know no one's there right now."

Hägerström gasped.

"But what about the alarm system? I'm sure they have an alarm in that place?"

"Relax—I'll take care of that."

24

Later. She was standing outside the front door of an apartment building on Björngårdsgatan. No, she thought: *the* apartment building—definitive form.

Midday. She had to be at the police station for questioning in twenty minutes. But she was planning on doing some investigating of her own before then. They'd have to tolerate her being late.

The elevator went only to the fifth floor; she had to walk the last flight of stairs to the loft apartment. The walls in the stairwell looked freshly painted.

She pulled out the key chain. It jangled.

Or maybe it was her hand that was shaking.

The door in front of her: two locks. One deadbolt lock and a regular door lock.

On the key chain in her hand: a total of seven keys. Four deadbolt keys, of which two were for their house at home. She recognized them.

In other words: two possible keys.

She picked up the first one. Inserted it into the lock.

Tried to turn it.

It didn't work.

She pulled it back out. Inserted it again. Tried to turn it.

No, she couldn't move it in the lock.

She picked up the other key. Raised it to the lock.

Inserted it.

Tried to turn it.

No.

That one didn't work either.

She tried again.

Fuck, fuck, fuck.

It wasn't the right key.

A sound: her cell phone—her cell phone was ringing.

She didn't recognize the number—it was the cop fuckers. She ignored the call. Natalie would be going to the station for questioning as arranged, they didn't have to worry.

She put the phone and the keys back into her bag.

She felt alone.

She remained standing there in front of the door to the apartment. She turned around. Started walking down the stairs.

Waited for the elevator. She heard the squeaking of the cables. It was on its way up.

The elevator door opened: a girl her own age stepped out of the elevator. They brushed by each other: the girl's Louis Vuitton purse—Natalie's Bottega Veneta bag.

The girl stared straight ahead. Didn't glance at Natalie. Natalie stepped into the elevator. Closed the door. Didn't press any button.

She peered out through the glass of the elevator door. The girl who'd just arrived started walking up the stairs. Up to the loft apartment. Natalie heard her unlock the door upstairs. She had the right keys, apparently.

Natalie took the elevator down. Opened the sliding door. Remained standing in the elevator for a few seconds. Listening.

Her head was pounding. With one pure, clear, determined thought: *I need to find out who that is. I have to go back up for that girl.*

25

No wheel loader.

No fucking wheel loader.

Jorge was screaming. Spraying saliva. Swearing salaciously.

Sergio was staring at him. Jorge kept on raging.

"Mierda! Joder! Hostias ya! Me cago en mi puta mala suerte! Le manda conjones! Me cago en su puta madre!"

He fell silent. Couldn't come up with enough swear words. Just stood there. Staring at the half-empty parking lot.

Nada. Zero wheel loader.

He called Tom again. "Where the fuck is wheel loader?"

Tom responded after thirty seconds. "Jimmy and Robert parked it there last night. They have no idea."

Jorge hung up. Looked down.

Vomit on the pavement. On the side of one of the parked cars. On his pants, his kicks.

His head was throbbing. His hands shaking. His pulse: like a shitty techno beat.

His stomach rumbled. Even though everything was already right there on the ground, stinking up the whole parking lot.

What the fuck were they gonna do now?

What the fuck was *he* gonna do now?

The wheel loader was the basis of the entire hit. It: a must.

They'd contemplated, ruminated. Finally: come up with the solution. The fucking wheel loader was gonna crush the sliding gate so they could bust through into Tomteboda's holiest of holy places. Force the gates to the loading docks, where they would unload the bags of valuables. Where the guards would be less cautious.

Open the door to the CIT heist of the decade.

And now it wasn't there.

They were supposed to strike in exactly four minutes—that was the plan. While the police were barricaded into their garages and the entrances and exits to downtown Stockholm were peppered with caltrops and burning cars.

The thoughts lurched through his mind.

His brain was screaming: *Abort—be smart about this! Don't take any risks!*

His heart was howling: *Crash the gate with the van instead! It's now or never!*

Get rich or die trying.

He refused to abort this thing—this was his retirement package. His dream. But they couldn't drive through the gates with the Benz van. It wouldn't be able to handle the impact. The gateposts were definitely too massive. Plus: it was indispensable—if it broke down, they were screwed.

They couldn't boost any of the other cars in the parking lot—the immobilizers used these days made it so that basically no one except Julian Assange hackers could boost newer buckets. And: they wouldn't be able to handle the gates either.

Jorge tried to concentrate. Covered his face with his hands.

Again: in his head: *J-boy, give up. Abort mission. Be smart now.*

Blow it off.

BLOW IT OFF.

He stared into his palms. Couldn't handle going back to the van. Heard talking in the background. Sergio, Mahmud. Rapid, stressed voices. Someone took the walkie-talkie from him. He heard Tom's voice through it. Buzz about cars. Sizes. Gates.

Jorge drifted off. Images pulsed past. Him and Paola on their way to school. They were walking by themselves. The last thing Mom always said before they left home was "*Caminar cogidos de la mano.*" Hold hands. Mom was always thinking of them—when Rodriguez didn't interfere, that is.

The underpasses under Malmvägen's residential area were completely covered in graffiti. The sun shone in through filthy windows. He looked out. Rhododendron bushes without any buds in the courtyards—the little punks'd destroyed them to use the buds for warfare: made good artillery. Junior high school kids playing hooky and broken park benches with gang names carved into them. Paola was stressed out. Pulling him along. She always wanted to be on time. Jorge never wanted to be on time.

Paola stopped. She took her backpack off. It was a nice backpack. She opened it and screamed.

Jorge looked at her, "What's wrong?"

"I forgot my homework at home!"

"Should we run home and get it?"

"No, no. We'll never make it on time."

He saw what was going to happen. Paola's face began to twitch. She squeezed her eyes shut. She screamed the same words over and over again.

"We'll never make it. We'll never make it."

And then came the tears.

No, he had to go back now. Back to Haga Södra, the parking lot. Back to shitty reality.

He looked up. Was gonna explain to the guys that it was time to lay down their arms. Abort this thing. Maybe they could try the same hit next week.

But before he could open his mouth to speak, Mahmud said, "Bro, we've got a suggestion."

Jorge couldn't handle any bullshit right now. "Not now," he said.

Mahmud placed a hand on his shoulder. "Listen, Babak's got the Range Rover. It's parked in Solna. It'll take three minutes to get it here. He's not the one registered on it anyway, and he said he'd consider loaning it out if he gets bills for his trouble. We can use it to bust through the gates. It should be able to handle it."

Jorge looked at Mahmud. Hard to break the negative thought circuit right now. "It can't take those gates," he said.

"It can. Babak thinks it can. And Tom thinks it can. You've driven it—it's the biggest Range Rover they make. Weighs over two and a half tons, V8 motor, four-wheel drive, body of steel, a grill that eats all other SUVs for breakfast."

"I know. But who's going to drive it here?"

"Babak—he's finished his shit by the pig station. He's on his way home now, he'll be there in two minutes."

"We won't make it."

"Come on, we might be max five minutes late total. It'll work anyway. *Walla.*"

"But what'll we do with it after?"

Mahmud grabbed Jorge's shoulder with his other hand too. "Come on, man."

Jorge looked up. Met Mahmud's eyes. No sad half-moon eyes anymore. Now: a gleam, a glowing ember. A gangsta gaze. His buddy believed in this.

Jorge swallowed, hard. His mouth still tasted like vomit.

Mahmud: his best *compadre*.

Mahmud: a real bro.

Mahmud: a guy he trusted.

Also: the Arab had some kind of gut feeling.

Jorge swallowed again. "Okay, we'll rock. He's gotta cover up the plates, and when we're done, we've gotta destroy the car. Does he understand that?"

Mahmud smiled, reacted right away. Switched on the talkie. "He says we roll."

Tom's voice on the other end. A new energy.

Jorge heard him talk with the others over their phones. Gushing orders, guidelines, the new plan.

Keeping rolling, that's all there was to it.

Range Rover Vogue versus Tomteboda's gates.

Six minutes and twenty seconds later. Jorge and Mahmud in the van. Babak and Sergio in the Range Rover in front of them. Less than three minutes behind schedule.

The Iranian'd stuck duct tape over the license plates. The postal terminal's gates were a hundred yards away. The time: eleven oh-five. The voices on the police radio that they'd put in the backseat: agitated. The city was burning. A state of war. Suspected bombs everywhere. The entire Essinge highway before the Eugenia Tunnel was backed up. Thirty-odd cars with ruined tires. Spike strips or caltrops. The cops were still clueless. Jimmy'd rigged the massive congestion like a hero—Jorge almost forgot the wheel loader clusterfuck. The road along Klarastrand was also a mess, total chaos. The traffic was moving slower than a kid crawling on all fours. Javier'd done his bit, same story there. But the northern exit out of Stockholm was clear. Open like a racetrack. Without police choppers in the air.

Also: the five-ohs' stressed-out radio calls, countywide orders, response preparations. Sabotage against the Stockholm police. J-boy heard it all. Tough luck, *pacos*. The orders were loud and clear: heightened alertness. It may be a question of a planned attack at a different location. It may be political activists. It may be a terrorist attack. Block all entrances and exits into the city. The cops'd been through this before: CIT veterans tended to create confusion and chaos. But never on this scale.

Jorge felt better. Actually: pumped. Turned to Mahmud, "*Loco*, let's blow this thing up. You want some?"

He held up a Red Line Baggie with some pills in it. "Roofies."

Mahmud grinned. "I already sampled my own stash."

Jorge nodded.

They waited.

The pills tasted bitter on his tongue, but better than the vomit taste.

The gate was closed. There were guards in the control booth next to it.

The gate was opened for an exiting yellow mail truck. Babak stepped on the gas in the Range Rover. Jorge heard the car rev. In first gear. They wouldn't make it through before the gate closed, he knew that. But according to both Tom and the Finn's calculations, the gate's mechanism was weaker when it wasn't completely closed. A wheel loader would definitely've made it. The question: Could Babak's car take the gate?

The Range Rover accelerated with a roar. Jorge waited to release the clutch, wanted to see how things went for the huge SUV in front of him first.

Thirty yards farther up: the gate. It was closing quickly. Still: in this moment, it felt slow. The Range Rover rammed into it with full force. A loud crash.

The Range Rover skidded.

He saw the gate sway on its hinges.

Realized: the Range Rover'd paved the way. Plowed through the gate. Cleared free passage.

There was a God.

Now: J-boy was back in the game.

He floored it.

Thirty yards farther up. Jorge drove through the busted gate.

He slowed down. Mahmud opened the side door. Tossed out a bag with text clearly printed on it: BOMB. They didn't want some idiot playing the hero trying to block their exit.

They had max three minutes now, and they were already late.

They drove straight ahead. Postal workers were screaming all around.

The summer sun's sweaty strength. Like J-boy. Strong. Sweaty. About to fry these clowns to a crisp.

He could do anything. Dared everything.

Loading docks number twenty-one and twenty-two had extra fencing around them. Sergio in the Range Rover—knew the way. Had watched Jorge's video footage at least five hundred times.

Jorge slowed the car down. Pulled the ski mask over his face. Grabbed the AK-47 and a duffel bag from the backseat.

Mahmud did the same. The Arab: like a real CIT pro—gray overalls, thick gloves, black balaclava. A fat Kalashnikov in his hands.

They climbed out of the car. Knew: no film in the surveillance cameras. *Verdad:* the insider was priceless.

Sergio rushed over. Wearing the same clothes as Jorge and Mahmud. In his hands: DeWalt's fattest model—the angle grinder from hell. Attacked the extra fencing that separated them from the loading docks. They couldn't drive the SUV through here, and they probably couldn't have driven the wheel loader through either—the concrete blocks in the bottom section of the fence were made to survive a small war.

Jorge saw a van parked on the other side, outside loading dock number twenty-two. Twenty-odd feet away. Completely black, no text or logo on it. It was the cash-in-transit vehicle. It was parked with its back to the loading dock. The gate was raised to the top. Two guards were opening a metal door but froze when they heard the screaming.

The insider's info was spot on.

Jorge looked over at the Range Rover: the front was severely buckled. The windshield was shattered. But none of the airbags'd been deployed. The Iranian was smart—he'd turned them off.

Jorge and Mahmud aimed their weapons through the fence. Held any potential mini-heroes at bay who thought they were gonna fuck with this hit. Kept the guards in sight who otherwise would've tried to bail. Babak was still sitting in the Range Rover—they hadn't had a balaclava for him. The Iranian hid his face as much as he could behind a hoodie he'd pulled up.

Twenty seconds. Sergio was through. Kicked the fence. A square piece fell out like an opening.

J-boy—rushed through, forward. Toward the metal door through which the guards'd disappeared. A wave through his body. Gangsta groove.

The door was unlocked from the inside. Again: the insider had delivered.

He saw a hallway. He knew his way around like it was his own bathroom.

Concrete walls. Bad lighting. A door at the other end. He opened it.

The reloading room: white walls. Guards. Carts with bags on them.

Now: he raised his weapon. Screamed in his best English: "This is a robbery! Open the door!"

Sergio was right behind him. A Walther in hand. Aimed at the guards too.

The door out toward the loading dock opened. The guards both inside and outside began to carry bags. Jorge tried to count: it might be as many as sixteen of them.

Outside: Mahmud was moving jerkily. Pointed with his gun. "Put the cases in the car."

The guards picked up one bag at a time. Climbed through the hole in the fence.

Meanwhile: Jorge spotted the other metal door. The door to the vault.

Mahmud took over outside. Waving the AK-47 around. Egged on the guards. Made them move.

Jorge set his bag down on the floor.

The big news: they'd solved the vault issue the day before yesterday.

Jorge'd been in touch with a guy: Mischa Bladman, JW's partner. A trickster with a face like a moon landscape—the dude's acne problems must've been worse than Freddy Krueger's when he was young.

Bladman said there were secure ways to reach JW. Jorge sent a message through Bladman. Jorge received an answer two days later. Yes, JW could get hold of people who could get hold of people who could get hold of classified blueprints from the City Planning Office. It was just a matter of price. Jorge offered a hundred thousand through JW's channel. Five days later: Bladman delivered the blueprints—JW was a God. Jorge drove them over to Gabbe's Pizzeria in Södertälje himself. The Finn let some explosives expert study the paperwork. He gave thumbs up.

So, now: Jorge pulled out an explosive cutting frame from the duffel.

The Finn'd been brief: "Firemen actually use these to bust through walls and stuff to save people. My guy's upped the explosive force ten times over."

Sergio helped Jorge set up the frame. They held up the diagram that the Finn'd made. Exactly how the frame was to be placed. Exactly how it was to be secured. Exactly how it was to be lit.

Jorge turned around. Peered out through the opening.

Now: four bags were already in the van.

Sergio's next job: he drilled into the wall. Jorge held up the explosive cutting frame. Sergio tightened the screws. It was secure.

One of the guards, a dude with a big gut, was still standing next to the cart with the bags of valuables. Trying to stall. Eyeing what they were doing.

Jorge knew: a strategy they used. Do everything slowly—allow the five-oh to make it to the scene.

He aimed the AK-47 straight at the gut-guard. Kept speaking in English, "Hurry up, or I'll blow your fucking head off."

The clown got moving.

Five bags in the van.

Mahmud was screaming. Vague stuff in Swenglish.

Sergio pressed the ignition button. They ran back out into the hallway.

Held their hands over their ears. Jorge saw Sergio's eyes through the ski mask. Gleaming.

Then came the explosion.

BOOM.

They ran back inside. Two guards on the floor. Smoke in the reloading room. The lights in the ceiling were out.

In the wall: a hole.

Jorge climbed inside. Had to crawl to fit through the hole. Heard Mahmud screaming to the two guards who were still loading their van.

Inside the vault: darkness.

He fumbled for the light switch. Thanked JW again: J-boy knew exactly where it was supposed to be.

He found it. Flipped the switch.

Still, nothing happened. He flipped the switch again. And again.

Cabrón—the explosion must've blown the circuit in the vault.

He looked around. The little bit of light seeping in through the hole in the wall illuminated a cloud of dust. There wasn't time to fumble around.

He took a few steps inside. Could make out tables. Chairs. Cabinets along the walls.

He tried to flash-accustom his eyes to the light. Impossible. All he could see was faint contours of objects.

Sergio popped his head in. "How's it look?"

"We blew the electricity," Jorge said. "And I don't have a flashlight. I can't see shit."

He could make out more tables. Counting machines. Crates on the floor. He saw something that could be bags. He fumbled his way there. Tripped. This was taking too long.

Two bags. Two feet high. He ran his hands over them. Sealed. The weight might be cash.

He grabbed them. Dragged them across the floor.

Back through the hole in the wall.

The guards were still lying down. Underneath one of them: blood on the floor.

He saw Sergio jump into the Range Rover. Jorge hoped it would start.

The guards who were still standing were loading the final bags into the Benz.

They were sweating. Good—they should be.

Thirteen bags.

He started crawling in through the hole again. There had to be more bags.

"We gotta go!" Mahmud screamed.

Jorge stopped. Already over by more than two minutes because of the time spent waiting for the Range Rover and blowing up the vault. The cops could be here any minute. Still: might be more bags in there.

Mahmud roared again, "For fuck's sake, let's go!"

His bro rushed up to him, grabbed Jorge's arm.

Jorge wanted to go back into the darkness. Mahmud pulled him.

No way it'd work. He slithered out. *Fuck*.

He threw the bags from the vault into the Benz. He felt around in his pocket. Pulled out the airsoft gun. Threw it on the floor—setting traps for the pigs.

Fifteen bags.

Mahmud roared. Game clock was going to zero.

He was standing still. Broad-legged. Prepared.

Aiming the Kalashnikov.

Sixteen bags.

Soooo many bags plus the sacks—there had to be a shit ton of cash in there.

Jorgelito, he didn't give a fuck about the vault right now. Soon: he'd be a very wealthy *blatte* anyway.

Seventeen bags.

A nasty tight nigga.

Eighteen.

A loaded Chilean with style.

They started the van.

Jorge heard sirens.

26

Hägerström was standing outside the door to the villa. At first he'd planned on breaking in through a window. But if Hansén saw a broken window, he'd realize there'd been an intruder. The door was better, if he could do it.

There was a sticker on the front door and on the windows: THIS HOUSE HAS AN ALARM SYSTEM. PAN WORLD SECURITY. But Torsfjäll had taken care of that part. The inspector had called Pan World Security and ordered that any alarms coming from the address during the next hour or so were to be ignored.

Hägerström took a chance. Hoped that his CO uniform would fool any possible neighbors or passersby. Prevent them from wondering why he was standing outside fiddling with the door lock. He had parked the car a ways off. Understood why JW had asked to be dropped off nearly half a mile from the house—he wanted to avoid some curious neighbor making the connection between Hansén and the prison car. This was Djursholm—a car from the Department of Corrections on these streets was more unusual than a Škoda.

Hägerström got out the electronic lock pick—the police's standard tool that Torsfjäll had just had delivered to him in a cab.

It would probably be able to take care of the front door. He inserted the tip of the pick in the bottom lock. Assa Abloy: a normal model. The lock pick made a spinning sound.

His mind drifted off.

The operation was making strides. Already before the trip in the transport car, JW had been asking him some questions now and then.

"What do you think, do you like Juan-les-Pins better than Cannes?"

"I'm thinking of buying an apartment on Kommendörsgatan when I get out. Do you think that's too far off the grid?"

"What do you think about the new Audi? Is it a little flashy, or is it just right?"

Isn't it a bit lame to drive an Audi? Hägerström thought. If you're going to drive a good car, why not drive a really good car? Otherwise you might as well just drive a regular old Volvo.

Then he felt ashamed: It was odd—the guy appeared endlessly confident and self-assured among his guys on the inside. But in relation to Hägerström, when they talked about this kind of thing, he was like an anxious seventeen-year-old. He almost got all maternal for the poor guy.

Hägerström snapped back into focus.

The lock made a clicking sound. The door opened. Behind it was a locked metal gate. He knew it would be considerably more secure. He got down on his knees in front of it. Pulled out another lock pick.

He tried to remember the course he'd taken in picking locks. He had read only one book, but he had practiced a lot. The secret to picking locks was three-part. Anyone could learn to pick a desk lock in a day. But picking real lock devices demanded the ability to concentrate, analytic intelligence, and above all, a mechanical sensitivity.

It was more difficult than he'd thought. But the teacher had said he was a natural.

The concentration part wasn't a problem. He was a former coastal ranger, internal affairs police investigator, a thinker. Concentration was part of his everyday existence. Even though he was often juggling many thoughts at once, he could focus when it came to locks.

But most of all, picking locks was about mechanical sensitivity. About learning to handle pressure. The problem was that most people learned to hold their body or hands in a certain way early on in life, no matter how much pressure you applied with them. But when it came to picking locks, the opposite was needed. You had to maintain the pressure at a very exact level. When you extracted the pick, the pressure against the pins had to be even. The lock picker moved his hand but kept the pressure completely steady.

He inserted the pick into the metal gate's lock.

Tried not to force the concentration, to ignore all the feelings that didn't concern the lock. There was a faint breeze on his face. A door slammed shut somewhere far away. A bird was chirping on a roof.

He felt the gravitation, the friction. Pins that moved a hundredth of a millimeter. A bolt that resisted. The pick was an extension of his fingertips and nerves. He maintained the exact same level of pressure against the pins.

He turned, slowly.

He felt the act of turning, the pick, the pins.

He felt the bolt move.

The lock clicked.

He grabbed hold of the metal gate.

It opened.

That's when the motion-sensor-triggered alarm went off. Blaring at a volume that was on the verge of unbearable.

Hägerström closed the door behind him. Walked up to the alarm system box that was mounted directly to the right of the door. Entered the code that Torsfjäll had given him, the one from Pan World Security.

The screaming alarm stopped as abruptly as it had begun.

He heard his own breathing. Remained standing in the hallway. Waited, in case a neighbor were to start yelling.

Nothing happened.

He looked around. A small rococo table and a sconce on the wall. No stool, but a set of stairs leading upstairs.

Hägerström walked farther into the house. A living room straight ahead. Genuine Persian carpets on the floor. More rococo furniture. Huge paintings on the walls: Bruno Liljefors, Anders Zorn, maybe a Strindberg. It looked like Mother's apartment, but with less taste. This felt vulgar.

He walked through a kitchen that was decorated in a rustic style. Some kind of white panel cabinets, matte metal handles. No invisible mechanisms or strange materials. A kitchen island in the middle of the room with induction stove plates and a fan above it that was about as big as Hägerström's Jaguar. A Moccamaster coffee machine, a dishwasher, fridge, freezer, and microwave from Miele. Four barstools around a tall table. Black and white stone slabs on the floor, they were warm—probably warm-water underfloor heating.

He moved on.

A hallway with four doors. A quick look into each of the rooms. A bedroom, a den. An office. Hägerström stepped inside.

This is where he might find interesting material. Inspector Torsfjäll ought to have gotten a search warrant right away. But he hadn't wanted to.

"It's better to have robust evidence before we even make the hit," the inspector told him over the phone. "Anyway, I've talked to Taxi Stockholm and put a tail on JW and Mr. Hansén. So we'll find out what they're up to no matter what."

The office looked ordinary. British oak furniture, a bookcase with three binders and some financial books in it, a desktop computer. Not much paperwork. Hägerström had hoped for more paperwork.

Not much of interest in the binders. A few old plane tickets, taxi receipts, hotel bills. It appeared as though Hansén traveled a lot: Liechtenstein, Zurich, Bahamas, Dubai.

Ding, ding.

The sound was coming from the computer. Hägerström checked it. It had switched on from standby mode. A reminder was flashing on the screen. *To do today: lunch with JW, call Nippe, call Bladman, dinner with Börje.*

JW and Bladman. There was obviously a theme to Hansén's social circle.

He looked up from the computer.

There was someone in the house.

He listened again.

Silence.

He wished he had his P226 on him.

He took a step toward the wall in order not to be visible from the doorway.

No sounds.

He took a careful step.

Still no sounds.

He picked up a pen from the desk. Held it out in front of him.

He walked out into the hallway.

Carefully.

Silently.

Maybe he had been wrong. Maybe what he had heard were sounds from outside.

He passed the kitchen.

Walked into the living room.

Something hard hit him in the back of the neck.

The force of the blow made Hägerström spin around. He dropped the pen, but before he fell, he saw a man dressed in black.

He heard a voice: "You fucking junkie—how the hell'd you shut off the alarm?"

Pain again. The man was kicking his back.

He tried to shield his head with his arms. Glimpsed a figure next to the one who was kicking. Speed-analyzed the situation. At least two attackers. Maybe they'd called the police, but if so, they shouldn't be this aggressive. At least one of them was armed with some sort of hard object, maybe with something more. But most important: they hadn't figured out what he was doing here. And they hadn't figured out who he was.

Another kick struck his back. But this time Hägerström was prepared. He blocked the blow. At the same time, he crawled back in the kitchen.

Another kick. Hägerström twisted his body—the kick missed. He threw himself after the leg, tried to slam into the back of the knee. He had been trained for this sort of thing, but that was a few years ago. The coastal rangers were taught an extremely stripped-down form of Krav Maga. Close combat training was basically nonexistent within the police force.

"Let go, you nasty fuck!" the man yelled.

Hägerström jerked his entire upper body. The man lost his balance. Fell.

Hägerström got up. Grabbed the coffee machine. He swung it with full force at the man's head.

The man roared.

The other one, who was also dressed in black, tried to make his way into the kitchen. They were standing in a narrow section of the room, just the way Hägerström wanted it. To face off against them one at a time.

The first man was holding his hand over his face. Still roaring. Blood was spraying from his forehead.

Guy number two came at Hägerström. He was large. Leather jacket. Black jeans. Crew cut.

He was holding a narrow object in his hand. Flipped out a blade.

A stiletto.

Hägerström noted that the man held the knife like someone who had been around the block a few times. His thumb against the flat side of the blade, windmilling his arm back and forth in front of his body.

"I'll take care of this whore!" he screamed.

Hägerström remained still. The man with the knife had a slight Eastern European accent. He lunged.

Hägerström moved to the side, blocked the stab. Followed along with the movement, forced the man's arm to the side. Tried to get his hand in a grip. Failed. The guy was *really* a pro, whipped forcefully as he pulled his arm back. Hägerström felt the pain in his hand but didn't look at it. He couldn't let himself get distracted now.

The first assailant tried to lunge at him again.

Simultaneously, another blow came slicing through the air.

Hägerström couldn't block with his arms. He twisted his body. The blade of the knife missed his cheek by an inch.

The man whose face was bleeding tried to grab him. Arms around him. He couldn't let it happen. Hägerström head-butted him with full force. Hopefully the blow landed where the coffee maker had already struck him. The man screamed like a coffee-scalded pig.

It was too late. Hägerström felt a pain in his side. Raw, stinging, worse than most of what he had ever experienced before.

The knife.

He couldn't hold his stomach. Couldn't lose control.

He hauled himself up onto the kitchen counter and kicked at the knife-man's groin.

A flash of pain through his stomach. The kick missed.

Hägerström saw his own blood on the floor. Or was it the other guy's?

The knife-man was fast. Another slice at his stomach.

A burning pain near his navel.

Hägerström wasn't screaming. He heard himself hiss, the same sound as when you put a fresh piece of tuna on the grill.

He gathered strength. All the force he was able to muster.

Held his hand straight. Slammed it into the man's eye while simultaneously kicking him in the groin again.

Classic combat technique in a panic situation: aim at weak spots.

The guy covered his face with his hands. Howled.

Hägerström took his chance. Shoved him aside. Pushed past.

Out of the kitchen. Out of the house.

Out onto the street.

His shirt was wet over the stomach.

It felt like there was a fire in there. As if he couldn't take another step.

He had time to think: *Maybe this is the end. Maybe I'll never get to see Pravat again.*

The Djursholm afternoon was completely calm.

He felt something dripping from him and onto the ground.

He ran toward his car.

27

Natalie positioned herself on the other side of Björngårdsgatan—kept her eyes glued to the entrance of the apartment building. She was waiting for the girl with the Louis Vuitton purse to walk out. She hoped that there wasn't a basement exit or some back way out of the building. She should really've been on her way to the police station a long time ago, but fuck the cops—they'd have to ask their questions some other time.

She was in luck. The door opened after less than fifteen minutes. The Louis Vuitton girl walked out. The monogrammed bag dangled in the crook of her arm. Fast steps on four-inch platform heels and a gaze that didn't even try to take in her surroundings—idiot.

Natalie followed her. She turned down onto Wollmar Yxkullsgatan toward the subway. The girl was clownishly made up. Dressed in a pink top, a short black jacket, tight blue jeans. She was difficult to place. On the one hand: the trashy top and platform shoes. On the other hand: the bag, which looked real.

They walked onto the subway platform. Just a guy with a stroller a ways off.

The girl stopped near the middle of the platform. Still with her gaze fixed straight ahead. She was staring at the ads on the other side of the tracks: H&M's bikini and bathing suit chicks and ads for cell phone plans with forty million free texts. The display said the next train would arrive in five minutes.

Two guys in their thirties pushing baby strollers started walking down the platform.

Natalie took a few steps forward: about thirty yards from the Louis Vuitton girl.

Another guy with a stroller came walking down the platform. It seemed to be some kind of religion here on the south side of the city—every guy had to have a stroller with a baby in it. The neighborhood was like one giant sect.

That's when the train pulled into the station. The girl got on. Natalie followed her.

The girl got off at T-Centralen and took the stairs down toward the blue subway line.

They walked the underground subway passageways. Got onto the moving walkways that transported people between the tunnels. It was different here than on Södermalm: no softy dads with mom complexes—an international feeling instead. The subway's blue line connected downtown with the ghettos. Natalie couldn't see a single person who looked typically Swedish. Still, she felt like she stood out here: none of these Somalis, Kurds, Arabs, Chileans, or Bosnians would question her Swedishness. Or rather, she could feel it, saw it in their eyes. They looked at her as though she were part of the system, part of this country: as though she were 100 percent Sven. Normally she was the *blatte*. Even if Louise, Tove, and the others never said it to her face.

A train pulled into the station. The girl got on. The car was packed. Natalie pushed her way in. The girl was standing fourteen feet off. Natalie examined her more closely. Her hair was bleached blond, and she had about an inch of dark roots peeking out. It was difficult to judge her natural hair color, but it was probably some variant of mousy. Her eyebrows were very plucked—you couldn't judge her natural hair color from them either. She had that tanning-bed tan—just like the one Viktor usually had. Even if she was hardly older than Natalie, she looked busted in some way. Worn out. Or maybe she was just nervous. She concluded: this chick was scared.

Natalie fished out her iPhone. Held it lazily in her hand. Pretended to surf or text. What she was actually doing was snapping photo upon photo. The Louis Vuitton girl got off in Solna. Natalie tailed her. Maintained a fifty-foot distance. Long escalators up to the surface—the blue subway line was at the bottom of the earth.

It was still nice out. The girl walked through the center of Solna, where all the shops were. Not so much as a glance over her shoulder. No suggestion of an increased stress level to her stride.

They left downtown Solna. The Råsunda soccer stadium towered on the other side like a UFO that'd parked in the wrong place. The girl walked down to an underpass under the road. Natalie didn't want to get too close. Waited for a few seconds. Then she walked down into the underpass. Just in time to see the girl disappear toward the buildings on the other side. Natalie jogged in order not to lose her. Hoped, pleaded, prayed that the Louis Vuitton girl wouldn't be paying too close attention.

She saw her, a hundred feet in the distance. Still walking. Apartment buildings. The girl slowed her steps. Walked into a building: Råsundavägen 31.

It was a four-story building. Key code pad beside the door. Natalie realized she'd reached the end of the road today. She wouldn't be able to get inside.

But it wasn't over. It was a start. She was already thinking about who the chick might be. She was going to dig into this thing until she found an answer.

28

They left Tomteboda exactly three minutes and twenty seconds after Babak's Range Rover'd paved the road. Two minutes and four seconds over the Finn's time frame.

The bomb bag they'd positioned by the gate was still standing there. The road was wide open.

They heard cop sirens.

They might be fucked now.

Still: no cruisers in sight yet. They must still be far away. Or else the pigs'd gotten stuck in the spike strip they'd planted out by the fork in the road.

They drove out toward Solna. First the Range Rover with Babak and Sergio in it. Followed by the van with Mahmud and Jorge in it.

Mahmud was working the wheel like a Formula 1 racer. Jorge was working the frequencies on the cop radio like a pig on *The Wire*. He was able to pick up all the police districts except for the surveillance frequencies—you needed special antennae for those. The Western region, frequency 79,000—they were first on the scene. The dispatchers were screaming like crazy. Calling ambulances, bomb experts, senior officers. Tried to figure out the escape route, modus operandi, if they could fly in helicopters from Gothenburg.

What wasn't according to the plan—that a security guard was lying on the floor, bloody. Above all: that they were bolting with *two* cars. Two cars that might be recognized. Two sets of descriptions of vehicles that were being wired out over the police radio. Two cars that they had to erase all their tracks from.

Still: so far, everything'd gone like a penalty kick at a wide-open goal, except for the fact that they'd blown out the lights in the vault. The guards'd taken it easy—fag Sweden didn't allow them to bear arms, but they all carried alarm buttons. J-boy and Co. got all the bags, lined up neatly with the handles facing out and the small, red LED that continued to blink as if nothing'd happened. Plus two bags with dough from the vault. Jorge decided to view them as a bonus.

Losers, *adiós.*

Five minutes later: they drove up behind Helenelund's cemetery. The drive out of the city'd been smooth sailing. Slow traffic: thanks to Jimmy and Javier for that—the main arteries were probably still in flames. No cop cars on the road: thanks to Jimmy, Tom, Robert, and Babak—the pigs were probably still trying to figure out how to disarm Jorge's fake bombs. No choppers: he thanked himself for that—felt bad for the dogs that'd died.

No surprises, except for the wheel loader: thank God for that.

He didn't know how he'd handle things with Jimmy and Robert when they met up: the wheel loader was probably not really their fault.

They turned up behind the chapel. Jorge's stomach was almost ready to blow again: what if the getaway cars weren't parked here either? What if the same shit happened as went down with the fucking wheel loader?

In front of them: the parking lot.

He saw it right away. The small truck was parked where it was supposed to be. A black Citroën. *Gracias a dios.*

They pulled the Benz van up close. Jumped out of the cars. Opened the van's back doors. Hauled over the sacks and bags with the valuables. One, two, three. They did it in no time. Four, five, six. The inside of the Citroën's cargo space was also covered wall-to-wall in aluminum foil. Seven, eight, nine. Jorge got a message from Tom over the walkie-talkie saying everyone was on their way home. Ten, eleven, twelve. They grabbed the jammer too. Thirteen, fourteen, fifteen. Mahmud and Sergio climbed into the Citroën—drove off to the apartment.

Two sacks plus maaaaany bags of bills on their way home to Daddy.

Now the final step. One of the most important—wiping out their own tracks.

Jorge got the fire extinguisher out from the van. Started spraying the inside of the Benz—that stuff got rid of fingerprints and corroded most DNA tracks. Babak was watching him.

"What do we do with my car?"

A question that was impossible to evade.

"I won't use all of the extinguisher," Jorge said. "You can have the last of it."

Babak glared at him. "What the fuck is wrong with you? You think I'm gonna take a bigger risk than anyone else? All I'm gonna get are the dregs of your fucking fire hose?"

Jorge continued to spray foam. Ignored the Iranian's bitching. "You or the front man for this car should call and report this thing stolen tonight at the latest."

"The fuck are you talking about?"

Jorge stopped spraying. "Stop bitching. When you used the car, you must've realized it was a risk. Now we gonna reduce that risk."

Babak kept on glaring at him. Jorge didn't wanna go at it now.

The Range Rover looked like a wreck—miracle that it'd made it all the way here. And even more of a miracle that no one'd reacted along the road.

Jorge stopped spraying foam. Babak grabbed the fire extinguisher from him. Jorge told him to start with the wheel, the instrument panel, and the seat. That was where you had the greatest risk of fingerprints and traces of DNA.

There was enough foam for everything in the front of the car.

"Fuck," Babak hissed. "I've driven people in the backseat too. There's probably mad hair, boogers, and shit back there."

Jorge didn't even want to deal with this *huevon.* Still, the Iranian was right. The van was secured: fire extinguisher goo covered all the surfaces. But the Range Rover was still a lethal threat. Even if it wasn't registered in Babak's name. The foam in the front seat wouldn't cut it.

They had to torch the fucking thing.

Again: this was not according to plan.

He opened the back door. Was still wearing gloves.

Fished around in the bag on the floor. He'd planned only on burning his clothes. He pulled out a bottle of lighter fluid—squeezed out more than half of it over the car's tan leather in the backseats.

He felt stressed. They'd already been here too long. More than five minutes. He picked up the matches.

His hands were shaking. He dropped a match. Difficult to do this while wearing worker gloves.

If Mahmud hadn't taken the weapons with him, they could have shot at the Range Rover until it caught fire. That's what they did in movies all the time, but now all they had to work with was matches. Old, soggy matches.

He pulled one glove off.

Fuck—his hand was shaking for real. Was it the roofies? Was it the rush from the robbery of the century? Was it the familiar criminal anxiety switched into panic mode?

One match finally flared up. He tossed it onto the backseat. Saw the lighter fluid catch fire.

Babak laughed. The flames flambéed his luxury interior.

Blue flames.

Jorge started taking off the jumpsuit he was wearing. Felt so good to take it off. The sun warmed him.

He pulled out a pair of jeans and a shirt from the duffel. Crammed the overalls, the gloves, and the ski mask into the bag. Sprinkled the last lighter fluid over it.

The bag, the clothes, the traces of Jorge Royale went up in flames.

Babak started bitching again, "Look man, the car's not lighting on fire."

Jorge looked up.

This was NOT according to plan.

The fire in the backseat'd gone out.

A minute later—as if they'd been there for three years. Jorge expected to hear sirens any minute. Cruisers with shrieking breaks. SWAT pigs with guns raised.

Babak unscrewed the cap to the tank of the car, stuffed sticks and grass down into the tank, and pushed in a piece of bark by the actual lid in order to let in oxygen.

Jorge picked up the matches again.

His hands: shaking worse than a vibrator turned on max speed.

Still, he succeeded. Lit four at once. Tossed them into the gas tank.

Stepped back quickly.

Waited for an explosion.

Nothing happened.

Finally: it looked promising. There was some smoke spiraling out of the opening in the tank.

They couldn't stay any longer.

One final thing before they split. There were still three security bags with valuables left on the ground. He picked them up.

"What the fuck is that?" Babak said.

Jorge walked toward the mini Fiat that'd been parked there the night before. Hauled the bags into the tiny trunk.

Babak repeated, "Weren't those supposed to go with Mahmud to the apartment?"

"This is our bonus," Jorge said. "Mahmud's in on it too, he knows about it. You want in?"

Babak grunted. But didn't talk back. X-tra cash *para los tres.*

Jorge started the car. They drove toward the apartment.

Hagalund. Blåkulla. All the apartment buildings looked like exact replicas of one another. Light blue, superhigh, crammed full of Iraqis, MMA fighters, and AIK soccer supporters. And chill *chicos*—J-boy knew a lot of good guys from here.

When he and Babak arrived, everyone was already there. Also: the Finn'd sent a guy over to check the booty. He was leaning against the wall, trying to look cool. They were gonna divide the cash up immediately—the Finn would get his cut.

Jorge followed Babak through the door. Was met with cheers.

Mahmud hugged him. Tom Lehtimäki held up a champagne bottle. Jimmy was jumping up and down.

At first Jorge was gonna say something about the wheel loader. But something inside him just let go. He smiled instead.

"Bros, we're fucking kings!"

They laughed, screamed, hugged each other again.

Even the Finn's guy looked happy.

"I don't wanna get all serious," Jorge said. "But we're not done yet. First, I have some questions. After that, we'll open these sacks and secured bags."

He gestured widely with his arm. The fifteen bags were lined up against one wall.

"Were the bags visible when you unloaded them?"

"No," Mahmud said. "We put them inside the duffel bags."

"Has everyone gotten rid of their cells?"

They nodded.

"Crushed and tossed the SIM cards?"

"Burned your clothes?"

"Dumped the angle grinder?"

They nodded again.

"Mahmud, d'you take care of the weapons?"

"They're in the bathroom. I took them apart and sprayed them with fire foam. They're ready to go."

"Good, when I'm done, you'll take them and toss the different parts where we decided."

Mahmud nodded.

"Has the jammer been on the whole time?"

They nodded.

"Do we have protective clothes, masks, and all that?"

Robert nodded.

"Did we prep boxes?"

Jimmy nodded.

Jorge raised his chin. Looked at the guys, one by one. He felt like a general. A gangster boss inspecting his army. A godfather rewarding his men.

"Then, gentlemen, it's time to open these bags."

* * *

Police Inspector
Jörgen Ljunggren
Granitvägen 28
Huddinge

REGARDING GROSSLY INAPPROPRIATE BEHAVIOR DURING A POLICE PROCEEDING

YOUR DOSSIER NUMBER: K-2930-2011-231

Undersigned represents Natalie Kranjic in the above-identified matter and hereby makes the following statement.

You are part of an investigation into the murder of Radovan Kranjic in Stockholm. In the context of this investigation, my client has been questioned by the police on four separate occasions. You have led the interrogation on all these occasions. My client has recorded the three most recent interrogations with the help of recording equipment that she brought with her.

I have had these interrogations transcribed and have thereby been able to note a great number of instances in which your behavior is grossly inappropriate. You also make yourself guilty of sexual harassment on at least three occasions.

For your information, my client is considering reporting you for the above-listed crimes as well as grave professional misconduct. She is also considering reporting you to the ombudsman at the Justice Ministry. Undersigned will be in touch with you again with additional information on any such legal action. Attached you will find excerpts of the transcribed police interrogations with my client.

My client also wants to stress that she, in order to show her good will, has only informed you privately at this point.

Stockholm as written above
Anders Nyberg, Esq.

Attachment

(TRANSCRIPT OF RECORDED INTERROGATION.)

"There we go, now I've turned off our little recorder here. So what we say from now on will not be included in the interrogation. Do you understand?"

"And why did you do that?"

"Because we want to cut the crap with you, you see. Talk about some serious things."

"Go ahead."

"We know who your old man was. We've been working on him for years. He wasn't one of God's best children—you know that, don't you? Frankly, he was a cowardly fucker who managed to scare people in this city. Isn't that right? But we're not scared."

"If that's how you're going to talk, I'm leaving."

"That's what you said last time too. But you won't. Listen to us. Your disgusting *daddy* ruined this city. People like him and you shouldn't even be sent back to where you came. You should just be shot, straight up."

(The sound of a chair scraping against the floor.)

"I said, I'm leaving."

"If you leave, I can guarantee that we won't work to find your father's murderer. You can forget that we'll lift a finger for him or you. So you'll stay right where you are, and you'll listen to me, you snotty little brat. What I wanna say is that we have to collaborate on both ends here. If you want us to make an effort to collar the gentleman who ground your dad into hamburger, we want some information from you. Do you understand?"

(TRANSCRIPT OF RECORDED INTERROGATION.)

"Okay, so I want to bring up some of the stuff we talked about last time too. As you can see, I've turned the recorder off."

"If you start your bullshit again, we're done for today."

"You know what I've said. You and me, we still want the same thing. We both wanna know who finished off your pop. If you want us to work on that, you're gonna have to collaborate."

"You're a pig. What do you want to hear?"

"Don't use that tone with me, you little slut. If you do, I won't be happy. I want to know the names of the guys who worked with your dad."

"Forget about it. If you call me that again, I don't care if you get hold of the murderer or not. We'll just end this little circus."

"I said, don't use that tone with me. Maybe you want to spend a night in a jail cell? Maybe have some fun with me on the cement floor?"

PART TWO

(A little over two months later)

29

Gate-out party for JW. The guy had been out for less than twenty-four hours.

Hägerström could have flashed his police badge and been let in. Then he realized: he didn't have a police badge anymore.

Instead, he mentioned JW's name to the bouncer and was waved through immediately. It couldn't be because JW was particularly well known in this place—after all, the guy had been locked up for over five years. But there were many other ways to put yourself at the head of the line. The premier method spelled out: money talks.

Stureplan: Stockholm's only real district for the party elite. This place was called Sturecompagniet. It was as far from moderation as you could get, miles away from the realities of ordinary Svens. A place that all Sweden loved to hate, but that everyone under thirty probably dreamed of getting into. It was jet-set-aspirational, glamorous—hetero-normative to the infinite power.

This was where JW had come six years ago in the pursuit of happiness. To become emperor of the silver-spoon-bred, tsar of the brats, flashy king of the Stureplan hill. And how had he done it? By becoming the royal purveyor of cocaine. JW was the high-class dealer everyone had wanted to know, the backslick brat who bathed in Benjamins. And then he fell, flat on his face. The eternal rule could never have been truer: the higher you climb, the harder you fall. Icarus ignites.

Hägerström wondered whom JW could have invited tonight.

The chaos was almost as great beyond the gatekeepers as outside the velvet rope. The place was crawling with people ten years his junior. Boys from the countryside, who had smeared so much gel in their hair that it would take two months to wash it out, were waving their Visa cards in the air—not even Gold Cards—wondering if they could pay the cover. The cashier shook her head. "Cash only, boys. How'd *you* get in, anyway?" Less green dudes from the inner city and the better suburbs were wearing tight jeans and their shirts unbuttoned. They glided past in the VIP line, pretended to be blue-blooded for real. But their shirts were shiny, and their shoes had rubber soles. Still, the hosts in dark suits and gloved hands ushered them in. Clusters of girls in clownish makeup who were probably underage were giggling relentlessly—so happy to have gotten in. Other chicks with more confident style and purses that cost two monthly police salaries swept past the cash registers with long strides, putting one foot in front of the other as though they were on a catwalk.

He thought about the girls he had tried to meet during his pre-Anna years. As soon as they had wanted to start dating for real or began talking about defining their relationship, he had pulled out. Of course he knew that he was turned on by guys, got hard for guys, even though he had no steady relationships. Instead, he was a regular at the Side Track Bar, the steam room at the S.A.T.S. gym, Zenit-gym on Mäster Samuelsgatan, US Video. He had visited the hill on Långholmen a few times on warm summer nights.

But he hoped he might get turned on by girls yet. It would be easier that way. Still, the thought of a permanent relationship with a woman made him anxious.

Then he thought of JW's sister. The girl who had hung out at Stureplan so much, the one who had apparently disappeared. Who JW had been looking for. Hägerström wondered what had happened. And how it had all affected JW.

Back to the present. It was Friday night, and Johan "JW" Westlund was celebrating that he had been freed. Gate-out bash for a former prince of Stureplan.

Again: Hägerström wondered who would be there.

He couldn't find him. Hägerström walked around and around, up and down. The place was larger than he remembered from the last time he had been there. That was eight years ago.

It was late—Hägerström had wanted JW to be good and tanked by the time he got there.

He had to push through the crowd, carefully but forcefully shove aside the teenage girls and men his age who were ogling those very same girls. The scars on his stomach strained even though they had healed beautifully.

The music was pounding, some Eurotechno that Hägerström didn't know the name of.

The crystal chandeliers hanging from the ceiling were gigantic.

The strobe lights on the dance floor caught people in photo-flashes.

He thought about Operation Tide.

The break-in into Gustaf Hansén's house had ended abruptly. When Hägerström fled the scene, he regretted having parked the transport vehicle so far away—for a while, he didn't think he was going to make it all the way. He might have lost as much as a quart of blood.

But afterward he was happy that the car had been parked where it was; otherwise the assailants would have seen that he fled in a car from the Department of Corrections. If JW had found that out, the whole operation would have been over.

Hägerström had driven away as well as he could. He had held one hand over his stomach. He had been able to make it only a couple hundred yards. Then he had stopped and called for an ambulance.

One day later the doctor came in to see him where he was lying in a bed in Danderyd's hospital.

The knife-man's first stab had given him a superficial flesh wound that needed only three stitches. The second stab had cut two inches deep, right below his navel. He had needed six stitches, she said, but he had also been incredibly lucky. A fraction of an inch to the side, and his liver could have been worthless for the rest of his life.

Hägerström was back at Salberga three days later. He told JW he had come down with an acute stomach bug and that was why he hadn't been able to drive him back to the prison. JW maintained his poker face—maybe he didn't even know that someone had been inside Hansén's house.

Unfortunately, the break-in didn't do much for Operation Tide—not as much as Hägerström and Torsfjäll had hoped. He hadn't had time to look around long enough before he was attacked. But at least they had come to understand three things. First of all: Gustaf Hansén was somehow connected to JW's business. Second of all: Gustaf Hansén was a shady person. He wasn't registered at the house where he appeared to live when he was in Sweden, and he apparently had two sets of alarm systems, one that went to a normal security company, and one that seemed to go to a service that was much more violent by nature.

Third of all: the reminder on Hansén's computer: *To do today: lunch with JW, call Nippe, call Bladman, dinner with Börje.* Bladman was mentioned. But also two other people: someone named Nippe and someone named Börje. Sure, it was possible that they had nothing to do with anything. But they could also be important.

Every single one of Hägerström's intuitive antennae were saying that there was more to be found in that house. But Torsfjäll wanted to wait to get an actual search warrant.

After Hägerström saw JW coming out of the house, Torsfjäll had been in touch with Taxi Stockholm and gotten the address where JW and Hansén had been dropped off: Restaurant Gondolen by Slussen. The inspector sent an undercover officer. The cop wasn't able to get any good photos but could report that the party at the restaurant had consisted of one younger and two middle-aged men who spoke Swedish. The table had been booked by someone named Niklas Creutz. A less-than-educated guess was that Niklas was Nippe.

What's more, Hägerström knew who he was. His sister, Tin-Tin, knew Nippe's sister. According to all the conventions, Nippe should not find himself in the same context as a convicted upstart—Nippe belonged to one of Sweden's wealthiest families. The Creutz clan owned the fifth largest bank, invoice, collection, and currency exchange empire in the country. It was strange.

JW approached Hägerström with open arms.

"Hey screwy, great to see ya."

Hägerström returned the embrace.

"I've got an open tab at the bar. Order whatever you like. This used to be my territory, I was a regular here. I've got a lot to make up for."

There was a table behind JW. On it were two large silver-colored buckets filled with ice. Two magnum bottles in each bucket. Drained champagne glasses. There were also small bottles of tonic water, Coke, and ginger ale, plus two half-empty bottles of vodka.

Eight men and four girls were sitting around the table. Hägerström recognized three of the guys. Crazy Tim and Charlie Nowak were there—both had gated out. They were beaming—as happy as JW was to be breathing free air again. And to even be sitting at a table at a place like this—it was a dream experience of a lifetime for boys like them. Hägerström hoped they would be able to handle having him show up here.

The third face he recognized did not really come as a surprise, not anymore anyway. It was Nippe.

Hägerström leaned over the table, greeted Crazy Tim and Charlie. They didn't seem to care that a CO was tagging along for the party. Maybe they knew that JW had used Hägerström on the inside.

"Hey, boys, I'm done with Salberga too. Did you know?"

They looked questioningly at him.

"I quit," Hägerström said.

They laughed. Raised their champagne glasses. Toasted freedom. Toasted their new ability to lock the bathroom door from the inside for the first time in years. Toasted the fact that they were going to take Stockholm by storm.

JW introduced Hägerström to the others. They all seemed to be pen pals, except for Nippe. Hägerström read their half-lazy gazes, their tattoos, their jeans and tight T-shirts. Their style was as out of place here as JW's backslick had been on the inside. But maybe not, on closer examination. Hägerström scanned the place one more time. Not everyone in here was rocking a bratty style. Many of the men were signaling other affiliations, money that didn't come from dull finance jobs.

Nippe leaned over and introduced himself to Hägerström.

"Hi, I'm Niklas Creutz."

A different manner of speaking, clear, well-enunciated Swedish. Those distinct upper-class sound markers: the long *a*'s, the slightly nasal voice. It was as far from prison idiom as you could get.

JW leaned over toward Hägerström. "We call him Nippe. He's an old friend of mine."

"Nice to meet you. My name is Martin Hägerström."

"It's a pleasure," Nippe said. "Are you Tin-Tin's big brother?"

"Yes," Hägerström said. "Do you know her?"

"My older sister is a good friend of hers. Have you met my sister, Hermine?"

Hägerström nodded. Smiled.

They felt a connection. Kinship.

Hägerström identified his goal for the night: to find out how Nippe was involved with JW.

No one else came to JW's gate-out bash. Hägerström almost felt bad for the guy—he obviously didn't have a lot of friends. More than five years in prison, and only eight people came to celebrate him—plus Hägerström, of course. But he was fake. Then it struck him that there might be loads of people who wanted to celebrate JW but didn't want to be seen with him in public.

Hägerström made his way over to the bar. Tried to push through the crowd. Bumpkins waved their Visa cards around. Flashy guys waved five-hundred-kronor bills. It took him fifteen minutes to get the attention of one of the bartenders. He ordered a bottle of Heineken. Said his name was Johan Westlund and that he needed his card. The bartender flipped through the credit cards that people had left in the bar. Returned. Put the card on the counter.

Hägerström picked it up. Looked it over. Four seconds. Memorized the card number. 3435 9433 2343 3497. MasterCard. Gold. Issued by a bank in the Bahamas: Arner Bank & Trust.

Hägerström gave the card back, then returned to his seat.

It was obvious that JW wanted to connect Hägerström with Nippe. He made conversation. Asked Hägerström questions just to accentuate his background. Martin Hägerström wasn't some middle-class Sven, that much was certain. He came from the same planet as Nippe. But Nippe had registered as much already after two seconds.

Nippe drank as much as everyone else. Hägerström didn't understand how he dared sit next to these thugs. If he was mixed up in JW's business, he ought to want to stay as far away as possible. The table was a stage. Hundreds of spectators were eyeing the lineup of men who were burning tens of thousands of kronor tonight.

Hägerström had gotten Nippe to take four shots, on top of the at least six glasses of champagne and three drinks he had already had. They had made enough small talk. JW was busy, he was talking to two girls. Nippe was drunk enough. It was time.

Hägerström took his chance, leaned over to him. "So, how do you know JW?"

A lucky question. Nippe started bubbling, like the champagne glass in his hand.

"Maybe I shouldn't be here. JW burned so many bridges. But he's a damn nice guy, you know."

"I agree."

Nippe was slurring his words. "You know, I knew him before he lost control. We used to party around here and stuff. And we went to the Stockholm School of Economics together too. He's a genius, did you know that? A mathematical and law genius. He was in the top three on every single exam. He studied law at the same time. He was one of those guys that the British investment banks come courting before they even finish their third semester."

Hägerström nodded, encouraged Nippe to continue.

"JW wasn't like the people who just studied in order to pass the exams with high enough grades. He learned stuff in order to use it right away, kind of like the entrepreneurial fucks from the countryside who're in the process of taking over SSE. The difference is that JW was like one of us, almost."

Nippe drained his glass. Hägerström sipped his.

He poured more. Thought: *Drink, Nippe, drink.*

Nippe gulped. "He wanted too much, JW. All that drug-dealing stuff was just rotten luck, if you ask me. JW was running a little too fast, you know? But he didn't mean any harm. So I thought I'd give him a chance. He's damn smart, and he's got a good heart. He's told me that he's already started loaning money to people in the prison world, guys who need fast cash. I don't think he should have to spend his time doing things like that."

Hägerström played along. "No, he's too good for that. I really like him. You know I worked at the prison, right?"

"Yeah, JW told me. How'd you end up there?"

Hägerström had been asked why he chose to become a cop thousands of times over the years. He'd stocked up on standard responses. One of them suited this situation perfectly.

"I'm kind of different, you know. I don't always like to do what everyone else does. I think people should find their own way in life. Right?"

"Totally. Totally."

Hägerström wanted to steer the conversation back to JW.

"But since I worked at the prison, I have to ask, wasn't it dangerous for JW to be lending out money?"

"I don't know. But he was pretty safe, protected by the walls, so to speak. Ha ha. You need to understand, I've never met anyone who's as hungry as JW is. For the rest of us, it's a question of appetite. For JW, it's a question of survival. Have you ever talked business with him? If you do, check out his eyes. It's like they're on fire. He knows that in order to become someone in this world, you need to accrue a fortune. Become a wealthy man, so to speak. Things might be different for you, Martin. You've been able to do what you want—you might not have to fight in order to become someone, because you already know you're someone. Everyone knows who your parents are. Everyone knows where your family comes from. That's not the way things are for JW."

"Maybe you're right."

Hägerström wondered where this was going. Nippe was being weirdly somber. Maybe he was trying to defend why he was collaborating with JW somehow. He tried a more direct tactic.

"I helped him a little bit while he was in prison. Maybe he told you that?"

"No. Helped how?"

"Some favors from time to time, you know. He has a business, as you yourself put it."

"Okay, well, that's great."

All Hägerström's feelers were on hyperalert. Did Nippe understand that he was an insider? Would he reveal anything?

"JW understands the system better than some criminal *blatte* ever will, you know? And he can be more straight and open than any lawyer or accountant could ever be. People need that. Even if we've switched government in this fucking Social Democratic country, we still have higher taxes than anywhere else in the world. All the sane people make sure to sign themselves up as residents of Malta or Andorra. Right?"

Nippe drained his glass again. He was slurring more and more. Hägerström had to come up with something soon, because this guy might be on the floor in a few minutes.

"I just have to say how damn nice it is that you want to help JW," Hägerström said. "I'm going to do my best to get him some clients too."

Nippe poured more champagne. Looked at Hägerström. His eyes were cloudy.

"Clients?"

"Yes, clients. Or whatever he's calling it."

Nippe looked nauseous. Still, Hägerström thought it seemed like he was registering what he was saying.

"Mmmm," Nippe said. He didn't say anything else.

This wouldn't work. Nippe was too drunk. He mumbled something about being tired and having to get up early on Saturday because he had a time booked at the Royal Tennis Hall. It sounded like a bad excuse. Hägerström regretted that he had fed him so many drinks.

As soon as Nippe Creutz went home, Crazy Tim, Charlie, and the others caught a second wind. It was as if they had been holding back before. The talk got cruder. The babe-watching intensified. The boozing escalated. They ordered a bottle of Dom Pérignon for thirty K.

They didn't seem to care that Hägerström, a former CO, was sitting there listening. They talked about how much you could make slinging coke, smart methods of flipping stolen goods, sweet streets in Berlin to go whore-hunting. They talked about mutual friends who had been collared, friends who had gated out, acquaintances who had died. JW said he was thinking of going to Thailand where he knew people. They discussed the CIT robbery in Tomteboda—according to them, it was a pale copy of the helicopter robbery—and the murder of Radovan Kranjic, new formations in the Stockholm jungle.

Hägerström tried to keep up as much as possible. But he couldn't pile it on too thick. The guys around the table knew he wasn't a gangster to begin with.

Two guys over by the bar were glaring at them. That's what Crazy Tim thought, anyway. They looked to be JW's age, wearing jackets with silk handkerchiefs peeking out of their breast pockets, pressed pants.

It was two-thirty in the morning. Crazy Tim was so drunk he was slurring his words. "Those tools over there, they've been staring at us all night. I'm gonna ask what their fucking problem is."

JW placed his hand on his arm. "Chill, Tim. I don't want any trouble tonight."

"Come on, man. I'm just gonna go ask them what they want."

JW held him back.

JW rose a half hour later. "Boys, it's time for me to go home."

The guys were trashed. Still, Crazy Tim asked if JW needed company.

JW thanked him. "No, I'm fine. But maybe you can follow me to get a cab, just to make sure there's no trouble?"

The question was directed at Hägerström.

"Absolutely."

A small breakthrough.

JW embraced Crazy Tim, Charlie, and the other guys. He and Hägerström walked together down the steps toward the exit. The place was still thick with people. Hägerström walked first, shoving people to the side with both arms. Cleared a path for JW.

It had been a good night, trust-creating. Interesting about Nippe. One of Hägerström and Torsfjäll's theories had been proven correct. Cards were issued by banks down there and used by people up here. And what was more, JW had pretty much asked Hägerström to be his bodyguard.

They didn't have any jackets to pick up in the coat check. The August night was cool but comfortable.

JW walked up to one of the bouncers. Said something into the guy's ear. He smiled.

Hägerström walked out onto the sidewalk. Tried to hail a cab. Could already feel the hangover tomorrow.

Every single cab was taken.

They both tried for five minutes, but it was a lost cause. There seemed to be a taxi drought tonight.

Finally JW said, "I think I'll walk. Feel like walking me home?"

It wasn't a question. It was an order.

They walked up Humlegårdsgatan. JW was renting an apartment on Narvavägen. But as he had told the guys tonight, "I swear, I'll buy something within three months. I've just got to find the right piece of property."

Crazy Tim and Charlie Nowak had just laughed—they didn't even play the same sport as JW, let alone in the same league.

When they reached Östermalmstorg, JW stopped. He pointed at two guys a ways off.

"There are those dudes that Crazy Tim wanted to jump."

Hägerström saw the guys, around twenty yards behind them. They were looking in JW's direction. Crazy Tim's irritation might have been justified—the grins on those boys' faces weren't friendly.

"They recognize me from back then," JW said. "Do you understand?"

Hägerström nodded. He thought about the double-cross JW used to play. Wondered if he actually felt more comfortable in his own skin now, when everyone already knew he had done time. When people no longer believed he was someone he wasn't.

The guys over there laughed. The sound echoed across the open square.

JW and Hägerström kept walking.

They reached Storgatan. But the entire time Hägerström could hear the guys' footsteps behind them—they were drawing closer, too quickly. He wondered what JW expected him to do about it.

After a few seconds, he turned around. "Is there something you want?"

The guys were only ten yards behind. They came walking toward them slowly. "What did you say? Did you say something?"

Hägerström and JW were standing very still.

"Don't worry about it," JW said. "My buddy's just had a little too much to drink."

The guys approached them. Blocked their path. Stopped.

One of them was slurring his words, "I recognize you. JW. Do you remember me?"

JW started walking around them. "No, I don't know who you are. But have a nice rest of your night."

The dude wasn't satisfied with that. He took a step closer to JW, slammed into him with his shoulder. JW stumbled. The guys burst out in hyena laughter.

Hägerström took a step forward. JW took a step back, fished out his phone.

"Calm down," Hägerström said.

The guy ignored him, turned to JW instead. "No normal person came to your little party tonight, did they?"

JW was standing three yards off to the side, talking quietly into his phone. Didn't even react to the guys' provocations.

"Go home and go to bed," Hägerström said. "You've had too much to drink."

The first guy turned to him. Got up close. Chest to chest. They were the same height.

"And who the fuck are you?"

Hägerström didn't respond, but tensed his entire body.

The guy was spraying spit as he spoke. "Huh? Who the fuck are you, you fucking joke? Do you know who that guy is you're hanging around with?"

Hägerström didn't say much, just tried to calm the guy down. "We don't want any trouble here tonight."

The guy wouldn't let up. They bickered back and forth for a while.

It was high time to get JW out of there. Hägerström began to walk backward, all the while keeping his eye on the guy.

It didn't work. The guy followed him. Continued his spit: "You fucking clown."

Meanwhile, in the corner of his eye, Hägerström saw guy number two readying himself to pounce. Shoved JW in the shoulder again.

Crossroads decision at lightning speed: either he took these guys down, or he and JW would be forced to bolt. The first alternative might get totally out of hand. The latter could equal a humiliation that JW would hate.

JW tumbled into a wall. Hägerström raised his voice: "I said, calm the fuck down."

He tried to make eye contact with JW, gauge what he wanted to do.

The guy near Hägerström yelled, "You fucking fag, who do you think you are?"

The words provoked him. Hägerström looked over at JW once again.

But it was too late. He heard yelling.

Crazy Tim was running toward them.

At the same time, the guy near Hägerström threw his body at him. His jacket fluttered. The dude's fist came flying. Just missed Hägerström's ear.

Crazy Tim reached them. Hägerström saw that he was holding something in his hand.

A spring baton.

He whipped the weapon, striking the guy in the back of the head. The dude collapsed onto the ground.

The other guy shoved JW again. Then tried to run over to his floored friend.

Hägerström's thoughts were raging. What was happening right now was not okay, but these cocky motherfuckers were acting like pigs.

Hägerström grabbed the guy. Shoved him. He teetered backward.

Crazy Tim threw himself over him. Rapped his face with the baton.

The guy lying on the ground began to stand up. Was on all fours.

Hägerström went over to him. Held him down with his knees and arms.

The brat looked up at him with cloudy eyes.

He was bleeding from the nose. "You fucking psycho."

Then he tried to knock Hägerström aside.

Oh, hell no. Hägerström felt the adrenaline begin to rush through his veins.

The guy tried to wrestle him to the ground.

Something in Hägerström snapped. He threw a punch in the guy's face.

Hard.

Felt a nose breaking.

He struck again.

Felt lips tearing.

He struck again.

Finally the guy lay still. Curled into the fetal position, arms raised above his head.

Hägerström got up. He was out of breath.

The other guy was also lying still on the ground.

JW and Crazy Tim were looking at Hägerström approvingly.

30

Natalie stretched her arms out as far as she could. Tried to feel the muscles in her back. It wasn't easy—the back's musculature was particularly difficult to pinpoint. She tried to elongate them, limber them up. Stretch like a pro.

The instructor was playing a slow song: Michael Jackson's "Heal the World."

Everyone around her was lying on mats on the floor, just like Natalie. Stretching their bodies. Their muscles. They were girls her own age, one or two middle-aged women, but only three guys. Guys didn't need classes at the gym the same way the girls did—they had their martial arts clubs, company soccer leagues, and floorball tournaments. They had more natural places where they got exercise than in front of a mirror in a windowless room. The whole gym thing was pretty crazy if you thought about it—a generation's feeble attempt to live up to its own sick body ideal. A generation of people who'd learned to be dissatisfied with themselves no matter what they looked like. Who sought some sort of meaning in their lives.

Natalie let the neg thoughts go. She knew what had meaning in her life.

The body pump class'd been hard—she liked to push herself. She could still feel her heart beating fast. Her body was warm. The sweat rose like steam from her head and arms. In the mirror that covered one wall, she could see that her face was red.

She reflected about the summer. A difficult time, with so many sleepless, tear-filled nights that she'd almost lost control. She'd isolated herself—couldn't deal with seeing Viktor too much, spent time with Louise and Tove only at her own house. She didn't go along with them to Saint-Tropez or Gotland. She didn't go along with them on their nighttime adventures around Stureplan. She didn't even go along with their jokes and sense of humor. She just wanted to become grounded in herself—become stable enough to handle law school in the fall.

She didn't want to involve them in what was truly important—finding out more about what happened to Dad. Who'd taken his life.

She'd called Goran in June, a few days after she'd trailed the Louis Vuitton chick to Solna.

They met up at Natalie's house. Talked briefly in the hallway. Goran wanted them to take a walk in the neighborhood. He leaned over and whispered in her ear, "For safety's sake."

Natalie understood. He was right. There was no reason to take risks.

She threaded her arms into her short leather jacket. They walked out.

The streets were empty. Summer vacations hadn't started yet, so her neighbors were at work.

Goran asked how she was feeling. Then he said that everything about Dad's death had been unnecessary. He said it in a different way than before. He didn't use any clichés about Dad being up in heaven among the heroes and so on. He cared.

They walked up to a wooded area where she used to play as a kid. Natalie liked this place. The trees, the rocks, and the pinecones belonged to her. This was her world.

She turned to him. "Goran, I want to ask you a favor."

They continued walking. Goran put some snuff under his lip.

"Like I said, I took those binders."

Goran picked his nose.

"There was some information about a weird apartment."

Goran scratched his ear.

"Don't you care about what I'm telling you?"

Goran turned to her. The snuff was dripping down over his teeth. "I've already told you. You're his daughter. I'll support you and help you in whatever you do, you know that. But you're the one who chooses the path. Not me."

Flashback: Goran's words in the parking lot outside the hospital after the meeting with Stefanovic. He'd promised her his loyalty. Promised to live according to promises made.

They talked for a while.

"The police aren't doing their job," Natalie said. "I don't really give a shit how they treat me. But they don't seem to have a clue who did this to Dad. So I want to deal with it now."

They discussed different strategies for how Natalie could get hold of information about the police's investigation. She'd recorded the most recent round of questioning. When she told Goran about that, he suggested she have a lawyer send a threatening letter to the police. And he would also see if he could help in other ways. Check with Thomas Andrén, the ex-cop who used to help Dad. He could put some hooks out among former colleagues. Pull some strings. Make it worth their while.

Natalie ruminated: she still hadn't told him about the girl she'd trailed. Should she go that far? Either Goran didn't know about the apartment, or no one wanted her to know about it. Still: she couldn't be alone in this.

She went out on a limb, all the way. Told him how she'd found the apartment. That she'd tried but failed to find the keys. That she'd gone there. That she'd seen a girl her own age enter and exit the apartment.

That she'd trailed the chick to Råsundavägen.

They stopped walking. There was a pile of pinecones on a rock.

"I want you to find out who this girl is," Natalie said. "And you need to be honest with me, even if it's something embarrassing."

Goran picked his nose again. He didn't have any manners.

"If it's embarrassing, let it be embarrassing. But I don't want to speak badly about the dead. A man is a man, that's all there is to it. And a man like your father probably needed places where he could be a man."

"I hear what you're saying."

"But when it comes to this apartment, all I can say is that I didn't know about it. I've never heard about it before."

Natalie looked at Goran. He was unshaved. Dressed in his usual style. Poor posture. He said he didn't know anything about the apartment. Still: she trusted this man. His entire being was radiating one and the same thing: *I care.*

Right now that felt so incredibly good.

"And the woman?" Natalie said.

"Not her either," he responded. "But that's no problem. I'll find out all there is to know about her."

———

Goran'd put Thomas on the case.

They installed Skype on their cell phones. Neither Goran nor Thomas was particularly good at computers, but they still knew about safety. The thing about Skype—the police couldn't listen in even if they'd tapped one of their phones.

The ex-cop'd called her two weeks later. "Hi, it's me. Thomas Andrén."

"I can see that. Have you gotten anywhere yet?"

"Somewhere, anyway. Her name is Melissa Cherkasova, she's originally from Belarus, but she's lived here for five years. She speaks Swedish and lives alone in that place in Solna. She is twenty-five years old and doesn't seem to have a regular job."

"So who is she? What does she do?"

"Let me put it this way: she meets men at hotels."

Natalie fell silent. Took a few breaths. "What men?"

"So far, I've seen her meet two different guys. Twice each. At the Sheraton Hotel."

"Who are they?"

"One's a Brit and just seems to come here on business. The other one is Swedish, middle-aged. I don't know much more about him. They don't come down to meet her, she goes up to their rooms. But I've got some photos of the old boys."

Natalie took a few more breaths.

"Thomas, find out everything you can about them."

* * *

K0202-2011-34445

INTERROGATION

Time: June 5, 0905-0916

Location: Södersjukhuset Hospital, Stockholm

Present: Stefan Rudjman Stefanovic (SR), Head Interrogator Inger Dalén (HI)

HI: I will begin by explaining to you that you are not suspected of any crime. This interrogation is purely informational, and you have been informed of the reason for it. So, this is in regard to the incident that took place a while ago on Skeppargatan.

SR: Mm, I know what this is about.

HI: Okay, I'm wondering if you might tell me how you knew Radovan Kranjic.

SR: We were superficial acquaintances.

HI: But you were in the car too, weren't you?

SR: Yes, that's pretty obvious, isn't it? That's why I'm lying in a bed here right now.

HI: Right. How are you feeling, by the way?

SR: I've been better.

HI: Okay, so let me ask you this: Why were you riding in the car with Radovan?

SR: We were going to pick up his daughter.

HI: And how well did you know Radovan?

SR: I've already answered that, we were acquaintances. "Hey, how you doing?" You know—not much more than that. And I can tell you straight off the bat that I won't have too many answers to your questions, because I don't know anything about all this. I hardly knew Radovan, I don't know anyone in his family, I don't have any idea about anything.

HI: Okay, but how did you become acquainted with Radovan to begin with?

SR: I don't remember.

HI: Was it many years ago or only a few months ago?

SR: I can't really remember.

HI: Did you do any business together?

SR: I don't think so.

HI: Have you been to his house?

SR: Once or twice.

HI: But do you know his daughter?

SR: I already told you, I don't. Am I under suspicion for something, or what? You're going on and on like I'm some fucking murderer. I was in the car, dammit, and I've been lying here in this place for over a week now. I'm the victim here, aren't I?

HI: You're right about that, formally you're the plaintiff in this investigation. But I still have to ask a few questions, as I'm sure you understand. We want to know as much as possible about Radovan in order to get to the bottom of this incident.

SR: Okay, but I don't remember any more. I've told you everything I know.

HI: All right, then I'll ask about some other things. At what time did you get into the car?

SR: Don't remember.

HI: Okay. But was Radovan already in the car when you got into it?

SR: Don't remember.

HI: For how long were you riding in the car together?

SR: No idea.

HI: Had you ridden in that car before?

SR: No comment.

HI: What'd you done previously during the night?

(Silence.)

HI: Do you not want to answer?

SR: I don't have anything more to say. We can end this now.

HI: Why? We're just trying to do as good a job as we can.

SR: No comment.

HI: Don't you want to help us solve this?

(Silence.)

HI: Well?

SR: No comment.

HI: Well, the fact that you don't want to cooperate might be perceived as a little strange.

(Silence.)

HI: All right, okay, I am going to take it that you don't want to say anything more. In that case, we'll end this interrogation. The time is 9:16.

31

Thailand. Pattaya. Queen Hotel. A fully private bungalow with a pool.

Jorge was lounging in bed. Staring up at the ceiling. It was decorated with painted pussies.

The air conditioning was buzzing—it sounded like it was dripping.

Thailand. Pattaya. Queen Hotel—100 percent whore den: when Jorge'd booked the rooms, the hotel'd asked if they wanted a *special reception*. He knew that would make the boys happy.

Eleven hours to Bangkok—they flew two days after the heist.

Two hours to Pattaya—they took a minibus. Pattaya was the biggest tourist nest near Bang-cock—easy to disappear into the crowd. Perfect stopover for robbers on the run.

Many weeks at Queen Hotel—the restaurant's menus included prices for girls. Thailand hadn't changed—the exact same feeling as the last time he'd been there, four years ago. The palm trees, the parasols, the pedophiles—everything a little too up close for comfort. The only difference: the last time he was here, they'd been playing the Police, Dire Straits, U2. Now: American R&B everywhere.

But the weather was sweet, and they were lying low.

Jorge turned over in bed. Grabbed the watch that was resting on the nightstand: it was heavy. An Audemars Piguet Royal Oak Offshore. The face was forty-four millimeters in diameter, nineteen millimeters thick. He hadn't been able to resist the temptation, despite the Finn's *mandamientos*. The day after the heist, he went to Nymans Ur on Biblioteksgatan. Shelled out for the freshest, phattest model they had. He could've ordered it online or bought it in Bangkok. But that wasn't the same—part of the thing: walking in and paying cash in the middle of Svenland's swankest street. Floss, get a receipt, a guarantee, and a Sven who bowed to him, smiled, and brownnosed until the shit came out of his ears.

Mahmud, Jimmy, and Javier were sitting at their regular hangout: Pattaya Sun Club. Were stretched out down by the beach. Akon blasting in the background.

Babak wasn't there—he was still sleeping.

Robert and Sergio hadn't wanted to roll to Thailand. They'd gone to other countries.

Tom wasn't there either—dude'd split for Bangkok to gamble. Jorge'd tried to forbid him to go—"You're not gonna be able to keep it together, *huevon*. You're gonna start betting higher and higher. I know you."

Tom just grinned. Claimed he could increase his dough tenfold at the casinos in Bangkok. The fact that Lehtimäki'd been bitten by the gambling bug—an understatement. Over the past few weeks, the dude'd bet on everything. Who got the most hits off a joint. Who could chug a bottle of vino the fastest. Which cockroach would be first to make it to the sugar cube he'd put under the table.

Jorge sat down. Lanterns that were lit at night: suspended from the palm trees. The wicker chairs creaked.

He wasn't hungry. Ordered a fresh-squeezed pineapple juice. Jimmy and Javier were chowing on breakfast. Mahmud claimed he was eating lunch. Jorge suspected he was doing all kinds of bullshit at night—peddling drugs to Brits, Germans, and Swedes who needed to escape their homelands in more ways than one.

Shades on. All the boys were bronzed. You could hardly make out Mahmud's tattoos. The ALBY FOREVER text on his forearm was starting to fade. He ought to touch it up.

Javier'd even gotten a sunburn. Whined that the girls he was getting weren't as fine. *Amigo:* out of control. *Hermano:* a sex addict or something. Going on nonstop about the best strip joints, the best hooker bars, the best go-go dancers. Bragged about the Kama Sutra, double-deckers, six-packs, shockers. Even babbled about *the lady boys*—the Thai version of trannies, they were everywhere. The other guys messed with him—called Javier *ibne*, banana-banger, Vietcong-cock-connoisseur.

Javier didn't seem to give a shit about the names they called him. "I'll do anything and anyone over fourteen. I don't give a shit if they're real chicks or not. They just gotta look good."

Jorge's juice arrived.

"Jorge," Jimmy said. "Listen to this shit."

Jorge put his shades on too. Closed his eyes. Pretended to listen.

Mahmud continued telling the story he was in the middle of: "So I was boozing like a *suedi*. Happy hour on top of happy hour, you know. Then that Russian chick showed up, the one I was hanging with the first few weeks we were here. Remember her?"

The others apparently knew whom he was talking about.

"I was sitting with some German *blattes*, good guys," Mahmud went on, "and she just, like, steps right up to me and goes, 'There you are.' And I'm like, 'Who are you?' And she's like, 'You can't sell like you're doing. This ain't your territory. You've gotta pay.' And I laughed. Like, who the fuck does she think she is, right?"

Jimmy grinned. "Maybe you hadn't been hard enough on her, Big Papa?"

"Shut it, man," Mahmud shot back. "What the fuck should I do? I hardly sold nothing. Just some weed to a few Germans and Brits. And five grams of coke to a guy from Gothenburg I met on the beach. The coke here comes like pieces of chalk—you break 'em up and hack 'em on your own. There can't be a monopoly on that."

Jorge leaned over. "What've I said?"

"I know, I know," Mahmud said. "But it was so little. I didn't think it would bother anyone, honest."

"How much she say you gotta pay?"

"I'm not gonna fucking pay."

Jorge interrupted him. "You're gonna pay. We don't wanna attract unnecessary attention."

"But Babak thought I should just fuck it."

Jorge raised his voice. "Okay, so Babak thought you should just fuck it, ignore whatever the bitch was saying? Smart. Wanksta's real fucking smart. I'm so damn tired of Babak, man. He thinks he's some hotshot just 'cause we used his ride. But he's not the one calling the shots. What else has he fucking done? Huh? If I say you pay, you pay. How much they want?"

"Ten thousand dollars."

"What?" Jorge spilled pineapple juice onto the wicker table's glass top. "They want ten thousand dollars?"

"Yes." Mahmud's voice: worried.

"How much've you been peddling, really?"

"Not much, honest."

Jimmy got involved. "That's not the thing. The thing is they've realized we're not regular tourists. They think we're trying to establish ourselves here since we've stayed so long."

The worry was washing over Jorge in waves. Ten thousand dollars—that was alotta bank. They were probably all thinking the same thing right now: the way the situation could've been.

Jorge saw images projected on the inside of his sunglasses. All the guys together in the living room of the apartment in Hagalund. Dressed in protective gear, plastic gloves, boots, and new ski masks. Dressed to handle a virus attack from hell.

One security bag in the middle of the floor.

Important to get the money out quick. The Finn's advice: get rid of the cash, fast. Stash it in a few safe places: 'cause no matter what happens—they can arrest you, convict you, shut you up for *muchos años* behind bars—but if you've kept the cheese somewhere safe, you've always gained something.

The Finn's guy was holding the ax. An LED was blinking its red light on each bag. Two holes on either side of the LED: you needed two different keys to open these bags.

Or else you did what the Finn's guy was about to do. Jorge was standing beside him. These days he knew more than most about CITs. But there was one thing he didn't know: he had no idea how all this "smart DNA" shit worked. The Finn didn't know too good either. They just knew that the bags might have ampuls in them, filled with something that could spread all over whoever opened them. Something the five-oh could use to find them, impossible to wash off. These particular bags were sprayed with CIT semen that would identify them like a rape kit. That's why the teams looked like HIV researchers right now.

The dude raised the ax.

Everyone stared.

Jorge already felt like he was coming down, even though it was just an hour or so since he'd taken the roofies.

The dude sliced the blade through the air.

A clicking sound. Jorge leaned down. Looked closely. The bag'd cracked near the opening on the short end. Just as they'd calculated. All they had to do was lift the lid.

The other guys leaned in as well. Jorge opened the bag.

Straightened his goggles. Looked down. Four plastic bags. Nothing that sprayed out. No sound. No powder, as far as he could tell. Maybe all the talk about smart DNA was just that, talk.

He opened the bags one by one. Set the booty on the table.

The guy the Finn'd sent was doing the same thing, counting bill by bill.

Mahmud was playing the announcer, using a loud voice. Eighty-one thousand Swedish kronor, cash. Thirty thousand euros. Ten thousand kronor in state-issued coupons. Seventeen thousand worth of scratch-and-wins.

Bad.

It was like some shitty comedy. A nasty cunt-parody.

But maybe there was more in the other bags and sacks.

They repeated the procedure, bag by bag. The Finn's man divided them up. Jorge checked for smart DNA. Jorge and Mahmud counted. The Finn's man recounted.

Three hours later, they'd gone through all the bags plus the sacks. Less than two and a half million kronor, total.

Them: stunned.

Them: tricked by the Postal Service. Maybe by the insider too.

Them: losers without borders.

Them: porked like passed-out virgins.

The only hope for J-boy right now: lottery luck—that there was an unexpected amount of cash in the three bags that he'd hidden away.

The bags that he, Mahmud, and now also Babak had stashed away from the Finn and the others.

32

Hägerström woke up the next morning to his cell phone ringing.

Unlisted number.

He picked up.

"Are you still sleeping?"

It was Inspector Torsfjäll. His voice sounded raspy and hoarse. Almost as if he too had been out partying the night before.

"Don't worry about it. I'm good," Hägerström said.

That was a lie in more ways than one. His entire body ached.

"I'm calling to see what's going on. We haven't spoken in a while."

Actually, they had an agreement stating that Torsfjäll would never be the one to call Hägerström first.

"I've tried to get hold of you," Hägerström said. "We've got to make up our minds. My assignment was formally supposed to end when JW gated out. And he gated out one day ago. So, what do I do now?"

Torsfjäll was silent for a few seconds. Then he said, "What do you think?" Hägerström thought about it. He had gathered good material over the past few months. He had copied the information every time JW asked him to be his errand boy. They had hundreds of bank account numbers, company names, banks, and names of lawyer front men in at least ten different countries. An enormous puzzle for Torsfjäll's economic crimes guy to piece together.

But this was the first time Hägerström was really starting to get close. The gate-out party last night, Nippe, the nighttime walk, what he had done to the guy on Storgatan.

Oh my God.

What had he done?

Hägerström pushed the thought out of his mind, said, "Things have been moving forward recently."

"I do believe you're thinking what I'm thinking. We don't have anything that would hold, so far. But you're well on your way. It's obvious that this little jewel is dealing with some really ugly business."

"But he won't let me in on the details."

"No, but the details we've already got will entertain the economic crimes auditor for a while. And according to my sources, Hansén is moving to Dubai this fall. That goes along with our theory that, as different countries get rid of bank secrecy, JW and Co. are forced to move their assets. And this Nippe guy, I've put a tail on him several times since we saw him have lunch with JW. By the way, did you get anything out of him last night?"

Hägerström wondered how Torsfjäll could know that he had talked to Nippe at the party. Actually, Hägerström hadn't even told Torsfjäll that he was going to JW's gate-out bash. Torsfjäll must have other sources.

"Yes and no," he said. "He was very intoxicated. But he confirmed that he knows JW well, and as he said, he wants to help JW. He didn't say what that so-called help might entail. But he sounded interested when I mentioned potential clients."

"Good."

Hägerström considered telling him about last night's assault. He looked down at his knuckles. Coagulated blood. Scabs in the process of forming. Maybe Torsfjäll already knew about all that.

The inspector said, "Either way, we've been able to deduce that Nippe is JW's Lord Moyne, so to speak. He comes from a good background, he's got safe money backing him up, and tons of connections. He's a good face for any operation. Possibly his dad's bank and currency exchange offices are involved somehow as well. It would be highly interesting, if that were the case. My guys've seen him at different bars and restaurants with at least seven different people, instead of meeting at his regular office. Of those seven people, we've seen five meet up a little later with guys working for Mischa Bladman. It's all connected."

"Yes, evidently."

"But unfortunately, we haven't seen any actual money exchanged. So in terms of hard evidence, this is all still pretty weak. You know, the National Economic Crimes Bureau doesn't exactly have a stellar record when it comes to getting people convicted."

"But it's still a start, isn't it?"

"Yes. And I've been able to get hold of the registration number for a company with the help of the information that you helped JW smuggle out. It's a Swedish company that we believe is controlled by Nippe Creutz. It sold a property in central Stockholm for four million euros two weeks ago. The buyer was a company that's registered in Andorra. That is also included in JW's documentation."

Torsfjäll paused for dramatic effect. Hägerström wondered what was coming next.

"So, my econ-investigator says the property was appraised at double that value two years ago, at over eight million euros. That means that Nippe's company sold an asset at a price seriously under market value. The buyers are probably paying the difference under the table. Nippe's company doesn't have to pay capital gains tax, and the buyers get an asset—paid for in half with dirty money—that they can sell and thereby get clean money in profit. And there you go: JW and Nippe helped someone launder four million euros."

"Aha. Well, that sounds like pretty robust evidence."

"Maybe. But real estate appraisal is not an exact science."

"But you said it's evident that JW planned the deal."

"Yes, but it could be claimed that he helped only with the numbers for the deal. That's not illegal."

Hägerström didn't say anything. He understood that this matter was a very complex crime.

"But even Mischa Bladman meets people on a regular basis," Torsfjäll went on. "The scoundrels he meets are of a shadier ilk than Nippe's contacts. People from the Yugo mafia, the Hells Angels, CIT robbers. They seem to have divided up the customers between them, so to speak."

"Do they use Nippe's company?"

"Maybe. Nippe was named CEO of World Change AB four months ago. The company is owned by his family. They have more than fifty currency-exchange offices all over the Nordic region. Since Nippe took office, the number of invoices from companies registered abroad has increased by eight hundred percent. We've been able to track more account numbers, invoice numbers, and transactions through the documentation that you smuggled out for JW."

"What does it mean?"

"It means that Bladman is having straw men, messengers, runners withdraw large sums in cash from the different offices. That pays for, among other things, illegal workers or laundering stolen money. Then the company covers up the withdrawals on the books by referring to the foreign invoices. But it's highly likely that they're fabricated."

"But I don't understand. Doesn't that mean we have solid proof?"

"As I said, we don't have anything that proves that Nippe or Bladman, specifically, knows anything about this or are directly involved. And we have simply been unable to decrypt a lot of the information that you helped JW smuggle out. There's no point in striking if we're only going to be able to arrest a bunch of half-pissed straw men."

Hägerström was sitting in silence.

"It's all on you," Torsfjäll said. "We have to get access to names of their clients. And we have to get access to their material. They must keep real accounts somewhere. That's the most important thing—without material we can't tie them to this stuff. You barely saw anything in the Hansén home. There might be some at Bladman's place, but I suspect they keep all their documentation somewhere else. The question is if you can get JW to reveal where."

"I'll try. So far he hasn't been too open with me."

"You'll have to keep luring him. Make him feel privileged."

"How do you mean?"

"Bring him along to something he'd like. A party with Princess Madeleine? A moose hunt? What the fuck do I know?"

They ended the conversation.

Hägerström thought for a few seconds. He was wondering what was happening to him. Was he losing his grip on things? As though it wasn't just that he was infiltrating JW's world, but it was infiltrating him as well. Should he bring JW along to a moose hunt? Bring him into his family, into his world for real?

He remembered a scene from *Donnie Brasco*. They were at a Japanese restaurant. Brasco freaked out at the waiter. His mafia friends beat the poor man, Brasco beat him even worse.

Hägerström picked at his scab-covered knuckles.

He closed his eyes. Felt as though it was rumbling outside.

33

Natalie was sitting in the Stockholm University library, trying to study. They'd had their first lectures this week. Legal methodology and theory. She knew that it would all be kind of bullshit in the beginning.

In front of her on the table: the thirtieth edition of Åke Blom's *Foundations of Law*. The lecturer was Mr. Blom himself—he'd referred to his own book as a classic. The old guy made a fortune on the fact that the students were forced to cough up the cash to buy new editions of his book year after year. That was the way the world worked.

Tove was sitting at the table behind Natalie. She was studying economics. Louise was sitting three rows farther up—notebook, law books, Post-it notes, page markers, rulers, calculator, and eighteen million different highlighters in front of her. Natalie's taste was more particular. She used a pencil to underline in her book, that was enough.

They'd found their corner of the library and agreed: this is where we sit; this is where we go to find each other. They were surrounded by similar-looking girls: well dressed, primped. Spiffy like Olivia Palermo, the lot of them. The Stockholm University library was far from dull. Natalie didn't have to read the fashion blogs—all the freshest styles were here. People cared about the way they looked—and the law girls looked the best.

Girls dominated the law school these days. The most dedicated, the most structured, the most grade-oriented. Law school was reading intensive, Louise said. Natalie was expecting to spend a lot of time sitting here over the next few years.

If only she could concentrate.

Her thoughts were churning like an espresso mill. This summer's discoveries—hers, Goran's, and Thomas's investigations. Thoughts about Dad.

After the threatening letter her lawyer'd sent, Natalie'd contacted one of the cops on her own. She hadn't sent a letter or e-mailed—just called. She pressed him like a pro. If he didn't grant her access to the investigative materials, she would submit the recordings. The notice to the parliamentary ombudsman would follow. Internal investigations, the rat squad—gross professional misconduct, sexual harassment. It was easy enough to predict the outcome. To put it simply: either the cop fucker messengered over the investigative material, or else he was finished as a police officer.

It'd been Goran's idea. And it'd worked—two days later, a messenger arrived with the paperwork from the investigation. A new situation: Natalie had five hundred pages of clues to go through.

Stefanovic'd called her four days ago. She didn't know how he knew, but he knew.

"You've gained access to something very important. Something you really shouldn't have. I'm assuming you know that?"

Natalie wasn't planning on playing the blushing little girl. "I believe I should have it. What they're investigating is my father's murder."

"Yes, and we're all mourning him. But this is about other things as well. Business, business contacts. Valuable, unfinished relationships. It wouldn't be good for that kind of thing to get out. You understand that, don't you?"

"Absolutely. And nothing I have will get out."

"Your father was a successful man. He built something in this city. And the state wants to take it from him. They're going through things that they shouldn't be going through. They're digging for stories that should remain buried. As I'm sure you've seen, I did everything I could, in my interrogation with the cops, to keep from giving them unnecessary information. I hope that's the way everyone is acting. It's not easy for you to know what information is important and what is just the pigs' attempt to ruin your father's business. Right?"

Natalie didn't respond.

Stefanovic lowered his voice.

"I want you to give me the investigation material and not try to play around on your own. I want you to leave this investigation alone. You should let the police do their job and let me do mine. Do you understand? I want you to drop your own little attempts to dig around in what happened to Kum."

Natalie refused to take it. She said she didn't have time to talk any longer—ended the call.

Called Goran immediately.

"Stefanovic is fucking crazy."

"He is not your friend."

"No, I knew that. But now he's calling me and asking me totally fucking openly to hand over the investigation material. And he's the one who didn't say shit to the cops in order to help. What should I do?"

Goran growled—he sounded like one of Viktor's cars. "Natalie, you have to choose your own path."

Natalie thought: *He is right.* She had to choose. She had to choose a life for herself.

And now: two more headaches to deal with. Her finances. And the situation at home.

The last few weeks. Stefanovic's predictions'd come true. Opened envelopes. Letters that were spread out over the entire kitchen table—the blue and black logos on the letterheads were ingrained in every Swedish person's consciousness: SEB, Handelsbanken, the tax authorities, the Enforcement Administration. And there was something from American Express and Beogradska Banka too.

Shit.

At first she thought: *Jebi ga*—fuck it. She hadn't had the energy to sit down with the stuff. But now she gathered the letters. Went through them, one by one.

SEB: overdrawn accounts. She thought: that was to be expected, she didn't give a shit about SEB. The Enforcement Administration'd already issued a seizure order for the estate's SEB account anyway.

Handelsbanken: endowment closed, the last securities, sold—nothing left in the account. She knew about that—she'd been the one who'd sold off the final assets in order to get cash.

The tax agency: memos about tax evasion in two different companies that'd belonged to Dad. Either way Natalie didn't give a shit—they'd hired a lawyer for that. He'd have to do his job. Anyway, it would take several years for the tax authorities to reach a decision.

The Enforcement Administration: new attempts at repossessing Dad's cars and his boat. Luckily, they were registered in other people's names. But the lawyer had to fight so the state didn't win.

The situation was unchanged—there was nothing for her to collect in Sweden anymore.

But there was worse news. American Express was informing them that both Natalie and Mom's cards were being revoked. The credit hadn't been paid in over three months.

And the worst was saved for last. A shit-storm. A lethal blow. A serious threat to everything they had and owned. Beogradska Banka: suggested that the property Dad owned in Serbia be sold off in order to cover the debt. It was mortgaged. And the accounts were empty, overdrawn, finito.

Natalie felt the worry in her gut: the house down there was nearly the last thing they had. Except for the cash that Dad'd left behind in the safe at home and in the safe deposit box in Switzerland. Natalie was happy that she and Mom'd emptied the safe before the economic crimes investigators'd paid a visit to their house.

And then she grew irritated: How could the accounts be empty? The last time she'd checked her balance, there'd been good coverage. No wonder American Express was complaining—the credit line was connected to Beogradska Banka. Everything depended on the assets down there—the stuff the Enforcement Administration in Sweden didn't know about.

Again: Who had access to the accounts in Serbia? Why had all the problems arisen after Dad was murdered? Either it was a pure coincidence, or else Dad's finances'd been rocky all along and he'd concealed that fact. Or someone was making this happen right now. And this other person must be someone who was able to control the accounts. Someone who'd had insight into Dad's finances, his tax solutions, his setup.

There weren't too many people to choose from.

There really weren't many.

After going through the letters, Natalie went in to see Mom. She was sitting in the den, as usual. She seemed to need TV more than sleeping pills ever since what'd happened to Dad. *Desperate Houswives*, *Cougar Town*, and movies featuring Hugh Grant played around the clock.

Natalie wanted to talk about their financial situation.

She put her hand on Mom's knee. "Hey, Mom. How are you?"

Mom didn't move a muscle. Her gaze was hazy, unfocused.

"Are you thinking about Dad?"

"No, don't worry about me."

"I think about him all the time."

"I understand."

They sat in silence for a little while. Watching Eva Longoria's fake smile.

Mom turned toward her. Her eyes weren't glazed over anymore. "You have to try to let him go."

"Maybe. But thinking about him gives me strength too."

"I think you're naïve. You only see what you want to see."

Natalie didn't understand what Mom was talking about. "Stop it," she said.

"No. You listen to me now."

Natalie rose, backed out of the den. She really didn't want to deal with Mom's nagging right now.

But it was too late. Mom exploded.

"You don't understand much, do you? You worshipped your father like a god. But do you really think he was a god?"

Natalie stopped in her tracks.

Mom raised her voice. "How do you think it's been for me, huh? Being treated like a damn trophy. Like a baby maker. And then like a nanny. I always had to guess what your dad was really up to. That I wasn't his only woman. Do you know what he did? What kind of a person he was? Huh? Answer me!"

Natalie stared at her. They'd fought many times. When she'd come home four hours past her curfew at night 'cause she'd gone with Louise to some afterparty, when Mom'd found Rizla papers and a Red Line Baggie in her jacket pocket, when she'd smelled vomit in the bathroom. When she'd discovered that she'd spent over ten thousand euros on Dad's card after a weekend in Paris when she was a senior in high school. But all those battles belonged to a far-gone past. During the past few years, she and Mom'd been like girlfriends. Like buddies who spent time together, went for coffee, watched movies, talked about the three Gs: guys, girls, garments. And not even back then, back when they'd been arguing, had Natalie heard anything like this. This was insane. This was scary.

Mom was screaming. A bunch of crap about Dad—what a sleaze he'd been, how he'd laughed at her straight in the face, ignored her. She didn't cry, but it was as though desperation were shooting from her eyes. She was beyond control. She was hysterical.

"I was twenty-one years old when I had you. Do you understand? Would you want to be a mom now, huh?"

Natalie tried to make her stop. "Mom, calm down."

It didn't work.

"You don't want to see who he was. You're naïve. Stupid and naïve. Your father was not a human being," she spit. "He was an animal."

That was enough. Natalie walked out into the hall. Raised her voice and directed it like a missile into the den: "Shut up. Now. If you say one more word about Dad, I'll kick you out of here."

Back at the university. Foundations of civil justice. *Pacta sunt servanda.* Contracts must be adhered to. Alliances must be kept. Honor must not be debased. Families may not be broken up. Bonds of friendship must be strengthened. People who can be expected to be loyal must remain loyal.

Fuck it.

Natalie rose from the table where she was sitting. Louise and Tove remained in their seats—looked after her as she walked toward the bathroom.

Her head was spinning. All the nerdy students around her were sitting with their heads buried in their books. Trying to appear important. What did it matter? Everyone was just playing the game—pretending that they had their lives under control. They were spoiled. They knew zilch about reality. They were princesses who'd never been forced to get their hands dirty.

There was wall-to-wall carpeting in the library. She opened the door to the bathroom. Heard her high heels click against the tiled floor in there.

She sat down on the covered toilet seat. Set her purse down. Hugged herself with her arms. The panic came in waves.

She leaned forward.

Ten minutes later—the floor was glistening with tears. She rose. Felt better. She could handle this. Her studies. Mom's crazy attacks. The grief after Dad.

Stefanovic's betrayal.

She had the investigation material. She was sitting on information. She would find out who'd ended Dad's life—and make sure that whoever was responsible would pay.

She looked at herself in the mirror. You could tell she'd been crying. She picked up her purse.

She was thinking about the summer. It was as though Viktor hadn't been able to handle Natalie's feelings after everything'd happened with Dad. She'd wanted to stay home—he'd wanted to go out for coffee, drink beer, or party. She'd wanted to watch movies or TV—he'd wanted to go to MMA events, celebrity parties, or the gym. They'd never been particularly in sync, but during the weeks after the murder it had grown painfully apparent.

When her thoughts weren't with Dad in the past, they were with Dad's world in the present. She spoke with Goran several times a week. They took frequent walks together: downtown or out by Natalie's home in Näsbypark. They divided up the work between them. They discussed Stefanovic's changed position. Milorad and Patrik's attitudes. Thomas's loyalties. They analyzed information. Bounced ideas back and forth constantly. How they ought to take control over Dad's bookkeeping. How long the money would last.

They had Thomas break into the loft apartment—it'd been cleared out. Someone'd carried out the furniture, broken down bookshelves, removed the Jacuzzi, even taken out the faucets from the shower and the sink. Natalie had to ask the lawyer who actually had the right to sell the place. Formally, a front man owned the place on paper. The lawyer told them, regretfully: the apartment was already sold—a new owner would get access to it soon. Nobody knew what the purchase price'd actually been, and it was impossible to get hold of the front man.

But there were moments of light in all the darkness. Leads. Among other things, the police'd confiscated the film from Dad's surveillance cameras at home. Stefanovic'd installed a bunch of them after the assassination attempt in the parking garage—each camera saved film for over forty-eight hours. Goran asked Thomas to get his hands on the footage.

Again: she had the threatening letter to the cop fuckers to thank.

Thomas analyzed the material. Natalie'd almost expected to see some assassin sneaking around the bushes with a gun in hand. Instead, she saw something else that unnerved her: during the two days in question, a green Volvo had driven past the house several times.

She blamed herself. Remembered first when she saw the films: she'd seen the green Volvo in the parking garage before the assassination attempt. And maybe she'd seen it once outside their house too? She should've been more on her guard, should've warned Dad that something was going on.

Thomas was keeping the men whom Melissa Cherkasova met at hotels under constant surveillance. Natalie'd even sat in her own car outside the Belarusian's apartment a few times. Jotted down when she'd come home and when she'd left, in a notebook. Tried her best to shadow her.

Thomas'd done some more research on the girl. Thank God for his old colleagues on the force. Melissa Cherkasova had permanent residency in Sweden. She'd been married to a fifty-year-old Swedish man for six months—that's how she'd been able to enter the country in the first place. She'd never been convicted of anything, but she'd been prosecuted for fraud four years ago. Thomas ordered the paperwork from the trial—apparently, Cherkasova'd gotten hold of two Swedish men's personal identification number and credit card information and then ordered flights to Belarus and France on their dime. The interesting part: neither of the two plaintiffs'd wanted to report her; the fraud was discovered by the credit card company. When it was time for the trial, they didn't even show up in court—Cherkasova was freed. She was registered not at Råsundavägen 31, where Natalie'd seen her, but at an address in Malmö, in the south of the country, in the home of a woman with a Belarusian name. But she spent so much time at the Stockholm address that it was obvious she was actually living there. Mostly, she stayed at home. Sometimes she traveled to various hotels at night. A few times they saw her go buy groceries. On one occasion she went to a home in Huddinge, and one time Natalie saw her walking with another woman who had a dog. As far as they could see, she never went back to Radovan's apartment on Södermalm again. What's more: they never saw her meet anyone who might be her pimp. And they couldn't find her services advertised anywhere on Internet. Neither Thomas nor his former cop colleagues could find any information in the police databases that suggested that Cherkasova was a prostitute. Maybe she hadn't had anything to do with the murder. Maybe it was a bogeywoman they were chasing.

On the other hand: the men she met were interesting. Thomas saw a total of six different dudes at three different hotels downtown. They always arrived alone. Cherkasova always arrived alone. One was a Brit—they couldn't find out much about him. He worked for a British aircraft manufacturer and lived alone in London. One was the guy from the Sheraton, whose room Cherkasova visited five times during the summer. Two of them were younger Swedish men—three or four times with them. The final two looked Indian or something like that—she met them four times each.

"This isn't some damn book or movie—this is for real," Thomas said. "Do you know what that means? It means that, most of the time, I'm just sitting in my car, on the phone, or in front of a computer. And I hate computers."

Natalie liked Thomas. She thought: *He is a former cop, but he doesn't talk like a cop. He talks like a human being.*

Thomas worked cautiously. Waited outside the hotels. Later at night he followed the men home. They lived all over the city. He got their addresses—everyone except the guy at the Sheraton. He was more careful. Always used some side entrance to leave the hotel. Thomas failed to get hold of him. The younger Swede was named Mattias Persson. He was twenty-nine years old, worked at an IT company, had been living with his eight-years-younger girlfriend for four years. The other Swede lived in Örebro and was single. One of the Indian-looking dudes was named Rabindranat Kadur, was forty-nine years old, a small business owner in the textile industry, married for twenty years to a Swedish woman. The other man wasn't Indian—he was from Iran, and his name was Farzan Habib. He was forty-five years old, worked as a travel agent, and had been divorced for eight years. Thomas couldn't find anything shady about those johns, but he kept on talking about his gut feeling: it was screaming at him that the guy from the Sheraton was interesting somehow. The guy was overly cautious.

At the end of July, Natalie had been close to giving up.

One morning her phone started ringing. A Skype call. Thomas.

Mom was eating breakfast in the kitchen. Natalie walked out into the garden. She never took these calls inside the house.

"Hi, it's me."

His face appeared on the screen. The office behind him: cluttered bookshelves, ugly wallpaper, crappy lighting. He was picking at his teeth while he spoke. If Dad had seen that, he would've ended the call right away—in his view: picking your teeth—only junkies and bums at bars in Belgrade did that, people who didn't understand the importance of brushing your teeth, people who'd never had dental care in their entire lives. For Dad, it was a matter of status: good teeth equaled a good background.

"A breakthrough today," Thomas said. "One of my contacts recognized the Sheraton man. His name's Bengt Svelander, fifty-two years old. He doesn't live in Stockholm."

"Fantastic. Do you know anything else about him?"

"That's the thing. This guy isn't just anybody. He's been a politician for years, is an elected member of Parliament, serves on a bunch of committees and shit."

"Damn."

"This is a guy with power. I'm going to keep my eye on that horndog."

Natalie got up. Studied her face in the mirror of the university bathroom. She'd been in there for twenty minutes. Louise and Tove must be wondering where she'd run off to. She'd finished putting on her makeup. Painted over the signs of sorrow. Her exterior was restored to a dignified level.

She opened the door. Outside: the history section. The surrounding shelves were filled with books about the Roman Empire. The rise and fall of the Kranjic Empire.

No, there would be no fall for her family. She had Goran. She had Thomas.

Natalie walked back to her table in the university library. The girls were still sitting where she'd left them. The exact same books, the same positions, their heads tilted at the same angle. Louise looked up.

"Where've you been?"

"I didn't feel good."

"Oh no. Let me know if there's anything you want to talk about, sweetie."

"I'm fine, thanks."

"Let's get a coffee. These criminal cases are starting to make my scalp crawl. Like, ruining my new highlights. Do you like them, by the way?"

They walked down toward Trean, a café situated in the third of the several university high-rises. The stairwell in the middle of the library: runway show for the poor philosophy students, linguists, and history of ideas scholars who would never be able to land chicks like Natalie, Tove, and Louise. Natalie felt her phone vibrate in her pocket. Skype.

She excused herself. Walked off a few yards. Saw how Tove and Louise looked at her funny. She tucked the earbuds into place. Saw Thomas's face. She whispered when she picked up.

"It's me," he said.

"I can see that."

"Another breakthrough. A *real* breakthrough."

Natalie held her breath. Three weeks'd passed since he'd identified the politician john. This call felt like it had something similar in store.

"I had someone tail Svelander. Followed his car into the city. No hotel meeting or anything. He went to Gondolen, you know—the luxury restaurant by Slussen. Does that ring any bells?"

Naturally, Natalie was familiar with the restaurant. She'd been there with Dad and Mom several times.

"I've been there."

"I suspected as much. 'Cause your Dad liked to bring people there. So anyway, this politician went into a private room. I couldn't see who was there to eat with him. But I saw a dear old friend leave the restaurant a few minutes after Svelander left."

"Who?" Natalie got a déjà-vu feeling. The same feeling as three weeks ago, when Thomas'd been tailing the john.

"Stefan Rudjman. Stefanovic."

"Oh, fuck."

"And the other interesting part is that twenty minutes later, I saw Stefanovic hand an envelope to someone named Johan 'JW' Westlund. Do you know who that is?"

"No."

"Ask anyone, they'll tell you he's not a reputable type. He just got out of prison, was convicted for gross narcotics crimes. But if you ask Goran, he'll be able to tell you a whole lot more about JW. He's well known as a money launderer, adviser, and investment specialist in the shady-to-pitch-black section of the economic spectrum. He works with Mischa Bladman, who has MB Accounting Consultant. Do you understand?"

"Yes."

"They're the ones who helped your Dad with, among other things, the holding company and the account in Switzerland."

Natalie didn't have coffee with the girls. She left the building instead.

Breathed in the sweet September air. Students were coming and going around her. She was standing still.

It felt like a wave was crashing through her body. Goran'd told her that she had to choose her own path—and what she was facing now was a turning point. She could continue studying law, hanging out with the girls, mourning Dad, and poking around a little in what had happened to him. Pretend that life was the same as it used to be.

Or she could do something important. Begin to act on her own. Transform the sorrow.

She felt the blood running through her veins, her heart pumping. She felt her overheated brain begin to be cooled by the air. She was strong—she was her father's daughter. She could do more, had more power than to just continue in the tracks reserved for ordinary people. Dad'd staked out a different path. Now it was her turn to walk it.

Take control. Take power.

* * *

SWEDISH ARMED FORCES

SWEDEC Designation:
Swedish EOD and Demining Center
383883:2011

Administrator/Client
Forensic Technician Lennart Dalgren
Stockholm Technical Squad
Preliminary Investigation
K-2930-2011-231

Identifying a Hand Grenade

BACKGROUND
SWEDEC has been asked to identify an object. The inquiry comes from the police force in Stockholm and is in regard to a hand grenade as well as other explosive devices that were used on Skeppargatan in Stockholm. The police have sent images and shrapnel fragments for identification. The Swedish Armed Forces

are responding with excerpts from EOD DC's database in regard to construction and function.

IDENTIFYING THE AMMUNITION OBJECT
The ammunition object has been identified as:
Type of ammunition: Fragmentation hand grenade
Classification: M52 P3
Country of origin: Former Yugoslavia

OTHER FRAGMENTS FROM EXPLOSIVE MATERIALS HAVE BEEN IDENTIFIED AS:

Type of explosive: malleable explosives, so-called plastic (putty) explosives.
Type: Semtex
Manufacturer: Semtin Glassworks
Country of origin: Czechoslovakia

ASSESSMENT
The attached images and fragments indicate clearly that the weapon in question is a hand grenade, model M52 P3, from the former Yugoslavia. It is probable that 1,000 grams of so called plastic explosives of the type labeled Semtex have been placed around the grenade.

DESCRIPTION OF THE CONSTRUCTION

M52 P3
M52 P3 is a hand grenade made to stop an attacker, to render the attacker unfit for battle, or to kill him. It does not have any function outside a military context. The grenade model in question is small and handy: 56mm in diameter, 105mm long, and weighs around 0.5 kilos. The grenade body is filled with TNT (100g).

The grenade has controlled fragmentation. It is smooth on the outside but has a grooved internal fragmentation surface. When the grenade is detonated, the parts are dislodged. It can rupture into both large and small fragments. The filler weight is 2.5 grams. There are 150 fragments, and they have a speed of 8,700 miles per second. If the hand grenade detonates on the ground and no object serves as a shield, there is a significant risk of fatal injury.

Semtex
Semtex is a type of plastic explosive that is composed of hydrogen and PETN. It is a doughlike mass that can be applied and

shaped according to the user's needs. Plastic explosives have a function beyond military life, for instance for use during explosions in larger construction projects. Semtex, manufactured by Semtin Glassworks, is delivered as a cartridge in a paper casing. The plastic explosive has a detonation speed of 4,800 miles per second and a density of 1.5 kg/dm3.

A detonator that has been secured on a fuse is commonly used to detonate the plastic explosive. The plastic explosive is difficult to start, which normally provides a high level of safety. However, in the event of a release of force—such as when a hand grenade explodes—the plastic explosive is ignited and detonates immediately.

PROCEEDINGS AT THE EVENT IN QUESTION

The most likely sequence of events is that the perpetrator replaced the pin in the hand grenade with a piece of wire that had been inserted under the catch. Then the perpetrator applied the plastic explosive under and on top of the grenade and placed it in front of the car's right front wheel, where the wire was placed so that it jutted out diagonally against the wheel. This was done very quickly. Most probably the perpetrator needed to pass the car and bend down in order to place the grenade with the applied plastic explosive in place. When the car was started and rolled forward, the tire pressed the wire aside, and after two seconds, the grenade and the plastic explosive were detonated. The explosion happened in a spot on the underside of the back of the car, since the car was able to roll about six feet prior to the detonation.

An alternative course of events is that the perpetrator rolled in or threw the grenade with the plastic explosive under the car from a few yards' distance. However, this scenario would have put the perpetrator in grave personal danger at the time of the attack. It also does not explain the traces of wire that have been found farther off at the scene of the crime.

A grenade of this kind and make without applied plastic explosives would, with great probability, have had difficulty breaking through the car's undercarriage with such force that a driver or a passenger sustained fatal injuries. Therefore the use of plastic explosives points to a perpetrator with solid knowledge of explosives, their power, and their directive explosive force.

34

Colorful lanterns were dangling from the trees. An Usher song swayed in the background.

Tom was back from Bangkok's casinos. It'd gone to hell, of course—after ten days he was dry-cleaned and folded, more in the red than a Muslim in flight school post 9/11. Had to take the minibus back to Pattaya—Jorge had to book the bus *and* pay for it.

Still, Jorge dug that Tom'd returned. Lehtimäki was the only one who wasn't sulking.

"I met a dude who's gonna teach me to cheat with dice. It's a big business down there. Dice, I mean," Tom said, and pretended to throw a set of dice onto the table.

Jorge laughed. "Lehtimäki, you're *loco,* man. You never give up."

"I'll give you four to one that I'll make it big on this dice thing," Tom said.

"I'll give you eight to one that you're gonna get ripped off," Jorge shot back.

Babak—awake for once—interjected, "Ey Jorge, you seem to know a lot about ripping people off."

Silence around the table. At that precise moment there was no music blaring from the speakers in the joint. Just the sound of the waves as they crashed against the beach. Washed up like the shitty mood.

Jorge knew: the same images in everyone's heads. The chopped-up security bags on the floor of the apartment. Next to them, in piles: less than a skimpy two and half million. After they divided it up: they were gonna feel flat broke. And still they didn't understand the full meaning of what Babak was alluding to when he said "ripping people off."

There'd been trouble back there in the apartment. Javier had complained. Robert just sat down, his hands in front of his face. Jimmy whined. Babak freaked for real: started messing with Mahmud. Demanded a bigger cut. The risk he'd taken. How they never would've been able to do it without the Range Rover.

The only one who didn't say anything was the Finn's guy. He just gathered up the Finn's cut. Shoved the bills into two duffels. Maybe he realized that no one, not even the insider, could've known how many bags or how much money there would be. That the only thing left to do was lick your wounds and prepare the next hit.

After the dude left: the fighting started up for real. Close to Chernobyl. Babak really went apeshit. Shoved Mahmud and Jorge. Tom and Robert had to restrain him. Everyone was pissed. Everyone was screaming. Everyone was complaining about their share.

Jorge kept his cool—sooo scared that Babak would say something about the bags he'd ferreted away.

It didn't help that Jorge promised to pay for their flights abroad. That he said he would have a talk with the Finn about it. Finally: Jorge cut back on his own share—gave each person thirty large extra.

And now here in Thailand: Babak was bitching again. Punches'd hung in the air at least ten times since they'd arrived in Pattaya. But still: Jorge didn't want to rumble with Babak.

"You gonna answer, or what?" Babak went on. "Who really ripped who off around here, huh? I took the biggest fucking risk of everybody, right? We used my car."

"We fucking had to—the wheel loader'd been towed by whoever owned it!"

"Yeah, I know they found it, but I'm the only one who's wanted for this, right?"

Babak suddenly fell silent.

Jorge looked up. Realized immediately: something was outa whack.

Two dudes were standing by their table. One Thai guy and one who looked Eastern European.

They said something to Mahmud in shitty English. Jorge did a rapid read: these were the people who were complaining that his buddy'd sold weed.

The Eastern guy took a step forward. "You gotta pay—you broke rules here. Try to take from our market."

Mahmud, in even shittier English: "What you talkin' about? I not done nothing like that."

The Thai dude positioned himself next to the Eastern dude, who leaned down over the table. "You gotta pay. That's it. We know you moved in here. And I don't give a fuck what you say. Tomorrow, latest, twelve o'clock. We come to your hotel."

Mahmud tried to protest again.

The dudes were already walking away from the table.

Mahmud got up. Followed them. The Arab: not a boy people could just walk over.

Five yards from the table. He overtook them. The Eastern guy turned around.

"Who the fuck do you think you are?" Mahmud said.

Jorge looked around. Saw the waitresses standing still over by the bar. Their dark eyes: wide. He followed their gazes. Farther off, by the entrance to the place: five Thai guys. Their style spoke for itself. Not big, no particular colors or clothes. Still, he clocked right away—knew enough about Thailand to see the small scars in their faces, the tattoos on their hands, the boots on their feet.

Jorge rose. Walked after Mahmud. Grabbed his shoulder. Held him back.

Said, "Okay, okay. My friend's gonna pay. Don't worry. Tomorrow at twelve, at the latest. You got my word."

Mahmud tried to say something in Swedish. Jorge, his voice sharp: "No, later."

The Russian or whatever he was seemed satisfied. They walked away.

Slow steps. Obvious control. Sending deliberate signals.

Tomorrow, at noon.

Later that night: Jorge was walking on the beach, along the water's edge. The other guys'd gone somewhere else. To their favorite strip joints, gambling dens, girls of the week.

He didn't understand what was happening. His brain checked out when he was with the others. He needed to be alone in order to think. Work things out. Make up his mind. What the fuck was he gonna do?

He read Swedish newspapers online every day. There had been big headlines at home in the days immediately following the hit. A NEW HELICOPTER ROBBERY. ROBBERS TRICK THE POLICE ONCE AGAIN. GUARD INJURED AFTER ROBBERY.

He thought it would calm down. The booty was small, after all. The media should catch on: there was nothing sexy about pocket money.

But then: GUARD IN CRITICAL CONDITION. RUTHLESSS ROBBERS. GUARD LOSES HIS EYESIGHT AND WILL BECOME WHEELCHAIR BOUND. FAMILY AND NATION IN SHOCK.

It was twisted. The fucking guard who'd been standing closest to the explosion: seriously wounded. Almost died.

Now: in a whole other league. Aggravated assault. Aggravated robbery, definitely. Attempted murder?

Joder—they never should've bothered with that vault. They'd been too rushed because of the fiasco with the wheel loader. Maybe the Finn'd received the blueprints with too little time to spare, hadn't had time to really check what explosive charge would work. Fucking Finn.

Idiots.

What's more, Babak was wanted and arrested in absentia—that's what the papers said, even if they didn't mention him by name. And in the latest article Jorge'd read, the cops hinted at what they were up to.

* * *

Today police confirmed that the technical analysis of one of the suspected getaway vehicles has yielded some results. The getaway car, a Range Rover, was also used to force open the gate at Tomteboda's postal terminal. The car, which was found aflame in a wooden area in Helenelund, outside central Stockholm, has long been the police's hottest lead.

Even though the Range Rover had been completely burned out, police technicians were able to secure certain traces from the backseat, which have now been subjected to analysis. The traces show DNA from persons with connections to the suspected perpetrator who has been arrested in absentia.

The police's press officer, Björn Gyllinge, made the following statement about the discoveries:

"This confirms our theory that something must have gone wrong. Why else would the robbers have used a car that had obvious links to them? It also illustrates how far the new DNA techniques have been developed. What we've used is called LCN analysis and is very advanced."

In LCN (Low Copy Number) DNA technique, samples with extremely small DNA traces are analyzed.

"We are able to use the technique on as few as ten cells,"

Jan Petterson, the laboratory manager at the national forensic lab, told *Aftonbladet*.

"All it takes is for someone to put a palm against a window, and we will be able to trace the DNA in the grease from the hand. It's almost like science fiction. But I want to add that we also have other evidence that ties the suspect to the robbery. We can't go into further detail at this time, as doing so could interfere with the investigation."

* * *

That familiar criminal anxiety.

Didn't help that Jorge was popping Valium, Atarax, benzo, and all kinds of Thai shit he got his hands on.

The criminal anxiety crawled all around him like a cockroach.

He remembered that the Thai customs authority'd photographed everyone who entered the country by the passport control area. He woke up with cold sweats over the fact that they'd been forced to shoot those nasty dogs by the helicopter base—the cops would try to trace the ammo. He nightmared about hand sweat that dripped DNA traces everywhere.

Jorge lost his appetite. Ran to the can seven, eight times a day. Lost weight like a needle junkie.

The criminal anxiety was fucking taking over.

And now: the Russian mafia with their Thai backup boys wanted to squeeze bills out of Mahmud.

Pattaya—he hated the place.

He walked past a beach party. Continued farther along the shore.

A soft breeze in his face. Chilled his nerves.

He knew what they had to do. What they should've done a long time ago.

They had to split tomorrow.

He would've preferred to wait a few days. But now it was too late.

He thought about Krabi, Koh Phi Phi, maybe Koh Lanta or Phuket.

Him and Mahmud knew the café business. They should be able to run some little joint down there. Become King Jorge Bhumibol instead of Bernadotte?

He turned up onto the boardwalk. Wanted to finish thinking over a glass of something.

A spot farther up. A blue sign: Poppy's Bar. Didn't look like a hooker joint. Neither Thai nor Russian girls in there.

A barstool at the bar. He sat down. Ordered a cup of tea. The bartender looked at him like he was a fag.

Next to him were a couple of backpacker chicks who must've ended up in the wrong place—Pattaya wasn't their scene. One had dreadlocks and a T-shirt with text across the chest: LISBETH SALANDER FOR PRESIDENT. Maybe she was Swedish.

He thought about his buddy JW. The jet set wannabe from the north. The guy Jorge'd gotten to know when they dealt coke together five years ago. A good friend. He knew he'd gated out a few days ago.

If he and Mahmud wanted to buy a place, they were gonna need help. Normally Tom Lehtimäki would've been perfect. But not right now: dude was in shitty shape—addicted to the rush of gambling like a teenager from Malmvägen craved sucking bong. Lehtimäki couldn't be trusted these days.

And the others? Javier just wanted to go out chasing chicks, with or without dicks. Jimmy was too stupid and was missing his old lady in Sweden too much. Babak was the devil in a pair of flip-flops. Jorge would've crushed the Iranian a long time ago—if he hadn't been sitting on the secret about how J-boy'd ripped off the Finn.

He needed someone else.

He called over the bartender. Asked for the phone number to Poppy's Bar.

He walked over to the backpacker chicks. Jorge tapped the one with the dreadlocks on the shoulder.

"Excuse me, can I ask you a favor?"

The girl replied in good English. But not good enough.

"Are you Swedish?" he asked.

The chick looked him over. The same reaction he always got down here—the Svens didn't think you could be on vacation just cause you were a *blatte*.

Jorge said, "I need to send a text to a friend in Sweden, but my phone's dead. You got a cell phone?"

The chick laughed. "Doesn't everyone these days?"

"Listen, it's an emergency. I'll pay you."

The chick smiled again. She had nice eyes: hazel, maybe. Hard to say in the blue-red-green lighting in Poppy's Bar.

She agreed. Her phone was a cheap make. It didn't matter.

Jorge fired off a text to the number he had for JW: *Yo man, it's your main Latino. Call 0066-384231433 if you've got a minute.*

It was afternoon in Sweden now.

Next morning. Early. It was only ten-thirty. Mahmud oughta be awake—after all, the Arab went to bed before midnight the night before. Jorge'd already packed his stuff.

He walked past the pool.

Mahmud's bungalow was 150 feet from his. He knocked on the door.

Mahmud's tired voice from inside: "Who is it?"

"It's me. Open up."

It took over five minutes for him to open the door. Boxers and a wife beater. Same paintings in the ceiling as in Jorge's bungalow. The room behind him was a royal mess. Shit, this could take some time.

"Man, we gotta go. Today, before noon."

"But fuck man, you said we were gonna pay those ching chong motherfuckers."

"No fucking way. We're going. I was thinking Krabi or Phuket. I've got ideas in the works, *amigo*."

Forty minutes later: Jorge'd helped Mahmud pack. The dude seemed to collect tanning oils, bootleg DVDs, and snort straws. But Jorge wanted to bring or toss everything. Not leave any unnecessary traces.

Mahmud didn't want to ditch the other guys. Jorge tried to talk him into it. Made promises. Assurances.

Guaranteed: "It's good for us to be apart for a while. There's just a bunch of bullshit with Babak all the time. Once we've established ourselves somewhere, they can join us."

They brought their suitcases over to the reception in the hotel next door. Ordered a minibus going south. It would depart in two hours. Then they walked back to Queen Hotel to check out.

It was eleven forty-five.

"Man," Mahmud said. "I'm gonna miss the pussies in the ceiling."

They were walking over to their Vespas. They had to be returned and paid for. Again: Jorge didn't want trouble.

He hopped onto his Vespa, started the engine.

Mahmud followed suit.

They drove out onto the main drag.

Ocean on their left. Clear air. Jorge thought: *Mahmud's probably not been up this early since we got here.*

Dust rose around the Vespas.

At that moment: the screaming of tires.

People yelling all around.

A large pickup, Toyota HiLux, driving too fast.

Straight toward Mahmud.

Mahmud tried to swerve. Drove up onto the sidewalk.

The Toyota was right behind him.

People were throwing themselves out of the way.

Jorge didn't know what to do.

He sped up, tried to stay close. Follow them.

The car nudged the back of Mahmud's Vespa.

The Vespa wobbled. Jorge yelled at him to try to drive down onto the beach.

The Vespa wobbled again.

People were running in every direction.

The engine in the enormous Toyota revved louder.

Hit him again. Pounded into the Vespa with full force.

Jorge saw Mahmud: frame by frame.

His buddy flew like a beach ball through the air.

A high arch.

The ocean in the background.

Mahmud hit the ground twenty feet farther away.

Everything died.

35

Hägerström was in his car, waiting for JW. He had been sitting here for an hour.

It wasn't the first time. JW had called him several times since the assault after the gate-out party and asked if he could chauffeur him around the city.

JW's driver's license had been revoked when he was convicted of possession and intent. And there were no opportunities to get a new license in the pen. That's how it always was for those just released back out into the wild: not only did they need to readjust to society after years of institutionalization, they were also homeless, had heavy fines to pay with the Enforcement Administration, and had no driver's license. What's more, they might not have had the best contact with honest friends and family during their prison years. Add on difficulties finding a job. More and more employers in Sweden were demanding to see an applicant's criminal record. They weren't exactly starting over from square one. They were starting at a major disadvantage.

JW swore that he would have a new driver's license within three months. But until then, there was one problem. He refused to take the subway. "It doesn't suit someone like me," he said when Hägerström suggested he buy a subway pass. Hägerström was familiar with the reasoning. His father hadn't ridden the subway in Stockholm a single time during his entire life. The pleb-way wasn't for him, as he liked to say.

So that's why Hägerström was driving JW around when he needed to get somewhere. Often to MB Accounting Consultant's office, to the gym, to different restaurants. Sometimes JW asked him to wait and sometimes just to sit outside his building and make sure no uninvited guests attempted to pay him a visit. Afterward JW slipped him one or several five-hundred-kronor bills.

It was a continuation of their relationship. A continuation of the infiltration.

And Hägerström had a clear goal: gather hard evidence proving what JW was up to.

He was bored sitting there in the car. Let his thoughts wander. Reminisced. Flipped through the pages of his own history.

He had enrolled in the Police Academy when he was twenty-one years old.

It was a strange time. *Über*-manly tests, homo jokes in the locker rooms, colleagues that he developed close bonds with. He was doing what he had always dreamed of doing: he was becoming a police officer. Meanwhile another secret dream was fulfilled.

After the summer party at the end of the first semester of school, he had boarded the night bus home. He was so drunk that he could hardly fish money out of his pocket to pay his fare. Normally he took a cab, but for some reason he wanted to take the bus tonight. It was four-thirty in the morning. The night bus was almost empty. Sitting in the very front were three giggly girls with wine stains on their white graduation dresses. That was all.

He found a seat farther back. Almost fell asleep. The girls got off at the next stop, and a guy got on. Hägerström was the only person left on the bus. More than forty empty seats, and yet the guy sat down next to him. It was a provocation. Or—Hägerström could usually tell by looking at guys if they were thinking the same thing he was—an invitation.

The guy crossed one leg over the other. He was wearing a parka and white jeans. Hägerström leaned against the window. Pretended to sleep. His body was tense all over. He almost felt sober.

It felt as though the guy were pressing his leg against his.

He hadn't been able to check the guy out before he sat down, but this just had to be something.

Did he dare do what he wanted to do?

The guy's leg against his leg. He was sweating.

Hägerström let his hand slip down, sort of fall, until it was next to his leg.

Brushed by the guy's hand.

Their fingertips met. They gripped each other's hands.

The guy leaned over and kissed Hägerström.

It was the first time his lips had touched another man's mouth.

Two stops later they got off. Home to Hägerström's house.

When he woke up the next day, the guy was gone. Hägerström never learned his name. But he never forgot that kiss on the bus.

He saw JW in the side mirror. He sort of kicked with his legs when he walked. The guy loved Hägerström's Jaguar. Hägerström noted that two other men also walked out of Riche, the restaurant where JW had been lunching. He made a mental note of their appearance.

JW sat down in the passenger seat.

Said, "Would you drive me to Bladman's office?"

Hägerström started the engine. "Of course."

He drove Hamngatan west, past Norrmalmstorg. Large banks and law firms all around. It ought to be time to strike now, he thought. Search Mischa Bladman's offices and JW's home. But Torsfjäll wanted to wait. He was certain: "They've got some other place where they keep the paperwork—they'd be idiots otherwise. You have to find out where. We need more evidence. You have to figure out where they keep the documents."

But so far Hägerström had never dropped JW off at any such place.

JW looked calm.

He opened his mouth. "Hägerström, you know a lot of people with money. Do you know the easiest way to launder money?"

Hägerström's ears pricked up. This was interesting.

"No."

"Go to the track or to the casino. You ask for someone who's just won. Everyone who wins gets a receipt, a voucher. Most of the time, you pay a hundred ten or a hundred twenty percent of the voucher's value. Big Brother is real sweet, handing out receipts for wins. If you run into problems with the cops or the tax man, you just show them the voucher. It shows where you got the money from."

"Smart. Do you know anyone who's done that for real?"

"I might, but that was mostly back in the day. I think it's better to play in a different league. Considering how much the state steals from people, it's more than right that the citizens strike back. Right?"

"I agree with you."

"At the races and the casino, you can only work with pocket money, really. So it's better to use other simple solutions, in case someone might be interested in that."

"Like what?"

"You make sure you put your money in different accounts, broken up in small enough parts that the banks' alert systems don't signal foul play. Then you transfer the money to a company with a foreign account in a country with bank secrecy. Then you let the foreign company loan money to yourself in Sweden. It's perfect. On paper, you don't have any income—you just have borrowed money, after all. And the best part is that you can deduct the interest you pay to your own foreign company from taxes. Pretty sweet, right?"

"Smart. So do you know someone who's done *that* in real life?"

"I might. But I wouldn't recommend all the mess of having lots of different accounts and making small deposits."

"So what would you do?"

"You've got to have connections in the bank and currency-exchange world. Get it? Connections."

Hägerström thought: maybe it was all happening. Maybe JW was going to start opening up for real.

"Yes, connections are everything," Hägerström said. "If you want, I'd be happy to introduce you to some people sometime."

"That'd be wonderful."

"But I'm curious—where did you learn this stuff?"

"I don't know about 'learned.' You know, I had some savings when I was doing time. I've worked with my own money. I started on a small scale. I didn't want to end up in trouble on the inside, like with that nigger who jumped me in Salberga—you remember. So when a dude asked me if I could help him with something, I said yes, in exchange for his protection. He had a few hundred thousand. And I never ask where it comes from. I think it's every individual's responsibility what they do with their money."

Hägerström nodded.

"The guy wanted his girlfriend and kid to be able to buy an apartment. That's easy enough to understand, he just wanted to help them out. But you can't quite buy real estate with cash—that's when people start asking questions. So we used the method I just told you about. I talked to a buddy who'd just gated out, asked him to go with the girlfriend, help her open bank accounts with four different banks. Those accounts were tied to the same account that was already controlled on the Isle of Man. She did the rest herself. She deposited four hundred thousand kronor per account over a few months, but never deposits larger than twenty grand a pop. After four months, the whole kitty was safely in the account on the Isle of Man, and she could buy herself a small one-bedroom in Sundbyberg."

Hägerström clapped his hands quietly.

"But that kind of thing would be even easier to do today," JW said. "Like I said: it's all about having the right connections. The currency-exchange offices are the best things God ever created."

"Bravo." He hoped JW would keep talking.

JW grinned. "You don't need to know more details than that. But tell your acquaintances that no one knows this like I do. And what's even more important: I've got all the right connections."

36

The attacks on Natalie's finances—the estate's finances. She had to understand how all the assets in Serbia'd been dissolved. She had to deal with the issue of cash assets in Switzerland. The solution was Mischa Bladman, or his crony, JW. They were the ones who'd set up Dad's financial system abroad.

On top of that was the fact that Thomas'd seen Stefanovic meet that JW guy right after he'd met with Svelander the john—JW was involved in some other way too. She wanted to know more. She had to meet JW.

Natalie spoke with Bladman—he was tight-lipped. "I know JW, we work together off and on. I can't say more about him than that. He doesn't have anything to do with this."

Natalie knew he was lying, but she also couldn't put too much pressure on Bladman—he was sitting on critical information.

Goran told her, "JW—he's Sweden's Bernie Madoff."

"Do you think he's on Stefanovic's side?" Natalie asked.

"I don't know. That guy's an independent contractor."

She asked him to get hold of JW. Goran promised to pull some strings.

He called back a few days later. "I've talked to that guy now. Or rather, I sent one of my guys. Explained to JW that we won't accept that any schemes or businesses that were begun by Kum are finished by anyone but us. But he wasn't too receptive. I think you have to speak to him personally."

A few days later, they met at a restaurant near the Royal Dramatic Theater, Teatergrillen.

She dug his choice of venue. Teatergrillen: international feel. Global class. Luxury packaging in a sweet way.

Drama details everywhere: abstract paintings, harlequins, masquerade masks with long noses, drapes that had that stage curtain feel to them. Round booths in half circles around the tables. Light-colored stone walls. Wall lamps shaped like drama masks, red wall-to-wall carpeting, red painted ceiling, red armchairs—like, everything was red. Except the tablecloths were white. A feeling of privacy—in just the right way. There were shielding walls like dividers behind the seats. You could see other diners in the restaurant, but they couldn't hear everything you said.

JW was sitting in the booth, waiting for her. He rose.

Shook her hand. Looked her in the eyes, deeply. She smiled. He didn't smile.

He was wearing pressed dark-gray-flannel pants, a double-breasted jacket, and a pale blue shirt with blue cufflinks that had gold crowns on them. His hair was slicked back, as though he'd just come out of the shower.

They sat down. JW ordered a martini. Natalie, a Bellini.

They looked over the wine list.

They talked shared acquaintances: Jet Set Carl and Hermine Creutz. They discussed nightclubs in Stockholm: the new bar at Sturecompagniet, the new upstairs at Clara's. They ticked off the party weeks at the top vacation destinations: Saint-Tropez and Båstad.

JW sounded like a major slickster—Natalie knew the guy'd just been released from prison after five years. Like, how posh was that?

JW ordered a bottle of wine that cost seven thousand kronor.

The food arrived. They started eating.

Natalie was surprised that the mood was so light, convivial. Goran's dude'd been a bit hard on JW, after all. She eyed him again. The guy: an actor. He played the archetype of a Stureplan brat. A Jet Set Carl copy. A climber made from concentrate. Still, there was something more to him, behind all that. JW's eyes were intelligent, gleaming.

Natalie inched closer to him on the seat. Their bodies were almost touching.

She speared a piece of fish on her fork but changed her mind and let it remain on her plate. "I want to discuss business with you, JW."

He took a sip of wine.

"I know you worked for Dad before you disappeared for a few years," Natalie went on. "I also know that you weren't always on his good side.

You made your mistake. But he let it slide, so you were able to help him with some of his finances. My dad understood people. He thought: you wouldn't rip us off one more time. No one does that."

The flame of the wax candle flickered gently.

She could tell by his eyes that he knew what she was talking about. Goran'd told her how JW'd become a kingpin in Dad's dealer stable. But at the very end, he'd tried to pull a fast one—rigged a deal with some other guys. Things went to hell, and the cops arrested both JW and the other guys. All of them got locked away for years.

"Take it easy," JW said. "That was a long time ago. But there's a lot of talk going around now, you know. About Stefanovic, Goran. You. I helped your father. But now I want the cards on the table. What is it you want?"

Natalie raised her fork with the fish once again. Popped it into her mouth. She finished chewing before she spoke.

"It's simple. I'm the one who's controlling all the businesses my dad started. That goes for all his business partners too."

JW's hands were completely still on the table. The cufflinks gleamed. Natalie noticed his nails. Real Swedish fingernails: unnecessarily short, unfiled, unpolished. *Dad's fingers never would've looked like that.*

JW leaned over. "You have to understand that I'm not like any other basement consultant. Normally when people want advice, they go see a more-or-less willing lawyer or accountant. Best-case scenario, they pretend they don't really know what it's all about. They're trained to be blue-eyed, and then they construct some system that's supposed to work. But things are different with me. My clients can speak openly with me, and my arrangements are designed with the specific intent of fulfilling my clients' wishes."

"But didn't you understand what I just said? All business coming from my dad will be controlled by me. Not by anyone else. That includes Stefanovic."

He understood—that much was obvious. But he explained that he didn't exactly know what Stefanovic did. Just that he made sure money was moved back and forth in the correct way. He refused to name people or banks. But Natalie already knew the main player: that horndog politician Bengt Svelander. Still, JW was open enough for Natalie to get something out of the conversation—he didn't deny his dealings with Stefanovic. The guy was a pro.

"You must also understand that I don't want any problems," JW said. "If I let you take this over, what do I tell your father's former crony? That's not how things work. The wheels have been set in motion, things are rolling along nicely right now. The current machinery works."

Natalie turned her head. Looked JW straight in the face. Didn't he understand? His head, that was what would be rolling if he didn't do what she told him to do.

The next day. Natalie was sitting in her Golf. Heading south. She was driving—kind of a bizarre feeling: next to her, folded over in order to fit, was Goran. When she picked him up near Gullmarsplan, he'd insisted. "You drive. It's your car, boss."

The same clothes as always: tracksuit and sneakers. But today he'd rolled up his sleeves. His beefy forearms revealed him for who he was: pale green ink—the double eagle and the Serbian Republic of Krajina's coat of arms. Natalie loved those arms—they'd held her that time down in the parking garage under the Globe Arena. When Dad'd been shot.

They turned off toward Huddinge. No traffic. Middle of the day, pre–rush hour. The person they were meeting should be home at this time. The person they were meeting should know certain important things.

The Golf was nice to drive. Not like one of Viktor's massive showroom vehicles that she borrowed sometimes, where a toe-flirt on the gas pedal made the motor erupt like an Icelandic volcano. Still, the Golf was powerful. Spirited, somehow.

Goran and she were silent. Natalie was focusing on finding the way. The GPS signaled a crossroads.

"Natalie, you're a good driver," Goran said.

"Thanks. You know who was my driving teacher?"

"I know. Him. *Izdanjik*."

"Yes, him. The traitor."

"Your dad was also a good driver."

"Maybe that is why he had way too many cars."

Goran grinned. Natalie cracked a smile. It was the first time she'd joked about Dad since his murder.

They were quiet for a few minutes.

Then Goran said, "You've got a sense of humor. Just like your dad.

And you understand people. Also just like your dad. I remember when he was going to hire me for his security guard company. Do you know what he did?"

"No."

"He set out a packet of cigarettes and a jar of dip on the table in front of me without saying why. The interview began. I held my hands in my lap throughout the entire interview. Because I knew his trick, I already knew him from before. The ones who spun the snuffbox or the packet of cigarettes never got the job. Your dad tested people that way."

"Why?"

"In the bars in Belgrade they sit all day, drinking, and smoking and spinning their packets of cigarettes. Unemployed, unwilling to work, lazy good-for-nothings. Your father didn't want to hire men like that. He wanted to surround himself with active people."

Natalie turned to him. "Goran, I'm glad I have you. I don't know where I'd be if it weren't for you. You can spin as many snuffboxes as you want with me."

Finally: the residential area. Small, flat homes. On average, about half the size of the houses at home in Näsbypark. This: *southern* Stockholm—the mere fact that there were suburbs out here was contrary to logic, somehow. She'd thought these territories contained only massive housing projects.

They drove along one of the streets with one-family homes. Parked: Volvos, Saabs, and Japanese family cars. Again: an entirely different car park from Näsbypark. Except for the Volvos, of course: they were everywhere in this country—but where she came from she mostly saw the SUV models and the S60s. Natalie thought that some Swedes were so retarded—loved Volvo like they loved the royal family, even if the car company hadn't had anything to do with Sweden for probably ten years.

Then she thought about the green Volvo that Thomas'd seen several times on the surveillance video footage from home. There'd been a huge mistake in the way the cameras'd been mounted: the area beyond the hedge and the road behind the hedge were clearly visible, but the lower part of the road was blocked. You couldn't see the car's license plate.

Thomas, Natalie, and Goran'd tried to make out other details that might lead them forward. It was an old S80, with normal wear, light-colored interior, no transponder by the rearview mirror. No car seats for kids, no junk on the instrument panel, tinted back windows with some kind of dark stain. It was like trying to identify a blade of grass on a soccer field.

Instead, they tried to make out who was sitting in it. It was a man, definitely. Pretty large build, with dark hair and deep-set eyes. And he was driving with gloves on. They couldn't make out much more than that, the images were pixilated. Still: Natalie was certain. The person driving the Volvo had something to do with the murder.

But they would never be able to identify the car without the license plate number.

Thirty yards farther up: the house they were going to.

She parked the Golf.

They climbed out.

The sky was blue-gray. The house was yellow-gray—like a filthy wall next to a highway.

Established: there was a connection here to Melissa Cherkasova. Both Natalie and Thomas'd seen her come to this house on several occasions. Go inside, come out again a few hours later. Most often in the middle of the day, when only the woman in the house was home.

Established: the woman's name was Martina Kjellson. Twenty-nine years old. On maternity leave with a one-year-old child. She ought to be home at this hour.

Natalie rang the doorbell.

The door opened after a long while. The woman's face was twisted into a question mark.

Natalie scanned her rapidly. Close-set eyes. Sweatpants. Peeling nail polish. A necklace around her neck: HOPE.

A baby on her arm.

Established: this was the right woman. The one that Cherkasova went to see.

Martina Kjellson raised her eyebrows.

"We were wondering if we might come in and speak with you for a minute," Natalie said.

The entire time: her gaze glued on Martina. Natalie saw it in her eyes right away—the same expression Cherkasova had: worry. Or really: terror.

"And what do you want to speak to me about?"

Goran: six feet behind her. Maybe it'd been stupid to bring him.

Natalie cut right to the chase: "We want to talk about Melissa Cherkasova. And we would very much like to come in."

Goran took a step forward.

The woman was gripping the front door. Obviously reluctant to open it any wider. Goran didn't give a shit—took another step forward. Grabbed hold of the door. Pushed it open. Herded the woman in front of him into the foyer.

Natalie closed the door behind them.

"You can't just come into my house like this. I don't have anything to do with you."

The foyer was tidy. A kitchen on the right. There were photos hanging on the walls: children and a sailboat. Natalie pointed toward the kitchen with a gesture of unquestionable authority. Martina went inside reluctantly.

"We just want to talk. We don't want to hurt you. I promise."

The woman remained standing where she was. Natalie asked her to sit down.

Martina set the baby down in a high chair standing beside the kitchen table. There was a clear plastic sheet under the chair—probably to protect the floor from the kid's mess.

"I don't have anything to do with you. I want you to leave," she repeated.

Natalie felt tired. "We're not going to leave until we've had a talk," she said.

She sat down. The woman sat down. Goran remained standing in the doorway.

The kitchen was nice, renovated. Black-and-white-checked-tile floor. Tan cabinet doors. A PH-lamp hanging down over the kitchen table.

"Tell me about Melissa Cherkasova," Natalie said.

"Why?"

"I know that you know her. We know that she's been here."

"So what do you want with her?"

Natalie felt the fatigue come over her again. Why was this woman making it so difficult for herself? She stood up—bumped into the table. An empty coffee cup trembled.

"I'm the one asking the questions today. If there's anything you don't understand, let me know. I just want you to tell me about this Cherkasova. And we don't have all day."

The baby was looking at her with wide eyes. Martina looked near tears.

"Promise you'll leave after."

Natalie sat back down. "Yes, yes."

"I only know her superficially. We met at a bar one night, maybe a year ago. She is a friend of a friend. Since then she's been here to have coffee with me, max three, four times. But that was a while ago now."

Natalie felt irritation replace the feeling of fatigue. "If you don't stop lying, things are going to get a whole lot less pleasant in here. I know that Cherkasova was here last week."

"Yes, that's possible. That might be true. We see each other now and then. She cares so much about little Tyra here. She loves kids."

"And more? I want to know more. Who is she, what does she do?"

"I think she's from Belarus, but she's lived here for quite a few years. She speaks good Swedish. She's studying Swedish and English, I think. Has had a few jobs here and there. She lives in Solna, so it takes a while for her to go through the entire city when she comes here."

Natalie felt the irritation rise again—it was crossing a line now. She leaned over. Stared Martina straight in the eyes.

"This is the last time I'm going to say it."

She took hold of Martina's hand. Turned her gaze toward the baby in the high chair.

"If you don't start talking now, something very, very unpleasant is going to happen. I like children too. I love cute little kids. But I also like people who cooperate. Those seem like conflicting interests here today. And now I want you to talk for real. Do you understand?"

Natalie looked at the woman again. What she saw in the woman's eyes was something different from what she'd seen there before. Not fear. Not terror. But hate—hate so thick you could cut it with a knife.

Still, she started talking.

"Okay, I think I know who you are. You people've never sent a girl like you before, but I still know. I know your type. And I have nothing to hide. I've put that life behind me. So since you want to know so bad, I'll tell you what I know about Melissa Cherkasova. And if you don't leave me alone after that, I'm going straight to the police. I swear, I don't care if you hurt me or my family. I'm going to make sure the police arrest you."

Natalie was sitting in silence. Satisfied that the woman'd started talking.

"Melissa and I are the same. Do you understand? I used to be like Melissa. And I've pulled myself up outa there on my own. Look at what I have now—everything I ever dreamed of. I have a husband, a home, a child. We have a nice car that's parked in the garage out there. I'm happy today. And Melissa could be here today too, but she wants to go further. I'm trying to make her understand that this life is enough. But you can never understand that kind of thing. You don't know what it's like to be at rock bottom."

Martina gestured with her hands while she talked. Natalie thought, *Maybe it's good for this woman to have someone to tell her story to.*

She wanted to appear understanding. "No, maybe not. But I'm a woman too. I respect what you're saying."

"I doubt that. And I doubt that you could ever truly understand. When I was seventeen years old, I'd gone through more than most people go through in their entire lives. I come from a shit family. I was beaten. Kicked out of the house. Put in a juvenile home. I've been used and tricked. I've tried every drug you can imagine, all but injecting heroin. I've been betrayed by everyone who I thought loved me. Finally I became what everyone already said I was. It started when I was studying for my GED. It was me and two other girls. We were invited to fancy places, got attention and drinks. But we were always expected to give something back, and it felt okay to do that. The sick thing was that it was one of the teachers who arranged everything. After that, it all just started spinning faster and faster, out of control. I could make three thousand kronor in a night, and sometimes I didn't even have to do anything with those men. There were a few of us who were Swedish, but most of the girls were from the East. I did it for a few years, but I always knew that I would quit when I'd saved up enough. And then something happened that turned everything upside down."

Natalie saw Goran moving out of the corner of her eye.

He took a step toward the kitchen table. Said, in Serbian, "She's talking too much. This isn't anything we should be listening to. Ask her to tell us about Cherkasova now."

Natalie shook her head. "No, I want to hear this."

"But I don't think it's a good idea. It might be things that'll upset you unnecessarily."

Natalie ignored him. Just nodded to Martina to keep going.

"One of the girls was from the north of the country, she tried to get smart. She started collecting information about the men we were seeing.

We were the top chicks, the elite escort service. We were the ones they sent when the men paid real well. We saw clients who were powerful, and this girl made sure to know who they were. She hid digital recorders in the nightstands, she hid Web cameras among the knickknacks in hotel rooms, and then she got some sort of spy camera. It looked like a pen. She snapped pictures of all of them. But you people found out what she was doing. And you couldn't tolerate that someone was trying to get ahead on their own. So you made sure she disappeared."

Natalie interrupted. "What the fuck are you talking about? Who is this 'you' that you're talking about?"

"Like I said: I don't know who you are. But I know that it was your people. Radovan Kranjic's people."

"That's enough," Goran said in Swedish. "Tell us about Cherkasova, not a bunch of other bullshit."

Natalie didn't know what to say. She leaned forward. Put her weight on her arms against the table. The baby was calm, sitting in the high chair and waving a rattle. Natalie looked at Goran. His face was relaxed, revealing nothing about what he was really thinking.

Nothing.

Maybe everyone but her already knew what this Cherkasova business was all about. Maybe she'd misjudged Goran. But that was a question for later. She would bring it up with him after they were done here. What she had to do now was remain calm.

Not show any emotion.

The woman started talking again. "Okay, okay, I'll tell you about Cherkasova. But you've got to understand where I'm coming from. I met Melissa at an event a couple of years ago. A huge party in an enormous house a few miles south of Stockholm. We started talking for real. I quit a few weeks later. She'd just started. We saw each other a few times after the party. Then a few years passed when we didn't talk at all. I met Magnus and started to live this life. But about a year ago, Melissa got in touch with me. She was still in that life, but she really wanted to quit. And the only thing I've done since is try to support her. Prepare her for getting out. She comes over now and then. We talk. I'm trying to guide her. She needs support. That's the only thing I can give her."

Natalie tried to concentrate. She said, "You mentioned Radovan Kranjic before. What is Melissa's connection to him?"

Martina looked as if she were actually thinking, hard. "I have no idea. I don't know if she'd ever even met Radovan. Most of us never met him.

We just knew that he was someone everyone was worried about. We only met the guys who kept the operation running, so to speak. Other men. She's never mentioned him. Anyway, I read that he's dead now."

"Yes, that's true. And Bengt Svelander, is that someone she's mentioned?"

"Svelander?"

"Yes, a client of hers."

"A client, okay. She never mentions them by name."

"He's a politician."

Martina looked as if she were thinking it over.

Natalie could tell by looking at her that she knew more.

"Politician? In Stockholm?"

"Yes."

"She's mentioned a politician. But you ought to know that."

"Why?"

"'Cause your people are the ones who asked her to record their sessions. I guess you've learned how much there is to gain by gathering information."

Silence in the kitchen.

The baby cooed.

"Okay," Natalie said. "This is what we're going to do. You're going to tell Melissa that we've been here. Tell her that, from now on, she can't give any more recordings to anyone but me or Goran. Not to anyone. Do you understand what I'm saying?"

Martina nodded.

* * *

***AFTONBLADET*, EVENING NEWSPAPER**

TAX HAVENS ALMOST ALL GONE

Forget the time when wealthy Swedes could hide their fortunes in tax havens like Isle of Man.

The tax authorities have now signed agreements with a number of countries and thereby been given access to information about bank accounts and transactions, according to Channel One's *Daily News*.

"There are not many places left where you can safely hide your money," says Jan-Erik Bäckman, chief analyst at the Swedish Tax Agency, to *Daily News*.

Can view account information

The agreements give the Swedish Tax Agency the opportunity to keep track of the way Swedes handle money abroad by viewing account statements, transactions, and information about credit and debit cards, among other ways.

So far this year alone, the Swedish Tax Agency has collected 850 million kronor from Swedish accounts abroad, according to *Daily News*. 160 private persons have been forced to pay a total of 500 million kronor in evaded taxes, as well as 100 million in additional tax penalties. What's more, 375 honest people have volunteered previously unreported gains, which has allowed the Swedish Tax Agency to collect an additional 250 million.

Liechtenstein is the latest in the group of countries that have signed agreements with the Swedish Tax Agency. The agreements also mean that a prosecutor's support is no longer needed to demand information from the different countries.

"We no longer need to have an ongoing criminal investigation in order to be able to ask questions about money and income abroad. Soon, there will not be any places left where you can hide capital," says Jan-Erik Bäckman to *Daily News*.

37

Samitivej Hospital Phuket. Jorge'd expected something totally different: simpler, dirtier, crappier. Instead: ill foyer, mad classy, soaring ceilings, phat flowers in fat vases on the floor. Chandeliers dangling from above and display cases with, like, Thai relics or some shit like that. Farther off: a piano. A dude in a black suit was playing *pling-plong, pling-plong*—mad ching-chong music. At a hospital—kind of *loco*, man.

The welcome desk was like at a deluxe hotel: a glass counter, dark wood paneling in the background, people standing in line, waiting politely. A receptionist in a white nurse's hat clapped her hands and said "*Kapun khap*"—like everyone else here did. But when Jorge started talking, she spoke perfect English.

Shit, this place was mad fly. But it cost too.

They knew right away: Mahmud al-Askori. Yes, sir. Unit four. We'll take you to the room.

Jorge was holding the flowers awkwardly in his hand.

The walls were painted a bright white, the place was deserted.

The nurse pressed a button.

The elevator doors were made of metal.

They boarded.

Jorge was staying in a budget hotel nearby. Phuket was more expensive than Pattaya. Mahmud's hospital bed was pricey.

The cash wouldn't last forever. The take'd been slim. And J-boy'd refrained from a large part to calm the guys down after the fiasco. Plus: life in Pattaya hadn't exactly been free.

He was thinking about going back to Swedeland to dig up the bills he and Mahmud'd buried in the woods. The ones that'd been in the security bags he'd stowed away. Six hundred Gs. Babak'd gotten two hundred and been happy with that. That's what he'd said anyway. But now?

Jorge hadn't seen Mahmud since he'd been run over by the Russians.

When they found out what'd happened, the mood among the boys'd hit a new record low.

Tom wanted to go back to Bangkok to gamble. Thought the whole gang needed a break from each other. Jimmy wanted to go home to Sweden. Didn't give a shit about anything, that was what he said. Especially after Jorge'd fucked it up even more royally. Jorge forbade him to leave—fuck, he was the one who'd fucked up the fucking wheel loader.

Javier whined, as usual.

And Babak totally went off his rocker. Completely flipped his shit. "You candy-ass motherfucker. You tricked Mahmud. Said we were gonna pay those assholes. Then you tried to make him bounce in the morning. How the fuck you think the Russian-Thai mafia were gonna react? Huh? Smile and help you find a fucking taxi?"

Babak could go *chinga su madre*. Jorge wasn't taking more shit from the Iranian—forget it. He turned on his heel and left. Expected Babak to yell something after him about the stolen bags.

Instead, Babak sprinted after him. Screamed so his spit sprayed like a sprinkler. Jorge ignored him. There was no energy left to fight now. And nothing came out about Jorge's rip-off.

He kept on walking away. The boys would have to choose. Him or Babak.

The day after: they split up. Tom and Jimmy left for Bangkok with the Iranian. Jorge and Javier left for Phuket.

That's really how it should've been from the get-go—robbers never stayed friends. Classic. A rule of thumb. Almost a *mandamiento.*

The ambulance'd driven Mahmud to the local hospital in Pattaya. But when they'd realized he was a Swedish citizen, they'd brought him here, to Phuket. Jorge and Javier followed. Waited to visit the Arab. First the hospital cunts said no, Mahmud was unconscious. Then they said the flu was spreading like wildfire in Thailand—risk of infection, blah blah blah. Then they said only family members were permitted to visit. If Jorge'd been a blond Sven, there'd've been none of this bullshit. As it was, he'd had to wait for over a week.

Mahmud's room: parquet floors, a hospital bed, a fridge, a leather armchair next to a window that looked out over the hospital park, dried flowers in a basket on a little table. Even paintings on the walls.

Could've been a hospital room anywhere in Sweden. But the difference: the parquet floor, the paintings, the fridge—they didn't have pimped shit like that in the socialist paradise. Thailand–Sweden: an unexpected victory—Thailand, three-zero.

The nurse was standing behind Jorge.

Mahmud was lying in the bed. Eyes shut. Still scabs and bandages on his face, a white neck thing around his throat, one arm bandaged, and a tube inserted into his hand. A green blanket covered the rest of his body.

Didn't look good.

Honest: brother was fucked.

Mahmud wasn't moving.

"*Habibi*, how you doing?"

Nothing happened.

Jorge walked over to the bed. Leaned down. "Yo, bro?"

Mahmud moved his hand. Opened one eye. Looked groggy.

"How you doing? Can you talk?"

Mahmud opened his other eye. Tried out a smile. It mostly looked like one side of his mouth was twitching.

Jorge held out the flowers. "I brought these. But you've gotta tell me if there's anything else you need."

Mahmud moved his arm slightly. Jorge understood: his bro was too tired to hold the flowers. Jorge gave them to the nurse instead.

Mahmud was speaking slowly. "Honest bro, I'm not feeling too hot."

"Fuck, *compadre*. But are you done with surgery and stuff?"

"I don't know. Ask her."

Jorge turned to the nurse. She spoke okay English.

"You should probably speak to the doctor. But I can at least tell you that Mr. al-Askori was unconscious until yesterday. He has broken both of his collarbones, a couple of ribs, and one arm. He has had stitches in his face, on his arm, and on his back. His right shoulder was dislocated, and he had a serious concussion."

"Concussion?"

"Yes, concussion. A serious one. He has had problems staying conscious, and he has headaches, is nauseous, has problems with his vision and balance."

Mahmud moved his hand again. "Tell her to leave now."

Jorge sent away the nurse. He pulled a chair up close to the bed. Sat down.

Mahmud was slurring his words. “I thank the Thai king and God for the morphine in this joint.”

Jorge looked down at him. A weak smile at least.

“Do you want me to get you other stuff?”

“No. My memory’ll apparently come back faster . . .”

Mahmud paused. Gathered strength.

“. . . if I don’t take a bunch of shit. But, bro, I can’t even remember the heist.”

They didn’t say anything, a few seconds passed.

Mahmud tried to say something. Word by word. Slowly.

“Jorge, thanks for comin’ up.”

“’Course, man, I’ll do anything for you. I was the one who guaranteed there was dough when they moved you. This hospital is private, you know. If we hadn’t made a little withdrawal from Tomteboda, we’d never be able to afford this luxury.”

Jorge’s turn to grin. Their eyes met. Mahmud looked insecure. Maybe sad. Maybe scared. The Arab was talking at half speed compared to normal. Maybe he was thinking the same thoughts that were rushing around in Jorge’s head. The big question: How the fuck was this gonna end?

Mahmud said, “Too bad we’re not nine-to-fivers.”

“Why?”

“Home and travel insurance.”

“Yeah, that’s true, they’ve got shit like that. But I’ve never met a real G from the hood who had home insurance.”

Jorge smoothed his hair back with one hand. Saw that look again in Mahmud’s eyes. Felt like someone was taking a knife to his heart. His buddy, his café brother, his best friend: obviously broken.

“Hey, by the way,” Jorge said. “Remember my buddy Eddie? He actually had home insurance. Then his place got broken into, someone wiped him clean. His new TV, over four hundred DVDs, the computer, his wife’s diamond earrings, his Cartier watch in eighteen carats with diamonds on every hour. Know what the insurance company said?”

“No.”

“Said that with his financial situation, no way he could’ve owned that shit. Said the whole thing was fraud. But I know that he owned that stuff ’cause I’ve seen it hundreds of times, and I know the shit wasn’t boosted. The gear was honest, straight through.”

Silence again. Jorge could hear Mahmud's breathing: his bro was wheezing.

He said, "We've split up."

Mahmud didn't respond.

"It didn't work anymore. Lots of fighting. Tom wanted to go to Bangkok again. Rollout. And your friend acted out one too many times."

"Too bad."

"That's how it is now. Me and Javier, we're here in Phuket. You check out in two days, that's what I think."

"Hope so."

Jorge thought: *Ten thousand baht per day, that's alotta dosh.*

Mahmud'd closed his eyes again. Leaned his head back.

Jorge was sitting still.

Thinking: Blackouts. Blurred vision. Nausea. *Joder*—his main man'd been transformed into a total goner. How was this gonna end?

Jorge tried to lighten the mood. "It'll all work out. We'll get a place here. Run it like the café at home. Settle down for a year or so."

Mahmud still had his eyes shut. "That'd be nice, *habibi.*"

Jorge thought about the substitute teachers he'd had in middle school. They came, they smiled, they thought they could change things. They pretended they were there to teach critical shit.

"You're important—you can be whatever you want to be."

After a few days: the subs started to get the game: the kids at this school didn't give a shit about their ideas, 'cause they'd already had forty other subs who'd talked the same smack. They looked more tired, they had outbursts, they yelled. When the week was over: you saw the panic in their eyes. Their body language revealed how broken they were. They started crying, ran out of the classroom, never came back.

The entire heist: like one of those substitute teacher weeks. Their plans'd been so tight, their ideas so rad, such ill planning. He'd thought he could change criminal history, become *legendario,* J-boy Royale, the king, the ghetto myth with the best cred in northern Europe. Then the hit happened, it didn't go too well. They got away but left a Range Rover with more DNA leads than a used razor blade. The loot: not small like a mosquito's cock, but smaller than expected. And then, then came the end of the story. Six guys in Thailand who could hardly keep it together. Started fighting with the Russian mafia. Wigged out. Split up.

Not just the familiar criminal anxiety.

Jorge felt the panic well up.

He wanted to cry, run away from here, never come back.

He took the elevator down. Had exchanged a few words with a nurse—Mahmud'd gotten some sort of infection, she said. He'd have to stay on for another two weeks, at least. But only if someone could pay.

Came as a shock—how long would this last? Still: Jorge promised he'd cover it. He had to write a guarantee, pay thirty thousand baht in advance.

He remembered that he'd promised Mahmud he'd call his sister, Jamila. Then he thought about his own sister, Paola. He'd called her from a pay phone, after Mahmud's accident. Needed to hear her voice. Make sure little Jorge was doing good, that Mom was alive. Ten minutes of talking, seven minutes of crying.

The elevator doors opened.

Jorge walked through the entrance hall.

The heat struck him in the face as he walked outside. From AC chill to heat from hell.

He needed to get more cash—100 percent.

He needed something to live on: a bar or a café. Keep what he'd promised Mahmud. But maybe his bro was totally out of commission.

He needed to stay here for a few years, until things'd calmed down at home.

He needed to talk more with JW.

He needed someone's help.

Someone who knew Thailand.

He had no idea who.

38

Hägerstrom leaned his head back. He felt a slight aching all through his back. There was nothing wrong with the airplane seat, but there was no legroom—cramped. He had been sitting like this for nine hours now. Read the airline magazine and a mystery by Roslund & Hellström, watched movies and a nature show on the little screen twelve inches from his face.

He was on his way into new territory for Operation Tide, literally and figuratively. An unexpected turn. He was on his way to Thailand, on an assignment for JW.

He rose and squeezed past the other passengers in his row. Stretched. Tried to straighten out his body.

It was a large plane with a set of stairs leading to the upper level, where the first-class people were seated. Hägerström wished he at least could have flown Economy Flex, but that would have aroused suspicion. A former CO simply didn't pay twenty-five thousand kronor for a trip to Thailand.

He looked out over the rows of seats. Hägerström had flown this route several times in his life. The plane was full of the usual mix of people. Middle-class Swedish families with kids running around and snotting and coughing in the aisles. Guys in groups of three and four who had been a little tipsy ever since check-in. Single men flying in khaki shorts and T-shirts who personified the image of Western pedophilia but might just be businessmen. Finally, there were the Thai women, alone or with children, who were on their way home to visit their families.

He closed his eyes. Tried to sleep. Instead, he started thinking about things he really didn't want to think about.

After the Police Academy, he had advanced quickly. Police officer, deputy police inspector. He had met guys now and then at gay haunts like Side Track Bar, Patricia, and Tip Top. He traveled to Amsterdam three times by himself and hung out at the Bent. But he never had any serious relationships. That wouldn't work. And on a few occasions, he even had sex with girls.

He lived a double life, a secret life, a closet life.

When he turned thirty, he rented out a restaurant and invited fifty people, including his parents and siblings. Had a birthday party. Ninety percent of the speeches were about how he was any mother-in-law's dream but never settled down. That he could get anyone he wanted but was never satisfied with anything. That he had not had a real relationship with a girl since high school.

He started thinking. His police colleagues moved in with their partners, had kids, got engaged, married. His old friends from childhood did all that but in reverse order: got engaged, married, had kids.

It had taken him a little over a year to understand that he too was longing for children. But he couldn't talk to anyone about it. Hägerström: former coastal ranger, career-hungry deputy inspector on the cusp of promotion who longed for a kid. That just didn't jibe. But the thoughts wouldn't leave him—every single day he thought about how he could meet a girl who it might be okay to be with.

But most of all, he just wanted to get away.

Three months later an offer arrived like a gift from the police gods. He was given the opportunity to take a leave of absence from work in order to accept a job abroad with the Nordic Coordination Unit in Bangkok.

It was a good time in his life. The job wasn't too intense, but it was interesting. Typical duties related to the extradition of Scandinavians on the run in Thailand and drug and child sex crimes. He learned tolerable Thai, and he learned about the Thai mentality. He hung out with the Scandinavian police officers in the unit and with some Swedes from the consulate. But his social life was, by and large, pretty meager. In his free time, he worked out or took walks around Bangkok. He spent a lot of time alone. Found gay bars and felt free.

When he had less than two months left of his service, he met Anna. She worked as a secretary at the consulate. They met at a cocktail party organized by the coordination unit. She was thirty-two years old, from Tyresö, and had worked previously as an executive secretary. They shared the same longing: children. Other than that, Hägerström wondered if they had ever shared anything at all.

And still, they began to see more and more of each other and actually became good friends. At the end of his service, she seduced him after they had been out for dinner. At the time he liked the idea: to try to start a relationship with someone who was a good friend and who also wanted to have children. Unfortunately, they had a harder time than expected getting pregnant, maybe partly because Hägerström so rarely wanted to try. After four years of agony, they adopted a boy. Thailand felt like the natural choice.

Pravat was about a year old when he came to them. Both Hägerström and Anna experienced the best days in their lives. They had done a lot of research, gone to informational meetings, partaken in discussion groups. He had felt prepared, and he knew he would be a good father. Anna was good too, she really was. The problem was that, other than the child, they didn't work together for shit. Their shared goal in life—to have a child—had been attained, but there was neither love nor sexual attraction between them.

Back on the plane. Ten rows farther up, a group of inebriated guys were playing loud music on a computer with external speakers. Nine rows up, a Thai woman was trying to ignore those very same guys. Two rows up, a father, whose kid had finally passed out in his arms, was snoring. All the drunk guys were wearing white T-shirts with NIKE across the front. Personally, Hägerström traveled in a white button-down shirt with the sleeves rolled up. He heard his father's voice in his head: *One always flies in a collar.*

If Göran had been on this flight, he would have forced his son to book Business Class in order to escape the hordes of white trash Swedes. But Father never would have used that expression, *white trash.* He might have called them trailer Svens.

Göran used to joke about airplanes.

"The black box is supposed to be able to handle anything. It's made so it can survive plane crashes into the ocean, into the desert, or right into the top of a mountain. So why don't they make the entire plane in the same material?"

That was pure Father humor.

Hägerström missed him.

He sat down. It was nine-thirty at night, Swedish time.

He tore the plastic wrapper off the blanket. It was purple with orange and yellow lines on it—like everything else on Thai Airways: the seats, the pillows, the carpeting on the floor, the uniforms the stewardesses wore, the logos on the wings of the airplane.

JW had called. He wondered if Hägerström was in the neighborhood, if he would give him a ride to the gym. Their relationship was built on each meeting the other halfway. Hägerström was a fine-familied fellow heading down on the class elevator. JW was a bad seed on his way up.

They cold talked for a while. Right before JW was about to get out, he said, "You know Thai, right?"

"Yes, I told you that, didn't I? I used to live there."

"Right, but there are, like, seven million guys who have Thai wives who don't even speak English."

"I'm not like that. I lived in Bangkok for over a year. I can speak Thai. Dammit, I know everything there is to know about Thailand. You want to know where the best chicks are, ask me. You want to know where you can buy a nine-millimeter for the best price, ask me. You want to know who you have to talk to in Klong Teuy in order not to end up in trouble, you ask Mr. Martin Hägerström."

"Great, buddy. I get your point. In that case, I've got a question for you."

"Shoot."

"You help me out, drive me around, make sure I'm feeling good."

"You know it."

"Do you have any other job going on right now?"

"No, but I've applied for a guard job in Stockholm."

"And when do you get that?"

"I don't even know if I'll get it, but if so, in four weeks."

"Okay, in that case, I'd like you to go to Thailand for a few weeks. What do you say?"

"Why?"

"I've got a buddy there who needs help with some business. He's wound up in trouble and needs someone who knows Thailand. I'll cover half the ticket. You understand?"

JW didn't really have to wonder—this was definitely an order.

Maybe it would lead somewhere. Right now Operation Tide had sort of stalled anyway.

39

She involved outsiders, for the first time.

Goran and Thomas'd advised her. Or rather, Thomas was the one who'd come up with the name: Gabriel Hanna. On the surface, he was known as a dealer of bulletproof vests, army boots, and paintball guns. Had two stores in Västerås, one in Örebro, and one in Eskilstuna. On top of that: Sweden's leading Web site for military gear. Bouncers, military fetishists, and cop wannabes loved him. But according to Thomas: in the underworld—Gabriel Hanna was more known as the real thing. Ammo king, dealer of warm metal, hot gear. The go-to source. To put it simply, Gabriel Hanna: the heaviest illegal arms dealer in central Sweden. Maybe in the entire country.

Natalie, Goran, and a young guy with a hoodie were walking down a hallway. A couple of Jack Vegas machines against the black-painted walls. A vending machine for soda. One for snacks and sandwiches. Then a narrow set of stairs leading up. When they reached the first flight up, the guy turned on the lights.

Natalie eyed the room. It was large. Stretched across the entire upstairs of the building. Beams in the ceiling. Linoleum on the floor. White textured wallpaper. There were four large gaming tables covered in green felt, one in each corner of the room. In the middle: a large, round roulette table in dark wood. Around the gaming tables were office chairs that gave off a 1980s feel: black poofy leather and armrests in some wood material. Posters for different online game companies and the magazine *Poker* were tacked up on the walls.

They'd stepped into Västerås Gaming Club. A half-shady gaming club for dudes who wanted to burn cash on poker, roulette, and dice. They should at least try to create a more glamorous feeling—that would benefit the gaming. On the other hand: these were the provinces. Maybe a roulette table was enough to make the country folk feel flashy.

Natalie and Goran sat down at one of the gaming tables. The leather of the chair seats made a whooshing sound like air was coming out of them. The dude spoke bad Swedish. "He come soon."

"We don't have all day," Goran said. "Call him."

The guy had a tattoo with an eagle with outstretched wings on his right forearm. Natalie knew: that was the standard Assyrian ink job.

The guy put his hands in his pockets. Repeated what he'd just said, "He come soon."

Then he walked down the stairs.

Goran'd warned her ahead of time. It was a game—who waits for whom. Who bends for whom. Who fucks whom in the ass. And right now they were the ones who wanted information, so they'd have to be the bottom for a while.

Twenty minutes later Gabriel Hanna came up the stairs with the guy in tow. He didn't look the way Natalie'd imagined. He was well dressed. Close shave. Neatly combed hair parted to the side. Pale blue shirt, dark blue jacket, and pressed chinos. Honestly: Hanna looked like a total lawyer, even reminded her of JW. The only thing that might separate him from the Stockholm style: fat stitching along the side of his shoes. Rubber soles. Above all: the shoes were super pointy. Natalie remembered something Louise liked to say: "You can buy a lot with money, but not taste."

Hanna grinned. Offered his hand.

"Hi, there. Nice that you could make it all the way here."

Västerås dialect. Pleasant style. Pleasant tone of voice, despite the dialect. Not exactly what Natalie'd expected from a dealer of something as illegal as weapons.

He sat down. Nodded at his guy, who left the room.

"I'm glad you could meet me," Natalie said.

She set the pile of papers from the investigation on the gaming table. According to Goran: if anyone in this country knew about illegal weapons, it was Hanna.

The little guy returned with three can's of Coke.

Hanna took them and turned to Natalie. "Would you like one?"

Goran's can made a popping sound when he opened it.

Gabriel Hanna teased, punned, made Kurd jokes. "Do you know why all Kurds do their homework on the roof?"

Natalie wanted to get right down to business.

Hanna answered his own question: "Because they want to get *high* marks!" He laughed at his own joke.

Then he began reading Natalie's paperwork. Silence in the Västerås Gaming Club for fifteen minutes.

The runner was playing with his cell phone. Goran was staring straight ahead. Natalie was thinking about Viktor. He also liked to laugh at his own jokes. They hadn't seen each other in a week. The last time they were together, he talked about his financial crisis and his new business ideas. Mostly Natalie wanted to fuck him. It made her forget all the shit for a while. But then Viktor'd started babbling about how he thought there were people in Thailand who were connected to the murder. That he knew some criminal dudes who'd gone there shortly after the event. Dudes who hadn't liked Dad.

Hanna flipped through the pages slowly. Held his body at the same angle, like a wax figurine. The weapons dealer was concentrating to the max.

Natalie thought: *Gabriel Hanna is the real stuff, a serious guy.* Professional style spiced with a sense of humor. Social competence, easy to like. She understood why he'd done so well. Maybe they could do business together sometime in the future. She thought about JW—she ought to see him again. He or Bladman had to give her the right information.

The minutes passed.

Hanna looked up. "I've been in this business long enough."

Goran turned to him. Natalie was listening.

"You can never be a hundred percent certain of anything," he said. "But I think I know where this ammunition, grenade, and putty come from."

One day later: Natalie climbed out of her Golf in the Lill Jansskogen forest. As usual: Goran in tow. She felt alone without him these days.

A strange place. It seemed hostile to her now, even though she'd been there plenty of times with Dad.

In front of her was a ski-jumping tower. Dad used to just call it the Tower. He'd bought the place a couple of years ago through a front man. A dilapidated old tower with a ski-jumping ramp attached to it, leading out over a slope in a clearing in the woods below. The actual ramp hadn't been used in thirty years. A mountain biking club used to hang out in the Tower. Dad had renovated the place. Torn down walls, built new stairs, fixed the floors. Installed a restaurant kitchen on the ground level. Brought in a chef and staff. It was perfect for conferences and corporate events.

And now Stefanovic'd turned it into his Batcave. The front man'd aligned himself with him—formally, there wasn't much that Natalie could do.

She felt the heat rise inside her with every step she took. Stefanovic: a fucking clown. Stefanovic: an asshole. An *izdajnik*.

She had to calm down. Play her cards right. Take three deep breaths.

She had to handle the situation like a pro.

At the top of the Tower: a large room. Windows facing in all directions. A view over the Lill Jansskogen forest. Over toward Östermalm. In the distance, you could see the town hall, church spires, and the high-rises around Hötorget. Farthest in the distance: a glimpse of the Globe Arena. Stockholm spread out before her. Her city. Her territory. Not the traitor's territory.

A sofa group, a table with six chairs around it, a minibar filled with bottles against the one windowless wall.

In the sofa group: Stefanovic.

Marko, Stefanovic's muscleman, was sitting on one of the chairs.

Stefanovic stood up. Kiss-kiss-kissed. Made some polite small talk, no heart in it.

Natalie thought his eyes looked more watery than usual. He was still wearing a Bluetooth earpiece in one ear.

Natalie sat down at the table. Goran remained standing by the door.

"We don't need an audience, do we?" Stefanovic asked.

He gestured toward his gorilla, Marko. The dude rose, walked out. Natalie nodded. Goran also left the room.

Her and Stefanovic.

"It's been a long time since I've been here," she said.

"It's a good place," he said.

"It's Dad's place."

"No, we both know that Christer Lindberg owns it."

She didn't care. Cut right to the chase: "Stefanovic, you were my father's right-hand man. I want you to tell me what's going on."

Stefanovic responded in Serbian, "I think you're going to need to be more precise. I've never hidden anything from you, sweetie. I promise."

He put his hand over his heart, as though he had one.

There was no reason to hide anything anymore.

"Okay, then I want you to explain to me who Melissa Cherkasova is."

Stefanovic didn't move a muscle. Total poker face.

"Natalie, honey, your father ran several businesses. Some lucrative, others less so, but you know that. Some were completely legal, some not. Some were geared toward everyone, some were just for men."

"I know what you're talking about."

"Good. Sometimes girls are needed to lighten the mood, make things nice. Especially international clients want beautiful women to be present at night, when you have dinner or go out to clubs. So: Melissa Cherkasova was a so-called escort. There's nothing strange about that. Why are you asking about her?"

"What else do you know about her?"

"Aren't you going to answer my question first?"

Natalie wasn't going to let herself be pushed around. "No," she said. "I want to know what else you know about Cherkasova."

"Okay, but then you're going to have to answer my question. And I don't know much, I can tell you that. I know that she stopped working for us several years ago. Your father might've had occasional contact with her after that. But now it's your turn to start answering."

Natalie didn't say anything. She thought about JW—the guy radiated something. And he'd helped her father and now Stefanovic with something beyond customary tax evasion.

She reviewed what she knew. She'd seen a green Volvo in the parking garage where Dad'd been shot, and a green Volvo'd been driving around on her street in the days before the murder. It could be the same vehicle. A man wearing gloves'd been driving the fucking car. Thomas'd tried to get the parking garage under the Globe Arena to produce images from its surveillance cameras—unfortunately they'd been deleted long ago. Natalie thought of Cherkasova, the whore who'd met the politician Bengt Svelander, who in turn had met Stefanovic at a restaurant downtown, who in turn had met JW. The former whore, Martina Kjellson, who claimed that Dad's people had been the ones who ordered Cherkasova to record her encounters with the politician. Thomas'd done more research on Svelander—the politician was serving on the Foreign Affairs Committee for Baltic Concessions.

Thomas'd explained, "They're the ones who decide over Sweden's economic zone in the Baltic Sea. And more important, who decide if the Russians are going to be allowed to build that enormous pipeline, Nordic Pipe, on the bottom of the ocean."

And now Stefanovic was sitting here, lying straight to her freshly made-up face.

Natalie finally spoke. "Stefanovic, let me say this. I know that something is going on that involves Cherkasova. But since you don't plan on telling me, I think we're done here for today. But I expect that, from now on, you will report to me about anything concerning a business that was started by my father. I don't mind if you do business of your own. But what's mine is mine."

This was the end—this was the beginning. She'd taken the step. Made her position clear. Stefanovic would have to get into line or disappear. Now she was waiting for his answer. She could feel her heart beating like a small bird's.

What would he respond?

She thought about Dad. His journey: rise and fall. How he'd beaten his way into Swedish society. Created a position for himself. Helped so many of his countrymen. Broken through the segregation: been accepted by the Swedes as a neighbor in the leafy suburb, as a power player in the city.

Stefanovic opened his mouth slowly. He smiled.

"Natalie, you have been like a daughter to me. And I considered Kum a real brother. You can be assured that I will honor him in everything that I do. But he would've had a good laugh today if he'd heard what you just said. You're a pretty girl. You're a sweet person. But not more than that. This business isn't for women."

Natalie waited for him to say more.

"Kum knew that," Stefanovic said. "And I know it. So I'm asking you now for the last time: stop acting like you're your father. Take Goran with you and leave—it's enough now. I've already told you not to get involved with that investigation. So listen to what I'm saying: Never come back here. Let go of what happened to your father. Never demand anything from me again. I don't want to be your enemy."

Natalie rose. Shook her head.

Stefanovic followed her with his eyes.

She opened the door.

Goran was standing outside. Maybe he understood what'd happened.

They walked down the stairs.

In her head: How would she do this?

She had no idea. But there was one thing she knew—Dad wouldn't have laughed at her today.

She heard his voice in her head: "*Little frog. You will take over.*"

*

Less than six months after I was in Stockholm last, I was back in a taxi, on my way from Arlanda Airport to the hotel. On my way to a job.

And it wasn't just the fact that I was back in Sweden again, in the same city as my last assignment. I was here for the same people as last time.

The same family.

It was improbable. But that's how it was.

I asked myself if it could really be a coincidence.

But this time I was planning on doing a cleaner job than the last time. The maid and the parking garage were two embarrassing memories.

In some languages we're called clean-up men. *A job should be clean when we finish, that's part of the nature of it all. The fact is that the failure in the garage during the martial arts gala was still bothering me tremendously. My lack of professionalism was eating away at me, my sloppy execution reminded me of the complexity of my operations. But there were more important problems too. The Swedish police were probably not done with their investigation yet. They should not have anything that pointed to me. But who knew—someone might've snapped a photo of me when I fired those shots. Someone could've happened to see me in the car outside Kranjic's home when I was scouting the area. Someone could've noted the license plate on the rental car, contacted the rental company, found the car, and searched for DNA in it. The car'd obviously been rented under another name, but still.*

The taxi driver'd posted some kind of taxi ID in a holder in front of the passenger seat. I read his name: Vassilij Rasztadovic, obviously from the former Yugoslavia. I didn't like the look of him. He reminded me of the judge who'd sentenced me to the gulag.

I addressed him in English, hid my accent as well as I could. It didn't really matter, anyway. I was traveling under a new name, with new documents and a new credit card. But I wanted to avoid unnecessary questions.

I was feeling relaxed when I stepped out of the car. The months I'd spent on Zanzibar'd done me good. I always stayed in the same bungalow, less than fifty yards from the beach. I always ate breakfast at the same hotel. I always jogged the same loop along the beach and up into the village. I had a woman there who, for some reason, agreed to wait for me. Or else I was the one waiting for her. She probably had others when I was gone.

I was rested.

I was concentrated.

I was excited for this job.

My assignment this time was to kill Natalie Kranjic.

40

Jorge and Javier were eating breakfast. Two pieces of toast slathered in a thick layer of Nutella.

This hotel: danker than the one in Pattaya.

Jorge's paper was burning up for real—Mahmud's hospital bills were eating away at his assets worse than Javier's hooker banging. Still, he was happy that Javier'd chosen to come with him.

The time: ten-thirty.

They were waiting for the new dude—his name was Martin. Last name: Hägerström. A real Sven name. The guy was a pure Sven—not like Jimmy and Tom, who were Svens but acted like they were children of the concrete. Martin Hägerström—how could you even have a name that was that Sven-like?

Right now Hägerström was still snoozing. He slept a lot, that dude.

Javier was talking about how tired he was, even though he'd had three cans of Krating Daeng, Thai Red Bull.

"So when you think Mahmud's gonna get out?"

"Last I was there, they said they didn't know. The screws in his arm've gotten twisted up somehow. And now he's got a hospital infection too. Know what that is?"

"Aren't you supposed to get well at hospitals?"

"Yeah, but diseases spread there too, smartass. A hospital infection, that's some bacteria called staph, that's what they told me. It's not good, man. And he's sharing a room now, 'cause it's too expensive with private. So he really wants to get out."

"*Comprendo*. Who he splitting with?"

"Different people. They come and go."

Javier took a sip of his fourth can. "Chicks?"

Jorge knew what was coming next—some joke about how Mahmud could get his dick wet. Jorge: really fucking tired of Javier's obsession.

Javier didn't wait for Jorge to respond: "'Cause if there're chicks, maybe he can get a quickie in now and then. When they're sleeping?"

"Mmm . . . but you, you little fairy, wouldn't bang if some she-male was in the room either, would you?"

Javier took a deliberately loud sip. "I love Thailand."

"Mahmud'll get out soon," Jorge said. "But I wanna have a place by then. So we can get started right away. And this Hägerström guy's gonna help me. You know, he got booted from the force. And he's helped my buddy with a bunch of stuff in Sweden. My buddy says we can trust him, but I don't trust some ex-*paco*."

"Never trust an ex-*paco*. But I don't know why you'd wanna run a place down here. I know the *dinero* is running out. But there are other, better things than working some joint."

"*Eres loco, huevon?* You saw what happened to Mahmud. We might have to stay here for a while, and I don't wanna do something that'll attract attention."

"Those Russian *putos*."

"Law of nature. At home too. We eat the Svens like gingersnaps. The Somalis and Iraqis eat us who came in the eighties like mini-baklavas. And the Russians eat us all like we're tiny pierogi with seeds on top. Russians."

Still: in the afternoon, Jorge met Martin Hägerström one on one. The next morning they were gonna have a meeting with a Thai guy who wanted to sell his sports bar. Jorge wanted to talk through the setup beforehand.

They were sitting in the hotel restaurant again. The Hägerström dude didn't look like the regular Europeans around here. A button-down shirt instead of a T-shirt. Real shoes instead of Crocs or flip-flops. Above all: pants instead of shorts. It made a good impression: Hägerström was more like the gooks than the tourists.

The ex-cop'd been here for nearly a week already, but he hadn't done much so far. Only talked briefly to Jorge about how he'd gotten hold of a list of real estate brokers and asked around among the Thai guys to see if anything was for sale—but so far that one guy was all there was. And Jorge needed to get something going soon.

But another thing: Hägerström'd brought an envelope for Jorge from Sweden. He said it was from JW. Jorge'd opened it—some folded documents. He unfolded them. The first was handwritten:

Hombre! I got hold of some information that might interest you. Check out the docs I included. And I understand times are tough. I'm sending some money in case you need it.

At the bottom: a code number for Western Union. One thousand euros. JW—*un compadre de verdad.*

And the documents were real special. Actually: top secret, classified shit. It was a copy from some cop registry. JW must have some sweet connect who'd gotten the material from the belly of the beast. Cops often leaked real bad—which proved: they were all hypocrites.

The five-oh were seriously onto them. The star of the show: him. First one page with lots of photos of him. Different aliases: J-boy, Jorge Bernadotte, Shawshank. His personal identification number, addresses to different apartments he'd lived in, what cars he'd owned, the last time he'd been fingerprinted. And more stuff: suspicions. Jorge Salinas Barrio: one of Stockholm's key players when it came to smuggling and dealing cocaine. Excerpts from the general reconnaissance register, paperwork from the customs police, the criminal records registry. "At present, Jorge Salinas Barrio can most likely be found in Thailand, according to the international unit and Interpol. No other information is available."

And then shit got a helluva less pleasant. They outlined his network, his acquaintances, his friends. Shit from the past: people he'd dealt to, people he'd bought from, dudes he'd done time with, dudes he'd threatened 'cause they tried to encroach on his territory. They listed everyone who'd visited him in the pen, bitches he'd banged, *hermanos* he'd lived with.

Then there was a special section: suspicions about the Tomteboda heist. He was connected to Babak, who was connected to the Range Rover. But other than that, they didn't have much. Jorge knew: there was also a preliminary investigation somewhere with a lot more info—but the worst of it oughta have made it into this compilation.

He breathed out.

Still: he almost got vertigo—the five-oh was sitting on so much info. It's like they almost knew more about him than he knew himself. He exhaled again: such a relief to be in Thailand.

The worst was saved for last: they listed his family. Mom's, Paola's, and his cousin Sergio's personal identification numbers, places of work, income situations, what kind of relationship Jorge had with them. Positive, neutral, negative. They even fucking listed Jorge Jr.'s day-care teachers. Four years old—what the fuck did he have to do with this?

Nasty. He hated the five-oh. Hated Sweden. Hated the kind of society that would drag an innocent child into this.

Hägerström was talking negotiation tactics. In Asia: always be polite, rock the *kapun khap* crap, don't look anyone in the eyes. Never get worked up. Don't say no, no, no and act all hard-line. Instead, say yes, yes, yes but then change your mind. Smile and pretend like you agree even though you are miles apart.

The ex-screw: "It doesn't matter if you're right. If they try to clean you out. Because if you get worked up, you show you've lost control. And then you're the one who's lost. If you do that, you'll have zero respect with the Thai guys. You always have to keep your cool."

Jorge listened, tried to take in Hägerström's advice. He was just gonna buy a café, then this Sven player could turn right back around and go home.

"They're never going to be able to show you anything in writing about their turnaround," Hägerström said. "So you or I have to get the right to check the place out from a distance for a few days. See how many people visit the place, calculate how much beer they sell, if they pay a protection fee to some Seedang family, check their daily takings."

Jorge laughed. "Who you think I am? That's how it is at home too. Everyone's tricking everyone. The only thing that matters is keeping your eye on the cash."

Still: he appreciated Sven Hägerström's thoughts. It was good to have him along.

The next day they negotiated with the Thai guy. They met at the sports bar. Jorge and Hägerström were sitting on one side of the table. The man and his two sons were sitting on the other.

All the talk was in Thai. Hägerström babbled on. Jorge followed his instructions: bowed and groveled like a twelve-year-old meeting the king. As soon as the Thai guy looked up, Jorge smeared a fat smile across his face.

The meeting took an hour and a half. Throughout, Hägerström explained what was happening.

There was a major problem—the guy wanted the money in cash, up front. No transfers, no installments. Hägerström was trying to get the guy to agree to a three-month plan, allow Jorge to get the place going.

The guy wouldn't budge—everything at once or nothing at all.

Fuck.

Fuck, fuck, fuck.

Jorge'd never be able to afford it.

Not even if he borrowed money from Javier, Jimmy, and Tom. He'd have to go back home and dig up the rest of the cash.

He could forget about that.

There was a knock on his door. One of the girls who usually worked the welcome desk looked in. Jorge was on the bed watching TV.

"Mister, there is a man wants to talk to you. Phone."

Jorge got up. Walked down to the reception area. There were no phones in the rooms in this place.

"Yo, what's up?"

It was Tom. He sounded stressed out. Jorge wondered what'd happened.

"It's crazy, man."

"What happened?"

"The Thai cops've arrested Babak."

"When? Why?"

Tom sounded like he was gonna cry.

"They took him away at night. Me and Jimmy were out partying. Apparently they just stepped right into his room. It's about the thing in Sweden."

"How do you know?"

"We got a message about where they'd taken him. A police station nearby. Do you know what Thai cop stations look like? Their arrest cells have bars that are totally open to the station's main entrance. You can go up and talk to the guys in there if you just pay the guards a little, like a thousand baht or something. So I just did that."

"Oh, fuck. Good thinking. What happened?"

"I talked to him for fifteen minutes. Babak's been informed that there's an international arrest warrant out against him. That they're gonna negotiate about extraditing him to Sweden. He's met a Thai lawyer too. It'll take at least two weeks before they're gonna be allowed to send him home. Thailand and Sweden apparently don't have extradition agreements, so everything's gotta go through embassies and shit. You follow?"

"Yeah, yeah. Fuck, man. What else he say?"

"He's not happy, Jorge. He's really fucking pissed off, you already know that. And now he's seen documents from Sweden that show the suspicions against him. You fucked him, man."

Jorge didn't understand what Tom was talking about. He'd ripped the Finn off, the other guys including Tom himself too. But he hadn't fucking ripped Babak off.

"They've got information about his car," Tom said. "The Range Rover. He found out it was chased by the cops a few weeks before the heist. With you and Mahmud in it. And with his hoodie in it. Now they've tied him to the fucking car even tighter. 'Cause the hoodie's been caught on film. And no one told Babak."

Jorge clocked the situation. Him: an idiot.

Him: AN IDIOT.

J-boy'd booked it from Babak's car when he and Mahmud'd had the gat with them. The thing: neither he nor his bro'd told Babak. And now it was boomeranging with full force.

"But fuck, man, nothing happened that time," he said. "That shit doesn't matter. Boy's gotta chill out."

"It doesn't matter what you think. Babak said if you don't help him at home in Sweden, he's gonna sing about you like a real canary."

"That's bullshit."

"You slow or what? He's gonna wrap you if you don't make sure he walks."

Brain freeze.

Thoughts short-circuited.

Hard-drive crash.

Jorge didn't know what to think.

What he was gonna do.

What he should say.

He thought he'd hit rock bottom.

And now this.

41

Hägerström had been here for about two weeks now. The food was giving him rushes of nostalgia. He liked the weather, the way the streets smelled, and how polite the Thai people were. But he missed Bangkok. Phuket was a particularly dank tourist trap. And the hotel might be the nastiest he had ever stayed at.

He met Jorge briefly on the first day. The guy told him why he had been called down here—it didn't exactly sound like his intentions were supercriminal. But Hägerström hoped he would find out more. At least one thing was certain: Jorge Salinas Barrio wasn't just anybody. JW had asked Hägerström to bring an envelope for the guy. He had opened it in secret and checked out the contents—a printout about Jorge from the police databases. JW must have some insider within the force who had leaked the document. That alone was unpleasant.

Over the next few days, Hägerström kept to himself. Mostly walked around the city and took trips out to the beach communities on the island. There were dozens of restaurants, bars, and cafés around every resort. Patong Beach, Karon Beach, Kata Beach. The Mai Khao and Nai Yang beaches alone made up over ten miles of waterfront property with more than five hundred prospective bars. He checked out places that might be interesting for Jorge. At night he tried the beer in the same places. Eyed the guests, the number of employees, tried to calculate the turnover in his head. He was waiting for Jorge to call on him again.

A week or so later, Hägerström was sitting at the restaurant next to the hotel.

He was thinking about Pravat. It was so strange: the tiny tot, Daddy's ragamuffin, his little boy was going to start school.

He thought about the nights when they had seen each other last.

Pravat had wanted to sleep in his bed. And Hägerström couldn't think of anything more peaceful than lying beside his sleeping son. It was as though Pravat's calm rocked his shaky soul to rest. The boy's snuffling sounds wrapped his demons in a haze of relaxation. Hägerström didn't worry about the investigation or even about the challenges he was facing personally. He was just calm. It was one of the best weekends of his life.

He looked up. Let the thoughts go. A voice nearby said something to him that might have been in Swedish: "*Sho bre.*"

It was Jorge's friend, Javier, who was standing beside the table. The guy pulled out a chair.

Hägerström looked at him.

"Bro, don't you get what I'm saying?"

"No."

"But you know the talk—you've been a screw."

The guy sat down. Hägerström kept glaring at him. Didn't know if Javier was messing with him or not.

"That's cool. But I speak Swedish too. Do you?"

Javier let roll a slow laugh. "I know three languages."

"Spanish, Swedish, and whatever that shit was?"

"No, that shit *was* Swedish, but I don't talk that ghetto lingo anymore. It's mostly baby Gs who say *sho bre* this and *yo brotha* that. I mean the third language, the international language."

Hägerström raised his eyebrows.

"The language of sex."

Hägerström raised his bottle of Singha. "Cheers to that."

Javier toasted in return.

"So, what're you doing here, really?"

Again—Hägerström didn't know what to say. He had no idea where he had this guy. He tried to gauge the mood, read Javier's slow drawl. He was different somehow.

"What? You know what a screw makes?"

"Better than we make here, that's for sure."

"Maybe, but it's all a bunch of crap. The Swedish government is pulling a fast one on us. We work like dogs, and what do we get for it?"

"At least you know you get *something*."

"I've worked hard. Know what I did before I became a screw?"

Javier shook his head.

"Come on, bro, guess."

Javier grinned.

The guy reminded him of Jorge, even though he'd seen so little of him. The same way of speaking, the same slang, the same way of moving. But still: Javier was mellower—there was a weed haze to his speech. Despite that, he had more intensity than Jorge. A gleam in his eye that seemed more inviting.

When, a half hour or so later, Javier found out that Hägerström had been a cop, he didn't seem surprised. Either Jorge had already told him. Or else he was just playing it cool.

A few nights later, Javier approached Hägerström again.

That day Hägerström had traveled around the peninsula with Jorge, walked along the beaches, and pointed out the places that were for sale. They had a list of real estate agents in Thai that Jorge had made notes on.

Javier sat down without asking if it was okay. He ordered a beer.

"So, you guys finding anything?"

Hägerström assumed he was talking about their search for real estate.

"There are a bunch of places for sale here. But you know, it's a matter of price and other conditions, about how secure the revenue stream might be and all that."

They chatted. Javier said some friends of theirs might be coming. Hägerström tried to get a sense of how long they had been in Thailand, what they were doing here, why they were here. Javier was straight with him, but still not: "You know, there's some stuff you just don't talk about."

Javier grilled him in return. Maybe he was trying to get something out of Hägerström. Where he came from. What prisons he had worked at. Why he had stopped working as a cop.

The guy was nice but far from exuberant. He couldn't expect that from someone who knew he was a former cop. Still, he was open, talked a lot about sex, about Thailand in general, and his childhood in Alby. Javier was no spring chicken, that much was clear.

Hägerström was going to ask Torsfjäll to look this guy up later in the week.

He played along. Served up his story for the thousandth time: he hated the police force these days. Maybe they had already looked him up—JW obviously had some insider. That wasn't a problem. Torsfjäll had entered Hägerström into the reconnaissance register for ongoing suspicions of possession, assault, and receiving stolen goods.

They kept boozing. Javier was talking more and more about how he wanted to take Hägerström out and show him the chicks in this Asian dump. Hägerström ducked as best he could. He didn't want to end up in a situation where he had to do something with a prostitute in order to prove himself. He considered maybe it was time to call it a night.

Javier let the subject drop for a while. They each ordered a fruity cocktail. Javier was babbling on about how a real G couldn't have a bunch of side interests. You couldn't care too much about music or sports if you wanted to become someone.

They kept talking. Javier shot questions at Hägerström between rounds. Did he have kids? What unit had he worked in when he was a cop? How had it felt to get booted?

Then after an hour or so, he started up again, "Come on, man. The chicks here are fine."

"Nah, let's stay here," Hägerström said. "I'm not up for it."

"Are you a homo, or what?"

Hägerström ignored him.

"Come on, *paco*, show some brass."

Hägerström just grinned.

"You wanna, I can tell. You wanna. I bet you've got a wife at home."

Hägerström shook his head.

"Come on now, man. Fuck it. Just cause you're a Sven, you don't gotta be so scared."

Finally, Hägerström said, "Let's go back to the hotel instead. There are chicks there too, right?"

He had to play this right. He really didn't want to end up in a sloppy situation with some woman. At the same time, he really needed to win this guy's trust. If he pussied out, he might lose too much of the ground he had just made.

They got up, paid, and walked the hundred or so yards back to the hotel where they were staying. Sat down at a table at the bar. The decorating job in the place was standard: colorful lights, palm leaves, and Buddha figurines everywhere. Hägerström was starting to feel intoxicated. Javier started talking about other stuff. The guy kept running back and forth to the bartender, ordering different drinks.

After a while, Javier said, "I wanna show you something."

"Okay, what?"

"Not here," Javier said. "Up in my room."

Hägerström wondered what this could be about.

They took the stairs. Javier's room was a mini-suite with a mini-bedroom and a mini–living room with a mini-pantry. Hägerström was surprised by how neat the place was. But maybe it was just the hotel staff doing their job.

Javier sat down on the small sofa. He had a drink in one hand that he had brought up from downstairs.

Hägerström walked over and stood by the window. Looked out over a construction site on the other side of the street: a new hotel. Bamboo scaffolding, tarps, and Dumpsters. Soon they would be starting up out there. The sound of drills and trucks driving back and forth.

Javier picked up his phone and started playing with it.

"Have a seat on the couch, man."

Hägerström wondered what was going to happen next. What was Javier going to show him?

There was a knock at the door.

Javier grinned. Opened the door.

Two Thai girls were standing out in the hall. Short skirts, short tank tops, hair up in ponytails.

Obvious what they were.

Javier's grin broadened. "This is my surprise. Now we're gonna have a real good time, you and me."

Suddenly Hägerström felt completely sober.

42

The blinds in the library were drawn. And it was dark outside too. Natalie'd turned the wall lamps on as well as the lamps that were perched on the low bookshelves. The wallpaper didn't reflect much of the light in the room. Everything took on a dark blue shimmer: the maps over Serbia and Montenegro, the paintings that depicted various battles and floods in Europe, and the icons of the old holy guys.

It felt like a movie. But it was for real.

Natalie was sitting in Dad's leather armchair.

Yes—*she* was sitting in it. And around her, sitting in the other armchairs, were Goran, Bogdan, Thomas, and a guy named Milorad. Dad's men.

Her men.

It was the first time she'd invited them into the library. The first time she'd called a meeting. This would make it all more or less official.

Natalie Kranjic was the new leader.

Goran already knew. She'd bounced ideas back and forth with him for weeks, and now Stefanovic's behavior was leaving her no choice. Thomas'd probably also guessed this would happen—but the fact that he was even sitting here was a big step. The dude was a Sven and had even been a cop—now he was in the boardroom with the others, in the innermost circle. But Natalie trusted him, he was safe and had been supporting her for months. But what was even more important: Goran maintained that her father'd felt the same way. That alone would have been reason enough.

Security'd been heightened, just like after Dad's first assassination attempt. All the surveillance cameras and alarms were set. The safe room was turned on. Patrik was living at their house full time. The schism with Stefanovic wasn't only under way—it was a fact. God only knew what that traitor might try to do.

Thomas and Milorad'd done the usual search for bugs. They'd

left their phones in the kitchen and taken the batteries out. They'd all arrived in different cars and parked them in different places. They wanted to avoid neighbors or someone else wondering what was going on. People in the area knew what'd happened to Radovan—they didn't want filth in their fancy suburb. They wanted to continue enjoying fraud-Näsbypark.

Natalie considered serving whiskey, the way Dad'd always done. But she decided against it. A new era. She was the one who would set the tone, make her mark. And she didn't like whiskey, so why should everyone drink it? She invited them to choose freely from the bar instead.

Bogdan poured a weak gin and tonic.

Thomas had a beer.

Milorad chose Coke.

Goran wanted whiskey. Johnnie Walker Blue Label—the same stuff Dad'd used to serve.

The men looked serious. At the same time, there was a mood of expectation in the air. Natalie thought she knew why. They wanted her to take control, clear things up.

She remembered how Dad'd served her whiskey in the library in front of a few of them. That was his signal: Natalie has my complete trust—and she should have your trust as well.

She'd told Mom to keep to the den or the kitchen. It felt weird to give her orders, especially considering the way things'd been between them lately. But there was no alternative, they couldn't have her running around in the middle of the meeting.

Natalie and the men made small talk for a bit, while she filled their glasses. Then she sat back down in the armchair.

"I'm grateful, and I'm as happy as I can be." She spoke Swedish, not Serbian. Mainly so that Thomas would understand, but also: she had new ideas.

"You know that I miss my father every single day," Natalie went on. "You know how I've been struggling with grief ever since it happened. You have respected that. You have supported me. But you also know that there are those who have handled this situation completely differently."

The four men nodded. Natalie paused. Eyed them.

Goran: in his regular tracksuit. Head tilted slightly up. Not in a cocky way, more to show that he was paying attention to what she was saying.

Bogdan: in a red shirt with a huge Polo Ralph Lauren figure on his chest. Bogdan's head moved constantly while Natalie spoke. He was nodding slowly: accepting what she was saying.

Thomas: in a shirt and jeans. Milorad was rocking jeans and a hoodie with a tribal pattern on it. Both were listening.

Natalie spoke. "First of all, I've gotten hold of material from the police investigation. The cops've analyzed fragments from the explosion and cartridges and stuff from the assassination attempt in the garage, and they've concluded that it's a matter of a certain kind of grenade, a certain kind of plastic explosive, and bullets from a certain kind of gun. After that, we contacted Gabriel Hanna—you know who that is. He says he knows where the gear's from. He sees a connection."

She paused again. Checked out the men's level of interest.

"According to Hanna, the grenade, the plastics, and the gun come from a restaurant called the Black & White Inn. He knows that they've been sitting on a store of precisely that kind of grenade, that they've had access to that particular type of plastic explosive, and that they received a batch of Russian guns at the beginning of the year."

An *aha* through the library. Everyone was familiar with the Black & White Inn. The pub was an institution in the underworld. A marketplace for all kinds of things. Goran'd explained to Natalie: the Black & White Inn—the best shopping in Stockholm if you're interested in self-defense or seriously injuring someone. But the thing was not that they were familiar with the Black & White Inn. The thing was that the pub was half-owned, through companies and front men, by Radovan's estate. And worst of all: Stefanovic'd basically run the place when Kum was alive.

The connection: Stefanovic and the Black & White Inn, the sale of the weapons that'd killed Dad. The connection: Stefanovic was trying to prevent Natalie from digging into the investigation. The connection: Stefanovic wanted to take over Dad's empire.

Still: circumstances spoke severely against the notion that Stefanovic was involved. He'd been sitting in the BMW himself when the explosion took place. He could've died as well, easy peasy.

So who was involved?

Natalie reported on other information that she'd found out by reading the investigation documents. The way both the assassination attempt and the final attack'd been handled pointed to someone with a military background, a pro. The perp'd used a grenade from the former Yugoslavia. Stefanovic'd contributed zilch in the interrogation with the police.

The men listened in silence. The information didn't come as a surprise. That it could be someone with a military background from the home country—expected. But again: the connection to the Black & White Inn was not expected.

Natalie continued to analyze the situation. Not just the murder—she wanted to get a sense of the whole picture. JW refused to give her full information and control. Beogradska Banka was giving her trouble. Someone must've leaked to the authorities, it couldn't be a coincidence. The Enforcement Administration was chasing after the estate with taxes, recovery orders, and repossession threats. She wasn't being paid any dividends from the businesses that were continuing to run in Radovan's name, except the ones that Goran and Bogdan were responsible for.

The men commented on the things she said. They added information. They wanted to know what they should do about the situation.

Natalie instructed Bogdan to go to Zurich and speak to the bank there, try to open the final reserves—Dad's company's safe deposit box. She gave him a power of attorney, hoped it would work. She didn't mention that the money here at home would run out within a month.

She remembered once when she'd been allowed to come along to Switzerland. Maybe eight years ago—she'd been a girl then. Different keys, codes, receptionists who smiled and spoke bad English. Safe deposit boxes en masse. Dad'd opened his, pulled it out, and brought it with him into a booth. Natalie'd had to wait outside.

She also told Bogdan to contact the coat checks he used to work with and inform them that payments were to be made only to him or one of his boys. She ordered Goran to inform the truckers who brought in the smuggled booze and cigarettes the same thing. From now on, you deliver only to Goran and to people Goran has approved. She asked Milorad to regain control over the amphetamine channels and their stolen goods business.

She would reconquer what was hers. Calculation: Stefanovic would perceive it as an open confrontation. Conclusion: a war would break out for real.

They had to be prepared.

They discussed the issue for a while. They had to make sure that all the underlings were on their guard. Got bulletproof vests, armed themselves, never went out alone. All jobs, even just selling smack, would be done in groups. Above all: Natalie would never be alone.

Finally: she brought up the Cherkasova story. The others squirmed uncomfortably in their seats.

She was clear: "I've understood what my father was doing. You don't have to be ashamed. I don't judge him, even if I'm not exactly overjoyed to hear that kind of thing. He was my father. That's enough for me."

Goran took over. "I've looked into this more. The politician, Svelander, is serving on a committee that decides over Baltic Sea issues. I've made the rounds. Your father was involved, that much I know."

Natalie: "How?"

"I don't exactly know yet. But Stefanovic has instructed this—eh . . . what word should I use?—prostitute, to film Svelander. The guy has influence over building permits in the Baltic Sea. And the Russians are building a gas pipe on the bottom of the sea. So Stefanovic wants to be able to blackmail that horndog with the films this woman is taking."

The men, reinspected: the determination in their eyes, their faint nods, their humming. They understood, they realized, they knew—this wasn't the usual small-scale shit. This was in a different league. Obvious. And Stefanovic was trying to run it on his own. Without giving Kum's daughter her share. What an asshole.

"This is about the Russians," Goran said. "Your father helped them by using this Cherkasova woman. Maybe he helped them in other ways too. And now Stefanovic is running the racket on his own. That's not okay."

"And where does this JW guy come into the picture?" Natalie asked. "We saw Stefanovic meet him."

Goran looked into her eyes. He knew they'd met up. She didn't know what he thought about that.

"I have no idea," he said. "But he builds money-laundering systems. Him and Bladman've got to start playing for us. And now when there's an open war with Stefanovic, they can't put their heads in the sand anymore. They've got to pick sides."

They ended the meeting. The men looked pleased—despite all the question marks. She'd finally taken control over the situation. They'd finally been given direction.

Nevertheless, she felt she had only herself to rely on. She was living in two worlds at once. The men were listening to her. Still, she was alone.

Alone with her grief.

Alone with the responsibility.

Alone with her hate.

Days passed. She put her law studies on hold. Worked frenetically. Reality was what mattered now. Called Goran, Bogdan, and Thomas several times every day. They called back from different phone numbers or Skype—they were security fascists. She appreciated that they were teaching her to be the same way. She talked, faxed, e-mailed American Express, SEB, Handelsbanken: at least saved something. She tried to get Beogradska Banka to understand that Bogdan was her representative, no one else. She studied the police investigation. She researched the Black & White Inn—mostly by talking to Thomas and Goran, but also through Mischa Bladman, who agreed to produce the bookkeeping and other documents. She looked up everything she could find about the politician who'd bought sex from Cherkasova, about Baltic Sea concessions, about the other men who paid for Melissa. She went around town and checked out restaurants, bars, pubs, and clubs that ought to get a visit paid to them by Bogdan or one of his men in order to put their coat checks under his protection. She tested out ideas about ways to import amphetamines, to cut the smack, to establish laboratories in Sweden instead of in the Baltics. This was all new for her—Milorad explained the whole setup, from the ground up. She schemed strategies for a meeting with Stefanovic—it was only a question of time before the shit hit the fan and he started to act. One thing was certain: she—they—needed money. Without cash, she couldn't continue running this project. Without cash, she wouldn't be able to handle a war with the traitor.

She woke up at six every morning. Went to bed past one every night. Drank eight cups of coffee every day, plus at least three cans of Red Bull, munched on valerian at night in order to sleep. She ate hard-boiled eggs and tomatoes. Lost weight. Told Viktor to stay away. She would call him "when I feel okay."

She chatted with the girls sporadically on Facebook. Wrote to Louise that she was feeling too low to go out.

Mischa Bladman played unaffected. He agreed to sit down with Natalie in order to help her gain a general understanding of Dad's company finances. Six of the companies'd folded. A few were dormant. Four remained. Kranjic Holding AB, the Demolition Experts in Nälsta AB, Clara's Kitchen & Bar, Teck Toe AB. Dad'd controlled a number of companies without being listed as the official owner—Bladman was obviously nervous, didn't want to discuss ownership shares right now. Didn't know what ass cheek to sit on. Mischa Bladman never said it, but Natalie understood—he'd been taking instructions from Stefanovic up until this point.

She ordered a close-fitting bulletproof vest. Goran provided her with gorillas to always have in tow: Adam and Sascha. Some nights she slept at hotels. They checked under her car, they always positioned her farthest from the window, they never let her be the first to enter anywhere. She studied the police investigation for the twentieth time. There had to be something there. She considered telling the police that she knew where the weapons'd come from. She sat through meetings with her lawyer and another tax lawyer. She drove to the Frihamnen harbor and checked out the dock and how the tankers from Tallinn arrived—maybe bags of amphetamine could be tossed from the boats? She drank six Coca-Colas a day, ate ginseng tablets every morning, and munched on painkillers to reduce the headache that took hold at five o'clock every afternoon.

One day Goran called. "He wants to see you again," he said.

"Good."

"Natalie, just take it easy."

They met four hours later. Same restaurant, Teatergrillen. Same red upholstery. Same lit candles. Same privacy.

Adam, her bodyguard, had to stay in the car.

JW was dressed in a dark gray suit and a green tie.

He got right to the heart of it: "This isn't good."

Natalie assumed he was referring to the situation between her and Stefanovic.

"Bladman is feeling pressured," he said.

"Let me do my business, and then you and Bladman can do yours," she said. "And the last time I saw you, you weren't too keen on cooperating."

"We cooperate with whoever it suits us to cooperate with. I have many clients. Your father was one of them. Now Stefanovic is one of them."

Natalie didn't plan on folding. She had to do what she had to do. At the same time, she needed JW's help. It was he and Bladman who'd helped Dad with everything that Stefanovic was now trying to take over. And he was involved in the Cherkasova-Svelander story.

"Give me a reason why I shouldn't take back what's mine," she said.

His eyes glittered. Maybe that was a weak smile at the corner of his mouth. "The right of ownership is the most important right we have. Trust me, I fight for it. But you also have to understand the reality of this situation. I can't decide between clients."

"You can have your principles, and I'll have mine. I'm going to take back what's mine. You and Bladman'll have to pick sides, that's all there is to it."

"We're not going to do that. But let me say this. You want something from me. I want several things from you. I think we're going to be able to solve this. Just give me some time."

He was different. Swedish—yet still the same talk and calm as in Dad's men. Playboy look—but despite that he played in the same world as she did. He'd done time—but he still ordered wine with the same style as Dad used to do. He was playing several different games at once. Just like her, maybe.

And the entire time: that glitter in his eyes. She'd never met anyone like him.

At night, she texted Viktor and asked him to come over. Mom was at yoga. They ordered pizzas that he picked up on the way over. Natalie cut off the crusts and ate—the LCHF diet'd been discarded for now.

Viktor wondered what was going on. Why she never wanted to get together. Why people said they'd seen her downtown with some other guy. Natalie tried to explain—the situation was bad again. It wasn't the same guy she was walking around with. It was different bodyguards.

Viktor kept whining. Natalie didn't want to talk more about it. Said, "Let's go into the den instead."

She turned the TV on and settled into the couch with her feet propped up on the coffee table. Viktor lay down beside her. A workplace reality series was playing on TV. You followed the lawyers at a criminal defense office in Stockholm.

Natalie put her arm on Viktor's thigh. "Want to move this into my bedroom?"

That was one way of putting it.

"Dammit Natalie, we haven't seen each other in over a week, we've hardly spoken, and now you want to fuck, just like that?"

"Stop."

He smiled. "I like you."

"Ditto," she said.

Still, he didn't do anything. Just sat there. Staring at the TV. A lawyer was babbling about how innocent his client was because the cocaine that'd been found was cut with lidocaine.

"Come on."

Viktor made a lame move to bend closer to her. He wasn't in the mood, that much was obvious. But Natalie didn't want to wait for him to get horned up. She unbuttoned his fly. He was wearing Polo Ralph Lauren boxers. She pulled out his slack cock. Massaged it.

Viktor slipped down low in the couch. She continued to caress him. He really didn't want to right now.

But that wasn't her problem. She ran her hand over his eyes, made him close them. She slipped down his foreskin. Licked the tip.

He made sounds. That was a good sign.

His cock hardened to midsize. She took it in her mouth. It tasted of shower gel and sweat.

He mumbled, "Shouldn't we go to your room?"

She ignored him. Continued sucking until he got fully erect.

She unbuttoned her own pants. Climbed on top of him.

"Not here," he said.

She ignored him, moved him inside her.

She supported her arms against his chest. Pressed away with her arms. Moved up and down and to the sides. Felt him inside her.

She closed her eyes. Her thoughts were rushing. She moved faster.

They were going to go to the Black & White Inn tomorrow to have a talk with the rats who'd sold the weapons that'd been used on Dad. It was time for the truth to come out.

Viktor was half-lying on the couch. Natalie continued to fuck him—faster and harder movements. She heard her own breathing.

Viktor was silent. She didn't give a shit about him.

She moved his hands up to her hips. Felt him grab hold of her. She pressed down as far as she could. His cock reached as deep as it would go.

She was close now.

Wiggled her butt. Pressed herself forward.

Up and down.

She saw masks and harlequins.

She saw a face on the inside of her eyelids.

Up and down.

She saw red drapes and flickering candles.

She saw the face again.

It was JW.

She saw JW.

43

Jorge: stressed like a drug mule with a full stomach.

Nervous like a babyface on his first day of school.

Wiggin' like a CIT robber on the lam. Which was exactly what he was.

Jorge's world: had come crashing down. Again. Mahmud was still in the hospital. The Thai fuckers who wanted to sell wanted all the cash at once. Babak was threatening to snitch like a bitch.

Life was shitting on Jorge. Life was sucking horse cock. Life was more unfair than a Swedish court's way of convicting addicts. He was tired. Rap-life remade as crap-life. G-life transformed into L-life. L as in loser.

Jorge's anxious thoughts were on repeat: maybe he should turn himself in. Call the cops and demand that they take him. Check into an arrest cell for a few months. Install himself behind bars again. Be interrogated around the clock. Be humiliated by fake-friendly cops who would try to get him to wrap his bros.

No.

NO.

He was J-boy. The king. He would handle this. They could count to nine—he would always get backup.

Plus: there was some light in the darkness. That Hägerström dude was being useful, even though he was an ex-cop. According to JW, police records showed that he was a bad boy, had fallen hard. No wonder he got booted from the pigsty.

Jorge was gonna buy a place in Phuket. Mahmud and Javier were waiting. And Tom and Jimmy would also need him sooner or later. He wouldn't let them down.

Now, today: the effect of too much shit—Jorge on the escalator on the way toward baggage claim at Arlanda Airport. No other way out: on his way home to Stockholm either to help the Iranian somehow or to dig up the cash and bring it back to Phuket. The alternatives were his for the picking. But he had to go home.

He'd made it through border control with his fake passport. Now: just customs left. This couldn't go wrong. He couldn't fuck this up.

On the walls: large photos of Stockholmers. Benny Andersson, Björn Borg, the King. And then the owner of a kebab stand. The latter: completely unknown *hombre*. WELCOME TO MY HOMETOWN, it said. Jorge thought: *The kebab nigga isn't even Swedish, how can he welcome anyone?*

Then: *Wrong thinking—the kebab guy is just as Swedish as me. And I don't have anything else—this is my hometown, my home. I belong here.*

His thoughts were interrupted. Someone rested a hand on his shoulder.

"Hi. Were we on the same plane?"

Jorge turned around. He recognized the hazel eyes immediately.

The girl with dreadlocks that he'd borrowed the phone from in the bar in Pattaya. She smiled.

"Yes, probably," Jorge said. "But I had to ride with the luggage."

She laughed. She had a nice mouth. "Well, shouldn't you be coming out on this baggage carousel then?"

"Yeah, but I crawled out and hid in your dreads. You didn't notice?"

They laughed together.

The girl asked where he'd been traveling over the past few weeks. Jorge told her the truth, that he'd been in Phuket. It sounded like she'd been around half the globe. Trekked in the jungle in Malaysia, visited orangutans in Indonesia, shopped electronics in Singapore, smoked weed in Vietnam.

She had a ring in her nose and was wearing a worn white T-shirt and hippie tie-dye pants. Jorge did some wishful thinking: if the customs guys didn't stop her to check for smokes, then there was no way they were gonna stop anyone on this flight.

They kept talking. The bags rolled out on the carousel. Jorge's arrived first. He picked it up. Set it down on the floor. Walked over to the girl, was just about to say goodbye. Then he stopped. Thought: *I'll wait for her instead.*

She noticed that he was waiting. Glanced at him. Smiled faintly. Asked if he had more bags.

Her bag arrived after another minute or so.

They walked together out toward the customs control area.

The girl asked where he was going in Stockholm. What he was doing. When he was going to get back on the road again. He felt worry pounding through his body. His stomach hurt. Vomit urges were pushing up his throat. He stared straight ahead. Saw the customs guys standing around, talking, fifty yards farther up. He tried to respond to the girl's questions.

He saw a dog, a German shepherd.

He saw it sniff at the bags that passed through customs.

He felt his own pulse pound faster than Little Jorge's baby heart.

He wasn't carrying any drugs. But the dog meant the customs guys were on their guard. That they were ready to pluck passersby for control. And a control would mean another scrutiny of his passport. He didn't think he was listed as wanted—if he were, it should've been noted in the documents that he'd gotten from JW through Hägerström. But they'd picked up Babak now—the situation could've changed.

They approached.

The sweat on his palms almost made him lose the grip on his suitcase.

The girl babbled on.

They walked toward the entrance to the customs area.

Nothing to declare.

He met the eyes of one of the customs agents. The guy's eyes bored straight into his.

But no reaction.

Jorge passed. The dog didn't even bother sniffing his bag.

They emerged on the other side.

A few Thai families and fat cabbies holding signs with names scribbled on them.

He was on Swedish soil again.

There was a God.

One day later. He was sitting at Paola's house. Örnsberg. Fall colors on the trees outside.

Little Jorge was crazy happy that he was there. Ran back and forth and wanted to show drawings he'd made.

Hijo predilecto. The best in the world.

In the kitchen. Jorge and Paola. Mom still didn't know that he was home.

Jorge'd rung the doorbell at midnight. At first Paola didn't want to let him in. Through the sliver of open door: thirty minutes of whispered discussion. Finally he was allowed to crash on the couch in the living room. She was still pissed at him.

But now: she'd just picked up Junior at day care. She was leaning over the kitchen table. Jorge looked at her. Her eyes were no longer filled with laughter. Her dimples were gone. Instead: two creases dragged down the corners of her mouth. She looked twice as old as the last time he'd seen her. She looked ten times sadder.

"I've still not gotten a decent job, and my unemployment is almost up. Do you understand what that means? That I'm living at subsistence level and am going to need to get help from welfare."

"I understand, things are rough. I promise, I'm gonna do everything I can for you."

Paola hissed, "Cut that crap. If you start with that again, you might as well just leave."

He didn't say anything.

She didn't say anything.

He looked around. On the counter: a SodaStream, a water boiler, a toaster. On the fridge: phone number to the local pizza place, day-care photos of Jorgito, and drawings. A pile with clothes on a chair. A beeping sound from the fridge—it probably needed to be switched out.

She lived nine-to-five. She didn't take any risks, had paid her taxes and her unemployment every year. But who was helping her now? Welfare, with four grand a month? That was a joke. Family was the only thing that mattered in these situations.

The insane part: right now Jorge envied her life.

He saw images. Him and Paola in the kitchen at home in Sollentuna when they were little. They were standing beside the toaster, waiting. A piece of toast each. When the slices popped up, they threw themselves at them. Grabbed the bread. Chased back to the table, hurled themselves over the butter knife that was standing in the package of butter. You had to be the first. First to butter your toast. That was their own private little morning competition. Both wanted the butter to melt as much as possible on their piece of toast.

Jorge reached his hands over the table. Brushed by Paola's elbows.

"*Hermana*, you're everything to me. I've made so many mistakes lately. But I'm back now. I'm going to set it all right. *Te prometo.*"

Paola just looked at him. Jorge couldn't read her eyes. Was she pissed again? Was she about to start crying? Did she understand all the love he felt?

He considered his own options. Either he tried to fix some sort of alibi for the Iranian—but he had no clue what Babak was gonna say when he was interrogated by the police about what he'd done on the CIT day. Or else he tried to free Babak. But with who? He wouldn't be able to do it alone. And now all his homies were abroad or straight. Except for JW—Jorge had to talk to him. Soon.

The other alternative: screw the Iranian, dig up his own and Mahmud's money in the woods, and go back to Thailand. Buy a place with Hägerström's help.

Fuck.

He regretted ever leaving his café life in Sweden. Who'd he think he was, anyway? All the fuckers, they just talked. About how easy it was to land mad gold. How easy it was to get loaded. But the criminal lifestyle was just as hard as a regular job. Or worse. Even more headaches, even more ulcers.

There were no easy roads. No broad paths. No life deluxe.

Everything was a lie.

Everything sucked cock.

Everything fucked him over and over.

He looked out the window: wind was blowing through the trees.

There was a STORM in his head.

44

The weather was nice, as usual. The shutter on the window created a faint striped light on the white wall. No paintings, no bookshelves, no curtains. Decorating wasn't exactly the main interest in this place.

A lot of thoughts were running through Hägerström'd head. At the same time, a single thought overshadowed the others. A thought that gave him a kind of peace.

The past few days'd been earth-shattering.

He thought about Pravat. Hägerström wrote him several postcards a week. An adult might think that was hysterical, but he knew Pravat liked the pictures and the greetings, especially since they came from Thailand. Pravat had begun to ask questions about what adoption was and how his had happened. They Skyped sometimes, Hägerström from an Internet café, Pravat from his computer at school. Hägerström explained that both he and Mom had worked here, and that was why they had chosen Pravat. "You were the one we wanted, we chose you with love," he said.

It was unclear if Pravat understood.

Hägerström could see his brother's text in front of his mind's eye. Carl wondered when he was going to come home—it was almost moose-hunting season. Hägerström didn't know. But if he made it home in time, he might be able to arrange something with JW and that hunt.

He thought about all the texts he had gotten from Torsfjäll. Short snippets of information about Jorge and Javier. Hägerström was always careful to delete the messages after he read them.

He thought about all the negotiations he and Jorge had had before Jorge left to go back to Sweden. They were done now. Jorge had put in an offer for a café, and after three days, the seller had accepted. They negotiated about the terms, mostly about how the payment was to be made. The deal now: payment in installments. Just what Jorge wanted—now he would get a chance to start the place up, make some revenue.

He wondered why Jorge hadn't come back from Sweden. He had promised to return to Phuket immediately. The seller was actually supposed to have received his dollars yesterday. Maybe it was hard to get flights.

Jorge's sudden trip home was obviously interesting. The first truly interesting thing that had happened since Hägerström got here. Because honestly, his stay here hadn't done shit for Operation Tide. Jorge never talked about JW. He didn't seem to know Mischa Bladman, or any of the Yugoslavs, or Nippe or Hansén. Torsfjäll said Jorge and Javier had probably been involved in the Tomteboda robbery earlier this year. It was very possible, but Jorge never hinted anything about it. He whined about being broke all the time. A friend of theirs was in a hospital nearby—Mahmud, whom Jorge visited every so often. Mostly the whole situation seemed pretty pathetic.

Maybe it was time to drop this investigation and go home—he had nothing to gain from being here right now.

Still, he had something fantastic to gain.

He thought back to the night when Javier had brought him up to his room.

The Thai girls had stepped into the living room in the suite. Javier had downed his drink. Yelled at Hägerström, "Ha ha—this is what you wanted, isn't it?"

He was standing stiff as an icicle hanging from a Stockholm roof. He thought: *What the fuck do I do now?*

One of the girls walked over to Hägerström. She had bangs and looked young. "You are very pretty, did you know that?" She spoke good English.

Hägerström responded in Thai, "I'm not interested tonight."

The girl giggled, told her friend that he knew their language.

Javier was sitting in the couch, cozying up to his girl. Hägerström saw that he had pulled out a Baggie with white powder.

He tried to smile. The girl put her arm on his shoulder and responded in Thai, "Come, let's go into the bedroom."

He saw Javier pour the white powder onto a DVD.

Hägerström didn't want to be in the same room as him. He led the girl into Javier's bedroom. She sat down on the bed. He remained standing by the side of the bed.

Before he had a chance to ask her if she wanted to leave with him, the door opened. Javier and his girl tumbled in. Hägerström saw coke rings around his nose.

They threw themselves onto the bed. Javier grabbed hold of Hägerström's arm in the fall. Tore him down with him.

The girls were giggling. Javier rolled around and wrestled Hägerström onto his back before he had a chance to sit up again.

"Come on, officer, don't be shy."

Hägerström's mind was searching for options. Evasions. He could just get up and leave without explaining why. Tomorrow he could say he hadn't been feeling well or something. He could try to get his girl back out into the living room again, away from Javier's eyes. Or else he could play along for a while and then try to escape when Javier was doing his thing.

He felt fuzzy. Drunk. His thoughts wouldn't crystallize. The room was spinning.

One of the girls started to unbutton his shirt. Javier was lying on his back in the wide bed; the other girl was in the process of pulling his pants off. Hägerström sat up. Set his feet down onto the floor. The girl pulled his shirt up. He was sitting with his back to Javier. Heard him moaning. The girl started to caress his chest.

He wanted to get one more look at Javier before he stood up and went back down to his hotel room. He twisted his torso, turned around. Javier was still lying on his back. The girl was sitting on top of him, on her knees, bent down. She had the tip of his cock in her mouth. Her long black hair framed the image, almost like a photograph. Hägerström sat, frozen. Just staring.

The girl next to him started unbuttoning his pants.

Javier raised his head. "What's up with you, man? You need help or what?"

Before Hägerström could react—or rather, probably before he *wanted* to react—Javier threw himself over to him and grabbed hold of his boxers. He put his hand inside. Pulled out Hägerström's cock.

He grew hard immediately

Javier laughed. The Thai girl standing over him looked up. The girl next to Hägerström bent down quickly, licked his cock. Hägerström shuddered. Javier was still holding his member.

The girl licked him again.

The whole time, Javier maintained a firm grip on his cock.

The girl raised her head.

Javier was lying on his stomach. Pushed himself up with his free hand.

Hägerström could usually recognize men who liked other men—he thought he could tell by their eyes. But he'd completely missed Javier. Now he knew what that gleam in his eye had been.

Javier opened his mouth.

Took Hägerström's cock in his mouth.

The next morning he woke up in Javier's bed. The Thai girls were gone. The sheets were crumpled. The AC was humming.

Hägerström turned over. He heard the door open, or close. He saw condoms and lube on the nightstand. He got up. He was naked. There was a faint burning in his ass.

Javier walked into the bedroom. A glass of juice in one hand. He laughed and said, "Yo man, it got pretty lively in here last night."

Hägerström felt unprepared. He had just had an incredible night with a megagangster. A man who, according to Torsfjäll's searches, had been convicted of countless violent crimes and drug offenses, was probably involved in the CIT heist of the year, and—above all—was someone he had been hired to infiltrate. This was a person he was supposed to trick at all times. Not fuck.

What should he say? Javier didn't seem to think there was anything strange about what had happened. He hadn't been open about his orientation with Jorge. A double agent, just like him. On the other hand: Jorge was in Sweden now. And he didn't know that Hägerström was playing a double-double game.

His boxers were at the foot of the bed. He put them on. At first, he wasn't going to say anything. Just leave and pretend like nothing happened.

But Javier beat him to it. "I've been to visit Mahmud at the hospital. They're gonna release him in a few days."

"Oh okay, good." Hägerström hadn't met Mahmud yet. He bent down for his pants.

Javier grinned. "So I think you should take those boxers off, have some juice, and we'll get back in bed."

Hägerström couldn't help but smile in return.

"That was nice of you, to get the juice and all," he said.

Javier threw himself onto the bed. "I was born nice. Let's have ourselves a quickie now, huh?"

Hägerström lay down next to him.

Javier kissed his chest.

Hägerström climbed out of his own bed. His bags were packed. He opened the door.

So much had happened in such short time. He had spent the days with Javier. They had smoked cigarettes, ordered takeout from Hägerström's favorite restaurant, and had lots of sex. They had talked about everything and nothing. Why Hägerström had been booted from the force, why Javier hated cops. Why Phuket was a dump while Bangkok was sweet. Why all the restaurants here had plastic chairs and their cashew nuts tasted like a favorite chocolate bar from home.

At night, they went out to eat. They didn't touch each other openly, but they brushed against each other all the time. Knee against knee. Hand against hip. Shoulder against shoulder. A flash of heat shot through Hägerström every time.

And today Jorge and Javier's friend, Mahmud, was being checked out from the hospital. That meant the end of Hägerström and Javier's little fling.

But Javier came up with an idea: "Let's go to Bangkok for a few days. Now that the Arab's out and can take care of himself, I don't have to stay in this dump anymore. You and me can have a better time somewhere else."

"All right," Hägerström said.

He would love to go to Bangkok. He would love to get more time with Javier. There was just one question: what the hell was he doing?

He walked down the stairs. Javier was already sitting in the taxi that was going to take them to the airport.

A few days in Bangkok. After that, nothing planned.

Five days passed. Hägerström and Javier spent every single minute together. They checked into a sweet hotel, Hägerström picked up the bill. They lay in bed and talked about Hägerström's Jaguar and about

Javier's dream car, Porsche Panamera. They talked about what it would be like to be a father—Hägerström didn't say anything about Pravat, but everything he said was based on his own experience.

They analyzed life behind bars—Javier from his perspective, and Hägerström from the screw side. They made love. They joked about the best ways to conceal weapons. Javier had gotten away clean from a search of his house once because he had painted his Glock yellow. The cops thought it was a toy gun. Idiots. They laughed, they made love again.

They went out to eat at restaurants where the food tasted like home. Hägerström guided them to the gay bars he had hung out at when he was working here in the foreign service. They strolled through the megamalls, eyed the shopping hysteria. They talked about the small altars in the 7-Eleven stores and the Buddha figurines that Western men wore around their necks.

Jorge was still in Sweden. Hägerström called the seller of the place in Phuket and negotiated an extension. Javier called Mahmud—the Arab was enjoying being out of the hospital, but he was wondering when Jorge or Javier were coming back to Phuket. Javier had paid the hospital bill with the last money Jorge had left.

Hägerström and Javier bought identical Ray-Ban shades. They walked around in tank tops and flip-flops. There was more than a ten-year age difference between them. They went to the temples by the river and looked at the enormous recumbent golden Buddha. They went to the floating market. They relaxed in the hotel room.

They walked hand in hand on the street.

It was the first time in Hägerström's life that he held another man's hand openly. But it wasn't just that. He was comfortable with this guy, enjoyed his company. Life was pretty wonderful. The only thing that bothered him was that he missed Pravat. But he definitely felt different with Javier than he had felt in a long time. It was like they met each other eye to eye, even though they were so different. As though it just clicked every time they spoke.

A completely impossible combination. An ex-cop, ex-screw with a super G. A Östermalm gentleman with a ghetto boy from the projects. Two macho men in a homo-relationship. An undercover agent with one of his targets.

He should have ended this on day one.

But he couldn't, didn't want to. And anyway, it wasn't all that bad. They were alone in Bangkok, no one would find them out. The whole thing could be kept separate from the rest of their lives and from Hägerström's operation. Maybe it would just peter out into a friendship anyway.

He thought about his brother. All Carl's friends were either from elementary school, high school, or his university years. He didn't have a single friend he had met after the age of twenty-three. And he was proud of that. "There's something weird about people who make a bunch of friends when they're adults," he liked to say. "Either they didn't have any friends when they were young, or else their friends don't want them around anymore. Definitely suspicious, in my opinion."

Hägerström thought about his father. He thought about his mother. All their friends were, like, from the beginning of time. All their friends lived the exact same lives they lived. Enormous flats within the same five-hundred-yard radius, enormous houses in the northern suburbs or estates in Sörmland. Nice summer homes in Torekov or the archipelago. Zero divorces. Zero acquaintances from non-European countries. Children who married each other in standard heterosexual marriages. Not a cop as far as the eye could see.

Hägerström forced himself to sober up on day six. He hadn't been in touch with Torsfjäll in over two weeks. The inspector had sent him texts, he had deleted them without responding.

But now he wrote, *In Bangkok with Javier. Mahmud out of the hospital. Jorge still gone.*

A response on his cell twenty seconds later. He was sitting on the toilet. His phone was on silent. Security was still everything.

Why haven't you been in touch. Call me.

He was down on the street fifteen minutes later. Told Javier that he had to call his mother, in private.

"Where've you been?" Torsfjäll asked.

Hägerström didn't know what to say. "When Mahmud was checked out of the hospital, Javier didn't need to stay in Phuket anymore and wanted to go to Bangkok. So I went with him."

"I understand. Stuff's been happening over here, at home. They've brought in a guy named Babak Behrang from Thailand. He's been arrested on suspicion of the CIT robbery in Tomteboda. And he's part of the same circle as Jorge, Mahmud, and the others down there. So it's just as I said: they're all involved in this robbery."

"That's not at all impossible, but they're very tight-lipped. They're pros, maybe. But they seem to be low on cash. And I haven't heard anyone mention any Babak."

"Yes, apparently the robbery didn't yield all that much. And so many of them were splitting that pie—there are more men down where you are who're connected to this. And the hypothesis the investigative team is working with is that there's a taskmaster somewhere in the background too. Their information points to a person who calls himself the Finn. They don't know who he is, but the feds suspect that he's behind several of the big CIT robberies over the past few years. Has anyone mentioned him?"

"Not a peep. They don't talk about that kind of thing with me."

"It might come. They've already interrogated that Babak guy three times here in Sweden."

"And what does he say?"

"Not much. But the investigators think that they're going to be able to crack him. And Jorge—what've you got on him?"

"Like I wrote in my text—he's still gone. He's in Sweden, as far as I know. No one's heard from him there?"

"No, and he's good at keeping his head down, that little fucker. He was on the run from prison for over a year, a few years back."

"So what do I do now?"

Torsfjäll fell silent for a few seconds and thought it over. "I'll get back to you with instructions. Maybe you'll have to stay in Thailand for a while longer, or maybe I'll want you to come home. Maybe I'll want you to try to get all the boys down there to go home so that we can pick them up here."

They hung up. Hägerström remained standing on the street for a few minutes. Cabs were dropping off tourists and Thai businessmen. Farther off, he saw large staircases winding up toward the elevated railway. A family with kids came walking toward him. He watched them.

The mom was pushing the double stroller. She flashed Hägerström a quick smile.

He went back up to Javier.

———

A few days later, as Hägerström came out of the shower, Javier was sitting on the bed. His previously suntanned chest had started to fade somewhat.

He was looking down at something.

Hägerström was completely naked.

Javier held up Hägerström's cell phone.

"What the fuck is this?"

Hägerström took the phone. How stupid could he have been, leaving it on like that?

Javier had obviously been snooping around while Hägerström was showering.

There was a new text. The sender was one of the numbers that Torsfjäll used.

It said, *Bring home as many as possible.*

45

Natalie was sitting across from Louise at Brasserie Godot on Grev Turegatan. Adam was waiting outside. She couldn't handle having the bodyguard with her when she hung out with Louise.

The place: creative wall paintings, designer lamps suspended from the ceilings, even more designy candelabras on the tables. The lighting set to perfection—strong enough to see everyone, soft enough to be flattering. The background music was chill: something jazzy, something with swing to it, something very of the moment. The price of the drinks: 150 kronor and up. The entrées averaged half a grand. Natalie didn't even want to think about the price of a bottle of Moët.

To put it simply: *very* flashy feel.

The crowd: accrued Aryan A-team. Crème de la crème, people who looked fresh and sun-kissed even though the autumn wind was whipping outside. People who summered in Saint-Tropez, on Gotland, or in Torekov. Natalie knew some and recognized even more. Jet Set Carl, Hermine, and so on. Definitely not anyone named anything like Natalie or close to Daniella or Danja. No one with parents born in the former Yugoslavia. Simple: ethnic wasn't welcome here.

A dude two tables over saw that she had raised her eyes. He flirted wildly with her.

Natalie turned back to Louise again. She was wearing a short-short skirt and a pair of Louboutins with heels like needles. Her top was covered in a cherry pattern. Natalie knew it had cost a fortune. Still: it revealed too much. As usual, Louise'd pushed up her already unreal tits so they were almost touching her chin.

Natalie looked down at her appetizer: duck liver terrine with pomegranate, port wine jelly, duck leg rillette, and toasted brioche. She yearned for regular cabbage salad.

Everything around her felt foreign. Silly. Almost repulsive. She felt like a tourist in this place. This wasn't her world anymore. In a way, it was as if she'd come home—she felt more comfortable sitting with the men in the library than she'd ever felt with Louise, Tove, and the others, even though they talked about much stranger things.

"Was yours good?" Louise asked.

Natalie picked at her food. "Mmm. It's fine."

"Did you see? Jet Set Carl is here."

The same old obsession with B-list celebs and Stureplan brats.

"Mmm."

"Did you see Fredrika over there?" Louise said. "She can't even walk in her shoes. Girls who walk in heels like they're doing lunges or something—that's the worst, right?"

Natalie glanced over at the girl Louise'd pointed out. She couldn't see anything strange about the way she was walking. The dude two tables over was trying to get her attention again. Natalie ignored him.

She thought about JW—wondered how he would've done it. The guy over there was so crude and unsophisticated.

JW'd been in her thoughts often, ever since they saw each other last. Okay, he was important for business. He might know something about the politician. But there were others who were more important. Still: she couldn't let JW go. She wanted to see him again. She got the feeling that he was there, in the background, all the time. Seemed to know more than anyone else. Seemed to be holding even more strings than Stefanovic. But it wasn't just that—she was tempted by who he was too. He exuded a kind of self-confidence that attracted her, very strongly. And what's more, he was a double player in so many ways—just like her.

Louise droned on. About new creams from Dior. A new nightclub in Paris. A new blog online. Natalie was only half-listening.

She floated away again.

Goran'd called yesterday. Thomas and he'd gone to the Black & White Inn a few days ago. Goran: was normally short, straightforward, and simple in a military way. But he'd provided a vivid description of what'd happened.

He'd walked straight up to the woman in the bar—everyone knew she was the gatekeeper for the side business at this place—and said, in Russian, "I wanna talk to you after closing. We'll wait."

At one o'clock, the place closed its doors. The bartender put the chairs on top of the table, started mopping the floor. The woman led Thomas and Goran behind the bar. Through the kitchen and out on the other side. The hallway smelled of disinfectant and garlic. A man emerged from a room. Delivered a quick pat-down. Then he went back inside. The woman opened another door. She, Goran, and Thomas sat down in dirty chairs in a small office. No frills. Got right down to it.

She asked them what they wanted to buy.

Goran responded in Swedish, "We want information."

The woman locked eyes with him. "I don't sell that."

"Do you know who we represent?"

The woman kept staring at him.

"We don't want trouble," he said. "You don't want trouble. But you know what happened to Kum Rado. We have to investigate it. Even your people must understand that. Right?"

The woman didn't respond.

He continued explaining. They knew from a certain secure source that Radovan'd been murdered with weapons and explosives purchased at the Black & White Inn. He wanted to know who'd bought the gear.

The woman'd still not dropped his gaze. "I have no idea. You know that. Who do you think I am? Someone who checks passport numbers and fingerprints on the people we do business with?"

Goran didn't cave. "Maybe not, but we have our own ways of checking that kind of thing. I want you to inform your people that we want to see all the objects he touched."

"What do you mean? You'll have to come back tomorrow."

"What we mean is that you're going to take out all the objects that he touched. And you can go ahead and call your people now."

That's how it'd gone down. Magically, the Black & White Inn agreed to Goran's demands, in exchange for ten grand in cash.

He'd walked back out to his car. Picked up the person who was waiting in the backseat: Ulf Bergström. Chemist formerly employed at the national forensic lab—these days partner in his own lab, Forensic Rapid Research AB. A private alternative to the government's forensic authority.

Ulf sat in that office all night. Brushed, taped, swabbed. According to the woman: the person who'd bought the weapons'd also handled a bag, two guns, and four grenades. It was almost six months ago. The chances of finding anything were less than getting a parking spot on Östermalm after ten o'clock on a Sunday night.

Still, it was worth a try.

Ulf Bergström'd promised to get back to them as soon as he had the test results.

They'd finished eating. Natalie suggested they have a cigarette in the outdoor seating area.

They walked out. Each lit a Marlboro Menthol. The air was cool. Infraheat billowed from suspended heaters.

A waiter came over with a tray with two glasses of champagne and said, "Courtesy of the man over there."

Natalie saw the flirt-dude wink at her.

"Do you know who that is?" Louise said.

"No."

"Me neither. But he doesn't seem too shabby, huh?"

Natalie just shook her head.

Louise asked how things were going with Viktor.

"We don't see each other too much, and he's kind of a pain."

"Oh no. Like, how?"

"I don't know. It's been so long. He annoys me. He doesn't understand that I'm sad sometimes and that I think about Dad. Either he just wants to go do stuff all the time, or else he's working like crazy. I don't have time for that. You know, I think he's a real loser."

"But maybe you should go away somewhere together, get some quality time."

Louise had bad suggestions. Natalie definitely didn't have time to go away right now.

"No, I don't want to do that. I can't right now. And besides, I'd just get even more annoyed at him. We argued yesterday."

"Oh, sweetie. About what?"

"He's jealous. Started going off about me seeing someone else and stuff. But that's just bullshit. I have an assistant sometimes, that's all. But Viktor doesn't get that. He thinks I screen his calls. That I can't explain what I've been doing. But that's bullshit too. It's just that I don't want to tell him everything."

"But can't you see where he's coming from, at least a little bit?"

"No, not after everything with Dad. And then he's got the balls to ask me if I could lend him money. Can you believe it?"

"Wow, what nerve!"

Louise checked herself. Her eyes flitted around. "That guy over there," she said. "He's waving to us again. He wants us to come over to his table. Wanna go?"

She pointed at the flirt guy. The dude: dark blazer, striped shirt unbuttoned at the neck, a pink tie with a loosened knot.

Natalie wasn't interested one iota.

"No, I think I'm gonna go home now," she said.

Louise looked disappointed. "Come on, sweetie. I think you should have some fun."

Natalie set her glass down. "Are you kidding me?"

Adam was keeping a safe distance, around four yards. They were walking toward his car, which was parked down on the short end of the Humlegården Park. The night was dark. Maybe forty degrees out. One of Natalie's contacts was bothering her.

She didn't regret having blown Louise off. Since Dad's murder, she didn't feel close to those girls anymore. Let them busy themselves with their little lives until they matured, in a few years.

Her thoughts were dancing through her head like the leaves in the park. Maybe she was drunk. Maybe she was just drained after all that'd been going on during the past few weeks. Maybe she needed to sit down in front of a computer and try to make some order out of everything that was happening.

The war was raging out there. Stefanovic's reaction after the meeting in the Tower'd been immediate. The lawyer that was dealing with Dad's estate'd received some nightly phone calls from an unknown man with some kind of Eastern accent. The person promised to gut the lawyer and his wife belly-up if he didn't give Stefanovic's front men back signatory rights for several of the companies. The day after: Marko and two other guys with baseball bats'd stepped into Dad's gym, Fitnesse Club, had really worked the place over. When the people working the front desk tried to stop the shit, they were jumped. Two were still in the hospital, one with life-threatening skull fractures. Two days after the assault: an amphetamine dealer found his dog's head in the trunk of his car with a Post-it note on the floor next to it: *Last warning. Don't sell to Kranjic.* The same week: several bars downtown received letters in the mail that smelled of gasoline. The message was clear enough: *No more business with Kranjic.*

Natalie thought: *Come on, Stefanovic, you're not Don Vito fucking Corleone. You're a goddamn loser.*

Goran told Natalie that they had to strike back. Of course they were going to strike back.

"But how?"

"We'll do what we usually do."

She let Goran command the details of the war. They tried to torch the Tower. Unfortunately the place survived with only minor damages. They hijacked a truckload of cigarettes that Stefanovic's people'd ordered. They slaughtered Stefanovic's best racehorse, Tima Efes. Put the horse head in a giant cooler and messengered it to him. They brought a bouncer who was connected with Stefanovic to a warehouse in Huddinge and cracked his kneecap with a hammer. That was a first revenge for the assault at Fitnesse Club.

Personally, Natalie was working like a maniac. She spoke to and e-mailed the banks every single day. She talked to Goran and Thomas. She gave orders to Bogdan and others. Planned excursions on the town with one of her bodyguards. She got in touch with people on the inside who were about to gate out, donated money to their wives. She donated money to the National Serbian Association in Stockholm. She donated money to the Näsbypark sporting club. Soon she wouldn't have a cent left—Bogdan had to go to Switzerland soon, very soon. She just had to sort everything out with JW first.

She took another step: she contacted Melissa Cherkasova.

Rang the doorbell at her apartment on Råsundavägen. Adam and Sascha in the background. It was three o'clock in the afternoon.

She knew Melissa was home. Sascha'd been sitting in a car, watching the apartment for ten hours. The girl'd entered the building but not come out.

The peephole grew dark. She heard a voice. Strong accent, yet still correct Swedish.

"What do you want?"

"I just want to talk. My name is Natalie Kranjic."

The voice on the other side sounded weak. "I know. You've already talked to me when you talked to Martina."

"Yes, but I want to talk to you directly. I promise nothing will happen to you."

There was a rustling with the door chain on the inside.

Melissa was standing there barefoot, wearing tight jeans and a loosely fitting T-shirt. Un-made-up, unstyled, uncertain.

The same look in her eyes as when Natalie'd followed her home.

Sascha closed the door behind them.

Melissa didn't show them into the apartment. Natalie tried to scope out the place. A small one-bedroom with a separate kitchen. She saw a couch and a coffee table. She saw a laptop and DVDs on the coffee table.

They remained standing in the hall.

"I know everything about you," Natalie said. "I know what you do. I know what you did with my father in the apartment on Björngårdsgatan. I know what you're doing with the politician Bengt Svelander. I know you're filming everything."

Melissa stared down at the floor.

"I don't mind what you do." Natalie went on. "But Martina's told you not to give any of the material to Stefanovic, right? Listen to me."

Natalie took a breath, then continued, "I'm not going to be involved in the kind of business you work in. I've told my men that Stefanovic can continue if he wants, but we're not going to be selling escort services anymore. You can also do whatever you want, but personally, I don't like that business. Do you understand?"

Melissa continued to stare down into the floor.

"But the material belongs to me. You are going to give it to me and not to Stefanovic."

Melissa didn't move.

"So," Natalie said. "Have you given anything to Stefanovic?"

Melissa's voice was even weaker than before, "No, not yet. But he wants it."

"Who's he going to give it to?"

"I have no idea."

"I understand. But in that case, you can give me the material now."

Melissa pointed at the computer. "I have to transfer the material to a DVD or USB in order for you to get it. It'll take an hour."

Natalie liked what she was hearing. But she didn't want to stand here waiting for a whole hour.

"In that case, we'll take your computer with us. I'll give it back soon."

"But you don't know which files they are," Melissa said. "There are hundreds, and many of them are blurry."

Natalie nodded. "Okay, this is what we'll do: you transfer the material and get in touch with me as soon as it's ready."

Back in the Stockholm night. She and Adam were walking along Humlegården Park.

Melissa hadn't been in touch. Natalie was starting to get impatient, but she had a lot of other stuff to deal with right now.

Two hundred yards farther down, she saw the white mushroom sculpture on Stureplan. The lights were bouncing up toward the park. Shouts from sloshed sluts sauntering to Sturecompagniet. Dudes desperate to party yelling at one another. The sound of cabs swishing by.

She was wondering what to do about Viktor.

At that moment: one of the cabs stopped right behind Natalie. The brakes screeched.

The back door flew open.

A man hurled himself out.

She turned around in the same instant that he caught up with her. He grabbed hold of her arm.

She heard Adam yell something.

She sucked in cool air.

One single thought: *Is this it?*

What was happening?

* * *

REPORT

STOCKHOLM COUNTY POLICE

Report processed by: Stockholm County Police
Dossier number: 2010-K30304-10
Date of report: October 2
Received by: Officer David Carlsson

Entered by: Officer David Carlsson
Report given by: Officer on duty

Crime Scene Area Code: 21A3049034900
STUREGATAN, HUMLEGÅRDEN PARK, STOCKHOLM

TIME OF CRIME
Saturday, September 29 at 23.00-23.10

CRIME/INCIDENT
Aggravated assault

SUMMARY

PLAINTIFF
Axel Jolie

WITNESSES
Saman Kurdo
Fredric Vik

SUSPECTS
Unknown

Description
Susp1: Middle-age man, large build, around 6'2", light brown hair in a side part, long black overcoat, dark jeans.

Susp2: Young woman, ca 5'9", long dark hair, dark clothes.

Description of Events
Dispatch received a call from Saman Kurdo. Police vehicles 2039 and 2048 arrived on the scene.

EVENT
The man in the bushes has regained consciousness when Officer David Carlsson and Officer Emma Skogsgren first arrive on the

scene. The person in question is Axel Jolie. He is intoxicated. He has sustained injuries to the face and head. He claims that he was attacked when he stopped in a taxi in order to speak with a woman he thought he knew. At this time, the suspected man (Susp1) threw himself forward and tore Jolie out of the cab. After that, Susp1 delivered blows to Jolie's face so that he lost his balance. Then Susp1 pulled out what he perceived as a firearm and forced Jolie into the park. The woman (Susp 2) remains by the men's side throughout and is yelling at Jolie. They walk about ten yards into the park.

Susp1 then pushes Jolie into some bushes. Jolie loses his balance once again. Susp1 kicks him in the stomach as well as several times in the head. After that, Susp2 enters the bushes. She strikes Jolie in the face several times with her open palm and yells. Then Jolie is forced to get on his knees and apologize. At that point, Susp2 kicks Jolie's penis. This causes terrible pain and Jolie loses consciousness.

INJURIES

Axel Jolie has swelling on the forehead and over the eyes as well as on his cheeks, as well as blood over his right eyebrow. He is bleeding on the inside of his cheek. He has a superficial wound on his left ear. He also has redness on his right arm as well as on his left thigh. He is in a state of shock. He did not want to show his penis.

WITNESS REPORTS

The taxi driver Saman Kurdo states that Axel Jolie got into the taxi by Linnégatan. He asked him to drive slowly and then to turn down on Sturegatan beside the Humlegården Park. It seemed as though he was looking for someone. When they saw the woman in question near the park, he asked Kurdo to pull up beside her and make a quick stop. Jolie threw himself out of the car and tried to talk to and grab hold of the woman. It did not seem to Kurdo as though the woman knew Jolie particularly well. She resisted. After a few seconds, a man jumped out and struck Jolie in the head. Jolie ended up on the pavement. Then they all ran into the park. Kurdo heard screams coming from the park. At that point, he called the police and tried to call for help from a man on the other side of the street.

Fredric Vik was called over by Saman Kurdo, who was standing beside his taxi on Sturegatan. At first, he did not understand what was happening. He walked over and asked Kurdo. Kurdo said there was an assault going on a ways into the park. Vik walked in toward the park, he heard sounds in there. Farther off, he saw two people walking away from the scene at a rapid pace. He did not see what they looked like. He looked around. He saw Jolie lying in some bushes. It appeared as though he was unconscious.

OTHER INFORMATION
Jolie is being driven to the Karolinska University Hospital to receive medical care and to document his injuries.

Jolie does not want to cooperate or give a closer description of Susp1 and Susp2. He claims that doing so might be dangerous for him. The descriptions are therefore only based on the information provided by the witness Saman Kurdo.

46

"*Sho bre*, good to see you man!"

Peppe in camouflage-colored carpenter pants, black Harley-Davidson hat, and a hoodie with writing across the chest: SUPPORT YOUR LOCAL BANDIDOS. The same silhouette as the last time they'd seen each other, at Babak's twenty-fifth-birthday bash: like a monkey. Overly broad shoulders and arms so long he could, like, scratch his heels without bending down.

They pounded each other on the back. Jorge couldn't help but like Peppe. They sat down at the table: McDonald's in Kungens Kurva.

Jorge ate two Quarter Pounders with cheese. Relished every bite of nongook grub.

An important meeting for Jorge. He wanted to borrow tools from Peppe to dig up the rest of the cash. With some *suerte:* he could have six hundred Gs in his hand tonight already. He just needed a chill Peppe and a few hours at the hiding spot.

Peppe let his mouth run, the usual. He worked as a carpenter. Jorge read him: it was mostly a facade, but there was nothing wrong with that—everyone needed a facade.

Peppe told him he was gonna be a father. "I usually jizz on her tits, so it's totally crazy man—how could that make a junior me?"

Peppe's sense of humor. Jorge congratulated him and grinned.

Peppe was wondering about Babak, Tom, and the others. Jorge ducked the subject as much as he could. Apparently Peppe didn't know that Babak'd been brought to Sweden. Though the newspapers'd been trumpeting it out for several days now: TWENTY-FIVE-YEAR-OLD SUSPECTED OF THE TOMTEBODA ROBBERY ARRESTED IN THAILAND.

Peppe buzzed about his usual smart plans. The fake invoices in the construction business, the tax man's latest check-up methods, employment agencies providing hard workers from Latin America who shoveled snow from the roofs for four euros an hour.

"Winter's just around the corner, you know. And every single coop board in this city is terrified that snow and ice is gonna go falling down on some poor sucker. They'll pay anything for some shoveling. We set up companies for the workers, then we hire them into the company where we have all the gear. The worker company pays the guys every single euro under the table. Our company'll never get hit if the tax man starts complaining."

"Sounds awesome," Jorge said. "So I'm guessing you've got a bunch of shovels and shit, right?"

It was dark out when Jorge parked the pickup. He'd borrowed it from Peppe. There was pro shit in the back. Big shovels, a stake, chains, tension straps, gloves, and coveralls.

He could sleep in the truck for a few days too. Peppe didn't need it right away.

Maybe everything would work out after all.

Being cautious was his highest *mandamiento* right now. He'd moved around like a homeless person during his days in Sweden. Stayed at Paola's place, with Mom, with Mahmud's sister, even with Rolando who'd turned Sven. He looked up the license plate number of every single car that acted funny—texted the road administration. Some citizen service shit: they responded with a text within three minutes. The registered owner of the car. You could tell right away if it was the police trying to scout in an undercover ride. He avoided his home hoods, not just at night. He didn't give anyone his prepaid phone number. He bought a pair of shades and added a hip-hop twist to his stride. Nailed the rhythm. Swung his arms. His right leg took a little extra turn with each step. Nigga with attitude. Feeling like he'd moved this way his whole life. Hopefully, it'd make him appear a little bit less like himself.

Everything reminded him of when he'd been on the lam last, from prison—except that time he'd maxed out: smeared himself with self-tanner too. "Shawshank." Babak could *chinga* his own fucking *madre*. *Concha*. Now he was the one in jail.

He climbed out of the car. The Sätra Forest. Firs and pines and leafy trees. The gravel crunched. He opened the back doors. The water tower was visible a hundred yards farther off—like a fat magic mushroom. He lit the headlamp. Tried to orient himself.

He let the glow from the lamp sweep across the leaves. The moss. The yellowed grass.

It was cold in the air. Maybe forty degrees. He shivered.

Branches from fir trees were hanging down low and obscuring the view. He walked back and forth. Kicked aside pinecones and tufts of grass.

He was looking for the place. The place where they'd hidden the gold that they'd never shown the other boys or the Finn.

He walked back to the road. Peered into the woods. Left, right. Right, left. The beam of light was like a tiny speck in a dark mass of fir trees.

Then he saw them. Three large stones in a row. Two inches between every stone. He remembered how they'd labored to get them in place. More than three hundred pounds per stone, for sure.

He approached them. Knew there was no point in trying to play World's Strongest Man. He bent down. Wound a tension strap twice around the largest stone, the one in the middle. Secured the chain in the strap. Dragged the chain to the car, thirteen feet away. Attached it to the trailer hitch.

Started the engine. Drove forward sloooowly.

It was too dark to see anything in the rearview mirror.

He opened the car door, leaned out, illuminated the spot with his headlamp. Followed the chain through the darkness. The stone'd moved. It was enough.

He jumped out. Got the stake and the shovel. Put the heavy work gloves on.

The stone'd been dragged a foot and a half. A round, flat indentation in the grass and earth where it'd been. He hacked with the stake.

He wasn't thinking about anything. Just shoveled and hacked. The only thing that mattered now: dig up the dough and head back to Thailand. He was planning on screwing the Iranian. Who gave a fuck if that idiot ratted him out? Who gave a fuck if the feds reported him more wanted than a suicide bomber? He had a working passport. *Un hermano* down there who'd been checked out of the hospital.

It all felt so easy.

Drenched in sweat. Messed-up feeling in his fingers. How could so many roots've had to time to grow in just one summer? He didn't remember all the small rocks, either. Where had they come from? Did rocks sprout in dirt holes or what?

He looked at his work. A pile of dirt beside a hole.

Three feet deep.

His back hurt.

He kept on digging.

Hacked with the stake to soften the earth. Crush the roots. Roll the stones away.

After about an hour: a plastic bag.

There'd been eight hundred in the security bags, but he'd given two hundred to that Iranian cunt. Where was the thanks for that now? What an idiot he'd been. He should've ended Babak right then and there.

He bent down.

His pulse: BPM in *prestissimo*. Sweat was running into his eyes. He felt that usual tight feeling in his belly. Dammit, he was so fucking tired of his stomach acting up.

He needed to climb down into the hole. He grabbed hold of the top of the bag. It needed to be dug up carefully.

He grabbed a smaller shovel in his other hand. Tried to dig with small, small movements. Didn't want to tear the bag.

He was at it for ten minutes.

Then: the bag was completely dirt-free. He picked it up.

Couldn't contain himself.

He felt the weight of six hundred large in five-hundred- and one-hundred-kronor bills.

He began to untie the bag.

47

It was dark.

Hägerström was thinking about the mistake he had made. He had left his cell phone out and forgotten to slide it closed. Normally, you needed a four-digit passcode to access his phone. But the phone apparently didn't lock when it was flipped open.

Javier was sitting with it in his hand. Curious, sticky-fingered, and gratuitously interested in Hägerström's life. You couldn't tell who had sent the message, but it was weird enough as it was.

Bring home as many as possible—that's what Torsfjäll had written. It was an order. Hägerström understood the reasoning. It was easier to arrest suspects in Sweden than to plow through tons of bureaucracy in order to get an international arrest warrant and then double the amount of bureaucracy again in order to get the Thai police to act.

He laughed and took the phone from Javier. "It's my sister. She wants me to bring home as many of those Thai emeralds as possible. You know they're insanely cheap here, right?"

Javier looked at him for a long time.

Then he stood up. He was also naked. Sinewy build and tattoos with an obvious gang theme covering half his body. ALBY FOREVER on one shoulder. A crucifix and a Mini-Uzi over his heart. And on his back: MAMÁ TRATÓ, Mom tried. That's the one Javier was proudest of. He loved his mother more than anything else in all of Alby. He didn't want to blame her for who he had become. A professional criminal, a concrete gangster. Bisexual.

Javier put his boxers on. He still hadn't said anything. Hägerström remained standing where he was, playing with his cell phone. Deleted the text. Double-checked that he hadn't forgotten to delete any others.

"Why haven't you said anything about the emeralds?" Javier asked.

"I didn't think about it."

"But all we've done is talk and talk. You told me about your sister. Why didn't you say anything?"

"What, you expect me to tell you about everything on my mind?"

Javier was silent again. He put his T-shirt on.

Finally he said, "'Cause I've got an *amigo*, Tom, and he's in the know about that kind of shit. He's been here in Bangkok a lot, gambled. Want me to call him?"

Inside, Hägerström breathed a sigh of relief.

That was the closest he had come to blowing his cover. He had to get it together.

An ad for HTC's new Androids were rolling on the big screen. Hägerström was sitting comfortably. There were only two other people in the theater.

When he was a teenager, he used to love the ads at the movies. It was almost like he and his friends could go to the movies just for the ads. But that was in the old Sweden, before the state allowed commercials on TV. Now it was just annoying. A trailer for some Swedish thriller started rolling. *Easy Money 2*. The actors seemed believable, for once—normally, Swedish thrillers didn't exactly tend to feel rooted in reality.

Hägerström was back in Stockholm. And now he was sitting in a movie theater, waiting for Torsfjäll.

He had decided to go back. The whole thing with Javier was crazy. Torsfjäll had ordered him to try to bring home as many of the others as possible. Babak was in custody and had been brought to Sweden. Jorge was already home, probably to scrounge up cash for the café deal. Hägerström didn't know anything about Mahmud, and it would take time to gain his trust since they had never met. There were other guys in Thailand too, he knew that. Tom Lehtimäki and Jimmy, but he had never met them. The only one he had managed to bring home was Javier.

Ten minutes later Torsfjäll lowered himself into the seat next to him. Hägerström didn't turn his head, but he sensed that the inspector was wearing his usual smile. Wide, blindingly white, and half-phony.

He leaned over and hissed into Hägerström's ear: "Is this really necessary? Couldn't we have met up in one of the apartments, like we usually do?"

Hägerström whispered back, "There's a leak somewhere. JW's gotten hold of tons of information that he sent down to Jorge. He could only've gotten it from someone with high rank in the feds. All kinds of database stuff."

"Sure, but that doesn't mean one of my people did it. You can trust the people who work for me."

Hägerström shook his head slowly. "You're not the one taking the risks."

Torsfjäll smiled again. He accepted.

"Have you had time to see JW yet?"

"No, I came home two days ago. But we've texted. We're getting together soon."

"How'd you manage to get Javier to come home?"

"It wasn't hard. He was pretty fed up with Thailand and thought that since Jorge'd been allowed to go home, he should be too. So it wasn't particularly hard to persuade him, especially when I covered his ticket."

"Good, very good. They've identified and arrested another two suspects in EU countries. Significantly easier to bring home than from that damn gook country. A guy named Sergio Salinas Morena, Jorge's cousin, in Spain. And a guy named Robert Progat in Serbia. They're going to be extradited into the country in a few days. Does Javier know that?"

"I don't think so. He hasn't said anything about it, anyway."

"Good. Do you know where he is now?"

Hägerström took his time answering. Thought back to the days with Javier in Bangkok. He already missed him. Less than two days had passed since they had parted ways at Arlanda.

He answered honestly, "I don't know where he is. But I'm seeing him tonight."

Torsfjäll propped one leg on top of the other.

They watched the film for a few seconds. The Hollywood actor in the lead was playing tennis.

Torsfjäll whispered, "Do you have any idea where Jorge is?"

"No. But I'm sure he's in Stockholm. Javier said Jorge probably has money hidden away somewhere."

"Can you get Javier to lead me to Jorge? Maybe tonight, when you're seeing him? I don't want to arrest Javier without being able to arrest

Jorge at the same time, because then we risk him disappearing across the border."

"I can try. But what kind of evidence do they have on these guys about Tomteboda? Am I going to have to be a witness, or do we have enough?"

"I'm under the impression that you're not going to have to be a witness. I mean, I want us to proceed with Operation Tide against JW and that Bladman guy. But I'm not the one in charge of the robbery investigation."

Hägerström envisioned the scenario. A price on his head. Jorge, Javier, JW—everyone would want to see him dead if his role in all this came to light. Maybe it was too late to think about that now, but the plan had always been for him to get hold of information that would suffice in and of itself. And as long as Inspector Torsfjäll was in charge of the operation, it shouldn't be a problem. But now the situation was different. The Tomteboda investigation was beyond Torsfjäll's control. The trip to Thailand might turn out to be the biggest mistake of his life.

He thought about Pravat.

Torsfjäll went on, as if it didn't matter: "The wire at Bladman's place has started to yield good results."

"What?"

"Two things. First of all, it's come to light that they have a storage location or an office somewhere other than at MB Accounting Consultant AB, just as I thought. They don't mention the address, but it's obvious that it exists somewhere. Did you take note of the addresses where you drove JW before you went to Thailand?"

Hägerström was lost in his own thoughts. Anonymous witnesses were not permitted in Sweden, but he might be able to testify under an assumed name—it depended on how complex his protective identity was. He had to think for a few seconds before he was able to respond to Torsfjäll's question. Of course he knew every single address he had driven JW to. Torsfjäll was going to look them up as soon as possible.

The inspector shifted in his seat. He whispered, "Second of all, a war has broken out within the Yugo mafia. After Radovan was murdered, one of his men, Stefanovic Rudjman, took over a segment of his business. Meanwhile, it seems that Radovan's daughter, Natalie Kranjic, also wants to take control of the empire. We've managed to pick up that this means JW and Bladman now have to decide who they're going to work for. It could get interesting. As I like to say: out of chaos, good police operations are born."

Hägerström was listening. He wasn't even watching the movie.

"We've got to tie this all up and finish the operation soon. They're making some major transfers. The economic-crimes guy is seeing patterns, and it appears to be as you and I observed earlier. They're moving large sums of money now. From countries that are about to give up on bank secrecy after pressure from the European Union and the United States, to nations that are still included on the blacklist. Countries where they can continue doing their business. We have to strike soon—there isn't much time left."

Torsfjäll kept talking. They discussed the operation. The prosecutor had been drawn in, and an investigatory group of five cops were spending all their time analyzing who was buying JW and Bladman's services. Nippe Creutz had a big network within his social stratum. Bladman had one that was equally large within his. Hansén was taking care of business on location. JW was the brain who controlled everything.

After a few minutes, Torsfjäll rose.

They had reached an agreement. Hägerström would inform him as soon as he knew where Javier and Jorge were. Preferably, he would be on site with them. All to guarantee that the arrest proceeded as smoothly as possible.

Torsfjäll repeated, "We've got to find out where they keep their second set of books."

Hägerström met up with Javier that night in a small studio in Alby that he had borrowed from a friend. *Scarface* posters on the walls and a collection of replicas of revolvers and guns that would have put any weapons-horny teenager into ecstasy.

They had sex in the narrow bed.

In Bangkok, they had made love several times a day. They had talked and hung out during the rest of the time. Sure, Hägerström had withheld a lot of things for security reasons, and Javier probably hadn't told him everything either, but still—they had been *close* down there.

This felt more rushed. Hägerström had nothing against fucking Javier or being fucked. But the contrast with their time in Thailand was weird. Or maybe it was understandable. They were home now: being openly together wasn't an option, either for Hägerström or for Javier.

They were lying in bed. Javier was smoking a cigarette. Hägerström was feeling low.

He said, "Do you know where Jorge is?"

Javier was blowing smoke rings. "Not a clue. Let him do whatever he came here to do and then go back. I'm gonna go back soon too. I'm just here to take a break, you know? What about you?"

"I did what I went to Thailand to do. I'm staying here."

"But can't you come, just for a week?"

"We'll see. It's not exactly free. But hey, do you have Jorge's number?"

"No. My boy's security-obsessed. I doubt he even has a phone now. Why you wanna talk to him?"

Hägerström had expected that question. "I'm not the one who wants to get in touch with him," he said. "It's the Thai guys down there—they're whining about the café deal. They've already pulled out once, but I got them to go back in. Now they want out again. Can't you ask around?"

The next day Hägerström went to Lidingö. He had called his lawyer first thing when he got back from Thailand, asked him to try to arrange a visitation time. Anna was unusually accommodating. Maybe that was her way of paying him back for keeping it cool for over four weeks. Over the past few years, angry legal letters, investigative meetings, and court dates had been legion. Not to mention all the angry texts and e-mails Hägerström and Anna exchanged every time they had to decide on times for pick-up and drop-off.

He picked his son up at school. They went to Pravat's favorite park. It was only thirty-five degrees outside. They played cowboys and Indians. Hägerström wished they were in Thailand playing instead.

Pravat told him about school. He was reading. He was drawing. He was writing letters.

They discussed how long snakes can get and whether Spiderman can fly or if he is just unusually good at jumping.

After the park, they went home to Hägerström's house. They ordered pizza and ate dinner in front of the TV. Hägerström tried to teach the boy not to chew with his mouth open, to cough into the nook of his arm, and not to put his elbows on the table. He felt like his mother.

———

The next day he got a text from Javier. *I got a hookup.*

Hägerström called him. "It's me."

"I've hit up so many homies for this, man—you wouldn't believe."

"Dope."

"His mom, his sis who had her panties all in a bunch—yikes. I talked to Rolando, an *amigo* of his from way back who's living real fucking nine-to-five. I've even talked to an old boy of J's from the inside, Peppe."

"And?"

"I got a number."

"You're an angel, in more ways than one. Would you call him and tell him I want to see him as soon as possible? The Thai guys want out of the deal. We have to talk."

Hägerström considered ending the call with some words of affection but changed his mind. Not because he had any indication that Javier's phone was tapped, but if it was, it could get complicated.

The following night. A cabbie hangout, the Mug, on Roslagsgatan. Open every day of the week, every hour of the day. Rumor had it the pea soup and pancakes on Thursdays were outstanding—a good old Swedish classic. Apparently the interior had not been changed since 1962. The Jack Vegas machines were supposed to bring luck to tired cabbies who had had trouble getting rides. The staff allowed smoking after midnight.

It was twelve-thirty at night. The place was half empty. Two men wearing leather taxi driver jackets were sitting on high chairs in front of one-armed bandits. Standing behind the counter was a fat man with a hairnet and his mouth half-open. His facial expression didn't exactly exude intelligence.

The café guy might be South American. Maybe that was why Jorge had picked this place for their meet-up.

Hägerström ordered an ordinary black coffee and sat down at one of the tables.

Outside, around the corner, in cars throughout the area and in the apartment across the street: cops. Heavy artillery was on the scene, ready to collar two of the country's most wanted men of the moment. Hägerström had informed Torsfjäll as soon as he had found out where they were meeting.

At least they would accomplish something, no matter what happened with Operation Tide. Arrest two professional criminals who had carried out the worst robbery of the year and wounded a guard for life. It would send a clear signal to the rabble, and to all the kids in the projects who wanted to become the rabble. *It's not worth it. The police always win in the end.*

At the same time, Hägerström had a bad feeling in his gut. Coming home had not made him any less confused. It was seven times worse now. He would make sure Javier got arrested and most likely sentenced to a long time in prison. Hägerström would personally ensure that he never saw him again.

It was insane.

The door opened. It was raining outside. Javier walked into the café. His hair was wet. Drops of water were running down his face and light stubble. He looked up at Hägerström and winked.

Hägerström closed his eyes for a few seconds—this was just too much.

When he opened his eyes again, Javier was by the counter, paying for a bottle of Coke Zero.

He turned around, "H, you been here before? You gotta say hi to Andrés here. A countryman."

Hägerström had been right. The man who worked at the café was from South America. Javier seemed high—he would be an easy snatch.

Five minutes later Jorge walked in through the door. He was wearing a black windbreaker and dark track pants. He had a backpack on his back, and all of him was dripping with rain.

Jorge walked straight over to Hägerström and Javier's table, without ordering anything at the counter.

Hägerström didn't need to inform anyone that Jorge had arrived. There were at least five officers on street corners all around, wearing concealed radios. By now, they would have communicated that the eagle had landed.

Jorge and Hägerström shook hands the regular way. Jorge swung his arm and slapped his hand into Javier's, concrete style.

Javier grinned. "Wazzup, bro?"

Jorge sat down. "Why the fuck d'you come home?"

Javier didn't seem to care. He really was stoned. "You went home. So. Why couldn't I fly home?"

"You know why."

"But Mahmud's been checked out of the hospital. I didn't need to be his nanny no more. He can take care of himself now. Know how hungry he was for anything but nurses?"

"Listen, you do what you want. But I'm gonna go back in a few days. I'm not taking any responsibility for you anymore. If you're wanted and you stay here, they'll pick you up sooner or later. You follow?"

Hägerström was surprised. They had never before been this open about their problems in front of him.

Jorge turned to Hägerström. "Screw, you wanna talk biz with me?"

"The buyers have been in touch again, complaining. You have the money now?"

"Yeah, I got it."

"Sweet. In that case it'll all work out."

"There's just one little problem," Jorge said. "But JW's gonna straighten it out for me."

They chatted for a few seconds.

There were screams in the doorway.

Hägerström knew roughly what was going to happen next.

A four-strong SWAT team rushing in, dressed in black. Balaclavas and helmets on their heads. The illest bulletproof-vest model strapped on their bodies. MP5s with laser sights trigger-ready in their hands.

They roared, "You're under arrest! Get down on the floor!"

48

Natalie got blood on her pants. Small dark spots over her knees. They might come out in the wash. If not, she'd throw the pants out. She didn't give a shit. What must be done, must be done. There would be more bloodstains to come.

She sat down on a plastic chair. Closed her eyes. Saw images from the past few days rolling across the inside of her eyelids.

By Sunday, Melissa still hadn't been in touch. Natalie waited until Monday. She called at night, from two different phones. Cherkasova's phone was off, there was no voice mail. She tried to call on Tuesday again. She asked Sascha to text her. Same deal: zero response.

That was when she decided to go to her house again.

Out there: the apartment complexes on one side, a large school on the other. Solna: not a ghetto burb like the southern territories or farther down on the blue subway line. Not a fancy burb like where Natalie lived or one of the other northern residential areas. Solna: somewhere in between. Like vanilla ice cream. Like 2 percent milk. Like Kungsholmen in relation to Östermalm and Södermalm.

Adam met her and Sascha on the street.

He had bags under his eyes. Said, "I've been waiting in the car since five p.m. yesterday. I haven't seen her go in or out."

"We'll see," Natalie said. She had a bad feeling about this. A small ache was growing in her stomach.

Adam knew the code to the downstairs door. He opened it.

There was no elevator. They walked up the stairs.

Natalie rang the doorbell. They waited.

Silence inside the apartment.

She rang the bell once more.

They knocked.

Adam pressed his ear to the door.

"It's completely quiet in there. Maybe she's sleeping."

They knocked again.

Nothing happened.

Adam felt the door handle.

The door was open.

This felt wrong.

Adam, like a mad Navy SEAL: pulled his gun and held it out in front of him.

This felt all kinds of wrong.

They walked in.

Natalie stood in the hallway, looked around. She could see into the living room. The couch pillows and the DVDs were on the floor. One bookcase'd been knocked over. The curtains'd been torn down. Paperbacks, framed photographs, small dolls, ashtrays, and packets of cigarette all over the room. Even a pizza carton'd been torn to shreds.

Fuck.

Sascha called from the kitchen. "Someone's really given this place a thorough once-over. I don't think we should touch anything."

She took a few steps toward the kitchen.

She heard Adam's voice. It was shaky.

"Natalie, come here."

He was in the bedroom. She went there. The grape-sized ache in her belly'd grown to the bulk of an orange.

The curtains were drawn. Dim light. All the dresser drawers'd been pulled out. Tops, skirts, socks, and panties on the floor.

It smelled strange. Melissa was lying on the bed with a bloody comforter over her. She had some sort of rag in her mouth.

Death'd painted her in its own nuance of gray—far from a flattering image. All the color was gone from her face. All the luster was gone from her skin. Everything sweet was gone from her eyes. Melissa'd looked scared the first time Natalie'd shadowed her. But the terror in her eyes now was completely different. No matter what death looked like, it hadn't looked good for Melissa Cherkasova. That was 100 percent certain.

Adam bent down and pulled away the comforter.

Melissa's body was ravaged. The sheets and mattress were bloody.

Her hands were bound with cable ties.

She had burn marks on her breasts and the insides of her thighs. She had bloody cuts on her arms and stomach. There was blood around her genitals. She had two bullet wounds in her chest.

Adam covered his mouth with his hand. Natalie felt the orange lump in her belly begin to move quickly. She ran to the toilet.

Thomas arrived half an hour later. He parked his van outside the entrance. Natalie and the boys were waiting in their car.

They walked in together.

The smell was more palpable now. Or else it was just that Natalie knew what was in there.

Thomas and Adam went into the bedroom. Natalie waited in the hall. Sascha was outside in the car, phone ready in case the cops showed up for some reason.

Thomas came back out. "Fucking pigs. Did you touch anything?"

"I've only touched door handles, nothing else. And I threw up in the toilet."

"I pulled the comforter off. Other than that, only door handles," Adam said.

Thomas crossed his arms in front of his chest. "Okay, we've got to clean up after ourselves. And then I think we should take care of the body, for safety's sake."

Thomas gave everyone orders. Pulled gear out of his duffel.

"Use these sponges. Wipe door handles, the sink, the bathroom floor, and any other surfaces you've been near. Use more disinfectant than you think you need. Tons. Put all the bedclothes in a garbage bag."

They worked for twenty minutes. Thomas: Mr. Wolf in *Pulp Fiction*, for real.

The big question: How would they get Cherkasova out of here?

They spread plastic on the floor and set the body down onto it. Thomas turned the bed upside down. It was a simple model, an ordinary foam mattress. He pulled out a jigsaw, plugged it in. Sawed the bed open from the underside. Lowered the body into the bed frame. It looked like a coffin. They covered it all with the mattress and more black plastic. Taped with a whole lot of duct tape.

Thomas walked out into the stairwell. Unscrewed every single lamp—in case of nosy neighbors. They carried the bed down the stairs. Melissa inside like a heavy luxury mattress.

Adam drove off with the body in the van.

Thomas said, "I don't think they got the material. She seems to have endured a lot. They wouldn't have done all that to her if they'd gotten the stuff. And I don't think there's anything in there. They looked everywhere."

Natalie looked up. She was still sitting. Standing in front of her were Goran, Bogdan, and Sascha. The cold storage room behind the kitchen at Restaurant Bistro 66. The place belonged to an old friend of Dad.

On the shelves: milk cartons, juice cartons, bunches of celery and other veggies, lots of limes and lemons. Cocktail fixings en masse. Large freezers on the floor.

Over the shelves: plastic wrap. On the floor: tarp. The entire room was covered in plastic.

It was a smart move—because on the floor was Marko.

Natalie got up. Four days'd passed since they found Melissa Cherkasova tortured and murdered in her apartment. Thomas'd finally found the material. A DVD taped to the back of a sewer pipe in the laundry room in the basement of the building. In total: twenty-seven mini-movies. Three different men, three different hotel rooms. Three different types of perversions. One of them was the politician, Svelander; one was unknown; one was a high-ranked police chief whom Thomas recognized. Svelander seemed to dig anal. The unknown Sven wanted to get sucked off. The final guy wanted to dress Melissa like a schoolgirl, handcuff her, and then do S&M stuff in three-hour sessions.

Natalie'd sent Sascha to inform Martina Kjellson. She would be told half of what'd actually happened: "Melissa is gone, and we're not the ones behind it. Don't try to contact her, don't contact the police or anyone else. We'll take care of this on our own."

Natalie saw sick images in her mind. Melissa's wide, staring eyes. The rag they'd stuffed in her mouth. Her wounded vagina.

Marko's jeans were bloody. His T-shirt was torn. A thick gold ring on his pinkie.

Natalie walked over to him. Goran'd just given him a once-over.

He whimpered, "Let me go now."

"Why?" she said.

He spat out a tooth. "I don't know anything about what happened to your father."

"Yes, I think you do."

"Fuck, no. I swear. I have no idea. He had alotta enemies. You could say he got what was coming to him."

What he'd just said: Natalie felt a storm rage inside her.

She kicked him in the face. He spat blood.

She got more blood on her pants.

"And what about Cherkasova?" she said.

Marko spat out yet another tooth. "Please, I'm not the one who killed her."

"I don't give a shit. You were the one who trashed Fitnesse Club and did what you did to the receptionists."

She kicked him again.

Yet another tooth hit the floor.

Goran screamed, "You've picked the wrong side, motherfucker!"

Natalie grabbed hold of Goran's baseball bat. Struck Marko across the legs, belly. Slammed the top of the bat down with full force in his face.

His nose turned to ground beef. He screamed.

Red was bubbling from his mouth. Blood. Teeth. Pieces of his lips.

Natalie raised her voice, "Shut up, you pig! What happened to my father?"

The storm inside her pounded against her forehead.

"I have no idea," Markos's voice sounded desperate.

She stomped on his forehead.

He cried, whimpered, begged for mercy.

Images of Melissa flashed by once again. She swung the baseball bat at his cock.

He howled like a maniac.

She hit him in the same place again.

He continued to scream. Cry. Cough.

She swung with both hands, like a golf club.

He made a peeping sound. That was all.

He grew silent.

Natalie dried the sweat from her forehead. Calmed down. Looked at Goran. "Cut off his pinkie with the ring on it and send it to Stefanovic. Then end him."

She walked out of cold storage room. Sascha in tow.

She wasn't showering in the regular shower near her room, she was using the one in the basement. Mom was sleeping. Sascha was upstairs. It was twelve-thirty at night.

She wet her hair and massaged shampoo into it: Redken All Soft. Leaned her head back and rinsed. The she squeezed the water from her hair, twisted it like a rag. Conditioner: same brand, Redken All Soft. She let it work for a while. Washed her body and arms. Filed her heels with a foot file that she'd forgotten was down here. Then she switched from the handheld shower to the overhead. Sat down on the floor. Let the warm water rain down over her. The glass shower door steamed up. She lathered herself with an extra amount of shower gel: Dermalogica Conditioning Body Wash. Washed while the water ran. There was foam all over the floor. She realized that she hadn't shaved her legs in several days. She opened the door to the shower. Stepped out, dripping over the floor. She looked for a razor in the bathroom cabinet. There was an unopened pack. She stepped back into the shower. Let the water run. Shaved her legs with slow strokes.

It felt good to relax.

She didn't think about the war with Stefanovic. She didn't think about Melissa. She didn't even think about Dad. She just enjoyed the heat and feeling her skin soften under the running water.

She saw JW's face in front of her.

She knew what he thought about her attacks against Stefanovic, even if he hadn't brought it up again.

JW was supposed to be in touch with her about some sort of plan—when they met at Teatergrillen the second time, he'd promised to help her. Partly by having Bladman disclose everything that had to do with Dad's assets and making sure to give her and her lawyer full jurisdiction, and partly by choosing a side: she wouldn't agree to them doing business with Stefanovic that actually belonged to her.

They'd spoken on the phone twice. He was slippery, said it took time. That it was difficult. Natalie wanted to call him again, and again, and again. Not just to make him deliver. She wanted to hear his voice too. Hear his excuses. Goran forbade her, but he didn't know how hard her heart started beating every time she saw an unknown number pop up on her cell phone display.

Later, she was sitting in the kitchen, still in her bathrobe. Eating cottage cheese with tomatoes. Half high on painkillers and valerian—but she still couldn't sleep. Made a few calls. Thomas. Goran. Things were happening all the time. News of what they'd done to Marko would break in two days max. They'd have to wait for Stefanovic's reaction. This ought to make him rethink things.

She put her phone down. Really had to go to bed now.

Before she got up, her phone rang again. Hidden number. Neither Goran, Bogdan, nor Thomas used a number like that. Not Adam either.

It was Viktor.

"Where the fuck have you been?"

Natalie didn't want to deal with his shit. "Home, and with the boys. Nothing strange."

Viktor sounded close to tears. "I haven't heard from you in a week."

"So?"

"I'm hearing strange things about you."

"If you're hearing strange things, it's bullshit."

"I heard that you were out with Louise and some dude, Axel Jolle or something like that, that he was hitting on you like crazy, and you just smiled. He bought you drinks, tried to take you home all night. You just took it."

"So, did you hear what we did later that night? Really interesting, actually."

"What did you do?"

Natalie took a bite of cottage cheese. "You haven't heard?"

"No, what happened? I swear, if you slept with him, it's over."

"All right, well then find out what happened before you call and whine to me."

She hung up. He had to cool it. If he bitched one more time, it was over.

Before she even had a chance to put the phone back down on the table, it rang again. A hidden number this time too. Had Viktor not gotten the message?

She didn't pick up.

Her phone beeped: a text. *You have one new voicemail.* She listened to it. "You have one new voicemail. Today, two-twenty-one a.m."

She had a feeling it would be something bad.

"This is Mischa Bladman. I'm speaking for me and for JW. Stop what you're doing. Your conflict is tearing the city apart. And now Moscow's getting fed up. They just called me and asked me to convey that they want to see results, they don't want any more fuss, no matter who has the material. Natalie, call me right away."

*

When the changes happened, there was a lot for us to do. The Russian economy was put through an acid test. If you wanted to get ahead, you had to jump at the right chance at the right time, have the right contacts, and be willing to walk over bodies. And that was exactly what made business boom in my industry.

There were a lot of people from KGB, GRU, Stasi, Securitate who were ready to solve people's problems. Personally I came from OMON, via my detour in the gulag—and was educated at the Gorkovskij Institute.

We reeducated ourselves quickly so that we suited the new market economy. When we'd learned the trade from a privatized perspective, we realized just how much work there was to do. Because what we were doing was actually the ultimate market liberalism: the survival of the fittest without state intervention.

And we came from the state, so when the state was reconfigured, we were already part of the reconfiguration. A lot of people thought the state would cease to exist in Russia. In fact, it grew stronger than ever. Us, the state, and the market—the bonds were unbreakable.

Some of the old sly foxes are dead now. Others have risen within the organizations, enabled the oligarchs to get to where they are today. Many have themselves become avtoritety *of rank: Orekhovskaya Banda, Izmaylovskaya, Malysjevskaya—those are just a few examples of groups that are controlled by people like me.*

Few of them are independent, few are as active as I am in my field.

In Italy people like us have always been needed. Sure, Cosa Nostra, 'Ndrangheta, and the Camorra mostly hire their own men, but they still need outsiders sometimes. There were jobs to do for the frogs in North Africa and les Dom-Tom. Proud France has always had a need to control its colonies and former vassal states. The power of oil and the longing for power is greater than most people understand. In Great Britain and Ireland our services were used when Northern Ireland's problems needed solving. We were also called in sometimes when the gangsters of London and Manchester needed to mark their territories. The Russians made headway in Scandinavia and Germany. They hired us when they needed to do some weeding in their own ranks.

I spent a little over three years in OMON before I was convicted. But it was enough. I became a master at what I do. We executed missions in Nagorno-Karabakh and in Georgia. I partook in the attack on Latvia's parliament. Those who heard my name and knew who I was all felt the same thing. Fear.

Bigger job offers started coming from Moscow. From former brothers in arms, from banks that had problems with government authorities, from oligarchs who ran into problems with one another. And later, after a few years, I got assignments all over Europe. It wasn't just recovery operations, reprimands, and private protection gigs. In 2001 I was given my first international mission: to execute a Turkish pimp in Frankfurt who was trying to take over the wrong streets.

By that time I knew how to kill, but I had yet to learn the organization around it all. If anyone in this industry were to study my methodology when I ended the Turk, they would laugh at my mistakes. But today, that's all history. Just like the failure in the parking garage.

I don't look back.

In Sweden time passed slowly. She'd learned from her father's mistakes. She was more careful than an avtoritet *in hot water with Putin.*

But that made no difference. I was paid to wait.

49

J-boy: the king with many names. El Bernadotto, El Bhumibolo, *El fucko the policía*. He had time to think: call me what you want—but you're never putting me away again.

FTP—Fuck the Police.

Four police officers dressed in black stormed the place. Helmets, bulletproof vests, MP5s pointed at Jorge, Javier, and Hägerström. Screaming like only pigs do. Ordered the cab drivers to get out, disappear. Two of them pushed Javier down to the floor. Two shoved Martin Hägerström down over the coffee table. Another two leaped in through the door. Threw themselves at Jorge.

He flung himself out of their reach.

Them: pros.

Them: yelling at him to get down on the floor.

Red dots of light from their laser sights danced over Jorge's body.

Them: losers.

Jorge threw himself straight for one of them. Fired off a jab. He wasn't really a fighter, but this time: luck—perfect hit. He could feel his knuckles smash into the pig's snout.

But the cop fucker hardly even flinched. Instead, he grabbed hold of Jorge's arms. Folded them behind his back. Doubled him over. The sound of cracking. Hurt like hell.

He screamed, "What the hell are you doing?"

Javier hollered from the floor, "Why the fuck you going *loco*?"

The Hägerström guy growled, "Take it easy, dammit."

The cops were efficient, did their thing. Cuffed Javier. Cuffed Hägerström.

They had to put up more of a fight with J-boy. He was really fucking pissed off now. The adrenaline tap was switched on: he became like the Hulk combined with some ill MMA fighter. Kicked, punched, tensed his whole body like a crazy person. Windmilled his arms, bit one of the cops in the finger, through his glove. Made himself impossible to cuff. Jorge: wild. Crazy. *LOCO.*

Still: they managed to get his arms behind his back again. A knee in his back. He thought he was going to break in half. He tasted the linoleum floor. Heard Javier yelling. Heard the metal sound of the handcuffs they were planning to put on him.

It was over now. The planning with his bros, the meetings with the Finn, the CIT—the heist of his life. The time in Thailand.

He thought of Mahmud: his café brother would be spared at least. He wondered if Tom and Jimmy were still over there.

They were holding his hand in some sort of grip. Applying pressure between his thumb and index finger. Started to put the cuffs on.

That's when something happened. A rapid movement. One of the cops fell to the side.

The other yelled something. Jorge turned his head. The pressure over his back eased. He looked up.

Andrés, the dude who worked in the joint, had thrown himself over one of the cops.

A wrestling match on the floor beside Jorge. One of the policemen tried to keep an arm on Jorge's back while pushing Andrés off at the same time. One of the cops who'd cuffed Hägerström threw himself into the tumult.

Andrés: a big dude. The cops had a problem on their hands.

J-boy: the Olympic sprinter, the ghetto cat with nine lives. The king with many names—this was his chance.

He pushed himself up.

Javier was lying with his arms on his back. Still with two pigs over him. Impossible to save his bro now.

Jorge ran out.

He heard the cops yelling in the background. But Andrés was a hero—was spread-eagle on top of two cops.

It was still raining outside. Dark despite the streetlights. Four uniforms were waiting for him. In the background: terrified taxi drivers who'd wound up in the middle of the ambush of the year and couldn't stop staring.

He pulled out his little surprise.

In the ditch with the money, he'd also hidden a Taurus nine-millimeter Parabellum—it'd been left over after the CIT. Now he was holding it in his hand.

He threw himself in the direction of one of the cabbies.

Shoved the piece up against the poor man's temple.

Screamed, "You move, and I'll blow his head off."

The four cops stopped.

He saw two undercover cars crawling slowly up the street.

He whispered to the cab driver. "Run in front of me as fast as you can, to your car."

The dude was maybe thirty years old. Dark stubble covered his cheeks.

Jorge pushed him in front of him with the gun. It looked real, an airsoft gun copy of a Parabellum model.

The cabbie started jogging.

"Faster," Jorge said.

Raindrops were hitting his face like small bullets. The cabbie was out of breath. For a few seconds, the five-oh stood as if frozen in place. Then they yelled for him to stop.

Jorge didn't care what they said. He yelled back for *them* to stop, or else he'd blow this guy into next year.

Thirty yards farther up the street: the cab.

He said, "Take out your car keys, unlock the car now."

The driver dug around in his jacket pocket while he ran. Fished out the key. The car made a clicking sound.

Jorge opened the driver-side door, shoved the cabbie inside. Sat down in the backseat. The entire time: the toy against the poor sucker's neck. He saw the cops a few yards off.

The driver turned the key in the lock. He sobbed. "I have kids. I have kids."

"Drive as fast as you can toward Odenplan."

Jorge almost fell over when the cabbie stepped on it. The cab: a Saab 9-5 with black leather interior. An evening paper shoved into the pocket in the seat in front of him. A sticker with rates on the window. The way all Swedish cabs looked inside.

The windshield wipers swept back and forth.

He saw the two black undercover cars driving behind them.

He felt calm. Leaned back. Let his thoughts flow.

He wondered why Andrés'd helped. Assaulting an officer, protecting a criminal, maybe something more. Andrés'd sentenced himself to the iron box in order to save Jorge. A true human being. An angel. Jorge would repay him.

He saw images in his mind's eye. The first time he'd been dragged home to Mom by the cops. He'd been eleven years old. Had been up to no good for months—him and his bros went store hopping every afternoon, boosted as much as they could carry. They often had to throw the shit in the trash. It was a sport.

And then one time, he was found out. He'd lifted two bags of candy. He and Sergio'd had to sit and wait in the back room until the cops came. But before they showed up, the store manager came in.

"Who do you think you are, you fucking niggers?"

Jorge stared at him.

The manager squeezed his cheeks together with his knuckles. It hurt.

"I think I'm gonna kick the shit out of you," he said.

Sergio got up. "Quit it."

True fact: he still loved Sergio for backing him up in that back room. Some dudes were just real by nature. Maybe Andrés was one of them.

The taxi drove up toward Odenplan. Made a sharp turn to the right. Up along Karlsbergsvägen. The tires screamed. The cop fuckers were still behind them. Jorge held on to the handle in the roof of the car.

He thought about the CIT cash he'd dug up in the woods. Sure: it was six hundred thousand. But *mierda:* most of it was dyed. It hadn't been the Finn's guy who'd helped open those security bags, he'd done it on his own. And he hadn't checked the bills as carefully as the other stacks either.

He'd called JW and asked if there was a way to clean the bills, or to put it more simply—he didn't need the paper to be white as fleece, he just needed to be able to exchange it and use it in Thailand. They met up, JW flipped through the piles of cash. Said, "There are ways to clean this, but it'll take a long time, all the drying and stuff. I recommend we exchange it at some exchange point where I've got connections. They'll take stuff like this, just give you a worse exchange rate. It'll take a few days."

Yet another setback. Jorge would be forced to stay in Sweden for too long. He regretted that now, more than ever.

The cab turned up on Norrbackagatan. Five-story buildings on all sides.

"Stop here, now," Jorge said. "And get out."

The undercover cars'd just turned up onto the street. Jorge heard sirens from the other direction.

He herded the driver in front of him. It'd stopped raining.

They walked over to the entrance of a building. Jorge kicked in the glass section of the door. Reached his left arm in. Opened the door from the inside. The whole time: he held the fake gun against the cabbie's head.

They walked inside. He told the cabbie to sit down.

He saw two cruisers stop, plus the undercover wheels. Cops leaped out. They were probably wondering what he was doing.

He opened the door to the building a few inches. Placed one of the cabbie's feet so that it was wedged in the crack in the door. It propped open the door. Jorge held up the gun, showed how he took the safety off. Then he hung the weapon by placing it on the door handle.

He looked at the driver. "You understand? If you pull your leg out, the door slams shut and then this piece might go off and fire at you."

The dude nodded. Jorge thought: *When this is over, I've gotta send this poor papa flowers and apologize.*

He ran up the stairwell in the building.

Heard cop cries echo through the door below.

50

Hägerström was sitting on the wrong side of the table. He had sat on the other side more times than he could count, where the head interrogator and the so-called interrogation witness—the other police officer—were now sitting. Inside, he was grinning at the situation. Today Deputy Inspector Martin Hägerström was not the one doing the interrogating; today he was the one being interrogated. Pravat used to say that he wanted them to play the opposite game. Today Hägerström was playing the opposite game with Deputy Inspector Jenny Flemström and Deputy Inspector Håkan Nilsson.

This should just be a routine interrogation, and then they ought to let him go. They weren't allowed to detain him for more than six hours without a decision from the prosecutor. And there was no way he could be suspected of anything. He had simply been having coffee with Jorge and Javier at the cabbie joint. He just happened to be in the wrong place at the wrong time.

Still, he was disappointed. Not in himself, really. After all, it wasn't his fault that the hit had turned into total chaos. The officers had acted unprofessionally. They ought to have had undercover officers positioned inside the joint, and they ought to have had cars blocking off the street outside. They ought to have cuffed Jorge first, not tried to cuff him *after* Hägerström.

He wondered if Jorge had gotten away.

He wondered how Javier was doing.

Deputy Inspector Flemström explained the formal guidelines for what was about to happen. "So, Martin, we're going to interrogate you now. You're a former police officer, so you know how this works. I will soon start the recorder. Do you want something to drink before we begin? Coffee? Water?"

Hägerström smiled inside once more. They were offering him

something to drink to make him feel comfortable. He shook his head, declined.

Jenny Flemström hit "record" on the Dictaphone.

"This is an interrogation with Martin Hägerström. Deputy Inspector Jenny Flemström and Deputy Inspector Håkan Nilsson are present. The date is October eighth, and it is three o'clock in the morning. We are recording the interrogation."

Hägerström looked at Flemström. She was holding a pen in one hand, clicking the ballpoint up and down.

"Tell us what you were doing at the Mug Café tonight."

"I was just there to grab a coffee with an acquaintance. His name is Javier."

"And how do you know him?"

"We got to know each other in Thailand a couple weeks ago, I haven't known him for long."

"Are you good friends?"

"No, we've known each other for such a short time."

"And how long were you in Thailand?"

"Around three weeks."

"What were you doing there?"

"Vacation. I used to work in Bangkok, so I know some people there."

"How did you get to know Javier?"

"We happened to be staying at the same hotel in Phuket."

"Did you spend a lot of time together?"

"Yes, by the end we were hanging out pretty much every day, but it was just for a few days."

"What's Javier's full name?"

"I have no idea."

"How can you not know what his last name is? Don't you think that sounds a little bit odd?"

"Not at all—we didn't have that type of relationship. We just drank beer and went to bars and stuff."

Flemström continued asking questions. She took notes. Nilsson was also taking notes in the background. When it was over, Hägerström was going to call Deputy Inspector Flemström and teach her some things about interrogation technique. She was too fast, wanted to move the interrogation along too quickly. She wasn't taking the time to establish patterns.

Maybe he ought to speak the truth, tell them he was an undercover operative in the middle of an important operation. But that might jeopardize the entire investigation. They were at a critical stage right now. So he just played along. He didn't have anything to fear: he was a regular police officer in an unusual situation.

Flemström moved into different territory. "Tell us a little bit about your background."

"What do you want to know?"

"What do you do for work?"

"I'm looking for work. Previously I worked as a corrections officer at the Salberga Penitentiary. And you know what I did before that. I was fired from the police force in the spring. I live in Stockholm and have a son who lives with his mother on Lidingö."

"Okay. And what kind of job are you looking for?"

"Guard jobs, CO jobs, stuff like that."

"And how do you support yourself?"

"I live cheaply, and I've saved up."

"Where do you live?"

"On Östermalm. In a coop apartment, a two-bedroom on Banérgatan."

Hägerström stared straight into Flemström's eyes. She reacted noticeably when he told her where he lived. He'd seen the same reaction many times from police colleagues. His housing situation didn't exactly signal middle class. But Flemström was most certainly thinking: *How can a former police officer and corrections officer afford to live in a coop on Östermalm?*

She went on. Leaned her torso across the table, toward Hägerström.

"And Jorge Salinas Barrio—how do you know him?"

"I don't know him."

"Have you ever met him before?"

"If you're referring to Javier's friend, then yes. We met once, also in Thailand."

"Does he know Javier well?"

"Yes, I think so. I think they're good friends. At least I know they knew each other before Thailand."

Deputy Inspector Flemström leaned back. Pleased with his answer. Again: entry-level interrogation technique. Lean in when you're attacking, lean back when you've gotten what you want.

"So what was he doing at the Mug Café?" she continued.

"I have no idea. I didn't know he was coming. Maybe Javier told him to come."

It was cold in the interrogation room. Hägerström glanced at the heater that was hanging on the wall. It was probably dead.

Flemström continued: "Babak Behrang—do you know him?"

"No."

"Have you heard of him?"

"No, no clue."

"Mahmud al-Askori—do you recognize that name?"

"No, never heard the name, never met him."

"Okay then. How about Robert Progat?"

"No, same story there."

"Tom Lehtimäki?"

"Same story. Who are they?"

Flemström's response came shooting back at him: "We're the ones asking the questions here."

Once again Hägerström noticed how unprofessional she was. The right technique would have been to try to connect with him, make him feel comfortable, make him feel he had nothing to fear. Not to cut him off like that. He looked at Håkan Nilsson, tried to see if he understood what Hägerström understood.

He basically got as much of a reaction as from the heater on the wall. Nilsson's gaze was ice cold.

He thought about Javier again. Hoped the officers hadn't seriously hurt him. Hägerström would be released soon. Javier would definitely remain—that was the point of the hit. It felt strange.

He thought about what he had done.

How would this end? How would he get to see Javier again?

* * *

From: Lennart Torsfjäll [lennart.torsfjall@polise.se]
To: Leif Hammarskiöld [leif.hammarskiold@polis.se]
Sent: October 8
Subject: Operation Tide; The Pillow Biter

DELETE THIS EMAIL AFTER READING!

Leif,

I am writing to you this early morning so that you won't be too shocked by tomorrow's headlines. Tonight a raid took place in which the operative with the internal alias Pillow Biter was involved.

As you know, the Pillow Biter's primary mission has been to infiltrate and gather information regarding serious economic crime. Thereby he has become close with Johan "JW" Westlund, who is suspected of being a leader in the large money-laundering scheme that the Economic Crimes Bureau is currently investigating within the framework of the Octopus Project (see my attached memo). Over the past few weeks, the Pillow Biter has also gained access to a group of professional criminals, so-called "New Swedes," who are suspected of carrying out the CIT robbery against Tomteboda. I personally steered him in that direction since I believe we can kill two birds with one stone.

One of the suspects was arrested during the raid, which took place around three hours ago. Another suspect, Jorge Salinas Barrio, succeeded in escaping under spectacular circumstances and is still at large, but intensive efforts are being taken even as this e-mail is being written. Due to the nature of the Tomteboda robbery and the Pillow Biter's background as a police officer, we can expect that the media will blow up tonight's police failures. Therefore I wanted to inform you as to why the Pillow Biter was on the scene of the raid. I sincerely hope that we will have succeeded in detaining Salinas Barrio by the time you read this, so that we don't have to be ridiculed further by our dear left-leaning media.

I want to add that the Pillow Biter's so-called orientation does not appear to have otherwise affected the operation.

I will call you tomorrow morning at nine o'clock as well. Do not hesitate to contact me at any time of the day or night.

Finally, I suggest that we continue to use our agreed-upon encryption key for these e-mails.

Lennart

51

Natalie's feet hurt—she'd bruised them kicking Marko.

It was nine o'clock at night. Not even twenty-four hours'd passed since she'd given that little traitor what he deserved. Even less time'd passed since Mischa Bladman'd called and told her that the Russians were getting involved. And at that point Bladman didn't even know what they'd done to Marko.

Still: he acted quickly. When she'd called back and told him she wanted to see JW, he set up a meeting right away.

And now here she was, sitting in one of the executive suites at the Hotel Diplomat, waiting. Natalie was actually glad Bladman'd called and whined about Moscow—that forced JW to see her again.

It was a corner suite, facing out toward the water in Nybroviken, apparently designed by some distinctive architect. A bedroom with a luxury bed, a living room with a luxury sofa, and a bathroom with its own steam sauna. Bathrobes from Pellevävare—thick and soft. Products from L'Occitane. Pale colors, simple patterns, sheer curtains that let in the autumn light. Parquet floors that creaked in an old-fashioned way, more authentic than their new floors at home in Näsbypark. There were fresh flowers everywhere, even in the bathroom.

Adam was sitting in the sofa, playing with his cell phone. He looked calm. Natalie knew he was carrying at least two weapons.

She'd opened the balcony doors. Fifth floor—ought to be safe. Adam in the living room, and one other guy down in the lobby—since the conflict with Stefanovic'd kicked into full gear, she actually felt safe only at home in her family's house and in hotel rooms.

But still, the fear was there, present all the time. Like chills along her spine, like a feeling that she was constantly being watched. She stopped drinking regular Red Bull and only downed Red Bull Energy Shot—not because it was that much stronger but because it took less time to ingest. She drank two at a time. She took valerian to come down.

She made chamomile tea to calm her nerves. She couldn't make up her mind. Did she want to crawl into bed and sleep, or did she want to stay awake twenty-four-seven?

She thought about the preliminary results from Ulf Bergström, the forensic technician at Forensic Rapid Research, the private lab they'd hired. He hadn't found any DNA he could use. But he'd found fingerprints on two guns at the Black & White Inn that were clear enough to be searchable. The person who bought the plastic explosives and the Russian weapons—probably a Stetjkin and the Glock—had also touched these guns. Natalie considered handing the information over to the police so that they could run the findings through their databases. Thomas dissuaded her. He wanted to try to do it on his own—maybe he could get access to the databases without having to involve the police formally. He thought he would know if it was possible in the next few days.

The hotel phone rang. Natalie picked it up.

"You have a visitor down here."

"Ask him to show ID."

There was silence on the phone for a moment, then the receptionist said, "Johan Westlund. He says he goes by JW."

"Okay, send him up."

At the very moment she hung up the phone, her cell rang. Her guy down in the lobby reported that JW was on his way up.

There was a knock at the door. Adam peered through the peephole. Opened the door.

Natalie took a deep breath—JW looked fantastic. His hair wasn't as tightly slicked back as the last time they'd seen each other. His overcoat and jacket fit like an extra skin over his shirt, which must've been made of insanely nice cotton—it gleamed even thought the light from outside was pale. His cufflinks had a green stone set in the middle. They matched the handkerchief that peeked out of his breast pocket.

But more than anything, it was his gaze. JW's eyes were glittering. Natalie thought, *He's so fucking hot. And he knows we're negotiating today.*

They embraced. He didn't smile. Natalie told him to keep his coat on and showed him out to the balcony.

They sat down. Natalie was wearing a pea coat and a scarf wrapped around her neck.

The situation was different today: her war with Stefanovic'd escalated for real. JW probably felt pressured to act. As it should be—all the bury-your-head-in-the-sand games were over now.

She cut right to it. "Your colleague told me that Moscow is getting fed up. Tell me more."

JW twiddled his thumbs. "I've already told you—you have to stop."

"Are you my boss or what?"

"No, but I'm not speaking for myself. Moscow is irritated."

"Tell me more, please."

"All this conflict isn't good for this city," he said. "For instance, Moscow believes you and Stefanovic are playing hide-and-seek with the information they need. I don't know any details, but it can't continue like that."

Natalie had to remain calm. She wasn't balanced—she felt excited, worried, and cool as ice all at the same time. The negotiation situation: so much was at stake. At the same time: she was visualizing JW in front of her, naked. She saw him kiss her. She was Natalie Kranjic—she set the rules of the game. She took what she wanted.

She said, "Come with me into the bedroom."

She could tell by his eyes that he understood.

They walked in through the living room. Adam didn't even look up.

They closed the bedroom door behind them.

She positioned herself close to JW. His face a head's length above hers. She took a tiny step forward.

"There's got to be a way for us to solve this, right?"

He bent his head down, she could feel his breath, it smelled of spearmint.

His face came up close against her. His chin brushed by her cheek.

She grabbed hold of his neck. Pressed him against her. Kissed him.

They threw themselves onto the bed. She rolled on top of him. He caressed her ass, hips, thighs.

He said, "You're so damn foxy."

She said, "You shouldn't play so tough."

He laughed.

She took off his jacket and began unbuttoning his shirt.

He kissed her neck. Then he kissed her forehead and eyelids.

The bed was even more comfortable than it looked. Natalie leaned back and stretched out. JW bit her earlobes and lips playfully.

He cupped her breasts in his hands.

She took his shirt off. JW was toned. Less than Viktor, but still with accentuated pecs and okay abs. She licked his nipples.

He groaned.

She pulled his fly down and pulled his cock out, licked the tip, took him in her mouth, held his cock at the root with one hand, and swallowed the entire length of him.

He groaned louder.

She didn't want him to come. She released him and crawled up. He unbuttoned her pants and pulled them down. She was wearing pink Hanky Panky panties.

She moved his head down toward her crotch.

He kissed the inside of her thighs. The outside of her panties—warm breath through them.

He slipped her panties off. Kissed her pussy.

She felt him spread her with his fingers.

His tongue carefully found its way down there.

He brought one hand up to her breasts, carefully pinched one of her nipples.

His tongue continued to swirl around down there. Slowly approached her clit.

She felt how he massaged her pussy with the fingers of his other hand.

Delivered wide-tongued licks, then with the thin tip of his tongue, to the side, back and forth, alternately. He moved it in circles.

She tensed her body. Almost squirmed away from him.

He licked faster and faster.

It was as though electric shocks were pulsing through her body.

His tongue was everywhere.

She screamed. Her body in convulsions.

She came.

They lay still. Her pulse was still racing.

A minute or so later she climbed on top of him, sat. She was wet. His cock slipped in easily.

He moved his pelvis. She moved in time with him.

Natalie felt him inside her.

She leaned forward. He grabbed hold of her ass.

In and out. He caressed her breasts.

The bed bounced to their rhythm.

She saw him breathing faster.

She felt sweat on her back.
Saw sweat on JW's brow.
They moved in time with each other.
His body pounded against the sheets.
She was close to coming again.
She felt the rush through her body.
Pulsing shocks through her pussy, through her belly, through her back.
Waves of pleasure washed over her heart.
She screamed.
It was unclear if he came as well.

They were lying next to each other. Hadn't said much yet.
Natalie said, "At least you're good for one thing."
"You too."
"Let's finish talking."
He smiled. "Okay, I think it'll go better now that we've broken the ice."
"What do you want in order to come over to my side?" she said.
JW stared up at the ceiling. "Your war has to end. It's ruining business. I want you to be as loyal to me in business as I will be to you. And I have a proposition."
Natalie waited.
"I want you to make sure that a certain thing happens," JW said.
"What?"
"I'll get to that. Be patient."
He smiled.

They talked. For a long time. Bounced ideas back and forth. JW offered propositions. Natalie told him what she needed help with—he already knew most of it. She wanted to understand exactly how he worked. He was unwilling to tell her.
Natalie said that if she didn't understand, they didn't have a deal.
He folded, explained his business—it took over an hour.
He was pedagogical, thorough. Almost seemed like he took pleasure in explaining. Showing how smart, multifaceted, advanced he was. Above all: how much money he was handling.

First: the key to success was transfers. Everything was ruled by transferal.

Transfers from one economic system to another. Transfers from dirty to clean areas. Transferal in a cycle. Transferal in three vital steps: placement, concealment, reintroduction. Without them, there was no closed circuit.

Again, the foundations: placement, stratification, and reintegration into the legal economy.

The first step: placement. The funds were almost always in cash. The cash had to be moved into the financial system somehow. Cash was lethal—nothing raised suspicions as quickly as a bunch of bills.

Step two: concealment. Stratification to distance the money from the source. They used several systems, several transactions. Companies, private persons, trusts, geographical areas with high levels of bank secrecy. Transfers between accounts in different banks around the world.

The final step: reintegration into the legal economy. Reintroducing the illicit capital so that it could be consumed or invested without risk. So that everything appeared clean and legal.

JW and his people were in control, creating plans, being consulted at every turn, every step of the way. "We don't just give advice, we implement the entire chain," he said. "We execute everything that I just told you about."

But now regulators within the EU and the OECD were applying pressure. Countries were implementing anti-terror laws to prevent shady transactions across borders. Many countries'd gotten rid of their bank secrecy laws. Switzerland had thrown in the towel years ago. Several Channel Islands gave up last year. Liechtenstein was on its way. Even most of the Swedish banks were much more careful now. No one wanted to become known as the dirty bank. Someone who wanted to make a deposit often had to answer questions and show valid ID if the bankers thought the transaction seemed unusual. Or if the bankers didn't understand the transaction's background, they began sniffing around. What was its purpose, where did the money come from, and what was it going to be used for? They wanted to see contracts, receipts, invoices, or other stuff that backed up your explanation. They wanted to know precisely who wanted to deposit what.

It was also increasingly difficult to use front men. The banks wanted proof that you owned more than 25 percent of the company, that you were the one who had the controlling interest. They wanted to know that you were the actual principal. Which was precisely what a criminal wanted to hide.

But JW had a good entry point—that's what he called it. The men in the currency-exchange group that he collaborated with made sure that the little birds behind the counters in the currency-exchange offices never asked questions.

Anyway, the main principle was to do only things that looked normal. Nothing that attracted attention. That created good relationships with bankers at other banks too. Created routines, trust. Once all that was in place, the deposit sums could be increased.

Bladman controlled three companies that did reasonably important business, in electronics, financial consulting, and catering. The important part: the companies actually had real customers, they had real income, they dealt with the real world. Front men were listed as the owners, but they could produce bank accounts, fake share books, and edited statements.

The electronics company had a Web site, a girl who manned a call center, even a small warehouse in Haninge. It sold laptops for fifteen million kronor a year. The thing: 80 percent of the sales were fake. Deposits were made into accounts without a sale taking place. The smart part: it all looked normal enough on the books. It wasn't so easy for the bank to see that eight out of ten deposits were made by the same twenty people.

The consulting company operated on the same principle. It had a real office space, a dude who was employed to help small business owners with their bookkeeping, real phone, and Internet plans. Companies all over Sweden paid for capital consulting. The company had a turnover of twenty million kronor per year. The thing, again: 80 percent of the time that the dude wrote invoices, no business'd been done. But the clients were real—that was a point of strength.

The catering firm rented space in a kitchen in a basement venue on Ringvägen. It employed a chef. It delivered lunches, dinners, and business buffets for thirteen million a year. Maaaaany employees, who were paid a salary. The thing: the chef was a gambling addict, and 80 percent of the grub was fictive. The employees were figments of the controller's imagination.

They had other companies too, where the business was fake all the way through. Antique furniture, tanning booths, and export companies—a lot was just on paper. It didn't matter—the companies looked like they had millions in turnaround every year. Cash-intensive industries—perfect. The banks thought everything appeared normal when the companies dumped ten grand a day into the service boxes. But the export company was best of all. All the payments came from abroad: its inflated invoices were matched by zero deliveries.

JW ran a tight ship, kept everything in check: you had to be careful about increasing the sums—they had to correspond with what the made-up companies might be expected to earn per day, and the deposits had to be made in old, wrinkly bills.

All together JW and Bladman had a large number of placement tools. Many ways to introduce illegal cash into the system.

But they didn't do everything via the companies. They deposited a lot straight off via errand boys—bums, alcoholics, and small-time criminals. Not junkies or gambling addicts—they couldn't be trusted. Cash deposits made directly with Western Union, Moneybooker, Forex, and, above all, the currency-exchange offices controlled by JW's business partner. They avoided the *hawala* joints and the Africa people—the terror hysteria was too rampant there. The errand boys made small deposits, under ten thousand kronor at a time, straight into the Swedish companies' accounts or to companies abroad. It ended up being a lot anyway: one dude could wander around town and make fifteen deposits in one day.

And last but not least: they often used mules directly. Loaded suitcases with one thousand tightly packed five-hundred-kronor bills, filled hidden compartments in cars with euros, let some down-and-out person travel with their stomach stuffed with diamonds. It was dangerous, of course—the mule could rip you off or be found out. That was why JW needed dangerous friends. He needed the support of the right organization. The mules had to be scared off from trying something stupid.

Summa summarum: JW claimed that he invested more than one hundred million per year in safe locations.

The second step was more refined. The actual stratification.

There were companies in Liechtenstein, the Cayman Islands, the Isle of Man, Dubai, and Panama. They'd even bought their own shell bank in Antigua where they were in control of the whole show. Northern White Bank Ltd.—JW loved the name. If suspicious eyes were ever turned on them, they could personally decide to shutter the entire bank and destroy the bookkeeping. Oops, we just had a fire—what terrible luck.

They opened bank accounts for the companies in the same countries or in other countries with better secrecy policies. They had walking accounts in more than ten countries through which they diverted deposits. The idea: the bank had clear instructions that all incoming money was automatically to be transferred to the next bank in the next country. But not too quickly. If a deposit was diverted directly, the honest bank could grow suspicious and its warning system would be set off. The instructions to the banks were to empty the accounts over ninety-day periods. Bit by bit. What was more: each bank got even clearer instructions that if some regulatory authority was in touch and asked about some transaction, it had to inform the bank in the other country, which then had to divert the money immediately. This method created tricky paths for Big Brother to follow. Even better: it created an early-warning system if something were to go to hell.

The setup and the structure varied depending on the client and the sum.

A significant portion was located in European countries or in the Caribbean. But according to JW, things were changing now. Actually, the best countries were Panama and certain emirate states.

Best of all: JW'd enrolled the perfect banker. He didn't want to mention him by name, but the guy'd apparently been CEO and head of a branch office in Danske Bank. An upstanding gentleman. A man from the real business world. "My man at the front," as JW called him.

The guy lived down in Liechtenstein but mostly traveled around the world. Ran the actual management company, Northern White Asset Management, and the shell bank, which took care of everything. The guy had connections with the offshore institutions and the law firms that helped get fake invoices, trust setups, certificates, and other documentation needed to create the impression that legitimate transactions were taking place.

He made sure the invoices were sent, that the banks issued credit cards. To put it simply: the guy held all the strings. And he created trust, both with the people down there and with the clients here at home.

Last but not least: integration. The reintegration of the money back into the legal economy. The final step. The most important step. Everyone wanted to be able to use their assets freely, without arousing suspicions.

JW'd been the brain behind the main setup. Many clients demanded special solutions. Sometimes a foreign company lent money to a client. The loan explained why the client suddenly could have so much money, from nowhere. Sometimes a foreign company bought property from a client at a crazy inflated price. The gains were totally legal, after all, even if it was taxable. Sometimes a trust was set up that made real investments on the stock exchange: the gains were white as snow even though the money that'd originally been invested was bloody. Sometimes a company in Panama simply paid for a client's health insurance, home, or new seventy-foot motorboat. How would the authorities in Sweden ever find out that the client had a Sunseeker yacht docked in a marina in Cannes?

But JW's favorite setup was entirely different. It was magically elegant. At the same time, awfully simple.

The money arrived at the client's company in some appropriate country. The company signed a contract through JW's Northern White Asset Management and opened a bank account in a bigger, better-known bank. That bank issued credit cards to Northern White Asset Management on behalf of the client's company. The credit cards were sent to the client in Sweden.

In other words: suddenly the client had access to a card connected to all the money he'd collected through bank robberies, blackmail, drugs, sex trafficking, or regular old tax evasion. And there was never an actual person's name on the card. No one could connect the client to all the money being spent. Everything went through the Northern White company instead.

It was so simple. It was so elegant.

JW grinned. "Personally, I have a MasterCard Gold. Issued by a bank in the Bahamas, Arner Bank and Trust. Big Brother will never know that I consume like an oligarch."

Natalie listened.

"We have more than two hundred clients in Sweden," JW said. "Everything from your father's people to the financial elite in Djursholm. Everyone wants to get away with it. And everyone does get away with it thanks to help from me, Bladman, and my deluxe guy down there."

Honestly, Natalie was impressed. By the size of the operation, the number of clients, and the complexity of it all. Most of all, she was impressed that he'd managed to run it all from prison.

"How'd you mange to do it from the inside?"

He laughed. "Let me put it this way: I had help."

He got up and got dressed.

Natalie sat on the edge of the bed. Put her panties on and fastened her bra.

"So you want the war to end," she said. "You want me to work with you. But you had another proposition. Something more you want from me. What?"

"Like I said: to begin with, I want you to hire only me in the future."

Natalie pulled her pants on. "That's not a problem."

"Second of all, I want your organization's full protection when shit hits the AC, so to speak."

She looked questioningly at him. Did he have in mind Melissa Cherkasova? The politician Bengt Svelander? The Russian's building project through Östersjön, the Nordic Pipe?

"You've already said that," Natalie said. "What more do you want?"

JW looked deeply into her eyes. "I want you to kill Stefanovic."

For a second or two, Natalie didn't know what to say. It was so direct, so unexpected, and so brutal to be coming from JW. But she recovered quickly—this was her reality.

"I'd want nothing more myself. But let me tell you, it's not so easy, ending that fucker."

"I've understood as much. But I can help you. He trusts me. I can give you what you need. In exchange, I will give you what you want."

JW rose, opened the door, and walked out.

Adam was still sitting on the couch, looked as if he hadn't moved a muscle.

Natalie gazed out through the window. Down onto the street.

She saw JW exit the hotel lobby. A white Audi pulled up next to him. She saw a man in the driver's seat.

He had light brown hair. Something about him felt strange—Natalie couldn't put her finger on what. He reminded her of Thomas.

She stared at the Audi.

She saw a sticker on the car's back window: HERTZ.

The car rolled off. The sticker was still visible through the back window.

It was a rental car. Probably because JW wanted to own as little as possible that could show up in some record.

Then she thought again. *A rental car.*

Anyone could rent a car. Of course.

What an idiot she'd been.

She grabbed her phone.

52

Jorge's head was filled with images.

How he'd run up the stairs. Heard screams from down below. Cops, the cabbie. Maybe neighbors.

Doors with names over the mail slot. Four on every landing.

No real plan, this wasn't his home turf, but he wasn't gonna fucking give up when he'd gotten this far. Shawshank—that's exactly who he was gonna be tonight.

The five-oh oughta be forced to stop for a few minutes: the cabbie down there with the toy gun pointing straight at his mug was like a stop block.

J-boy panted. His heart was beating faster than he was running.

How many stories did this building have, anyway?

The answer came immediately. He was standing in front of a door that seemed to be made out of plywood. It was locked. The end of the stairwell. Didn't look like there were any apartments up here. But there were boxes on the floor, some kind of generator, and a bunch of cables. He picked up the generator. It probably weighed over a hundred pounds. It felt like his back was breaking.

He staggered. Almost fell. Then straightened up. Held the generator bulk in front of him in a cramped grip. Thundered straight into the closed door.

The sound: like the building was crashing down around him. Lots of dust. A rattling noise. He'd slam-dunked the generator straight through the door. Two-zero to Jorge.

He looked around. The sheet of plywood behind him was hanging on one hinge. He understood why there were boxes and a generator outside the door—someone was in the process of turning this attic into a massive apartment.

High ceilings. Beams up there. Three large holes in three different spots in the ceiling covered with hard plastic. Irregular pillars everywhere. Paintbrushes, cables, and worker's gloves in large crates standing on the filthy gray protective paper that was covering the floor. Building machines, ladders, and wooden boards were leaning up against the white-painted walls.

Jorge didn't have time to loiter and look around—as he grabbed a ladder, he just had time to think: the Svens loved their renovated attic apartments the way his homies loved their tricked-out Benzes. Everyone wanted something to pimp. Everyone wanted something to brag about. The elevator didn't go all the way up, and there were five flights of stairs to walk, maybe with a stroller—who gave? You couldn't stand upright in half the square footage because the ceilings were so slanted—who gave? *Who gave* that the windows were set so deep, they had to live in semidarkness year round? The Svens: just as horny for status as everyone else—they were just into weirder shit.

He propped up the ladder. Climbed toward one of the holes in the ceiling. Struck the hard plastic with a screwdriver he'd found in one of the crates. They were obviously building skylights here.

He slipped the screwdriver in under the edge of the plastic. The ladder swayed. He bent the plastic back. Pulled on it. Tore off small nails and tape.

He heard voices yelling down in the stairwell. They were on their way up.

He got a good grip with his fingers. The hard plastic cut into his skin. He didn't give a shit. He used both hands and put his whole weight into it. It was bulging inward now. He climbed one more step up the ladder.

Felt the cold night air hit his face. He slipped his backpack off.

The ladder swayed.

He almost lost his grip.

He managed to press aside enough of the plastic to haul himself up. Pushed the backpack out.

Both elbows on the roof now. He was standing on tiptoes on the ladder. He pulled his torso up. He tore himself on some nails that were still stuck in the material.

The hard plastic scraped his back. He kicked the ladder to the side.

Pulled the rest of his body up and out. It'd started to rain again.

The roof was probably slippery as hell.

He hunched down. Slipped forward a few feet. Tried to get a look down at the street. He didn't need to: the cop cars were projecting a light show that colored the building facades blue all the way up here.

The *culos* down there could mobilize as much as they wanted—Shawshank was on the go.

He reached the edge of the roof. The next building over: not as tall. The roof: over ten feet down.

They didn't seem to have followed him up onto the roof.

He jumped. Flew.

As though he were floating through the air. Ice-cold drops of rain pecked holes in his face. He was seeing things in slow motion. He saw himself fall. He saw his foot twist in the grass beyond the wall. Saw himself running from the Österåker Pen, toward freedom. Pain in his ankle, shooting up through his leg. His steps, all fucked up.

It couldn't happen again. He landed.

His arms and feet broke the fall. Like a cat.

Like Spider-Man.

Sprint. Faster.

His back was completely soaked. The backpack was bouncing up and down. Was it rain or was it sweat? In the middle of the mad rush: a thought about his sweat. His smell now: sharp, strong, stressed.

Onward, across the next rooftop.

He pushed himself.

Never slow down, J-boy—never slow down. Life is yours to take.

Farther up, he saw the end of the street block. To jump over to the next building: impossible. At least fifty feet. He had to get down somehow.

He looked around. Slid down to the edge of the roof. Feet first. Terrified of losing his grip.

He placed one foot on the drainpipe. Put his weight on it. It seemed stable.

He stepped down onto it with his other foot. Folded his body down. Tried to hold on to a roof tile with one hand.

Bent his head down. Looked over the edge of the roof. Shit—at least sixty-five feet down. He got mad vertigo.

Then he looked again. Directly below him: a balcony.

There was a God.

Jorge opened his eyes. The images disappeared. One day and five hours since he'd fled from the cop ambush.

He'd busted the balcony window carefully. Opened it. Slipped soundlessly through the apartment. Maybe someone was sleeping in there. The front door was easy to open from the inside. He crept down the stairs. There were two entrances downstairs—one led to the court-yard exit. He chose that one. Leaped over a couple fences to other inner courtyards. Emerged on the other side of the block.

The street outside was dead quiet.

He spent the night and the next day outside. Roaming back and forth in a mall. Pocketed candy bars at ICA Supermarket and bought a prepaid phone card. Wondered who he dared call.

Pulled a classic move: bought a personal identification number from a junkie by Fridhemsplan for one grand. The night shelters invoiced the junkie's welfare officer. The dude lost his welfare checks—but would rather have easy money for horse.

Jorge checked into Karisma Care by Fridhemsplan for the night, under his new name.

And that was where he was now. An uncomfortable mattress. Lots of uneasy people all around him. Didn't matter—he'd made it.

He got up. Walked out to the common room. Wooden chairs and a dank old couch. A TV in one corner. A pay phone in another. Dudes who looked like they were sixty years old but were probably not a day over thirty. A small reception area. A large message board across from the welcome desk, peppered with ads for *Situation Stockholm*: opportuni-ties to sell the magazine that profited a cause for the homeless. Courses at the community college: discount for homeless people. Information packets about welfare programs. Bikram yoga classes in Mälarhöjden.

Fuck that shit.

Jorge set his backpack down on the floor. In it: a passport and twelve hundred five-hundred-kronor bills. He had to give JW the cash so he could exchange them. Then he had to get a ticket back to Thailand.

He was tired.

Called Paola from the pay phone. Gave her his new number. Didn't tell her anything about what'd happened. Just couldn't muster the energy for that right now.

He called Mahmud in Thailand. His buddy already knew J-boy'd picked up the six hundred Gs. He explained everything that'd hap-pened the night before. Javier arrested. The Hägerström Sven maybe arrested too. Everything fucked all to hell.

Mahmud bitched: "Babak's gonna rat you out, man. Maybe me too. What the fuck you gonna do about it?" And: "You can't just leave Javier there." And: "Can't you help them escape?"

Jorge: didn't have any answers. They ended the call.

He sat down again.

What the fuck was he gonna do?

He leaned back.

One of the dudes in the common room looked like Björn, his old teacher in the after-school program when he was a kid.

Gray beard. Bald on top of his head. White hairs on the side. Kind eyes.

Jorge: maybe eight years old. Björn: the teacher who was a God at drawing. All the boys asked him to draw things for them. Submarines, camels, Ferrari cars. Björn blinked. The wrinkles near his eyes spread all over his face. He looked like Santa Claus.

Jorge and his crew beat up the weaker kids. Explained to the girls who talked back that they were whores. Ran amok in the nap room: glued the pillows to the floor with Super Glue they'd swiped from shop class. Pooped in buckets that they set out in the air vents so the place reeked for a week. Teachers and after-school people tried to get them in line. Talk to them. Yell at them. Write made-up contracts for how they were supposed to behave.

No one gave a shit. The Sven staff were like yappy poodles. All the boys had to put up with real fists at home anyway. The after-school people's attempts at disciplining them were just pathetic.

The only one they respected was Björn. They remained cool with him. And if he told them off, they obeyed immediately.

Björn: like a wise old man.

Jorge wished he could be here now. To draw something for him.

Just a submarine.

That would've been enough.

53

They had released Hägerström right after the interrogation. Naturally. They couldn't have anything on him, except possibly that he had lost control on Östermalmstorg. But they didn't ask any questions about that little blunder.

Maybe they would call him in for questioning again. Maybe they would put a tail on him. He had to be careful. Had to talk to Inspector Torsfjäll.

As soon as he turned his phone on, it beeped. Missed calls. New voicemails. Message icons popped up on the screen.

JW and Torsfjäll had both tried to reach him. Both with about the same questions: *What the fuck happened? How did Jorge get away?*

Hägerström arranged a time to meet JW at Sturehof. He walked there from home. It was cold outside. On the way, he bought a new phone with a new plan—his old one would most probably be tapped soon. He called Torsfjäll.

At first, the inspector didn't want to talk. Hägerström told him he was calling from a new SIM card. Torsfjäll made a one-eighty. Instead of being monosyllabic, reluctant: the inspector became half-crazed.

"How the fuck could this happen?"

Hägerström tried to respond.

Torsfjäll screamed, "Have you seen the headlines today? Have you seen that the online papers are mentioning you by name?"

Hägerström tried to say something.

"It's damn fucking lucky that our little operation is really UC," Torsfjäll went on, "or else I'd be drowning in phone calls today, like some fucking press secretary. Fuck these Commie journalists—they're totally consequence neutral. They don't give a fuck about what they might be messing up."

Hägerström tired to calm the inspector down. There were good aspects to the whole thing.

Torsfjäll wouldn't let up. "I'm getting pretty fucking tired of this operation. I'm considering dropping it. We managed to cuff this Javier guy. Our economic crime investigator might have enough pinned on JW. I'm so fucking tired today. What kind of fucking cop clowns do we have in this country anyway? Huh? They act like fucking fairies. They can't go into a regular café and arrest two people? How hard can it be? Fucking fags."

Hägerström counted. Torsfjäll'd managed to say *fuck* ten times in less than thirty seconds. He tried to get some calming words in edgewise.

Finally the inspector settled down.

"In one way, it's good the papers are writing what they're writing," Hägerström said. "It'll raise my credibility with Jorge and JW's people. They'll see that I'm involved for real. We'll get Jorge, I'm sure of it. Don't worry."

"But that little nigger could go back to Thailand any minute. He obviously has a passport."

"Yes, but his bills are dyed. And JW's supposed to help him with that. Do you understand? He's going to be in touch with JW. And I've got eyes on JW. We're going to be able to cuff Jorge. And maybe JW too, at least for attempted money laundering."

Torsfjäll sounded a little pleased. "Okay, you have a point. But this playboy isn't going to get convicted just for money laundering—we're going to get him for heavier shit. You just have to find out where they keep their material."

"Believe me, I'm trying. And there's one more thing. I've got a little surprise for JW today. Something he's been nagging me about. Something that might make him use me even more."

Two days later. The second Monday in October. Always. Anyone serious would be out in the woods today. The offices downtown were half-empty. The rutting season for moose was over. Meaning: moose hunt time.

Hägerström's surprise: he had arranged for JW to be invited to a moose hunt, followed by dinner at Carl's estate, Avesjö.

A beautiful fall day. A long day in the woods. Meet-up at eight in the morning. There were twelve of them, in total. They were hunting with dogs. Two hired dog handlers flushed through the stand. The hunters were posted in elevated blinds surrounding the area. Three stands during the day: three times three hours. Early lunch in the hunting lodge. They ate goulash soup in plastic cans, standing up. A recap between every stand. Some of them smoked cigarettes. Most drank coffee. The dog handlers gave them a rundown, discussed the best car route to the next place, prepped the rifles. They talked hunting, mutual acquaintances, and business throughout.

By the end of the day, a bull moose and two calves had been taken down—Hägerström was one of the heroes. He was the one who'd shot the young bull.

For Hägerström, the hunt meant another kind of victory. He and JW had sat together in a blind all day. JW was carrying his own class-one rifle that he had borrowed from Hägerström's brother. A Blaser R93 with a luxury riflescope: Swarovski Z6.

JW was in seventh heaven.

Hägerström saw that he was struggling not to appear too impressed.

But he was even more exhilarated than when he had gated out.

And above all: these were JW hunting grounds, business-wise.

That night there was a dinner at Avesjö. Hägerström, Carl, JW, and nine of Carl's friends. Hägerström recognized most of them. Carl lived according to the principle that new friends are not real friends. Fredric Adlercreutz was there, of course. He acted normal toward Hägerström. *Maybe*, Hägerström thought, *he is also gay.*

There were three new faces that Hägerström didn't know. Carl's business contacts—they were exempt from his rule.

This was the first time Hägerström had brought a friend. JW was more than ten years younger than he, but Carl was a few years younger than Hägerström, so the age difference between the two was not as great.

Catering staff prepared the meal. The dog handlers were sent home. Dinner was served. The appetizer: potato pancakes with sour cream and bleak roe.

Only the gentlemen remained. Carl's closest friends. All lawyers, finance guys, real estate moguls.

They had all made the same life choice: career was number one.

They all had the same background.

They were all sitting on inherited money or had wives with even more inherited money.

Hägerström eyed JW.

The others were wearing jeans and French-cuff shirts. Some had blazers on. Loafers or brown boat shoes on their feet. All were well dressed and yet relaxed. Ten years ago these boys used to be the biggest playboys in town; now they didn't need to prove anything to each other anymore. They were adults.

JW, on the other hand, was sporting a pair of red chinos with knife-sharp creases and a white shirt with a dark blue blazer. Berluti shoes flown in from Paris. He topped it all off with gold cufflinks with the Swedish royal crowns on a red background.

Might just be superficial details. After all, the basic foundation was the same. But Hägerström saw it. And he knew that Carl saw it. JW was just a little *too much*. He wondered if JW himself perceived the difference.

The others had well-cut manes, but their hair was casually tousled after an entire day under a hunter's hat in a moose blind.

JW, on the other hand, had obviously been to the bathroom and groomed himself. His hair was slicked back like a helmet.

They were sitting on refurbished rococo chairs covered in zebra skin. Carl's wife had an interest in interior decorating. There was a white tablecloth on the table. Above the plates were three different crystal glasses from Orrefors that Hägerström recognized. They had been his and Tin-Tin's wedding present to Carl when he got married six years ago. Real silver cutlery, plates and napkins that Carl's wife had inherited from her grandmother—the Fogelklou family crest was embroidered on them in curlicue lettering. There were huge candelabras with lit candles placed on the table. Hägerström recognized them too. They were from his maternal grandmother, Countess Cronhielm af Hakunge.

JW's eyes were as large as the gold-rimmed saucers on the table.

Hägerström thought the guy had to learn to play it cool.

Carl welcomed everyone. "I want us to raise our glasses and toast a successful hunt today. Even if I didn't manage to take anything down this year. Ha ha."

Everyone raised their glasses, sipped the wine that was served with the appetizer: Chablis Cuvée Tour du Roy Vieilles Vignes.

Hägerström continued to study JW.

He fumbled for his knife and fork. Glanced around the table to see which bread plate was his. Wiped his mouth too frequently with the linen napkin.

The guy sitting on JW's other side, Hugo Murray, raised his glass to Hägerström.

"Cheers to you, Martin. You're the only damn one who shot something worthwhile today."

Martin raised his glass. Looked Hugo in the eyes. Nodded. Smiled. Said, "And who shot the raghorn last year?"

Hugo laughed. Nodded. Tilted his glass toward Hägerström. Looked around. The others also raised their glasses. Everyone allowed their gaze to travel around the table, meeting each person's eyes the correct Swedish way. Then they set their glasses down again. No clinking when you toasted—that was gauche.

Paintings hung on the walls. Count Gustaf Cronhielm af Hakunge, the original. The same old guy that Hägerström had on the wall at home. Except that in this painting, he was holding up two pheasants that he had shot. Portraits of his three sons, one of them Hägerström's grandfather. The old man had died when Hägerström was four years old. A new photo was hanging on one short end of the room: a photo of Father in the motorboat with Vreta Bay in the background.

Hägerström thought of what Father would have said if he'd seen him and Javier hand in hand in Bangkok.

They continued eating. Hägerström pricked up his ears. He heard Hugo talking to JW.

"So what do you do when you're not hiding out next to Martin in a blind?"

"I manage my money, like everyone else."

Hugo laughed politely. JW laughed painfully.

"Sure, right. And what do you do when you're not managing your money?"

"I work in asset management."

Hugo was less polite, more interested for real. "Oh really? You run solo, or what?"

"Yes, you could say that. I work with a guy down in Liechtenstein, Gustaf Hansén. Do you know him?"

"No, I don't think so. How old is he?"

"Around forty-five."

"Was he at SEB before?"

"No, Danske Bank."

"Okay. He might be Carl-Johan's uncle. Do you know Carl-Johan Hansén?"

The waitresses served the main course. Boeuf bourguignon with moose and almond potatoes. The meat had been shot at Avesjö last year, of course. The wine: Chambolle-Musigny 2006, straight from Carl's wine cellar.

JW and Hugo kept the conversation going.

Hägerström continued to listen in.

"So what do you do?" JW asked.

"I'm at Invest Capital. I keep myself busy there."

"Okay. What division?"

"Trading."

JW tried to play right back at him: "So do you know Nippe Creutz? His sister's boyfriend's at Invest Capital, I think."

Hugo looked like a question mark. "I haven't heard anything about that. But I've been on paternity leave lately."

"Nice?"

"Absolutely. I made Friday dinner for my wife and kids. That's about where I draw the line, though. But it was great. The nannies need a break too now and then. Ha ha."

Hägerström wondered if JW knew that Hugo Murray practically owned Invest Capital.

He heard Hugo turn the question game back around. Interrogate JW.

"Where did you go to college?"

"Where did you go to high school?"

"Where do your parents summer?"

JW navigated skillfully.

"I lived abroad."

"I went to an American high school in Belgium."

"They have a little place in Provence."

Hägerström thought: It wasn't just the clothes, the coif, and the cufflinks. A truth was crystallizing. No outsider could ever really enter the world he was from. It didn't matter how much money you made, that you lived at the right address, dressed the right way, were overly friendly, or could name-drop hundreds of names. It didn't matter if you hunted, were a member of the Värmdö Golf Club, bought a summer house on the most expensive street in Torekov, or drove the flashiest cars.

It was impossible. Entrance: barred. You would never become one of them for real. Because they were like a family. You wouldn't fool anyone with perfect table manners, the correct right-wing political sympathies, membership in Nya Sällskapet Gentleman's Club, or condescending comments about the plebs in boroughs like Farsta. They saw through you—because *if we don't know your parents or your siblings, or at least have heard of your family's estate in Sörmland, you are not one of us. Either you belong with us or you don't.* The only way in was through the right birth canal.

Hägerström had been a cop, then a corrections officer. How well did that fit into Carl's world? He didn't dress like the others, he didn't live like them. He was a fucking homosexual. Still, they accepted him like a brother—because they knew where he came from. Their parents knew his parents. Their grandparents had known his grandparents. They saw his ancestors on the wall. They knew they could trust him.

The dinner ended. They rose from the table. Went into the smoking room. Carl distributed cigars. There were hunting trophies and more paintings of old Cornhielm af Hakunge men on the walls.

They drank cognac and calvados. They talked business and hunting.

JW did well. They liked him. Even if he wasn't one of them, he wanted to be. That was okay.

Hägerström heard how he filled in the five empty years of his life—the years he had actually been doing time. He talked about jobs at American banks and contacts with tax havens. He described the beach in Nassau, the restaurants in George Town, and the hotels in Panama. In passing, JW mentioned how one could be a little bit smart about things. Maybe invest something through someone down there, not let bureaucratic Sweden take such a big piece of the pie.

Hägerström could see curiosity in a few of the men's eyes. He wanted JW to keep trying to recruit potential customers.

He couldn't hear everything JW said during the rest of the night. But he heard him talking to Fredric.

"I love Panama. They have those bearer shares there, sort of like promissory notes, but ten times better. It means that the owners of the companies can be completely anonymous. You know, the holder of the share certificate is the owner of the company, but his name isn't listed in any record anywhere, and he doesn't have to be registered on the share certificate. Not even the bank needs to know who the owner is. It'll be like in the good old days, when there were Swiss numbered accounts. There aren't too many countries in the world where that works anymore."

Fredric didn't look uninterested.

"For example," JW went on, "you can add three hobos as board members, so the real owner's name isn't listed on the board either. The owner can even designate them by proxy. You can have a law firm down there that takes care of all the paperwork. Authorities around the world can go ahead and track as many transactions as they like—they'll still never find out who the owner is. It's fantastic. Right?"

A few hours later Hägerström and JW were in a taxi on their way into the city. It was two o'clock in the morning. They were sitting in the backseat.

JW was half-boozed and wholly happy.

"That was so awesome, Martin. So damn nice of you to bring me, man."

As expected. JW would be indebted to Hägerström now. JW would want to get even closer to him, because what he had just experienced was his own personal paradise.

But above all, JW would want Hägerström to connect him with some of those men again.

He said, "Wonder what's happening to Javier?"

JW grinned. "Who cares? He'll be convicted. Idiot, that's what I think."

It was pitch-black outside. The woods, fields, residential areas on Värmdö looked cold.

Right before they were about to leave, Carl had asked Hägerström to come upstairs with him for a moment.

He had looked Hägerström in the eyes, deeply.

"Martin, who is this guy you dragged along?"

"Why, what do you mean?"

"Did you become friends with him when you were working in the prison, or what?"

"What's your problem? He's a nice guy. Everyone here likes him."

"I don't care about that. Hugo told me who he is. Do you know who he is?"

"Quit it, Carl. What the fuck is your problem?"

"Your buddy, JW, who has been wined and dined in my home tonight, has done lots of years for possession. And now here he is, talking to Hugo Murray, Fredric, and other guys about doing dirty business with Gustaf Hansén, opening accounts in offshore companies in Panama and shit like that."

"It's not that bad. Fredric wanted to see him again."

"If so, that's on him," Carl said. "I think it's embarrassing."

Hägerström felt he was very near a breakthrough. JW not only trusted him and saw that he could get him customers, he wanted to be close to him. Now Hägerström just needed one tiny bit of information: where he kept his secret books. Evidence that would hold up. Physical documents that could show everything he was involved in.

They drove across the bridge toward Nacka. The water below was dark. At a distance, the windows of the houses gleamed like small candles. This area hadn't been this densely populated when Hägerström was a kid. He remembered the old Värmdö road. It used to take two hours to get to Avesjö. These days it took forty-five minutes.

JW turned to face him. Focused his gaze. His voice was dead serious. "Why, Martin? Why?"

Hägerström wondered what he meant.

"Why?" JW said again. "Why've you worked as a cop and a screw when you've got all that?"

"What do you mean?"

"You've got everything anyone could ever dream of. Money, friends, family. Why've you worked those jobs?"

Hägerström ran his hand through his hair. "I have my brother, and I might have certain habits, what do I know. But you have to understand: I don't have any money. I'm pretty much broke. The only thing I own is my apartment, and it's heavily mortgaged. I did something seriously stupid a few years ago. I don't really want to go into it, but the result is that I don't have any money saved up. The opposite actually. I'm desperate for cash."

JW leaned back. "Still, if I were you, I wouldn't have worked as a screw."

"No, but I don't do that anymore."

"So you need money?"

Hägerström cracked a crooked smile. "More than ever."

"I might have a job for you," JW said. "It's a piece of cake. All you have to do is bring a bag to a place for me. I'll give you thirty large for it."

54

Natalie was with Sascha in a rented Passat. On their way to a Hertz on Vasagatan.

Not to return the car. Not to complain about anything. Instead: to check if Hertz'd rented out a green Volvo in mid-April and, if so, to whom.

The thing: Natalie'd checked the film from the surveillance cameras more than ten times. It was impossible to make out the license plate number on the green Volvo. But last week, when she'd stood on the hotel balcony and seen JW get picked up in a rental car, it'd all clicked: a Hertz sticker on the car's rear window. The dark spot on the rear window of the green Volvo could be just such a sticker.

They'd been to Avis yesterday. They said they didn't have any green cars in their fleet. The day before that, they'd stopped by Europcar. They had Volvos in their fleet. Natalie hassled them, argued, threatened—*We have to know if you rented out a green Volvo in April.* It took several hours. They rummaged through archives, ran searches through their databases. Europcar concluded: they had green cars in April, but they were all parked in their garage up in the north of the country.

Natalie wouldn't give up, so today it was Hertz's turn.

Also, Thomas'd called that morning. He'd gotten results from the database searches he'd arranged. The fingerprints that Forensic Rapid Research'd found at the Black & White Inn.

He didn't want to take the information over the phone. They were going to meet up as soon as she could. After Hertz.

Sascha parked the car. The curb was painted yellow: parking forbidden. Sascha was in personal bankruptcy anyway—he'd have to take on any eventual parking ticket.

First he walked around, scouted the scene. The Hertz office was five yards farther up the street.

Since the Marko thing: the war with Stefanovic'd reached a new level. Nothing'd happened yet, but all her advisers agreed: Stefanovic was only licking his wounds. He was definitely not laying down his arms. The opposite—*izdajnik* would try to strike back ten times harder.

Natalie switched her car out every other day. When she spent the night in her house, she slept in the safe room that Stefanovic'd had built—fate's irony. Other nights she moved between the Hotel Diplomat, the Strand, and different Clarion hotels around the city. Sometimes she slept in Thomas's den. His wife, Åsa, was supersweet. Their son, Sander, was a cutie.

She drank eight Red Bull Shots a day and seven cups of coffee. She stopped taking valerian at night—munched on Sonata mixed with Xanax instead. She washed her hair only once a week, used dry shampoo the rest of the time. She only wore light makeup. She started eating white bread again for the first time in three years—the LCHF diet was for little girls. She didn't work out, quit Facebook, and switched her cell phone out every fifth day.

She'd dumped Viktor a few days ago.

Not a big deal. He'd called to ask if she wanted to have dinner. Maybe he wanted to apologize for his behavior.

She told him the truth. "We've grown apart."

He was silent.

She offered up the number-one breakup cliché: "It's not you, it's me."

Viktor was breathing heavily.

"I've change a lot since Dad was murdered," she said. "I can't have a normal relationship right now. There's too much else going on. I'm sorry."

Viktor was about to say something. He sucked in air.

Natalie interrupted him. "There's no point for us to keep in touch and stuff. That'll just be weird. I like you as a friend, Viktor. Really, I do."

"Is it that guy from Brasserie Godot?" Viktor asked.

"Oh, get a grip. Didn't you do what I told you to do? Didn't you look up what happened to him?"

"Just tell me. Is it him?"

Natalie thought of JW in the hotel bed at the Diplomat. They'd gotten together two more times, at different hotels.

Her voice hardened. "Didn't you hear what I just said? It's not about someone else. It's only about me. I'm not the same person I was six months ago. I was a girl then. I'm an adult now."

Viktor was making strange sounds. Maybe he was crying.

Natalie ended the conversation.

She felt relieved. At the same time, irritated.

She followed Sascha into the Hertz office.

Two guys in their thirties were manning the counter. One of them—with a shaved head—was helping a customer. The other—with long hair tied back in a ponytail—was sitting at a computer. Looked fake-busy—wanted Natalie to get in line.

She looked around. On the walls: old Hertz ads from the American 1950s. Men in hats and women in long skirts: SEE MORE, DO MORE, HAVE MORE FUN . . . THE HERTZ RENT-A-CAR-WAY! THE HERTZ IDEA HAS BECOME . . . THE HERTZ HABIT. More: posters with images of the cars you could rent. Volvo S80—they had it in several different models. And colors?

A couch in pleather against the wall. The customer at the counter kept talking. Natalie waited for five minutes. The guy with the shaved head didn't get freed up. Natalie wanted to do this the soft way, but still, she didn't want to wait any longer.

She leaned over the counter, eyed the ponytail guy in front of the computer. White, short-sleeved shirt with a name plaque pinned to his breast.

"Anton," she said. "May I ask you something?"

The guy almost jumped in surprise.

"Absolutely."

"I'm going to need some special help. I have some questions about different cars that you've rented out."

"How do you mean?"

Natalie glanced to the side. The customer and the other Hertz guy were busy with each other. "I think it's best if we take it in your office."

Anton was reluctant. Natalie coaxed him. Explained that she was a big Hertz customer—that much was true: but she was never the one listed on the actual rental contracts.

Finally Anton caved. Natalie and Sascha were invited to follow him behind the counter.

An office slash kitchen. A sink in one corner, coffee cups, a coffee maker, and a mini-fridge. A small table and four chairs. The other half of the room: a wide desk with two office chairs on either side. Phones, computers, lots of binders.

Anton remained standing in the middle of the office. "So what can I do for you?"

"I'm interested in knowing whether you've rented out a green Volvo S80 at some point during the first half of April this year," Natalie said. "And if so, to whom."

Anton crossed his arms over his chest. "Unfortunately, we don't release information about other customers."

Natalie didn't want any bullshit. "But Avis releases that kind of information."

"Well, we're not Avis. We want our customers to feel safe with Hertz."

"But do you have green Volvo S80s in your fleet?"

"That I can say that we do, yes."

"Did you have that car in April this year?"

"The answer is yes."

"How many of those cars were in Stockholm? You can check that, can't you?"

Anton scratched his head. He had an earring in his right ear. The guy looked like Anders Borg, the ponytailed Swedish finance minister.

"Yeah, that shouldn't be a problem. But why do you want to know all of this?"

Natalie pulled the same story that she'd told Avis and Europcar. "We're hunting down a hit-and-run. There was an accident in Östermalm on April fourteenth, a child was killed. The police have still not been able to identify the car, so now we're trying to take matters into our own hands. I assume Hertz will cooperate for such a cause."

Anton continued to scratch his head. "Oh, wow. Well, let me take a look."

He sat down at one of the computers. Typed on the keyboard. Clicked on different windows and icons with the mouse.

There were the same vintage ads on the walls in here as out by the counter.

Natalie thought of her agreement with JW. He'd said that he didn't dare break free from Stefanovic unless someone got rid of him. She'd asked him what, then, he needed her protection for. The answer was something entirely different. A grand coup: JW was planning on blind-siding his customers. Screwing over the people who'd put money in his hands. Given him the sensitive responsibility of laundering their money. And there wasn't exactly a risk that his customers would go to the police.

His idea was simple. Genius. Insanely dangerous.

She had to think it over. On the other hand: she had to kill Stefanovic. JW was the key.

And also: she needed him—it felt as though he were her mirror image. As if he truly understood her, saw inside her, knew who she was. She felt for him. Maybe too much.

And if she could get a percentage of his rip-off scheme, all her problems would be solved. Except for the one question: who'd murdered Dad?

Anton pushed his chair back. "We had a total of two hundred rentals of Volvo S80s during the entire month of April. Prior to April fourteenth, we had eighty-five rentals. I'm not entirely sure, but I think we had two green cars here in Stockholm. That means that we had seven green Volvo rentals prior to April fourteenth."

Natalie thought: the guy wasn't stupid.

"Can I see who the seven renters were?" she asked.

"I told you, you can't do that. We have a privacy policy."

There were three ways to deal with this. She could set Sasha loose on him—she would get what she wanted but risk police reports and other crap like that. The second alternative was to show this Anton guy her tougher side. Threaten to set Sascha loose to him, threaten to chop off his ugly ponytail and stuff it down his throat.

Natalie chose a third way. She placed four five-hundred-kronor bills on the desk.

Anton just stared.

"If you give me a printout of who rented those seven cars, you can go buy yourself something nice this afternoon."

She and Sascha were still sitting in the car on Vasagatan.

She'd never thought Anton would break bad—the guy seemed more blue-eyed than a Swedish tourist in Marrakech. He just smiled, pocketed the five-hundred-kronor bills, sat back down in front of the computer, hit the keyboard, and printed seven pages.

He gave them to Natalie in a plastic folder with the Hertz logo on it.

She couldn't wait. She climbed into the backseat. Retrieved the blurry image from the surveillance cameras of the green Volvo and its driver on the seat. Picked up the seven printed pages that Anton'd give her and held them in her hand. The thing: Hertz always made a digital copy of the customer's driver's license.

Shit.

Six men and one woman.

The driver's license photos were bad. Black and white, blurry, difficult to make out. She weeded out the woman straight away.

Held them up to the light. Against the seat. Placed the printouts next to each other, one by one.

The image from the surveillance camera was beside them.

John Johansson, Kurt Sjögren, Kevin Whales, Daniel Wengelin, Tor Jonasson, Hamed Ghasemi.

Process of elimination. Hamed was out immediately. The dude was too dark.

She compared again. Kevin Whales was young, born in 1990. The man captured by the surveillance camera was older, had a wider face. She weeded out Whales.

Four remained.

Fuck, the surveillance images were so crappy. Why even have those cameras if you can't recognize a person in a car from less than two hundred feet?

She ranked the photos. One to five.

Daniel Wengelin: straw blond, thin. Thirty-six years old. A one—he wasn't anywhere close to the man in the car.

Tor Jonasson: a two. The hair color was right but not the rest.

John Johansson and Kurt Sjögren: both were fours.

Both were possible.

She told Sascha to drive to see Thomas.

They met up at her house. Thomas was already there. He was sitting in the kitchen.

They went into the library—they had serious business to discuss.

She said, "So what've they found?"

"There are a lot of people in the police force who hate me. But others actually understand why I've done what I've done. They know that

I'm still an honorable man. So I gave the fingerprint results to a buddy, along with an envelope with some extra gratitude in it. He entered the fingerprint results into an ongoing project he's working on. Doing that enabled him to pass the stuff to the Nordic Cooperation Committee and Interpol. Then they could run searches through their databases based on the fingerprints from the Black & White Inn."

Natalie felt her pulse pounding in her temples.

"They've come up with three hits. A murder in Berlin last year, an assassination attempt of a Russian politician. And another murder in Lyon seven years ago."

Natalie wasn't breathing.

Thomas said, "They suspect the same person."

He picked up an envelope, opened it. Placed a document on the table.

A printout from Interpol's *Wanted* database. First: a few lines of general information. Then a name: Semjon Averin. Then two photographs, front and profile shots.

There was more text, but she was only looking at the person in the photograph.

A clear face: it was the same person as John Johansson.

* * *

OIPC–ICPO INTERPOL

RED NOTICE
[image]

Legal Status
Current Surname: Averin (son of Michail)
Current Given Name: Semjon
Sex: Male
Date of birth: April 4, 1966
Place of birth: Kurgan, Uralskij
Nationality: Russia
Known aliases: Florencio Primo, Sergey Batista, Volk ("The Wolf")

Physical Description
Height: 187 cm
Weight: 97 kg
Hair color: Dark
Eye color: Brown

Crimes
Murder, attempted murder, illegal weapons possession, conspiracy

Arrest warrant issued by:
Moskovskij gorodskoj sug, Moscow, Russia
Tribunal de Police, Paris, France

COMMENTS
Semjon Averin was born in the city of Kurgan in Siberia. His father, Michail Averin, served as a high-ranking officer in the Russian Air Force. His mother, Sonja, was a Communist activist. Semjon Averin's parents divorced when he was young. His father is reported to have severely abused the boy on two occasions.

After finishing school, Averin applied to the Russian military. After completing two years of basic training, he was accepted to OMON (Otrjad Militsii Osobogo Naznatjenija). OMON is made up of a large number of special units within the national police in Russia. OMON was created in the former Soviet Union and is today under direct orders from the Ministry of Internal Affairs (MVD). Every Russian police department has an OMON force that is deployed in high-risk situations such as, for example, hostage dramas, kidnappings, riots, terror threats, and so on.

However, Averin was fired from the unit after only fourteen months of service, for unknown reasons. He returned to Kurgan and found work there as a gravedigger. In 1989 he married and had a daughter. Shortly thereafter, he was charged with rape and sentenced to eight years in the gulag. On the same day that he was to be transported to the gulag, he was allowed to pay a visit to his wife. Averin managed to escape from the third floor of a building where the visit was taking place. After a number of months on the run, he was found 120 kilometers north of Kurgan, was arrested and brought to the gulag. Even though Averin had the right to serve his time in a special unit reserved for former members of the military and/or police, he was placed in an ordinary unit, probably because of his high escape risk.

According to unverified rumor, the other inmates, when they

learned of his background within the police, sentenced him to death. He survived a number of murder attempts in the prison camp and was forced to fight for his life on numerous occasions. He was given his nickname, Volk ("The Wolf"), by the other inmates because he had a reputation for biting his opponents in the throat when he was attacked. After some time, they left him alone because he was considered dangerous.

Averin escaped from the gulag in 1992. He returned to Kurgan, where he is suspected of having joined the local criminal organization. He is suspected of participating in the murder of the rival organization's leader, Dima Romanovitj, in the city of Tjumen. In 1994 Averin is believed to have moved to Moscow.

From 1994 to 2002 Averin is suspected of having participated in various illegal activities in the service of different organizations and associations. The allegations include attempted murder, blackmail, assault, and illegal weapons possession. However, these allegations have not been proven. After this period of time, Averin is formally suspected of the following:

- Murder of the Algerian citizen Hassan Saber, Lyon, 2003. Fingerprints have been found on a weapon, a pistol of the model Stetjkin APS, which was discovered in a water tank on the roof of the apartment building where Hassan Saber lived. Hassan Saber was known to French police as one of the leading figures in the sex trade in Lyon. He had been shot in the eyes with three bullets from the pistol in question.
- Assassination attempt on the regional Russian politician Alexandr Glinka, 2007. In 2006 Glinka was elected mayor of Novgorod. His primary campaign promise was to fight corruption in the region. In June 2007 Glinka's service car exploded outside his home. Glinka had not yet climbed into the car. His chauffeur sustained serious, but not life-threatening, injuries. Russian police estimate that the charge, which consisted of a grenade and plastic explosives, had somehow been set off prematurely and was also placed incorrectly. Semjon Averin was spotted by witnesses in a car near the scene of the crime.
- Murder of German citizen Özcan Cetin, 2012. Finally, Averin's fingerprints were found on a soda can in an apartment in Berlin where the German citizen Özcan Cetin was found murdered and tortured.

To conclude, the police have not been able to make any personal or other connections between Averin and any of the victims Saber, Glinka, or Cetin. Because of this circumstance and the ways the crimes were executed, as well as the fact that they were committed in disparate parts of Europe, Averin is suspected of carrying out so-called contract killings.

Averin is not included in any DNA database.

NOTE
Despite what has been written above, the person in question should be considered innocent until proven guilty.

55

At Arlanda Airport again. Jorge thought about the chick with the dreadlocks that he'd met when he was returning to Svenland. Insane coincidence that they'd run into each other.

Now: already too long in Swedeville. J-boy'd done what he'd come here to do. The cash'd been dug up. Six hundred G's for this G.

Now: time to go back. Figure out the café down there. Settle down. Let the years pass by. Chill with Mahmud.

His loss: Javier'd been collared—nothing Jorge could do about that. The *blatte*'d been an idiot for coming home. Still, he felt bad for Javier's sake.

He'd given the dough to JW. His bro'd promised to Mr. Clean that shit. Instead of exchanging it or laundering it, he was gonna get it down to some account in Liechtenstein, then into an Asian bank. Shit, his buddy JW was cool—was only charging forty big ones for his trouble. Jorge was gonna get a credit card tied to the cash. *Guapo.*

After his escape over the rooftops in Vasastan—Jorge's jumpiness'd reached new levels. He saw dark Saab 9-5s—UC cop-car giveaways—every minute. Texted the National Road Administration ten times a day.

He dreamed twisted nightmares every night. Every other time he saw Javier in a cell in jail—they were hosing him down with fire hoses. Screaming, "Where is Jorge? Talk!" Every other time he saw Babak calling the Finn from a cell phone he'd smuggled in behind the bars: "Jorge played you."

Jorge'd stayed at a new homeless shelter every night. He'd bought a winter hat and pulled it down low over his ears. He bought a Palestine scarf and pulled it up high over his chin. Go ahead, let 'em think he was Taimour Abdulwahab with a political fixation—as long as no one recognized him.

All he'd been waiting for was today: the flight to Bangkok was taking off at four o'clock.

Jorge: Shawshank.

Still a king?

Still J. Bernadotte Bhumibol?

Hardly—all he wanted now was to get away. Screw everything. Babak could go ahead and rat him out—the prosecutor wouldn't bother chasing him all the way to Phuket. Little Jorge and Paola would have to survive on their own for a few years. Javier would have to lie as well as he could to duck a charge.

Jorge was outa here.

He was sitting in the departure hall in terminal five. Nasty markup on croissants and orange juice. The plane was departing in one hour. Thailand—*estoy esperando!* Checked in and ready. Just carry-on, a passport with a proven success rate, a car magazine to read on the plane: nice. He hadn't passed through security yet. The less time inside the terminal the better—he felt trapped in there.

He'd actually called his mom. Said *adíos*. Explained that he loved her, Paola, and Jorgito more than anything. She just cried. After they hung up, Jorge saw two words on the insides of his eyelids: *Mama trató*—Mom, you tried.

Crumbs from the croissant were getting everywhere. He was sitting so that he could see a screen with the flight info. Fifty-five minutes to go.

He thought of what Mahmud used to say: "Ride gangster, die gangster."

And now: how would Jorge die? In a dank apartment in Phuket? As a café king in a fat bungalow on the beach? In a Swedish prison? He didn't know, and right now he just didn't give a shit. As long as he made it onto this plane.

Javier thoughts again. He was leaving his friend here. But the ground rules had been clear: everyone had to deal with their own shit on their own. He couldn't be his boy's mama, couldn't wipe the Latino's ass for him.

Then he remembered his most recent conversation with Mahmud.

"I'm coming back, the day after tomorrow."

"Okay, good. And the dough?"

"Done. JW's taking care of it."

"Great."

"Anything you want me to bring over from here? Some food, dick?"

"I've got a dick already, thanks. But can you buy some of that fish candy?"

Jorge smiled inside.

Now: fifty minutes till the plate took off. He missed Mahmud.

A vibration in his pocket. Someone was calling his phone. It was Paola's number.

Her voice sounded stressed. She was almost whispering.

"Jorge."

"Yes, what's wrong?"

"They're here."

"Who?"

"They're pounding on the door. They say they're gonna break it down if you don't come here and pay."

"Who says that?"

Jorge heard his own voice: weak. Felt his head: growing hot.

Paola said, "They're from someone called the Finn. They say you ripped them off. I told them you're not in Sweden, but they don't believe me."

In Jorge's head: bad images. Paola's frightened eyes. Jorgito with bruises on his face. What the fuck was he gonna do?

He heard screaming in the background. He heard Paola yell, "Beat it! Jorge isn't here!"

He heard pounding sounds.

"Jorge, what should I do?"

"Is Jorgito there too?"

"Yes, I locked him in his room. What should I say?"

Jorge looked at the screen farther off. Forty minutes until takeoff. Forty minutes until peace and quiet.

He was holding his passport and boarding pass in one hand. Cell phone in the other. The screams in the background. The pounding. He couldn't even hear what Paola was trying to say.

Mahmud's saying in his head: *Ride gangster, die gangster*—but what kind of a G leaves his sister in the lurch?

Jorge yelled into the phone, "Don't open the door. I'm coming."

The taxi was driving eighty-five miles an hour. Jorge'd flashed an extra five-hundred-kronor bill. The cabbie promised to drive as fast as he dared.

It would take at least thirty-five minutes to get to Hägersten. Jorge tried to visualize Paola's door. How thick could it be? What could it be made of? Wouldn't the neighbors react if someone tried to break it down? Should he call the police?

The final thought felt unreal: he'd never called the police in his entire life.

He called Paola again. She picked up: the noise in the background was even worse now. But her crying was the worst.

He screamed, "Paola, you have to call the police! You HAVE TO! I'm hanging up now, and then you call me back when you've talked to the cops."

They hung up.

Jorge waited.

Not too much traffic on the highway. He stared down at his phone's display.

Was there anyone he could call who could get there faster? Fuck, everyone he knew who might have had his back was abroad, in jail, or had become ruler-straight. Except for that Hägerström guy and JW—but no, they weren't the right caliber for this.

His screen remained dark. Why didn't she call him back?

Jorge entered the most recently dialed number.

Signals went through.

It went to her voicemail.

He called again. One, two, three signals.

She picked up this time. No noise in the background. Paola was crying. "They're inside now, do you understand? I've locked myself in with Jorgito in his room."

"I'm on my way. Did you call the police?"

The call was cut off.

Jorge tried to call again.

Only: "*You've reached Paola. You know what to do after the beep.*"

He was holding the phone tightly in his hand.

Then he did something he never thought he'd do.

He called the five-oh.

Twenty minutes to get to Paola's door.

The taxi driver tore through more than three red lights. The worst minutes of his life.

He saw the cop car down on the street.

He ran up the stairs.

The crowbar marks on the door were clearly visible. The door was ajar.

He heard men's voices from inside the apartment.

He peered in. Glimpsed two cops in there.

He hoped they'd made it on time. But he couldn't go in if there were cops in there. He tried to listen. Paola's voice? Jorgito's voice?

He didn't hear anything.

Jorge walked down the stairs.

He called Paola.

Signals went through.

A man picked up. "Who is it?"

Jorge hoped it was one of the cops.

"It's Paola's brother."

The voice said, "We've got her and the kid."

He clocked right away—he'd been too late.

He said, "You fucking cunts. Release her and the child. They haven't done anything."

The voice said, "The Finn wants his money. The Finn knows you ripped him off."

The voice had a slight accent. Jorge couldn't place it.

"What the fuck is he talking about? I haven't ripped him off."

"We know. Canaries've been singing from jail. You stashed away three bags. The Finn wants his money."

Joder. Maricón.

Motherfuckingcocksucker.

No words were enough—the Babak-*puta* must've snitched. Jorge wondered how the info'd leaked out. The Iranian was locked up, top security, all restrictions applied.

"Release my sis and the child."

"We'll make an exchange. You bring the cash you stole, eight hundred thousand. We bring what you want."

"When?"

"As soon as you like."

"Where?"

"We'll call you about that. You got the dough?"

Jorge envisioned the two hundred he'd given to Babak and the bag with six hundred that he'd handed over to JW to launder in offshore accounts.

He responded, "Yes."

56

Now they ought to have a watertight case.

Two days after the moose hunt at Avesjö, JW called Hägerström.

"Thanks for a good time. It was great, really great."

Hägerström waited for something more. They discussed the hunt and the gentlemen's dinner that followed for about five minutes. Then. There it was. JW's order: "Come to Bladman's accounting firm—you know where it is. You've dropped me off there tons of times. Bring a duffel bag, a backpack, or some other small bag."

Hägerström drove there. Torsfjäll had ordered him, for the first time, to wear a wire.

JW was waiting for him down on the street.

"This isn't where we're going."

He followed JW. They walked around the block and stopped in front of the entrance to a regular residential building. JW punched a code into the keypad. They walked up the stairs. An ordinary door, it said ANDERSSON on the mail slot. JW unlocked the door, and they stepped inside.

It was a small apartment. Two rooms. The walls were covered with bookshelves filled with binders. Hägerström tried not to stare. He felt elated.

Superbingo—this had to be the secret cache. The double set of books that Torsfjäll had been so convinced that they had.

Finally. Operation Tide would soon come to an end.

One of the rooms held a desk. They sat down on either side of it.

JW set a backpack on the table. Hägerström recognized it; it was the one he had seen Jorge lugging around.

JW opened the backpack. Inside was a white plastic bag containing something that looked like a carton of milk.

He set the bag down on the table.

"Here, take this and put it in your bag."

Hägerström stared.

JW grinned. "Take it easy. I actually don't know exactly what it is. But I know it's not drugs or chemical weapons or anything."

He placed an envelope on the table.

"This is your ticket. The flight leaves tomorrow at nine o'clock, going to Zurich. From there you'll take an express train to Liechtenstein. That's where you'll leave the bag. Then you go back to Zurich and take a plane home, at five o'clock CET."

Hägerström put the plastic bag into his bag. It weighed less than a carton of milk would. He was 99 percent sure that there was cash in the bag.

"You'll get half now and the rest when you come home," JW said. "The only thing you need to do is go through customs in Zurich and then take the train. At the train station, you'll lock the plastic bag in a storage box. That's all."

Hägerström put the envelope into the inner pocket of his jacket. "That sounds easier than shooting a moose, anyway."

"It's ten times easier. Believe me, there's nothing to worry about."

That afternoon he met Torsfjäll at one of the apartments where they used to meet up pre-Thailand. They opened the bag together, both of them wearing latex gloves.

"He's asked me to be a mule—it's on record," Hägerström said. "And I know where they keep their material. Now we've finally got him."

Torsfjäll put the stacks of bills on the table. "Let us listen, and let us see."

They listened to the recording. Then they counted the bills carefully: six hundred thousand kronor. Most of the bills were dyed. Torsfjäll held up a couple of five-hundred-kronor bills, examined them with a magnifying glass that he fished out of his briefcase. He turned every bill over several times—inspected the numbers, the dye stains.

He said, "I'm not sure that what JW said will yield all that much. But this is money from the Tomteboda robbery. This is Jorge's money, definitely."

"Yes, and what's even better, I'll take the stuff down to Liechtenstein, and we'll see who picks it up. We'll arrest that person, while we arrest JW at the same time and hit up their secret location."

"No. We have to wait. If we arrest JW now, Jorge will disappear."

"But finding him may prove difficult."

"Yes, he's obviously managed to get this money to JW without you knowing about it. He's going to leave any minute now, whether or not we arrest JW. But if we take JW, he'll disappear immediately. We've kept the streets around Arlanda under top surveillance over the past few days, but that fucker's smart."

They talked for another few minutes. Then Torsfjäll wanted to end the meeting. The inspector took the bag with the bills. He was going to prepare them, as he put it.

The next morning they met up again in the same apartment. It wasn't even five-thirty a.m. When Pravat was little, he used to wake up at this hour all the time. Hägerström would bring him into the living room, put him on the couch, and lie down on the edge so Pravat wouldn't fall down. And then Pravat would sit there playing with balls and blocks while Hägerström half-snoozed for another half an hour.

Torsfjäll pulled the bag from his briefcase and handed it over to Hägerström.

"It's the same bills, but they've all been sprayed with smart DNA. We can follow them to the end of the world. Whoever touches them will get this stuff on their fingers, and it'll stick for at least three days."

Hägerström agreed. It was clever. But he still didn't understand why they weren't going to arrest JW now. Jorge was probably on his way back to Thailand. If they arrested JW, it would stress him out even more, make him less cautious. And if they had people at Arlanda, there was nothing to worry about. What's more, he ought to be able to get hold of Jorge on his own before then, if he used JW.

There was something off about Torsfjäll's reasoning—but there wasn't time to discuss it with the inspector right now. Hägerström had to go to Zurich.

He didn't run into any trouble at Arlanda. He was dressed in a suit, no tie. He had put the bag with the money in an old suitcase that his father had given him twenty years ago. Perfect, because there was a metal thread inside each bill. All together they would set off the metal detector if he brought it along as a carry-on. He filled the rest of the bag with shirts, pants, and underwear.

He had a one-way ticket. Having a return flight on the same day would've seemed odd with all that luggage.

On the plane, his thoughts were spinning.

He thought of Thailand. Of his brother and his friends. In his mind's eye, he saw JW's impressed expression. He missed Pravat. He hated the fact that longing for the boy had become his normal state of being.

He thought of his father. In 1996 Hägerström had been an assistant police officer for a year. He'd met a guy, Christopher, a couple of times at a club on Sveavägen. They would dance, drink vodka drinks, and go home to Hägerström's place and fuck. Hägerström brought Christopher to Avesjö one weekend in November. It was before Carl had taken the place over. The estate was more or less empty during the winters. Father usually asked the groundskeeper to stop by once a week, that was all.

Hägerström picked Christopher up outside his apartment on Tulegatan. He was thin with bleached-blond hair. A toned-down femmeness that Hägerström liked.

They drove out to Värmdö. Hägerström played Backstreet Boys in the car. Dug the music ironically. Winked at Christopher. "*When we're alone, girl, I wanna push up/ Can I get it?*"

Hägerström disarmed the alarm in the house. Turned on the lights. Got settled. They cooked Asian food for dinner. Christopher said he wanted to drink ABC—anything but Chardonnay. Hägerström got a couple bottles of Sauvignon Blanc from Father's wine cellar. They talked about how they dealt with their sexuality. About when they had had their first experiences with men. About which places in Stockholm were serious and which were just dirty.

At night, they lay down on the bed in Hägerström's parents' room. Made out. Rolled around on the king-sized bed and kissed. They closed their eyes and let their hands find their way.

Christopher produced a bottle of lube, as if by magic. They made love.

Suddenly, in the middle of it all, Hägerström heard a sound from the ground floor.

He tore out of bed.

Someone called from down there, "Hello?"

He called back, "Who is it?"

"Göran. Is it you, Martin?"

Hägerström threw his boxers on. Walked out of the room.

Called, "I'm coming down." Whispered to Christopher to get out of the bedroom.

It was too late. Father was already walking up the stairs.

Hägerström met him in the upstairs hallway.

"What are you doing here?"

Hägerström said, "I'm here with a friend. I was asleep. Didn't know you were coming out here tonight."

Father looked at him. Shook his head. "You were asleep already? It's only eight-thirty."

Back on the plane. Hägerström missed his father. Even if they hadn't had a close connection or been similar in any way, his father's love had always been unconditional. It's not like he ever said anything. His father didn't talk about feelings like that. But you could still feel it—in his way of talking with his children, looking at them, hugging them when they hadn't seen each other in a while.

Hägerström thought of Javier again. The tattoos on his back, his tanned arms and back. His laughter. He didn't want to think about him, but he couldn't stop.

It felt like he needed him now.

The plane landed according to schedule. Hägerström waited for his bag. It looked untouched—he had put a piece of tape over the opening as a control mechanism. He rolled it through customs without incident.

The express train pulled into the station fifteen minutes later. The seats were incredibly comfortable.

When he arrived at the station, he walked straight to the storage boxes. He put the bag with the money in box number 432 and inserted four one-euro coins into the slot. He bought a *Vanity Fair* and took the train back to the Zurich airport. He had a seat at a café and waited for his return flight. JW was supposed to have booked it during the day.

The flight home departed according to schedule. Hägerström had delivered twelve hundred DNA-marked bills in less than twelve hours. Door to door.

When he got home, he was tired. Sat down in front of the TV. A dance competition was playing on one of the channels.

His cell phone rang.

A panting voice. At first he couldn't hear who it was.

"Yo, Hägerström. I gotta see you. I got mad problems."

"Who is it?"

"It's me, Jorge. We gotta meet up right now, man."

He wondered what had happened. Jorge sounded like he was on the verge of tears.

Hägerström was only thinking one thing: *Now the case must be completely finished.*

Now they could arrest Jorge. Which meant that there was no reason to wait to arrest JW.

It was finally time to reel them in.

* * *

From: Lennart Torsfjäll [lennart.torsfjall@polis.se]
To: Leif Hammarskiöld [leif.hammarskiold@polis.se]
Sent: October 15
Subject: Operation Tide, The Pillow Biter, etc.

DELETE THIS EMAIL AFTER READING

Leif,

Thank you for a pleasant conversation yesterday. The decision we discussed—waiting to arrest Johan "JW" Westlund—has proven to be very fortuitous.

We have strong evidence against JW thanks to the hand-off money that was given to the Pillow Biter. The prosecutor will, without a doubt, issue a search warrant both for JW's house and for Bladman's official and unofficial office spaces. The money was delivered by the Pillow Biter to a box at the train station in Vaduz, Liechtenstein. Before he left, however, I took care of the money and replaced it with fake bills. It will probably take a few days before this fact is discovered, as it involves Swedish currency. The real money is now available for you and I to split according to our agreement.

Previously, I believed that we could arrest JW and Jorge Salinas Barrio now. However, the latter contacted the Pillow Biter this morning to ask for his help in dealing with a recently arisen situation. The person who is suspected of planning and controlling the Tomteboda robbery—only known as “The Finn”—has kidnapped Salinas Barrio’s sister and nephew. There is obviously some form of aggressive discord between them. This leads me to conclude that we ought to wait yet another few days to arrest JW and Salinas Barrio. After all, the possibility has hereby arisen of actually arresting and bringing to justice the so-called brain behind the Tomteboda robbery. The Finn is probably also responsible for a large number of other cash-in-transit robberies over recent years (see the attached report). I foresee great triumphs for the police department, and not least for you. What do you think?

I would be grateful if you would get back to me about this as soon as possible.

Lennart

57

Goran'd booked a chamber separée at the casino. Honestly—Natalie wasn't so sure anymore that Gabriel Hanna's Gaming Club in Västerås was lame in comparison. Casino Cosmopol—it was big and state-run, claimed to be superlegal—but the Stockholm casino still felt shabby.

Maybe it'd been top-notch when it opened seven years ago. Now: the mirrors'd lost their shine, the buttons on the gambling machines were worn down, and the original color of the wall-to-wall carpeting was impossible to determine.

On the walls: ads for Christmas banquets and a New Year's dinner. Seafood tower for two for 799 kronor. The jackpot at the casino right now: 32,900,000 kronor—at max bet: 37.50 kronor. At the same time: informational posters: DO YOU THINK YOU GAMBLE TOO MUCH?—WWW.CURBYOURPLAYING.COM. Standard Swedish hypocrisy in a shrimp shell—lure the poor devils here with seafood and fat jackpots so they gamble and make money for the state, but at the same time, pretend that it'd really be best if they didn't come here at all.

The place was occupied by three different factions: one-third antiquated hags, one-third Asians, and one-third dudes in short-sleeved button-downs. Natalie heard Louise's voice in her head: "*Go ahead, joke and be happy—but never wear a short-sleeved shirt to a casino.*" She was glad they had their own room.

They were sitting around a gaming table. A croupier dealt the cards. Natalie didn't get any.

She, Goran, and Thomas plus two others around the table.

One: Dad's old business colleague from Belgrade, Ivan Hasdic. The other: his bodyguard.

Both Adam and Sascha were sitting outside the room, and there was another guy stationed down in the foyer. Security was doubled today.

Ivan Hasdic put his cards facedown on the table. Folded up one corner—looked without moving his eyes.

Natalie checked him out. Hasdic: the cigarette king, the smuggling legend, the wandering Serb. Goran'd told her: Radovan started doing business with Hasdic already in the mid-1990s. They knew each other from the war down there. Dad'd brought in his first thirty thousand packs of cigarettes in a truck that carried aluminum rods. Earned a krona per cancer stick on average, after the truckers and the customs guys'd gotten their cut. Okay money. Their relationship'd developed. Dad began to receive trucks with cigarettes regularly. A few years later Hasdic ran into trouble with the authorities down there. Dad arranged so that he got a temporary residence permit in Sweden, could keep away from allegations of incitement to murder long enough for the police to drop the charges against him. Hasdic moved around, lived in Austria, England, Russia, Romania. He shipped clean goods to Dad—Dad shipped stolen flat-screen TVs to Hasdic. Hasdic sorted things out with one of the pimp kings in Romania—Dad helped Hasdic buy race horses that, over the years, made over two million euros in prize money. Hasdic sent reliable guys when Dad needed reinforcements—Dad arranged so that Nacka municipality hired Hasdic's workers when they were going to build a new heating plant.

Back then: Ivan Hasdic'd loved Radovan Kranjic as his own brother.

Today: Ivan Hasdic was one of the most important men in the Serbian underworld.

Now: Ivan Hasdic'd promised to help Natalie as much as he could.

Natalie's Serbian was broken. "Kum Ivan," she said, "I want to thank you for coming. I want to welcome you to Sweden. The last time we saw each other was during even less pleasant times. We had no opportunity to speak."

Ivan'd been present at Dad's funeral, but had flown back that very same afternoon.

Natalie stood up. Walked over to him and handed over a bottle of Johnnie Walker Blue Label.

Ivan kissed her cheeks: right, left, right.

He thanked her for the bottle. He pulled the usual your-eyes-are-so-beautiful flattery. He said how much she reminded him of her father. Asked about her mom. Natalie avoided the questions about Mom—their relationship was ice cold.

They sat back down.

Natalie went straight to the point. She began by explaining what she knew about Dad's murder. What she'd found about Semjon Averin, alias John Johansson, alias Volk, the Wolf.

She went on for over an hour.

The entire time Ivan looked at his cards. Continued to play with Goran and Thomas. Continued to flip his chips. Played with the fabric bag, which was constantly being filled. But Natalie could tell by looking at him that he was listening. Sometimes he nodded faintly. Sometimes he scratched his chin as though to try to remember something.

Actually: What did she know that was of value today that she hadn't known a month ago? Okay, she knew that the murderer was a hired assassin who had a certain name. Still: she hadn't come any closer to the central question—who'd given Averin the job? Who had hired him? Who was really behind Dad's murder?

Maybe it was the Russians. Maybe it was some Swedish gang.

At the same time, her entire body screamed: Stefanovic. The connection with the Black & White Inn, the planned takeover of Dad's empire, the encroachment on their finances that happened at the exact same time as the murder. And more: Stefanovic's way of responding during the police interrogations, and the fact that no one but Stefanovic and possibly Mom could've known that Dad was going to be at Skeppargatan that night.

When Natalie'd finished talking, Ivan put his cards down. He looked up. Met her eyes, but his gaze was distant, as though he were staring far away through the door.

He was wearing a shirt that looked gray, but it was probably supposed to resemble white. His hands were rough, and the knuckles looked worn, like old leather gloves. His hair was gray. It was difficult to say how old he was—he had scars and wrinkles all over his face. And Hadic's face was just like everything else: gray.

But his voice had a certain rhythm to it. A calm, safe, secure tone.

"It's not good, what you're telling me," he said. "Not good at all."

He picked up the deck of cards again. Dealt the cards onto the table. Goran and Thomas looked as if they didn't know what to do. Ivan gestured with his hand—keep playing.

They played a round. The croupier dealt new cards.

"The Wolf could be here now, in Stockholm," Ivan said.

Natalie put her hands in her lap. Tried to relax.

"Goran briefed me beforehand," he went on. "I've talked to people at home and asked around. I can say that the Wolf Averin is very dangerous. Besides the crimes that Interpol has obviously connected him to, he has carried out at least ten similar attacks that I've found out about from other sources. And there are probably more that my sources are not aware of but that the current authorities in Russia know about. He is educated, he has gathered experience over the years, and he uses different identities. They say he works in the high-end segment. That is, he doesn't take any jobs for less than fifty thousand euros. In Russia, they call him a superkiller. It's been explained to me that only four other assassins have been given that title prior to the Wolf."

He fell silent for a brief moment, letting the gravity of the situation sink in.

"According to my sources, he came to Scandinavia a couple of weeks ago. We know that he picked up weapons in Denmark, and we know that he visited an apartment brothel in Malmö. So unfortunately, a lot speaks for him having made his way north, here. And I might add, there is a great risk that he is here to hurt you."

Ivan continued speaking. He described details of other attacks he'd been informed of. He told them about the Wolf's reputation in Eastern Europe. Averin was a so-called freelancer—he didn't belong to any organization. He was hired by *avtoritety*—the Russian mafia—oligarchs, and Central European crime syndicates when the need arose.

"Normally, I would say: we'll track down his mother and father. We'll track down his siblings and cut their throats. The problem is that the Wolf Averin doesn't have any relatives that anyone seems to know about, except for his daughter. But she has changed her identity. His former wife and parents have been dead for a long time. And if they were alive, he wouldn't care."

Natalie felt cold. She looked down at her hands. They were trembling.

"Kum Hasdic—what do you advise?" she asked.

Ivan responded quickly. "If Stefanovic is behind this, you must liquidate him as quickly as you can. The only way is to strike hard and fast. If the Wolf Averin understands that he is no longer going to be paid by his employer, he will stop hunting you. That is the only advice I can give. And if there is trouble, I promise to support you as best I can."

Natalie thought: *There is only one way forward.*

Stefanovic's fate was already sealed.

She just had to understand how JW wanted it to be done.

The following day she met JW at one of the hotels where she stayed. He was driven there by the same man she'd seen pick him up by the Hotel Diplomat. She got the same vibes again, the same ones she got around Thomas. But with this guy, her gut was screaming "*Cop!*" even louder.

She and JW were lying on the hotel bed. Freshly kissed. Freshly licked. Freshly fucked.

JW explained the plan he was imagining for his big econ-bust.

Really, it was the same basic factors that'd set everything in motion. Several of the jurisdictions JW used had changed their policies. Gotten rid of their supersecrecy, let in international police and EU inspection committees, the UN and OECD. Switzerland'd given up a long time go. The Caribbean'd fallen about six months ago. The British Virgin Islands and the Cayman Islands were the latest examples. Liechtenstein'd just signed a contract about bank transparency. And now the haven-above-all-havens, Panama, was beginning to waver. The country's president'd signed a contract about transparency with the United States. Within a few years, the EU would get the same insight. So JW had to move the clients' money. He'd set up new companies in better countries: Dubai, Macao, Vanuatu, Liberia. JW and his people'd worked hard. Contacted new banks, issued new credit cards to their clients. They made an asset transfer of everything in Northern White Asset Management, moved it to a newly started company in Dubai: Snow Asset Management. After that, the money had to be transferred without setting off the banks' warning systems.

Natalie understood only about half of what JW told her, but she got the basic idea.

Half the clients' funds'd been moved. Gustad Hansén'd been working like a maniac from down there. Traveled among the countries like a fucking foreign minister. Met bank people, lawyers, management people in air-conditioned offices. JW and Bladman took care of the paperwork. Filled out forms for banks and law firms. Filed applications for new credit cards. Wrote letters and invoices. Confirmed that the deposits'd been made, faxed signatures, answered questions from clients, like, a hundred times a day.

So far, the clients who'd had their money moved were happy. JW & Co.'d transferred over eight million euros. That created a solid foundation to stand on. Confidence in what they were doing.

But the truth: an equal amount still had to be transferred. Those clients were impatient. Anxious.

And JW was prepared.

He'd been planning this for over a year. Created companies, trusts, accounts tied to accounts—but without activating them. Without transferring a single krona so far.

But soon it would be time: JW would set the ball in motion. Press the button and trigger a chain of transfers. To make a long story short: eight million euros would be transferred from already-existing accounts all over the world into new accounts—and from there into accounts that JW controlled. The clients' money would become JW's money.

He would become eight million euros richer in one day. A huge scam. A ridiculous robbery. A superswindle, like taken out of a movie.

"They're going to kill you," Natalie said. "Even if I help you, there are going to be so many people who want your head on a plate."

JW stretched. He looked visibly pleased.

"First of all: none of them can go to the police with it. But they're going to be angry, you're right about that."

His smile was roguish, and his eyes sparkled.

"Second of all: everything I've done has been done in Hansén's name."

"Okay, sure, but he isn't exactly going to sit on his hands when he finds out about this."

"Yes, he is going to be sitting very still. In his car. Gustaf Hansén will be found in his Ferrari at the bottom of the Mediterranean with over two percent alcohol content in his blood. A tragic accident. To those who got swindled, it's going to appear as though some client did it."

Natalie didn't know if she should grin or stare.

"But you're still right," JW said. "Even if I've made sure that everything points to Hansén, people are going to be mad at me. I'm mixed up in it, after all. That's why I always need support from people like you. In my industry, you need dangerous friends. So I'm going to need your help, Natalie. I really am."

———

Thirty minutes later. Rekissed. Relicked. Refucked.

After JW's financial run-through: to have sex with him felt like playing with a loaded gun. He was almost *too* slippery. Too calculating. Too smart.

The entire setup was on a whole new level. Okay, she still had a lot to learn—but she heard Goran, Bogdan, and the others talking almost every single day. She'd discussed many plans, ideas—but JW's coup beat anything she could even have dreamed of.

But now they needed to talk about the other thing.

"I've done what you said," Natalie said. "My men approached that politician, Svelander, with the videos of him and the hooker. He got scared. Pleaded and begged. Said we could have anything we wanted."

JW said, "Good, 'cause then the Russians'll go crazy. Those videos actually belong to them. And they need them for their gas pipe. I've tried to set up a meeting with them and Stefanovic. The Russians want you to calm down. That's all—they demand that you end the war, they want the material, and they want to take care of Svelander on their own. In a few days, I'll get the time and place."

"In a few days." Natalie fell silent.

Soon it was time. There would be a meeting with Stefanovic. A meeting that the traitor would fully believe'd been planned by objective persons. A situation in which he would feel safe.

But really: a meeting where Natalie would be present and would do what she had to do.

Stefanovic would be eliminated.

For Dad's sake.

58

Jorge'd answered yes to the question.

"Do you have the money?"

"Yes."

How could he've said that he had the cash? *Cómo?*

Him: an idiot?

Him: a cunt? Got his own sister and his *sobrino* kidnapped.

Jorge'd been crushed many times in his life. When he'd been forced to crawl back into the cage. When the wheel loader'd been missing before the CIT. When he and the boys'd realized that they'd combed home less than two and a half million.

But this: Paola and Jorgito—holier than God. More important than anything else in the world.

Again: How could he've said that he had the cash?

The fucking cash was floating around somewhere in Europe right now. A café in Thailand: worth zero in comparison. A credit card connected to the dough: worth zero million in comparison.

He slept like shit. Checked out of the homeless shelter at four in the morning. Wandered around the city. Oozed angst. Oozed self-loathing.

He sat down on a park bench in Tantolunden. He rode the loop on a night bus. He heard the birds chirping as though there were something out there in the world to be happy about.

J-boy—the loser.

Ghetto cockroach, betrayer.

Shawshank—what did that matter now?

He saw people going to work. Moms pushing baby carriages. Dads rubbing their eyes. The city was waking up.

Jorge just wanted to sleep.

Later on, he called JW—worth a try.

"Can I get the shit back? Something's happened."

JW sounded fed up. "Why?"

Jorge told him quickly what'd happened his sister and Junior.

"I'm very sorry for you. What fucking pigs, man. But it'll take too long to get the gear home. A few weeks, at least."

Jorge ended the call.

The same question over and over again: How could he've said that he had the fucking cash?

Still: his wandering during the night on the town'd awakened a weak, crappy little idea. A teeny-weeny little plan.

Maybe.

There was an image on his phone. An MMS he'd sent JW four days ago. Crap lighting, the plastic bag around it, shit focus. It was a picture of the money. Clear enough—it was *maaaany* stacks of bills.

He would need help. But from whom? Mahmud, Jimmy, and Tom were still in Thailand. Eddie was still locked up. Elliot was living in Germany now—apparently he had three kids there, with three different babymamas. Rolando wasn't even an option. And JW? The dude was too weak for this kinda thing.

He could think of only one person: the Sven who reeked of pork. The man with the most Sven name in Svenland. Martin the ex-screw-ex-cop Hägerström.

It wasn't good. But it'd have to do.

Later. Cold as Santa's ass. Jorge remembered the last time he'd been on the lam, when he'd crashed in people's summer shacks. This was worse—he was colder inside this time around.

He pressed the button for the buzzer.

A canned voice: "The Practice."

"Hi. I wanna see Jörn Burtig the lawyer, please."

"He's not in at the moment. Can I take a message?"

"It's about his client, Babak Behrang. Can I come up and wait?"

"There probably isn't any point. He's in court and won't be back until five o'clock."

Jorge kept roaming around the city. He had nowhere to go now. He pulled his hat down even farther. Pulled his scarf up higher. Let people thing he was *loco*. Let them think whatever they wanted. Just as long as they didn't call the five-oh.

With Hägerström's help and the photo of the cash, Babak might accept. Maybe it would all work out.

He walked down to the water.

Looked out over the city. What kind of a place was this, anyway?

He'd run a café in the inner city for almost a year. Smoked weed with some niggas on Tomtebogatan tons of times. Partied at Stureplan. Boosted shit from the sports apparel stores around Sergelstorg as a kid. *Chinga*'d pretty *chicas* in tiny condos on the south side. He knew the inner city. He belonged here.

Still: it didn't want him. He could feel it everywhere. People stared. Gripped their purses tighter. Pulled their cell phones out, prepared themselves. The inner city: too white for him. The inner city: as though there were an Israeli wall between it and him.

He tried to imagine what it would be like to mix Chillentuna with downtown. What it would look like if he brought half of Sollentuna here. To the fancy streets, the old buildings, and the trendy restaurants. Just half. How would it feel if he filled the place up with Latinos, Somalis, Kurds? If he exchanged every other clinically clean 7-Eleven with one of the homey tobacco stores on Malmvägen? Removed half the purebred Labradors and put in a few pit bulls? Exchanged the church spires for basement mosques? Removed the elite high schools and brought in the chaos classes, where the fifth graders hadn't even learned to read yet but where the atmosphere swayed with creativity? Replaced some of the polite, boring, faggy feeling with pure emotions and authentic experiences?

He never even should've tried. *La dolce vita*—not for him. He should've just kept being a coffee man. Now he had to finish what he'd started.

Life deluxe—to turn everything back to square one. Paola and Jorgito back to their normal lives.

Later: the air was even colder.

He pressed the button. The same canned-sounding voice.

He was buzzed in. Two flights up, an ordinary stairwell.

The door to the law firm clicked.

He stepped inside.

Sick office—honest: Jorge hadn't been inside a law firm in ten years, probably. The last times he'd seen his lawyer, he'd been locked up in jail. Sat in a sweaty, windowless room in order to run through things before the trial.

Red chairs, white walls, a lot of glass. A long desk in the reception area, two receptionists. The firm's phat logo on the wall behind the welcome desk.

"How can I help you?"

Jorge removed the scarf from over his mouth. "I wanna see Jörn Burtig. He's supposed to be here now."

"He's here, but I don't know if he's able to see you. What is this in regard to, and who may I say is calling for him?"

"Say it's about his client Babak Behrang and that it's very, very important."

Twenty minutes later: Jorge was sitting in a worn-looking leather armchair. Not as minimalistic in here. Piles of documents, books, papers, computers. Paperweights, paintings, framed photos from newspapers.

Jörn Burtig on the other side of the table. Babak Behrang's defense attorney.

According to the chatter on the inside: one of the city's best.

They shook hands. Burtig rested one leg on top of the other, leaned back in his chair.

Burtig said, "Okay, Jorge. I'm in a bit of a rush. But I understand that you want to talk about Babak. What's this about?"

The lawyer wasn't from Stockholm, you could tell by his accent.

Jorge took his hat off. "I know Babak well. My last name is Salinas Barrio. Do you know who I am?"

The lawyer leaned back farther.

"I know who you are. And since I know that now, I have to ask you to leave. We can't sit and have a meeting like this. You are one of the coaccused in the same case as my client, Babak. That means the police are looking for you. But that's not the problem, I can assure you—I have no problem having meetings with wanted persons. No, the problem is that Babak is being held with restrictions on communication. That means he is not permitted to bring in or out any information that has to do with the case. And I am not allowed to do it for him. So with all due respect, I have to ask you to leave."

"I know what restrictions are, believe me."

"Good. Then you know that if I bring information in or out to Babak, I will be guilty of an ethical violation, which means that I risk losing my license to practice. So I would like you to leave before you've even said anything."

"But can't I say what I want, and then you do what you want?"

"No, I would rather not hear anything. If I do, I'll wind up in trouble with other rules of professional conduct, loyalty to my client, and things like that. Do you understand? There will be trouble. You have to leave. Now. I'm sorry."

Jorge didn't know what to do. The fucking lawyer was shutting him down. What an asshole.

"But just listen anyway," he said.

The lawyer stood up. "No, thank you."

Jorge raised his voice. "I know Babak somehow got a bunch of lies out to a guy called the Finn. But tell Babak this: I want him to take back whatever he said. I want him to make the Finn stop hunting me."

The lawyer held the door open.

"I'm prepared to help Babak if he does that," Jorge went on. "Tell him to make sure he gets sick so he's transferred to Huddinge Hospital. Just say that, and I'll do the rest."

"No, thank you. It's time for you to leave now." The lawyer grabbed Jorge's arm.

Jorge rose. Reluctantly. "Just tell him to get himself to Huddinge and he'll get a hundred Gs."

Jorge held up his cell phone. The picture of the money in front of Burtig's face.

The lawyer pushed Jorge out the door.

Jorge said, "I'll give you fifty Gs too."

Jörn Burtig, Esquire, didn't even so much as glance at the photo.

59

They could have arrested Jorge yesterday already, when Hägerström met him. Jorge had explained what happened. Apparently Babak had talked smack about Jorge. Then that had leaked out from jail somehow. The shit had hit the fan, big time. A crazy fucker called the Finn had kidnapped his sister and nephew.

Jorge had tried to talk to Babak's lawyer but got the cold shoulder. Now he was close to a breakdown. Hägerström could see it in his eyes, they were bloodshot, wide-open, intense. Desperation mixed with panic.

Torsfjäll got all worked up. Now they'd be able to pluck the Finn too. That would mean a major victory for the Stockholm police. And a guaranteed promotion for Hägerström. An enormous victory for society versus the rabble.

But Jorge didn't want help with the Finn, he told Hägerström. He needed to free Javier.

"Listen, all my homies are in Thailand. I need to get Javier out. Then I hope he can help me with this Finn fucker. And maybe you can help me with that too. But first Javier's gotta get out."

Jorge almost spat on Hägerström when he spoke.

"Will you help me? I'll pay you as soon as I get back to Thailand."

Hägerström's heart was doing flips in his chest. Free Javier: he envisioned Javier and himself at home at his apartment. They were laughing, kissing, holding each other.

On the other hand, it was a completely insane idea. Rescue missions were always dangerous. Meant threats, weapons, violence. He had to talk to Torsfjäll.

But he already knew what his answer was going to be.

He promised to think it over and called Torsfjäll immediately.

The inspector had blown off Jorge's arrest when he understood that the Finn was within reach. But this proposed rescue mission came as a surprise even to him. He wondered if Hägerström was sure that it would lead them to the Finn.

Hägerström couldn't be 100 percent, but still. Jorge's sister and nephew were being held captive by this Finn guy. And Jorge had said he needed Javier's help. That must lead them to the Finn.

And the fact was, Hägerström didn't care whether it led them to the Finn. He wanted to see Javier again so badly.

Now he and Jorge were sitting in the waiting room of another law firm, Skogwall & Partners. Bert T. Skogwall, who was Javier's lawyer, would see them shortly.

Oak paneling covered the walls. Heavy British leather armchairs on authentic Persian carpets. Spotlights in the ceiling illuminated antique paintings.

It reminded Hägerström of his dad's waiting room.

Three minutes later they were sitting in the corner room of a magnificent apartment, alias the law office. Kommendörsgatan and Grevgatan stretched out below them. An address of which Lottie would have approved.

The room was perfectly decorated. Either Bert T. Skogwall was a color genius, or he was good at hiring the right decorator. The walls were olive green. The bookcases were filled with legal books whose spines all seemed to be different shades of brown. There were frosted-glass doors on some of the shelves: probably more books behind them. On the floor: an old Isfahan. The fact that it was well worn made it appear even more expensive. Two paintings hung behind the desk, both consisting of large circles of color in different shades. They might be Damien Hirsts.

Hägerström sat down. His cell phone was switched on in his pocket.

He thought of his brother. Bert T. Skogwall looked different. Carl always wore a dark suit and muted ties. The attorney sitting across from Hägerström and Jorge obviously didn't believe in *less is more*.

Instead, Skogwall was wearing a pink shirt, yellow slacks, and a green tie. His cufflinks were enormous, and the diamond on his tie clip looked like it had been taken from Tin-Tin's engagement ring. In other words, at least two carats.

Hägerström thought: *This attorney looks like Pravat's box of paints.*

Jorge said, "Do you know who I am?"

Bert T. Skogwall spoke with an indeterminate dialect. "Naturally. You are Jorge Salinas Barrio. Known for your latest escape over Stockholm's rooftops. You are arrested in absentia. You are coaccused with my client, Javier."

Jorge nodded in time with the attorney's words.

"And now I'm wondering what it is you want."

"I just want you to convey one thing to Javier. Just two sentences."

"You know that he has communication restrictions."

"Yes, I know. Is that a problem?"

The attorney was twirling a pen. It looked like it was made of gold.

"That depends. Bringing information in and out is very risky. I would risk losing my license to practice."

"I know. But I'm not the kind of guy who creates problems. If you help me, I will help your client."

"That sounds good. But I need to know that it will benefit me too."

Jorge slid an envelope across the table. The lawyer picked it up. Opened it carefully, looked inside. Counted the bills that Jorge had slipped inside.

He put the envelope into the inner pocket of his blazer.

"Okay, what do you want me to pass on?"

"He has to get himself transferred to Huddinge's closed psychiatric ward. And you have to inform me exactly when it's going to happen."

Hägerström's ears were larger than a lop-eared rabbit's. The wire he was wearing felt warm.

The lawyer raised his eyebrows. "That last bit, about me informing you, was not part of our agreement."

"Maybe not," Jorge said. "But we've recorded this conversation on a cell phone. So now it is part of our agreement."

60

Ivan Hasdic'd gone back home. His final words: "I want you to know that you are always welcome to come down to us if things don't work out the way you want them to up here. We'll take care of you, until things've calmed down."

Natalie kissed him on the cheeks. In her head: another image. A glimmer of hope. Everything would calm down quickly, after she'd done what had to be done. Stefanovic's honchos would lay down their arms. Her finances would return to their normal state, or better. Her men could focus on their regular jobs again—smuggling, amphetamine sales, run-of-the-mill racketeering.

Today JW was supposed to have pushed his buttons, made his phone calls, sent his e-mails. Faxed the monkeys—that's what he called the men managing the assets down there. Hopefully, he would've succeeded in hauling over all eight million euros to accounts that were connected to other accounts that were connected to accounts. Ones and zeros that were transferred far beyond what could be controlled. The money would've been moved through so many banks, exchange offices, trusts, and jurisdictions that it would be harder to find than a dropped contact lens on the floor of a nightclub on a Saturday night. And what was more, all the trails would point to that Gustaf Hansén guy. His name was on countless documents connected to the first accounts in the chain. Many of the powers of attorney that'd been faxed out today looked as though they were signed by him. A large part of the online controls today: verified by security tokens that'd been issued to him. Not everyone would fall for it—but Natalie'd have to deal with the rest.

And for that, she wanted 10 percent.

But most important of all: tomorrow they were going to see the Russians and Stefanovic.

JW'd managed to arrange a meeting. That was when Natalie was planning on dealing with the traitor. She knew how.

She was lying in the safe room tonight.

She couldn't sleep. The room was around two hundred square feet large. Just barely fit a pullout couch, two chairs, and a small table. The couch was pulled out: the mattress was hard and uncomfortable. She turned the bedside lamp on, looked around.

There were four monitors on one wall. One monitor showed what the camera above the front door captured: the gravel path, the gate farther in the distance. The second one showed the view from the camera above the kitchen entrance: the deck, a section of the garden, the illuminated lawn. The third one showed the set of stairs that led down to the rec room. She glimpsed Mom's paintings of the king and the brass railing. The final screen showed what the camera just outside the safe room captured—the rec room with the couch, the projection screen in the ceiling, and the treadmill. The windows up by the ceiling were barred. Adam was sitting in an armchair with his cell phone in hand. He was awake.

A phone was hanging beside the monitors, and next to it was a laminated piece of paper with important telephone numbers: SOS, the police, Adam, Sascha, Patrik, Goran, Thomas. Stefanovic's name was at the very top, but had been crossed out. There was an alarm button to G4S and other buttons to control the alarm system in the house. There was an extra cell phone on a hanger and a Maglite flashlight. There was a fire extinguisher in one corner. Two gas masks were hanging on one hook. A stun gun was hanging on another.

There was a plastic bin on the floor. She knew what was inside it: four bottles of water, one bag of nuts, Wasa bread with cream cheese, and a few cans of food. There was a first aid kit, a toiletry kit, a packet of wet wipes, a cell phone charger, and a map of Stockholm. There was also a change of clothes for Natalie.

The aim was that you would be able to survive at least twenty-four hours in there.

She remembered what Thomas'd said: "If something happens, you should first try to escape. The safe room should be your absolute last resort—it's not a bomb-safe bunker. It can stop an intruder only for a certain amount of time, until we or the police arrive."

Natalie tried to relax. Neither Stefanovic nor the Wolf Averin should be trying anything tonight—they were supposed to meet with Moscow tomorrow, after all. Eye to eye, just her, Stefanovic, JW, and the Russians.

Nothing should be happening tonight.

Still, she couldn't sleep.

The house was so quiet. She eyed one of the screens again. Adam was still awake.

There was another bodyguard up there somewhere, Dani. Just to be on the safe side.

Mom was in Germany. Natalie'd sent her off to stay with relatives ten days ago. They hadn't been in touch since. Was easiest that way.

She thought about Semjon Averin. He'd looked so self-confident and relaxed in the blurry image from the surveillance camera when he was driving the Volvo. He looked even more self-confident in the passport photo in John Johansson's name. As though nothing in the world could move him. Averin's attitude reminded her of Dad's. Would she ever be able to feel the same way? Maybe.

She remembered one time when she'd been to the Solvalla race-track with Dad. Two old geezers from the municipal environmental and building committee had been there too—Dad wanted to build an addition on their house.

Nice atmosphere in the air. Ads for Agria animal insurance wallpa-pered the area. Hot dogs, beer, and betting slips in everyone's hands. The speakers announced the day's upcoming race. Natalie was seven-teen years old.

They were sitting in the Congress Bar and Restaurant: an à la carte restaurant in seven stories, right in front of the finish line. The nic-est part of Solvalla: white linen tablecloths, wall-to-wall carpeting, low music playing in the background, flat-screen TVs, and tons of slips on the tables. Most of the people there were men in their fifties and sixties—just like the municipal guys who were shoving their faces with foie gras and sipping champagne across from Dad and Natalie.

The speakers blazoned out the special event of the day. Björn and Olle Goop's horse was going to run a victory lap for the audience. Peo-ple applauded. Natalie wasn't interested. She regarded the men around the table.

They talked about building permits, detailed planning, and God knew what else. She wasn't really listening, but she remembered that one of the municipal guys'd said, "I think it's important that Näsbypark is a living, dynamic place. That we don't make it too difficult for people to change their houses to suit their needs."

The other municipal guy'd raised his glass. "Cheers to that."

Dad'd pushed two envelopes across the table to the men. Raised his own glass. "No one could agree with you more than I do."

His face was relaxed, confident. Total assurance that he knew what he was doing and that he was doing the right thing. Natalie hadn't thought about it back then. She'd just accepted that that was the way Dad looked when he did business. But now she wondered—was it perhaps just a mask that he put on when he needed to?

Goran'd called an hour ago.

"Natalie, where are you?"

"I'm in Näsbypark. Sleeping in the bunker tonight."

"Good. Who's there with you?"

"Adam and Dani. Adam's being switched out at three o'clock."

"Natalie"—Goran was breathing heavily—"I heard that you're going to meet with Stefanovic and try to make up."

Maybe there was worry in his voice. Maybe it was irritation.

She said, "Yes, that's true. I think it's best that we end this war."

"You're right. That's probably best. But is JW somehow involved in setting this up?"

"Yes."

Goran was breathing heavily again. "Natalie, listen to me. You have my support, no matter what you do. But be careful with this JW guy. I've said it before, don't trust him. There are things you don't know about him. Things you don't want to know."

"Like what?"

"I can't talk about that now. But *veruj mi*, be careful."

Natalie reached for the glass of water on the floor. She picked up a tablet of Xanax. "Tell me now."

"Natalie, you have to listen to me," Goran said. "I love you. Now is not a good time to tell you. But I'll explain soon. Good night."

They hung up. Natalie popped the pill in her mouth. Gulped water.

Leaned her head back on the pillow.

She turned off the bedside lamp. Thought: *What does Goran have against JW?*

* * *

SWEDISH BANKER DEAD IN CAR ACCIDENT IN MONTE CARLO

Gustaf Hansén, a banker who was active in Liechtenstein and Switzerland, died on Sunday in a car accident in Monte Carlo.

Gustaf Hansén stopped working at Danske Bank five years ago after accusations of fraud. The tax authorities began an investigation that was dropped two years ago. Hansén had been living in Liechtenstein for four years. He was known for his great interest in cars.

Hansén was driving a Ferrari California Cabriolet at the time of the accident. He had a high alcohol content in his blood. According to sources within the Monaco police force, there is no suspicion of foul play.

Gustaf Hansén was forty-six years old.

61

There was no time.

His sister and nephew: had been kidnapped for forty-four hours now.

No time.

Jorge didn't give a shit about anything—he was ready *now*. Time was a luxury. The CIT planning'd been detailed like a book: What'd that led to? *Nada.*

Now this motherfucking Latino was running on routine. Now he was going on his G-gene. Now he just had to act fast.

Sin mandamiento, sin reglas. There was no time for planning, for thinking ahead, for tight co-dees. No time. His plans'd grown out of a night on a mattress at a homeless shelter. How much was he thinking ahead? Half a day. And tight buds? He was gonna use an ex-cop, *oooo yeah*.

He thought: *Let whatever happens, happen. I'm prepared to die for you, Paola and Jorgito.*

Violence can solve most things.

You are me, and I am you. My blood will absolve us all from sin.

Jesus—*joder*: he was gonna sacrifice himself if need be.

He was gonna break Javier out, and then he was gonna settle the score with the Finn—get Paola and Jorgito.

He met Hägerström by the main entrance to Huddinge Hospital. Thirty degrees in the air. Maybe the scarf Jorge'd wrapped several times around his neck didn't look that shady after all.

Hägerström was wearing a glossy down jacket. Jorge thought it looked gay.

Jorge was rocking baggy track pants and a cardigan. He was carrying a duffel bag.

A new Taurus gun was stuffed in his pants pocket. The same kind of gat that'd saved him once before. That the poor cabbie'd tasted against his temple.

His cell phone was in his other pants pocket. Bert T. Skogwall, Esquire'd, called thirty minutes ago. Informed him that Javier was now being moved to the closed psychiatric ward at Huddinge. Javier'd started acting weird as early as last night. Been awake all night, banging on his cell door. Cut himself and bled all over the cell. In the morning: the staff found him smeared with his own excrement with a rope made out of torn prison clothes wrapped around his neck. Javier—obviously psychologically unstable. Obviously: a risk to himself. The staff at the Kronoberg jail couldn't guarantee that he wouldn't try to take his own life—he had to be sent to receive proper care.

Javier: a homie. The dude knew how to handle the Department of Corrections. The lawyer briefed Jorge. Javier'd tied a T-shirt tightly around his upper arms so that the veins were clearly visible. Made a tiny cut in the crook of his arm, squeezed out a few drops of blood. Mixed the blood with water and simply splashed the cell with it. Then he shit on toilet paper and hid it under his bed. It stank. Finally, he mixed coffee dregs with bread—the right shit color. Smeared himself and everything around him like a toddler with finger paint.

Jorge and Hägerström took the stairs down.

Within an hour, one of the Department of Corrections's transport vehicles ought to be pulling into the back of Huddinge's closed psychiatric unit.

Jorge and Hägerström would play welcome committee.

But before then: they were gonna fix something.

They continued down the stairs. Continued out through the parking garage. Out on the other side. They jumped over a few concrete blocks. They saw it, behind a metal fence ten yards off.

Jorge set the duffel down. Pulled out a pair of bolt cutters that he'd lifted forty minutes ago in the Flemingsberg Mall.

Began cutting a hole in the fence.

The ambulance garage was behind there. Jorge saw the large garage gates. One was open. He could see two ambulances parked right inside.

A hole in the wall large enough so that they could bend it back and climb through.

It was calm outside the ambulance garage. Where were all the ambulance drivers? Where were all the bleeding, screaming patients?

Hägerström said, "This is not where the transports drive into. They arrive upstairs, outside the ER."

Jorge thought: *Okay, maybe it would've been smarter to carjack an ambulance up there.* But it was too late for that now.

They walked into the garage. At least ten ambulances in different models were lined up. Even one that looked like a truck.

Jorge thought: *If anyone were to ask me to draw an ambulance, I would draw a white car with a red cross on it*—but not a single one of the real ambulances was white. They were all yellow with green color fields and blue symbols on them.

He asked Hägerström to position himself behind one of the cars.

He pulled the Palestinian scarf up over his mouth and nose. Positioned himself next to the gray metal door that appeared to be the only entrance to the garage, aside from the route they'd just used.

He waited.

Seconds ticked.

Minutes passed.

He held his hand over the fake gun.

A fluorescent in the ceiling flashed. There were pipes and cables on the walls.

Jorge remembered when Mahmud'd been picked up by the EMTs on the street in Pattaya. Jorge'd thought his friend was dead. But now Mahmud was waiting for him in Thailand.

And Javier was waiting for J-boy in a transport car en route from jail.

It was like one of the computer games that he'd played as a kid. You shot a figure on the uppermost part of the screen. The figure fell down and destroyed two other figures lower down, just by falling on top of them.

Domino effects. All of life, every single thing you did, was like popping computer game dudes. Everything could affect something else. Everything was connected.

He was scared: all the shit he'd set in motion. All the people who were waiting for him. What if he'd taken other steps in life? What if he'd never saved Denny Vadúr there in the Ping-Pong room and never gotten in touch with the Finn? Something good—saving someone from a beating. Had led to something else good—a recipe for a CIT heist. A talk with Mahmud one night at the café. Led to something half-ass—two and a half million in booty. A small decision—to trick someone: led to the worst thing he'd ever been through. Again: everything seemed to be connected. It was like one giant complicated web of connections and people. Where did it all begin, really?

What if he'd learned to draw like Björn?

What if he'd tested heroine that time when Ashur tried?

What if he'd listened more to Mom? Who would've been waiting for him then?

Maybe the same people would've been waiting for him, after all. But they would've been waiting for something good. Not for him to attack the first best person who walked in through the door of an ambulance garage.

62

Hägerström was crouching behind one of the ambulances.

He saw Jorge standing by the side of the garage entrance. His face was hidden by his hat and scarf, only his dark eyes peeked out. And in those eyes, Hägerström saw the same thing he had seen when they met at the law firm: desperation, panic. Except now the panic almost seemed to have taken over.

Torsfjäll was informed about the situation. Jorge wanted to free Javier so that Javier could help him settle the score with the Finn and get his sister and nephew back. A rescue mission was a dangerous operation, but Torsfjäll had said, "The ends justify the means in this industry. That's just how it has to be, or else us cops would never get anywhere. This will lead us to the brain behind the CIT robbery."

The inspector was right. Within twenty-four hours, they ought to have Jorge, Javier, the Finn, Bladman, and JW, each in a cruiser on his way to be placed in custody. As long as Jorge didn't totally lose it. As long as no one was injured unnecessarily. As long as Hägerström could control this thing.

At the same time, he longed for Javier. It was as though he had a mosquito bite—in the heart. Every other minute it itched so badly that he had to muster all his concentration not to feel too much.

A few seconds passed.

The gray metal door opened. An ambulance driver walked out. Green clothes with yellow reflectors over the shoulders. A radio attached to her breast pocket. A Bluetooth earpiece hanging around her neck.

Hägerström saw how Jorge took a step forward, raised the Taurus pistol. Pressed it against the woman's head. Covered her mouth with his hand. He leaned over and whispered something in her ear.

Everything was so quiet. Hägerström had expected Jorge to yell and carry on. Wave the gun around. That the person who walked out through the door would cry or scream something.

Ten seconds later Jorge was beside him. A pair of keys in his hand. They ran to an ambulance. Jumped in. Hägerström climbed into the driver's seat.

He used the keys to start the engine.

The window was open. Jorge kept the fake gun aimed at the ambulance woman the entire time. She was still standing by the entrance. Her cell phone and the radio on the floor in front of her, destroyed.

One of the two garage doors was already open. Hägerström carefully put the vehicle in drive.

Rolled out of the garage.

Ten minutes later. Huddinge's closed forensic psychiatric ward was only five hundred yards from the ambulance garage in a separate fenced-in building—they didn't want the criminal crazies in the same building as the regular spooks, plus, of course: they had to keep them from escaping. Hägerström and Jorge had parked the ambulance two hundred yards from the insane asylum, in a staff parking lot.

Now they were sitting in a different car, an old Opel. Jorge said he'd boosted it earlier that day. They saw the driveway and the entrance to the closed ward twenty yards off.

Soon one of the cars from the Department of Corrections ought to pull in with Javier.

Jorge was smoking a cigarette. The window was rolled down. Still, he didn't bother blowing the smoke out through the opening. Stared straight ahead instead.

Hägerström said, "Are you okay?"

Jorge exhaled smoke. "I've got a Kalashnikov in the duffel. Can you work one of those?"

Hägerström nodded. He thought: *It's better that I have the real weapon.*

Jorge grabbed the duffel from the backseat and pulled out the assault rifle.

He held it low so that no passersby could see that they were handling a real AK-47.

He handed Hägerström the weapon. Images from his military service flickered past. Coastal rangers were educated in intelligence service work on enemy territory. If you came across an enemy weapon, you needed to be able to handle it as well as you could your own.

He ran his finger along the bolt. This was a model with an elongated barrel. Probably from some Eastern Bloc country. The magazine box was altered so that you could use Russian military ammo made for a Mosin-Nagent rifle.

Jorge looked at him. Handed over the magazine.

They waited. The weapon was resting in Hägerström's lap. Loaded and ready.

Huddinge's closed forensic psychiatric ward was in a one-story concrete building with a worn-looking facade and barred windows. The building was surrounded by a well-maintained lawn. Where the lawn ended, a six-foot fence with barbed wire at the top began. There were surveillance cameras attached to the fence and to metal rods in the lawn. He didn't see any movement in the building.

The visitors' entrance was located on the other side. Here by the gates that were used for transport, everything appeared quiet as the grave.

"According to that dirty lawyer," Jorge said, "he should've come by now."

"Yeah, but you can never trust lawyers. He'll be here. And I know the Department of Corrections—everything takes longer than you think. I promise."

Five minutes later a Volvo V70 pulled up to the gates. It was painted red, white, and blue. The Department of Corrections's logo on its side.

It was a prisoner transport vehicle. Hopefully, it was *that* prisoner transport vehicle.

The back windows were tinted. Impossible to see whom they were transporting.

Hägerström turned on the engine.

Started the Opel with a jerk. The car jumped forward fifteen feet.

He turned in front of the transport vehicle. Blocked the entrance through the gates.

It was all in now. They took a chance that it actually was Javier back there in the vehicle.

Jorge threw himself out. Hägerström opened the car door, also jumped out.

Jorge was holding the Taurus pistol with both hands.

Hägerström hesitated for a millisecond. Then he saw Javier's face in front of him. He raised the assault rifle.

Jorge pressed his gun to the driver's-side window. Yelled, "Open the back door now!"

Hägerström caught a glimpse of a terrified face in there.

Then one of the backseat doors opened. He could see Javier back there, sandwiched between two transport guards. His hands were cuffed, and there was a chain running from the handcuffs to a broad leather belt around his waist.

Jorge pointed with the gun. "Let him out."

Hägerström kept the AK-47 pointed at the two staffers in the backseat throughout.

Javier pushed his way past the guard sitting closest to the door.

Hägerström met his eyes. They glittered.

Jorge screamed, "Blow out the wheels!"

Hägerström hesitated.

Jorge repeated, "I said, blow out the wheels!"

Hägerström squeezed the trigger gently.

He fired off a shot. The noise sounded familiar.

The front tires of the transport vehicle deflated.

An hour later: they were sitting at Hägerström's place.

Hägerström said, "Damn, the sound of the sirens is still ringing in my ears."

Javier laughed. "Shit, so fucking elegant, man. We were probably making a hundred and ten when you stepped on it."

They told and retold. Javier had jumped into the Opel. They had driven two hundred yards and then switched to the boosted ambulance. Blared the sirens and the lights. Taken the highway toward the city. Plowed through traffic like a car on Pravat's toy racetrack. At Årsta they switched to a car that Hägerström had rented.

Jorge had left them there. He was going to call Hägerström's place as soon as he knew what the deal was. He didn't mention any details, but Hägerström understood what he meant.

Javier's teeth glowed white. They were sitting on Hägerström's couch. It was the first time Javier had ever been to his house. There hadn't been any alternative. Jorge was homeless, and taking Javier to some relative's place would be hopeless—that was the first place the police would look. What was more: according to Jorge, they were going to take care of the thing tonight and then go back to Thailand. It was just a matter of a few hours.

It had taken thirty-five minutes to file, cut, snip, and break apart Javier's cuffs. But now his hands were free. They had lost all their tan. Hägerström thought his skin looked clean, like milk.

Javier took his hand. Smiled.

Hägerström curled up on the couch.

Javier rested his head on his shoulder.

They were lying in the bedroom. The curtains were pulled. Hägerström knew that the street outside was crawling with UCs. The plan was that they would follow Javier to Jorge who would lead them to the Finn.

But right now he and Javier were an island in time. Hägerström was planning on making the most of these minutes.

They talked. They had had sex about a half hour ago.

Javier told him about the interrogations in jail.

Hägerström told him about the interrogation he had gone through.

It was a strange feeling—he felt like he was twenty-one years old again. The conversations felt so important, so filled with meaning, so honest. They talked about reality. About things that had happened, things that meant something, for real. But what kinds of things? They were talking exclusively about Hägerström's fake life in the gangster world. It was bizarre.

An hour or so later, his home phone rang. It was Jorge, who wanted to talk to Javier.

Javier went into the kitchen. Hägerström tried to listen in. Only heard mumbling and short responses.

Javier returned to the bedroom.

"We've gotta go. It's payback time for me. Jorge really needs help."

Hägerström sat up. "He said there was some shit with his sister. What's going on?"

"Someone's fucking with him. We gotta bounce. They're settling the score. He needs our help."

Hägerström shook his head. "I can't come."

"Why not?"

"I'm taking care of my son tonight. I can't cancel. Sorry, I just can't come."

Javier looked at him quickly but didn't seem to take it very hard. He was still so fucking happy to be free.

Actually, Hägerström was going to see JW in a few hours. Drive him to the meeting with Radovan Kranjic's daughter and a few others—he didn't really know who. The only thing he knew was that as soon as Jorge, Javier, and the Finn had been arrested, JW was going to be collared too. And there would be a search of Bladman's office and all his properties, including the secret one.

Javier dressed and left.

In his mind's eye, Hägerström saw the caravan of scouts who were trailing him down on the street.

* * *

From: Leif Hammarskiöld [leif.hammarskiold@polis.se]
To: Lennart Torsfjäll [lennart.torsfjall@polise.se]
Sent: October 17
Priority: HIGH
Subject: Re: Operation Tide, The Pillow Biter etc.

Lennart,

First of all, I was just informed about the freeing of Javier. How the hell did this happen? Shooting like a crazy man with an assault rifle? Don't you have any control over the Pillow Biter? Make sure that Javier, Jorge, and if need be the Pillow Biter, are arrested immediately. If the Commie press finds out about the real situation here, they'll eat us alive.

Second of all, the economic crimes investigators just informed me that they've received an alarm from a number of banks about a series of transactions that were made by Gustaf Hansén and/or JW and/or Bladman over the last few days. They have also succeeded in getting hold of names of a few of the implicated companies, and in around a dozen cases, these can be connected to physical people in Sweden.

I also want to mention that Hansén has apparently been found dead. At this time, the Monaco police confirm that they do not suspect any foul play.

Lennart, this information is EXTREMELY sensitive.

We have seen names in this mess that neither you nor I want dragged through the mud. Your men must be extremely careful and meticulous at the planned hit toward JW and/or Bladman. There is a great deal of material that must not see the light of day.

I want you to keep it all under strict control and naturally away from the prosecutor's eye. Call me about this as soon as possible!

Delete this e-mail, as usual.

Leif

63

The Radisson Blu Arlandia Hotel: one point two miles from Arlanda Airport. According to JW: the Russians wanted it that way. They were only staying for a few hours. The good thing: Natalie was apparently meeting the ones who were really in charge. Not some hooligans stationed in Sweden. Not some underlings without any decision-making power.

She stepped into the conference room.

A man approached and ran a metal detector over her body. It crackled—but didn't beep. He brushed her arms, body, and legs with his hand.

The man's hand was covered in black tattoos.

Goran, Thomas, and Adam were sitting on the sofas in the hotel lobby. Sascha was sitting in a car outside the entrance.

She'd seen Milorad and a couple of Stefanovic's men in another sofa group.

Thomas'd also pointed and told her that an old police colleague of his was sitting in the lobby: "He was fired six months ago, but I actually don't know what he's doing here."

But Natalie knew who it was: JW's driver. The dude who'd been giving her bad vibes. Thomas said, "I think it seems strange."

Natalie couldn't blow things off now. If JW trusted that driver, she would have to too.

The agreement: just her and Stefanovic—eye to eye—in the conference room. Plus JW and the Russians as mediators.

She looked around. An oval wooden table with steel legs. White walls with framed photographs of airplanes. Spotlights in the ceiling. Typical midrange-hotel feel—Natalie'd stayed at so many different places over the past few weeks that she'd become hypersensitive to white walls and Scandinavian design.

It was dark outside. The curtains were pulled closed.

On the table: five glasses and a bottle of Absolut Vodka.

At the table: JW and two middle-aged men. The Russians.

Natalie didn't know much about the people she was meeting. But Thomas and Goran'd told her the little that they knew. And JW'd said a few words too.

Solntsevskaya Bratva: one of the most powerful syndicates. Possibly the biggest mafia in the world. Almost certainly: the most influential organization in Russia—with a global focus. Probably the most dangerous people in the world.

Goran'd told her that her dad'd maintained close relations with *avtoritety*. But it wasn't as Natalie'd originally thought—that the Russians'd contacted Dad to get help with something. It was the other way around. Dad'd contacted them many years ago with the following message: "*I've got holds on people in Sweden who may be of interest to you. I am happy to sell you information when you need it.*"

That made her proud. She felt like an equal. Her dad hadn't just been some errand boy for *avtoritety*. He'd taken the initiative, offered them something they were willing to pay for.

They introduced themselves as Vladimir Michailov and Sergey Barsykov. Responsible for Scandinavia.

They shook her hand. JW's eyes flashed.

The man who'd patted her down acted as interpreter.

Vladimir Michailov said, "Welcome. I hope vodka is all right?"

Natalie responded in Russian, "*Da.*"

They were properly dressed. But differently from JW or Gabriel Hanna—the suits the Russians wore were probably expensive, but they rocked a different style: shinier fabrics, broader shoulders, wider pants. She thought of Semjon the Wolf Averin.

Goran'd advised her to wear jewelry—a two-carat diamond in a simple setting around her neck—it'd been a twentieth birthday present from Dad. In her ears: her Tiffany's studs. On her finger: a signet ring with the Kranjic family crest engraved in it.

She hung up her coat. Under: a silk top with a dark blazer.

In the inner pocket was the comb. Thomas'd given it to her this morning. It was made of carbon fiber and was sealed inside a leather case. The thing: the handle'd been sharpened to a point. Natalie'd tested it out on a piece of paper at home—it cut like a warm knife through hair gel.

The door opened. Stefanovic walked in.

The same procedure: the interpreter guy swept the metal detector over him. Ran his hands over his body. He appeared clean: not even a cell phone.

They were beyond time and space now. They were on Russian territory. Maybe.

Vladimir Michailov welcomed Stefanovic.

He poured vodka into the glasses.

The other Russian was sitting silently, chewing gum.

Vladimir raised his glass. "*Na zdorovje.*"

They threw back the vodka.

"First of all," Vladimir said, "I want to thank Mr. J. Westlund who was able to arrange this meeting."

JW looked at Natalie. Then he looked at Stefanovic.

Vladimir went on. "Look each other in the eyes now. Because we don't want any more fighting."

Natalie looked straight across the table, met Stefanovic's gaze. It was like staring straight into the eyes of a shark.

"There are one million people I would rather look at right now," she said. "But I am doing it for your sake."

Stefanovic snorted.

In the corner of her eye: she saw Sergey Barsykov flash a quick smile, then go right on with his gum chewing.

Vladimir said, "Calm down. Let us talk instead. We're here to do business. We have cooperated with your father for years. Our cooperation has been profitable for all parties. I truly regret his fate."

He lowered his head in a respectful gesture, then said, "But life goes on. And business goes on. Our interest in the Nordic countries grows with every year. Russian industry is expanding. Our export balances are increasing. But there are a lot of prejudices against us out in the world. So we often need help in order to get a fair business relationship on its feet."

He explained for a few minutes. Told them about Nordic Pipe. The aim was to facilitate the energy supply to Central and Eastern Europe. To avoid the recurring fights with Ukraine about gas prices, fights that made the price of electricity higher for all consumers. About building two thousand miles of double pipes from Russian Viborg to German Greifswald. It was a question of nearly eight hundred miles of gas pipe running at the bottom of the Baltic Sea in order to pump more than 1,700 billion cubic feet of natural gas per year.

The numbers didn't mean much to Natalie. But one thing was clear: what they were discussing was high-level business.

"We're doing something for this country too, but not a lot of people seem to understand that. For instance, when we lay down the pipe, we're also cleaning up old mines. We've picked up more than eleven mines from the bottom of the ocean. But no one has thanked us for that."

Natalie and Stefanovic were both nodding. They hadn't come here for a lecture about the politics of natural gas.

"In order to do this," Vladimir said, "we need help. We have already passed and will need to pass through many obstacles."

The interpreter listed Swedish words. Natalie was unsure whether he knew what he was saying. Expert studies, descriptions of environmental consequences, official hearings. The Espoo Convention, county boards, the Swedish EPA, the Swedish Defense Research Institute, the Swedish Maritime Administration, and the Swedish Department of Transportation.

But this much was certain: what they had on their hands was an extremely complicated decision-making process. Many people had to be influenced and nudged in the right direction.

Natalie thought of the people she'd met over the past few months. The weapons dealer Gabriel Hanna and the woman at the Black & White Inn. Her allies, Goran, Thomas, Ivan Hasdic, and the others. She thought of the women, Melissa Cherkasova and Martina Kjellsson. And now the Russians.

So many people were mixed up in this web of business. People who saw her as a leader. Someone who was in charge. Who gave orders.

But who was she, really? She'd never dreamed of being the head of a large organization. And when she reflected, she didn't even know what she'd dreamed of being. Everything was blank—everything'd been possible. But maybe leading was what she was meant to do.

Vladimir was approaching the end of his monologue.

"We don't care who we collaborate with, as long as it goes smoothly. The recent fighting between the two of you is impeding our business. People are getting nervous. Important people don't want to accept our services or our gifts. Decisions are being delayed, which in turn delays Nordic Pipe. Your disagreement is costing a lot of money, every day."

Natalie glanced at Sergey Barsykov. He seemed to have spit out his gum.

"Now you have to agree somehow," Vladimir said. "You, Kranjic, have material that we need. And so do you, Stefanovic."

The final bit came as something of a surprise, that Stefanovic also had material. But it wasn't so strange—the bribe and blackmail work must've been happening on many fronts at once.

The Russians and JW rose. The plan was to allow Natalie and Stefanovic to discuss things on their own. How they chose to divide up the market in Stockholm was their business. Solntsevskaya Bratva would let them settle their business on their own. According to Vladimir, they had no alternatives—when they returned to the conference room in two hours, she and Stefanovic must have reached an agreement.

Natalie remained in her seat.

Stefanovic was seated across from her.

"Okay," he said. "You hear what they want. Let us talk."

Natalie fumbled in her inner pocket.

The comb was resting safely in its case.

64

Jorge didn't give a shit about the cold.

Cold didn't exist to him. Too many scars in his personal history. Too many raw memories.

Jorge: had seen most things. Dudes who'd been cut, friends on bad trips, girls who'd been fucked with a gun to their head. Stockholm's underworld: his home. His school. His day care.

But now: this was different.

Tonight—him: prepared to die.

Tonight: *You are me, and I am you. My blood cleanses us all from sin.*

His mother didn't know anything yet. Jorge'd called her—told her Paola and Jorgito'd gone away for a few days.

It was time.

He and Javier were sitting in a freshly boosted Citroën. The E20 highway southbound. On their way to Taxinge. Past Södertälje. A gravel pit.

The Finn's honcho'd informed them of the meeting place an hour ago. "Bring the money, come alone."

Jorge'd borrowed five thousand from JW yesterday. The cash was resting atop piles of fake bills that he'd cut himself. Rubber bands around them. The Finn would never fall for it—but that wasn't the point. If it worked for a few seconds, that would be enough.

Javier: not as serious. Said: "What a rescue, *huevon*. Even if they pick me up tomorrow, it was worth it."

Jorge could hardly think about what was gonna happen later. Right now it was all about the shit with the Finn.

"Why couldn't Hägerström come?" Jorge said.

Javier drummed his fingers on his knees. "He said he had to take care of his son."

Jorge thought: Hägerström was shady. Why could he come to Javier's rescue mission but not to the meeting with the Finn? Why hadn't he said anything about a kid to Jorge, while he'd told Javier he was gonna be with his son?

"He's got a kid?"

Javier nodded. "Sure. I've seen pictures of his son at his crib. His place is banging, man."

Again: the Hägerström dude was weird. Jorge could understand why he might not want to be part of this now—maybe a rescue mission with an AK-47 was enough for one day. And maybe the ex-screw really was gonna be with his son. But why'd he never mentioned the kid before? And how could he afford to live it up like that?

One more thing was itching Jorge's head. Hägerström'd brought a bunch of secret police docs to Thailand from JW. Jorge remembered how he'd opened the envelope and unfolded the documents before reading them.

Nothing strange about that—ordinarily. But a couple of days ago, Jorge'd met up with JW and handed over the six hundred large. He'd received an envelope in return. He'd opened it and peered inside. A folded piece of paper, he could see the text—the name of a bank.

JW'd said, "We'll be professional about this. You'll get invoices and information from us. Check it—we even fold the letters the real way."

Jorge had asked, "What you mean?"

JW showed him. "You always fold letters so the text is facing out."

Jorge hadn't made the connection. Until now: Hägerström must've secretly opened the envelope that JW'd sent down to Thailand, read it, and put it back. But folded the documents in a different way than JW had.

But then maybe that wasn't strange. If someone sent a secret envelope with Jorge, he would've done everything in his power to sneak a peek too.

But overall?

An ex-pig, ex-screw who'd remade himself as a G-wannabe? How likely was that?

He turned to Javier. "Fuck man, I don't trust Hägerström."

"I do. *Hombre* just rescued me twelve hours ago. What else I gotta know?"

"But he's shady, man."

"Who isn't shady?"

"He's been a cop, a screw. He turned up from nowhere down in Thailand."

"*Calmate.* I said, he freed me. And he wasn't just in Thailand for your sake. He had his own biz too."

"What biz?"

"Buying emeralds and shit."

"How do you know that?"

"He told me. He got a bunch of texts from his sis about buying stuff like that. 'Bring 'em home,' stuff like that."

They kept driving. The darkness outside: as black as Jorge's thoughts.

The underworld was not his world anymore. Paola, Jorgito—they were his world.

He just wanted to solve this shit with the Finn, then go back to Thailand. Live the café life again.

Still: that Hägerström dude was messing with his focus.

He picked up his phone.

Four signals. Then JW's voice.

"Yes, hello."

"Yo, it's me."

"Hey, I'm kind of busy right now. Everything cool?"

"No. What're you doing?"

"I'm waiting for a really important meeting to end. I'm at a hotel near Arlanda."

"Your buddy, that Hägerström guy. There's something mad wack about him."

"Why? He's here with me now."

"What did you say?"

"I said, he's here with me now. At the hotel."

Fifteen minutes later. They stopped the car.

Javier got out. Jorge's conversation with JW'd ended quickly. JW was busy. Jorge'd only had time to explain about the weird texts that Javier'd seen in Thailand.

Fuck that now. He had things to settle.

Let JW deal with his own shit.

Still: he was happy that Hägerström wasn't with them now.

He turned to Javier. "You take the forty-seven. Go up over there.

Look for the lights from this car or some other car. Find a spot where you got good eyes on me and the Finn."

Javier wasn't grinning. Was just holding the assault rifle. He understood now: shit was real. Jorge felt stiffer than stiff.

He started the car back up again. The bulletproof vest he was wearing was heavy.

He drove in through the mountains of sand.

All around him: the gravel pit. Heaps of sand, rocks, gravel. Everything covered in a white layer of powdery frost. Or maybe it was a thin layer of snow. What was the difference, anyway? Washed-out shadows. Dark boulders. Facing him: a machine, at least twenty meters high. Some kind of stone crusher.

Silence.

A lonely place.

A place where no one would see them.

A good place for the Finn.

Jorge turned the car's headlights off.

The darkness—his friend.

He remained sitting in the car. Picked up his phone. Called Javier.

Whispered: "D'you find a place?"

Lights from the road that led in toward the gravel pit. Two cars.

Jorge switched on the Citroën's high beams.

They drove in. The back car stopped at the entrance to the gravel pit. Blocked the exit.

The lead car pulled up. Stopped. Kept the lights on.

Jorge's phone rang.

A voice: "Kill your lights. Get out of the car."

Jorge opened the door. Climbed out. Was blinded by the headlights from the other car.

He squinted. Heard car doors opening.

Two men emerged.

He walked sixteen feet toward them.

One dude in a leather jacket and a black beanie.

One dude in a down jacket and a baseball cap.

They were standing thirty feet away now. It was hard to make out their faces in the strong backlight. Arms hanging down at their sides.

The baseball cap dude said, "You got the cash?"

"Yeah, you saw the pic I sent. You got my sis and the kid?"

"Yeah, yeah. They're back there, in the other car."

Silence. The baseball cap guy raised one of his arms. Jorge glimpsed the silhouette of a gun.

"Neither of you is the Finn," Jorge said. "I can hear that."

"No."

"Is he here?"

"None of your fucking business."

"No Finn, no deal."

The baseball cap guy didn't say anything.

Jorge remained silent.

Steam was billowing out of their mouths.

Finally the baseball cap guy said, "All right, the Finn's here. He's in the other car too."

Jorge said, "I want him to get out."

65

The Yugo elite and the UC elite were rubbing elbows on the sofas in the lobby of the Radisson Blu Arlandia Hotel.

Hägerström was sitting with JW in one sofa group. They were waiting for the meeting between Natalie Kranjic and Stefan Stefanovic Rudjman, taking place in one of the upstairs conference rooms, to end.

Hägerström had seen three other men come downstairs with JW—they looked like they were from Russia or Eastern Europe. They had disappeared by now. Maybe they were outside. Maybe they were sitting in some room in the hotel. He didn't know who they were.

But he knew who the rest of the dudes down here were.

Stefanovic's men were sitting on one sofa.

Kranjic's men were sitting on another sofa. Hägerström knew their names: Goran and Adam. Then a surprise: Thomas Andrén, his old friend and colleague. Hägerström had never suspected that Andrén had sunk this low.

Their eyes met. Thomas didn't give anything away, but he must have been wondering what Hägerström was doing here.

On the rest of the sofas, by the check-in counter, upstairs, outside the entrance, and in the bar: schools of civvies. Torsfjäll had promised that this would be the hit of the century. As soon as they got a green light from the other unit—who were at the gravel pit with Jorge, Javier, and the Finn—shit would go down.

JW seemed to be in a good mood. He was playing with his phone. Firing off texts, e-mailing, surfing. He answered phone calls, walked around the lobby talking on his phone out of Hägerström's earshot. He appeared indifferent to all the Yugo mafiosos sitting off time in the sofas.

Hägerström thought of Javier. He was with Jorge now. He hoped he would take it easy.

JW sat back down in the sofa. "Your sister—she's a real estate agent, right?"

"Yep."

"You got her number?" he asked. "I'd like to ask her something. I'm in the market for a place."

Hägerström wondered what JW wanted to ask Tin-Tin about right now. He hadn't said anything previously about buying an apartment. And Hägerström didn't want to get his family mixed up in this. On the other hand, JW had already been to a moose hunt with Carl.

He gave JW Tin-Tin's number.

JW typed it into his phone. Walked off a few yards.

Hägerström saw him talking on the phone.

66

Natalie and Stefanovic were talking. Back and forth.

He seemed seriously prepared to split up the Stockholm market.

"Natalie, we don't really have anything against each other. Things just turned sour after your dad was murdered. All I'm saying is that I think the work I've put in should pay off."

She listened.

"You get the coat checks," he said. "You get the speed. I won't get mixed up in any of that. I'll take the cigarettes and the booze."

They kept talking. Discussed the turnover in each industry. Discussed which men were best suited. From where they got their most stable income. Where the police were most active right now.

"We can both use Bladman's services. He doesn't have anything to do with this."

Natalie thought about JW—Bladman's crony was involved in much bigger business than Stefanovic appeared to know. He probably wouldn't be interested in Stefanovic's small-time stuff anymore.

She said, "And the material that I have, that the Russians want—which one of us will get to use that?"

Stefanovic sighed. "Your dad and I worked like maniacs on all that, believe me. We've been working this on both ends—with a carrot and with a stick, as they say. Bribes and blackmail. We've used Bladman's services to ship millions to the right guys. At the same time, we noticed that those same guys went to the right parties, met the right girls. So we set it up so that some of the girls recorded what they did with the guys. We had to have a lot of talks with those girls, let me tell you."

Natalie had already figured out what he was talking about.

"So we've got those old guys on the hook," Stefanovic went on. "They get money. The Russians make them do what the Russians want them to do. And if they start to fuss, we send them unpleasant e-mails with images and movies of seventeen-year-old Romanians licking their assholes."

"And Melissa Cherkasova?"

"No point discussing her now. That won't solve our problem, will it? If you want to go there, I can bring up how I felt when you sent me Marko's finger. We've got an hour to get somewhere. If we're going to start talking about Cherkasova, we'll both get in trouble with the Russians."

"Okay, we can let it go for now. But I won't tolerate that kind of thing going forward."

"You're at the beginning of your career. You'll see. Everything isn't that simple."

They let the subject drop. Continued discussing other business, markets, areas that were ripe for expansion. Stefanovic wanted to keep the ski jumping tower—run a legal conference business there. He thought he had good connections in the home country when it came to selling stolen Swedish electronics. He thought it was fair for him to keep running the girl business—he was the one who'd built it up, after all.

Natalie thought: *Economically speaking, this might be good.* Maybe they could actually reach an agreement. Maybe she didn't have to do what she'd come here to do.

It was obvious: it would make life easier. They would be able to work without interfering with each other. Okay, their territories would be smaller, but they would be able to focus. Develop. Increase the margins. It would send an important message to all the amateurs trying to become something in the Stockholm jungle: Kranjic is still the queen of the hill.

Then she thought: fuck me backward—I'm never going to strike a deal with this man. He killed my father.

Stefanovic kept talking. The point: the two of them were alone in the room.

Natalie: twenty-two years old. Thin. Attractive. Above all: a woman. In Stefanovic's eyes: she was anything but threatening. Her men were dangerous. Her power could be dangerous. But just her, alone—Stefanovic had watched her grow up, he had taught her how to drive. He had been her chauffeur. Her jack-of-all-trades. An older brother.

He didn't feel any fear. He felt safe with her.

Natalie rose. Took her blazer off. Rolled up the sleeves of her top.

Walked around to his side of the table.

Stefanovic looked at her.

"Listen, I think we can agree," she said. "For the Russians' sake, if nothing else. Let me look you in the eye, up close. I want to see that you're serious about this."

Stefanovic looked up at her. He smiled.

"Of course I'm serious."

Natalie pulled out the comb that she'd transferred to her back pocket. Gripped the top of it, the actual comb part.

Stefanovic looked at her. Saw that she had rolled up her sleeves. Maybe saw that she was holding something narrow, dark, plastic-looking.

He said, "What do you want?"

Natalie stabbed him in the throat with the blade of the comb.

She felt it push in, deep. Stefanovic batted his arms.

She dodged his fists.

She stabbed him again.

67

Six hundred large, that's all it was—to the Finn, it couldn't really be that much cash.

The dude didn't need to get out of the car for the money's sake. Still: the Finn fucker didn't want two innocent lives on his conscience. Above all: the Finn fucker didn't want the brass on his ass for this. A felony. Looking at alotta time.

Jorge'd counted on that: the dude would be ready to face him, just to get this shit over with.

Risky business. Dirty business. No one wanted to stay here longer than necessary.

He heard a car door slam.

Someone emerged from the back car.

Slow steps. A man. Long coat. Dark pants. No hat.

The man came closer. The backlight made Jorge's eyes sting.

He looked ordinary enough. Thin, light-colored hair. Piggy up-nose. Cloudy eyes.

Maybe thirty-five years old. Thirty feet away.

He opened his mouth, "Quit fucking around. I'll get Paola and the kid if you get the money."

Jorge recognized the voice. It was the Finn.

"Okay," he said.

Jorge turned around. Walked back to the Citroën.

Opened the back door. Checked his phone when he leaned over to get the duffel with the money and the fake bills. A text from Javier: *I see you. Waiting to see Paola and Junior.*

Good. Jorge hauled the duffel out. Retraced his steps.

The guy with the beanie and the guy with the baseball cap remained glued to their spots.

He heard a quiet voice farther off. Saw the Finn approaching. With Paola and Jorgito walking in front of him.

Junior wasn't wearing enough clothes, just a T-shirt and jeans. Fucking Finn fag.

Thirty feet between them. Paola was silent.

Jorge set the duffel down. "Here's the money."

The Finn signaled with his hand.

The guy in the baseball cap walked over to the bag. Stooped down by Jorge's feet.

Opened the bag. Jorge knew what he would see: stacks of five-hundred-kronor bills, at least on top.

The baseball cap guy didn't flip through the stacks. They'd already seen the photo Jorge'd sent with all the bills.

The dude called to the Finn, "It's green."

The Finn's quiet voice: "Good."

Jorge saw Paola and Jorgito begin to walk toward him.

Twenty-five feet.

Fifteen feet.

The baseball cap dude was still hunched over the bag. Three feet from Jorge.

Paola and Jorgito, six feet from Jorge.

He reached for his nephew.

Scooped him up in his arms. Jorgito was cold.

He began to cry.

The baseball cap guy picked up the bag. Walked back toward the Finn.

Jorge carried Junior toward the car while he pushed Paola in front of him.

The Citroën was clearly visible in the light from the other car.

A dozen or so feet left.

He heard the Finn's voice: "What the fuck is this?"

He opened the car door. Pushed Paola inside. Tried to make his body as broad as possible over Jorgito.

The Finn yelled, "You little whore! This is fucking Monopoly money!"

Noise. New lights.

The smatter of bullets.

Jorge threw himself at the car.

Sounds echoed. Everywhere.

He felt a pain in his back.

68

They had been waiting for one and a half hours now. JW said they had to be done up there within two hours.

Hägerström could feel the mood in the air. The sofa groups were vibrating with tension. Toss a match in here, and the hotel would explode like an atom bomb.

He tried to relax. JW kept running around, talking on the phone the entire time.

Hägerström's thoughts drifted off.

The floor in the kitchen at home on Banérgatan. Pravat, twelve and a half months old. They had just picked him up in northern Thailand.

Hägerström had been lying on his back. Anna was out grocery shopping.

He let Pravat climb over him. Stand up with his help. Hold on to him.

Pravat gurgled, da-da-da'ed, spoke in his own language. He was wearing learn-to-walk diapers and a striped shirt from the high-end children's store Polarn & Pyret. Hägerström felt Pravat's little hands and nails on his arms. It was one of the best sensations he knew.

He'd pushed his body carefully to the side. Pravat held on to him but was relatively stable on his feet. Hägerström pushed himself to the side a little more. Suddenly Pravat let go of him. Raised his arms straight out in the air, bent his knees, and straightened his legs. He was standing on his own. Entirely on his own.

Hägerström had cheered. Pravat laughed, almost seeming aware of his own feat. To have stood up on his own for the first time in his life.

Hägerström looked up, scanned the lobby again.

The elevator doors opened.

Natalie Kranjic walked out. She was wearing a dark coat.
She approached JW.
Hägerström heard her say, "We're done."
Movement on the sofas. Different men stood up. Looked at Natalie and JW.
Waited for signals. What would happen now?
Natalie didn't say anything more. She waved to Adam.
The beefy man walked up to her.
They strode toward the exit together.
Hägerström saw swift movements among the people in the lobby.
It was time.
He saw the civvies by the elevator take deep breaths. He thought he heard faint radio commands through hidden earpieces from the ones who were waiting outside. He smelled sweat, didn't know if it was coming from the cops or the mafiosos.
Natalie and Adam walked out through the automatic doors.
That's when everything around them exploded.

69

Natalie was done. Adam walked out through the hotel doors first.

Outside, night had fallen. There were a lot of cars to the left, in the hotel parking lot.

Adam pointed. "My car is over there."

Her hands began to shake. The effort of walking calmly through the hotel lobby backfired.

She'd inspected herself closely before she took the elevator down. Her hand and forearm were bloody, which was to be expected. She'd washed up in the restroom in the hallway outside the conference room, for probably five minutes. Scrutinized every millimeter of skin until she was completely clean of blood.

Someone would discover Stefanovic within a few minutes. Either the Russians or one of his own men. Let that be as it may. She'd avenged Dad.

She saw Adam's car: an Audi.

A man came walking toward her from the other side of the car.

Natalie stared into his eyes.

A broad face. Gray eyes. Light-brown hair.

Effortless self-confidence. A calm, relaxed gaze.

It was Semjon Averin.

He was holding something. Natalie didn't have time to see what it was.

Then: all hell broke loose around them.

She saw rapid movements out of the corner of her eye.

Heard screaming, "This is the police! Get down on the ground!"

She saw Adam stare, wide-eyed.

She saw Semjon Averin raise his arm.

70

The pain was gone now. The cold on his face, gone.
Jorge was lying flat on the ground.
He knew so many things.
He knew nothing.
He: shot in the back.
He: on his way somewhere.
He drifted off again.

You are me and I am you. My blood cleanses us all from sin.
Moments in the present once again. Too tired to open his eyes.
He heard strange noises. Faint, fuzzy sounds.
Paola oughta've made it, inside the car.
And Jorgito?
Sálvame.
He didn't know.
Couldn't take it.
He should've said good-bye to Mom.
He should've told Javier.
A life.
His life.
A life deluxe.
It felt as though he was bleeding from the mouth.
Didn't matter.
He felt calm now.
Relaxed.

EPILOGUE

(Four months later)

Hägerström was lying in his bed. It was firm, hard. He looked up at the wall.

Two photos of Pravat, secured with tape. He had taken one of them himself, in Humlegården a year ago. It was a close-up of Pravat's face, with the park in the background. Pravat had sent him the second one. At the center of the photo was a large Lego fortress with figures standing atop the wall. Pravat was posing behind the castle—proud of his fine creation.

Hägerström looked out. The prison yard was gravelly and bleak.

His trial had lasted four days, ending two weeks ago. He had been in jail until then. Now he was here, in Kumla. Compared every single detail to the Salberga Penitentiary, where he had worked. Back then he had thought things like freshly painted walls, clean showers, and a working television set were just baloney. Now he longed for a single surface that didn't feel dirty.

He hadn't fought the charges. The evidence was robust. The prison transport guards were able to identify him, and they had found gunpowder on his jacket. Still, his lawyer did a good job. The prosecutor wanted to get Hägerström convicted for attempted murder. Four shots fired with an assault rifle at the tires of a transport vehicle belonging to the Department of Corrections on the seventeenth of October last year. According to the prosecutor, fortuitous circumstance was the only thing that had prevented the loss of life. But Hägerström had been a coastal ranger, he knew how to handle assault rifles. The lawyer was able to prove that there had never been any real risk to the transport guards' lives.

He was convicted of attempted aggravated assault instead. Three years in prison.

The day after Hägerström was arrested at the Radisson Blu Arlandia Hotel, Torsfjäll had visited him in the jail cell.

The inspector had entered the cell alone. Only detectives on the case and his lawyer were actually permitted to see him, but Torsfjäll apparently had his ways.

"Good afternoon."

Hägerström greeted him. "Hi. Great that you managed to get in."

Torsfjäll remained standing. There were no chairs in the cell. Only a simple mattress on the floor.

The inspector shook Hägerström's hand. "Have they interrogated you yet?"

"Just superficially. But I haven't said anything about Operation Tide. I was waiting for you."

"Good, because there's nothing to say."

Hägerström stared at the inspector. His teeth didn't look as white as they used to.

"What the fuck made you think you could shoot at a prison transport vehicle?"

Hägerström's thoughts came to a halt. Torsfjäll was speaking in a completely different tone than usual.

"It was part of the job."

"Committing crimes like you did—that is never part of the job."

"Okay, well. What do you mean there's nothing to say about my role as a UC operative?"

"Because you've never been one. You were fired from the police force. You've been a civilian all this time."

"What the fuck are you talking about?"

"I'm talking about what we talked about the entire time—that you were fired from the police force. Isn't that right?"

"That's not what we said. I was fired formally. But I've still been on the force informally."

Torsfjäll's eyes were dead. He didn't even try to meet Hägerström's gaze.

"There is no such distinction within the police force."

Hägerström could hear his own breathing.

"That was part of the agreement, was it not?" Torsfjäll said. "You've taken risks. I'm grateful for that. But you knew what you were getting yourself into. Really, you should just be damn happy you haven't been convicted of more. Just think about it: engaging in unlawful monetary transactions, aggravated assault, harboring a fugitive. You could've gotten many more years for everything you've done."

Hägerström said, "That's highfalutin bullshit."

The inspector set a voice recorder on the table. Pressed the "play" button.

A recording. Hägerström heard his own voice midsentence. Then he heard Torsfjäll's voice: *"You are not a police officer anymore. You are a corrections officer with an assignment. You have to act on your own without immunity."*

The inspector switched off the recorder. "See, I told you you weren't a police officer any longer."

Hägerström just stared. He remembered that conversation. But at the time he had interpreted it completely differently.

"And you must understand too," Torsfjäll went on, "that if I were to admit that I had ordered this, we would never be able to carry out similar operations again. And besides, if this came out, it would ruin my career. That would be a shame."

The inspector was a sly fucker.

Hägerström had only one question left: "What happened to JW?"

Torsfjäll stood up.

"You fuck-up," he said.

Back in his cell. Hägerström had been a fool.

Yet given that he had not been a member of the police force, he had gotten off light, just as Torsfjäll said.

Hägerström could have tried to convince the police investigators that he had been a UC operative, that he had believed he was employed by the police force the entire time and had acted only according to instructions from Inspector Lennart Torsfjäll. But what were the chances that they would believe him? It would be meaningless to try to dig up e-mails or texts from Torsfjäll since his computer and phone had been confiscated. He would have deleted anything important a long time ago.

He could at least have tried to get the police investigators to understand that he had been a civilian infiltrator. But same story there. How great were the chances that they would believe him?

And he had another, more important reason to not even try. If he were to say he'd been an infiltrator, he would be taking another risk: an enormous price on his head. JW, Jorge, Javier, and the others would pay anything to see him cut down, snuffed out. Dead.

Without Torsfjäll's support to get a secure hidden identity, he would be an easy target.

It was a fucking terrible choice to make. He could say he'd been an infiltrator and maybe get away with a shorter prison sentence but live under a death threat for the rest of his life. Or he could take on the role of a criminal and live with that reputation for the rest of his life.

He concluded that it was better to keep his mouth shut. Keep on pretending. Play the part.

So he never said anything to the police.

He never explained that his criminal record had been filled with fictitious incidents.

He never told anyone that he had met Mrado Slovovic, or about all his meetings with Torsfjäll in various apartments.

He didn't even try to make them understand why he'd seen to it that those guys in the unit in Salberga were transferred, so that JW would be left alone.

He just did what Javier would have done. He squeezed his mouth shut and breathed through his nose. Didn't answer any of the police's questions.

He wondered why Torsfjäll had used and tricked him. He could come up with only one answer. The higher-ups in the force would never have greenlighted a project that used a police officer like that—so the only way to do it was to make Hägerström a civilian.

He would never be able to work as a police officer again. Nor as a corrections officer. The question was what kind of job he would be able to get. He would definitely not be granted increased custody of his son. Convicted of attempted aggravated assault—good luck.

He gazed up at the photos of Pravat again. Pravat, proud of his Lego fortress. That was all so far away right now. One day Hägerström would tell him what had really happened.

He picked up a newspaper from the table.

Unfolded it.

The centerfold was a picture of Javier, on his way into a courtroom. He was trying to hide his face with a state-issue towel.

The headline: THE LAST DAY IN THE TOMTEBODA ROBBERY TRIAL.

Hägerström didn't know what Javier thought about it all—they hadn't been able to talk. But he hoped Javier would end up in the same prison. Maybe they could make their own little life on the inside, somehow.

Hägerström was grateful for his inherited money. But would he see any more of that? Lottie wasn't happy. She was coming to visit him in two hours—he would learn more then.

Right now the minutes were dragging worse than during a hunting stand.

He tried not to wonder what his brother and sister must be thinking. Their brother, Martin, former police officer, former corrections officer, now a convicted felon. They might have been able to handle a conviction for aggravated drunk driving or some white-collar crime, but after this they would probably never speak to him again.

It was a miracle that Lottie was coming to visit at all.

An hour and forty-five minutes later: a knock on his door. A screw opened. Led him to the visiting room.

The walls were painted white. A couch with burgundy vinyl upholstery. A wooden table with two wooden chairs. A tray on the table. A couple plastic mugs, stacked inside one another, plastic spoons, a Thermos made of some kind of plastic material with hot water in it, a plastic jar of Nescafé, a box of Lipton tea bags. Nothing metal. Nothing that could be used to injure someone else, or injure the inmate himself. Standard.

The door opened.

His mother looked confused.

Lottie appeared older than when he had seen her last. Her hair was grayer, the wrinkles around her eyes deeper.

Hägerström said, "Come in."

She was wearing tan slacks and a cashmere cardigan. She had a silk scarf tied around her neck. Hägerström recognized the pattern—Hermès, of course.

She walked over to him. No kisses on the cheeks, no polite one-liners, no nice-cardigan comments. They just hugged each other. For a long time.

Hägerström breathed in her scent. Her perfume. Her hair touched his cheek.

He closed his eyes. Saw Pravat running toward her at home in her flat. How she had scooped him up, calling, "*My little golden nugget.*"

He said, "I'm sorry, Mother."

They sat down.

"Me too," Lottie said.

Hägerström had made up his mind. He was going to put all the cards on the table. Tell her the truth.

They had an hour. He spoke quickly. He told her how Torsfjäll had contacted him. How he had learned as much as possible about JW. How he had been fired from the police because of some made-up fight outside a hot dog stand. The grounds for his termination had all been fake. He explained how Torsfjäll had gotten him a position at the Salberga Penitentiary. How he had done everything to wheedle his way in, become friends with JW. How he had even brought him along on a moose hunt at Carl's place.

Lottie listened.

Hägerström tried to see if she believed him.

She didn't move a muscle.

When he was finished, he said, "You may not believe me, Mother. But I want you to contact a man named Mrado Slovocic and ask him a single question: Who did I ask him about when he was cooperating with the police?"

Lottie nodded.

She didn't say anything for a while. Then she said, "And Pravat?"

It was as though everything he had just said was insignificant—the only thing that mattered was his relationship with Pravat. In a way, it was a relief. She didn't care if he was an infiltrator or not. To her, his world was foreign no matter what. The simple fact that he had chosen to become a police officer more than fifteen years ago remained inexplicable.

"When I'm released," Hägerström said, "I'm going to buy a house in Lidingö. In the area where Anna lives. That's all I know now."

"And what else?"

Hägerström wondered what she meant. But there was one more thing he wanted to tell her now. It was time. He had promised himself. He was going to put *all* the cards on the table.

"There's one more thing I want to tell you, Mother."

She played with her scarf. Lowered her gaze.

Hägerström thought of the J. A. G. Acke paintings hanging in her home. The three young naked men standing on a cliff in the middle of the ocean.

"I am homosexual."

Lottie looked up.

"Martin." Pause. "I've known that for twenty years."

The police'd tried to interrogate her to pieces.

"What were you doing at the hotel?"

"What were you doing in the conference room?"

"Who else was there with you?"

"Did you see anything happen to Stefanovic?"

She had answered evasively throughout, insinuated that someone else'd murdered him. The cops weren't idiots—they sensed intuitively that she was lying, but they couldn't know about what.

She was held in custody for three months. Finally they were forced to let her go.

She'd been in the conference room. But so had JW and three unknown Russian men. There was no way to prove that she, specifically, had been the one who murdered Stefanovic—there were no DNA traces or fingerprints on the weapon, she'd wiped it meticulously. There were no traces on her person. None of the men who'd been down in the lobby would talk to the police—general praxis according to their code of honor. And above all: the Russians were gone—they were suitable as perps.

She was sitting in the library, waiting for a meeting to begin.

She didn't think about Dad as much anymore. She didn't see Melissa Cherkasova's face as often when she was about to fall asleep.

She'd done the only thing that was possible to do. Punished the one who had to be punished.

Stefanovic'd looked surprised, there in the conference room, when she stabbed him the first time. Then he'd been seized with panic.

The filed comb handle sank in so easily. She needed only one more jab in order to be on the safe side. She waited for a few minutes after he'd collapsed. There was blood all over the floor.

No one outside the room appeared to've reacted. The men were all sitting one flight down, waiting.

And then, in the parking lot, she'd met Semjon Averin eye to eye.

But her blessing in disguise: the police crackdown'd exploded around her.

Natalie'd had to spend three months behind bars because the hotel was rammed chock-full of cops. Still, she thanked them—if they hadn't been there, she would've ended up like Dad. The Wolf Averin would've shot her in the head from a distance of less than fifteen feet.

They arrested JW and his driver, Hägerström. They arrested several of the men, both hers and Stefanovic's. They didn't manage to arrest the Russians or the interpreter. And they didn't manage to arrest Averin. They must've been surprised when he showed up, or else they never even discovered that he was there.

She didn't know.

She leaned back in the armchair. On the drink table were bottles of Johnnie Walker Blue Label, Glenfiddich, vodka, gin, Coca-Cola, and tonic water.

She poured a glass of Blue Label.

They ought to be here in ten minutes.

She thought about JW.

There must've been a leak somewhere. Why else'd all the cops been there? Maybe it was that driver, Hägerström. Jorge, JW's buddy, had called JW in the lobby. Started talking about how he shouldn't trust him.

JW'd called about a few things, like that stuff with Hägerström's sister. What Jorge'd said checked out—Hägerström'd lied about some weird stuff. JW was paranoid as usual—didn't take any risks. He'd called Mischa Bladman immediately.

Which was the right thing to do. Twenty minutes after the hit against the Radisson Blu Arlandia, the police had arrived at the doorstep of MB Accounting Consultant's offices. Apparently they also knew the location of its secret office.

More than fifteen police officers stormed in, pushed Bladman up against the wall. Searched the office and the extra office with a magnifying glass.

But they didn't find anything.

Bladman was a hero. In no time, he and a couple of assistants'd deleted the hard drives, made sure the most important binders disappeared, and emptied out the archives in the office and the bookshelves in the secret office. They'd gotten rid of all material that might serve as evidence.

JW was released from custody at the same time she was. Free as a bird.

He'd called her and told her the story. The white-collar cops had a lot of material, but his name, account, or signature didn't appear anywhere. The front man, Hansén, had done a thorough job. And Bladman'd acted with extreme speed.

And now JW was abroad somewhere. Letting things cool down.

Right now there were just a few too many people who were pissed off here at home.

Eighty lost millions had a tendency to create some frustration.

But he would come back—he'd promised Natalie he would.

She longed for him.

The door to the library opened.

Goran stepped inside.

They kissed each other on the cheeks.

Natalie poured a glass of whiskey for him. He sat down.

"The others are coming, any minute now."

"Good."

He said, "Ivan Hasdic's guy called. They're sending gear up tomorrow. It should be here on Thursday."

Natalie took a sip of her whiskey.

"Good," she repeated.

They sat in silence for a little while.

Goran said, "And I had Darko have a talk with your ex, Viktor."

"And what did he say?"

"Darko had to explain things to him, be very clear. But now they've reached an agreement, and he understands the consequences. He's not going to do anything that disappoints anyone."

Natalie leaned back. "Good," she said for the third time. She knew that JW would be pleased.

The library'd turned out nice. She'd put up new wallpaper. Pale green instead of the former dark color. New bookshelves along the walls—lighter, with square compartments for the books. She'd let the paintings remain. Europe and the Balkans. The Danube. The battle of Kosovo Polje. The portraits of the old holy guys. The maps of Serbia and Montenegro.

But she'd also hung a new painting: a framed, engraved map of Stockholm, dated 1803.

The city had been significantly smaller back then. The Old Town, the northern parts, Södermalm, and certain parts of Norrmalm'd been developed. Back then, everything else had been a vegetable garden.

Stockholm: it was her territory now. Her business.

She used to wonder who she was. Was she a girl who'd been forced to grow up too quickly? Was she a woman who'd taken on her rightful role in life? Was she a student or a criminal? Serb or Swede?

Now she knew who she was—she was a Stockholmer. One hundred percent.

She was Natalie Kranjic. Radovan Kranjic's daughter.

She was the new Kum.

She was Queen of Stockholm.

It oughta be here in ten minutes. He knew how it usually worked. The court faxed the verdict to the office in the jail. The office in the jail sent a messenger up to the unit. Someone in the unit delivered it to the prisoner.

The trial'd taken four weeks.

Him, Javier, Babak, Robert, and Sergio. And the Finn. Lined up next to their lawyers in the Stockholm District Court's security room.

The media were there for the first few days, behind Plexiglas. They lost interest when the long cross-examinations began.

The charges were complicated. Basically, the prosecutor wanted to nail them, hard.

* * *

On June 6 of this year, Jorge Salinas Barrio, Javier Fernández, Babak Behrang, Robert Progat, and Sergio Salinas Morena, together and in collaboration with others, with the use of violence and the threat of violence that the plaintiffs perceived as dangerous, unlawfully stole a number of so-called security bags containing cash and lottery tickets that, all together, equaled a value totaling 4,231,432 kronor (of which 2,560,300 was in cash), and in connection with this act, intentionally injured the guard Suleyman Basak seriously by detonating explosives in his vicinity.

Anders "The Finn" Ohlsson instigated and controlled the abovementioned offenses by ordering the robbery and instructing the perpetrators.

* * *

Additional charges were added because of the cabbie who'd had a fake gat pressed against his temple when Jorge fled through the city, and because of the Javier rescue mission. Where Hägerström'd been involved too.

In her closing arguments, the prosecutor'd recommended that Javier, Babak, and Sergio be sentenced to eight years.

She'd recommended twelve for Jorge.

Honestly, Jorge was sorry the guard'd been blinded and was wheelchair bound. But fuck, that hadn't been on purpose—it had been the Finn's fault, his shitty planning. And the cabbie—he'd never been in any real danger. It had just been an airsoft gun. 'Course, he hadn't known that.

The prosecutor and the lawyers'd been warring like maniacs.

The DNA evidence: palm grease from Jorge in the Range Rover.

Strands of Babak's hair in an apartment where a walkie-talkie'd also been found.

Sergio's skin cells inside a found ski mask.

Strange texts on Robert's cell phone.

Maps of the Klarastrand highway found on the hard drive in Javier's home computer.

And why had most of them left Sweden in the days immediately following the robbery?

There was no so-called direct evidence against any of them.

But the pattern, the connections, the bad explanations. Still, the prosecutor needed more robust evidence. And to provide it, there was nothing better than witnesses. She had a trump card there, unfortunately—they called in that Viktor fucker. The dude'd babbled like a greenhorn in the police interrogations. His words on the witness stand could get them all convicted.

Jorge's lawyer told them that both Babak and Sergio were screwed. For Jorge, it was fifty-fifty.

A lot depended on what Viktor would say in his witness testimony.

And for the Finn: the prosecutor referred to a dyed bill that'd been found in one of the pizzerias he ran—it was weaker than weak. But no matter what, the dude would still get convicted for the shots against Jorge, Jorgito, and Paola. Attempted murder—that was enough to put him away for at least eight years.

Jorge thought of the gravel pit.

He'd survived: opened his eyes in the ICU at Huddinge Hospital. Thanked God he'd been wearing a bulletproof vest. His kidneys and liver'd made it through, even though two bullets'd burrowed into his back.

Whatever the verdict was, no matter how many years he got—he was an intact human being.

Paola'd made it into the car, thrown herself inside.

And Jorgito'd been shielded by Jorge's body.

They were alive.

Jorge's plan was clear. If he was freed, he'd bounce. Maybe to some other, bigger place than Thailand. The cops knew he'd been there. Somehow they also knew he'd wanted to buy a place there. Maybe that Hägerström dude'd snitched.

But still, not.

The guy'd apparently been slammed with three years for freeing Javier.

Also: if the guy'd been a rat, he would've told the cops what Jorge'd done during that rescue mission. But not a word from Hägerström. So weirdly enough: thanks to the ex-screw, Jorge'd probably walk on that charge.

In the courtroom the other day, Javier'd whispered something strange to Jorge: "If I'm convicted, I'm gonna try to end up in the same cage as Martin. And if I walk, I'm gonna visit him right away."

It was weird. Jorge glanced down at the documents in front of Javier.

He'd been doodling. Drawn stick figures and old tags. But one other thing—in the margin, Javier'd written: *Martin*.

They were better bros than Jorge'd realized. Much better.

Jorge thought about the conversation he'd just had over the jailhouse phone.

He remembered the number by heart: the dreadlock chick he'd met in Phuket and at Arlanda.

The phone signals sounded different than in Sweden.

Then he heard her voice.

"Hi, this is Sara."

"Hey, my name's Jorge. Last time we met was at Arlanda, I don't know if you remember me."

For some reason he had butterflies in his stomach. Not in the usual, bad way. This was different.

"'Course I do. I was just thinking about you. Where in the world are you?"

"I don't know yet. You?"

"Indonesia. Why don't you come here?"

"That'd be sweet. I'm just waiting to hear about a thing. A real important thing I gotta know first."

* * *

STOCKHOLM'S DISTRICT COURT

VERDICT CASE NUMBER 931-11

Unit 55

PARTIES

Prosecutor
Chief Prosecutor Birgitta Söderström
City Prosecutor's Office of Stockholm

Plaintiff
Security Guard Suleyman Basak
Gröndalsvägen 172
117 69 Stockholm
Security Guard Peter Lindström
Pilbågsvägen 3
184 60 Åkersberga
Security Guard Johan Carlén
Backluravägen 29C
149 43 Nynäshamn
Taxi Driver Pabli Gomez
Bredängsvägen 200
127 32 Skärholmen
Police Officer Olof Johansson
Tätorpsvägen 54
128 31 Skarpnäck

Defendant (number of defendants: 6)
Jorge Salinas Barrio
The Kronoberg Jail

EXPLANATION OF VERDICT (A SELECTION)
Regarding Jorge Salinas Barrio, the prosecutor has relied on circumstantial evidence. Above all, that Jorge Salinas Barrio is a close friend of several of the co-defendants, that he left Sweden after the robbery, and the fact that a certain receipt was found in his apartment. The prosecutor has also relied on testimony from the witness Viktor (confidential).

First of all, the District Court notes that the circumstance that Jorge Salinas Barrio is a close friend of several of the co-defendants is not in and of itself a circumstance with particularly high probative value with regard to his involvement in the Tomteboda robbery in any of the ways which the prosecutor has claimed.

The fact that he left Sweden shortly after the robbery took place is of course a circumstance that may suggest that he wanted to flee the country because he had partaken in the robbery. However, no certain conclusion can be drawn that this is in fact the case. Therefore, this circumstance also does not have significant probative value.

The piece of evidence that is of most interest is the receipt from the ICA grocery store in the Sollentuna Mall for thirty rolls of aluminum foil that was found in Jorge Salinas Barrio's apartment along with DNA traces that were found in the burned-out Range Rover, which was used to force open the gates at Tomteboda at the time of the robbery. Fingerprints from Babak Behrang and Sergio Salinas Morena were found in the same vehicle.

To begin with, the District Court wishes to remind the jury of the evidentiary standard in a criminal case. In order to be able to convict a defendant, the prosecutor must prove beyond a reasonable doubt that the events took place in the way that the prosecution claims in its indictment. The duty of satisfying the requisite standard of proof rests solely with the prosecutor.

The fact that a receipt for aluminum foil was found in Jorge Salinas Barrio's home is very troubling for him. He has told the District Court that he thinks the receipt ended up at his apartment when a friend, whom he does not want to name, was at his house for a party. Fingerprints have been found on the receipt, but they do not match Jorge Salinas Barrio's fingerprints. It should be added that, according to the prosecutor, Jorge Salinas Barrio is also a close friend of several of the co-defendants. Even though Jorge Salinas Barrio's explanation may appear to have been invented after the fact, primarily because he does not wish to disclose his friend's name, the District Court cannot rule out this alternate theory of what happened.

The same conclusion applies regarding the DNA traces from him that were found in the Range Rover. Jorge Salinas Barrio has confirmed that he is close friends with, among others, Babak Behrang, and that he borrowed his car for his café business. This is also supported by a number of witness testimonies. The District Court cannot rule out that the events unfolded in the manner he claims.

The District Court now moves on to evaluate the witness, Viktor. The witness gave, in the District Court, a completely different testimony than the statement he gave during the police interrogation, to which the prosecutor has referred. During the police interrogation, he said, among other things, that he was involved during an early stage of the planning of the robbery, and that Jorge Salinas Barrio was the one in charge of the robbers. The prosecutor has requested that this testimony be used, rather than his later testimony that was made under oath in court. The reason is that Viktor may have been subjected to external pressures, in the form of threats or force, to recant his testimony. However, the prosecutor has not been able to establish who could have threatened or forced Viktor to change his testimony in court. No other evidence has been provided to support the prosecutor's assertion.

The statements that Viktor gave during the police interrogation and in the District Court are conflicting. They are also, in many respects, impossible to verify. When it comes to the aspects that can be supported, however, parts of both testimonies diverge from the other available evidence.

In view of the above, and in adherence to the strict evidentiary standard applicable in criminal cases, the overall circumstances of the case—even though they are very troublesome for Jorge Salinas Barrio—are not sufficient to support the charges beyond a reasonable doubt.

The charge against Jorge Salinas Barrio for aggravated robbery shall therefore be dismissed. The charges for aggravated assault and attempted aggrevated assault during the mission to free Javier Fernández shall also be dismissed. He shall be convincted only of aggravated assault of the taxi driver Pablo Gomez.

This court holds that the defendant is guilty of aggravated assault of the taxi driver Pablo Gomez, assaulting an officer (Olof Johansson), as well as criminal damage, and shall be sentenced to one year in prison. Including the four months already served in jail, and the option to be released on parole after serving two-thirds of the sentence, Jorge Salinas Barrio will serve a total of four further months in prison.

HOW TO APPEAL, see attachment (DV400)

*

I was sitting on the front step of my bungalow. A pineapple cocktail in hand. A folded Izvestiya *on the table next to me.*

The ocean was bluer than usual. As though, today, the water were coloring the sky and not the other way around.

My woman was somewhere, I didn't know exactly where. She said she was going to visit her sister on the other side of the island. But I followed her once when she said the same thing. She went to see a British man who lives a mile farther down the beach.

I was starting to get restless. Four months in a row on this island was too much for me. I used to say that I loved boredom, but maybe that was just an excuse to do what I do.

But now I was forced to wait for the circus over in Sweden to settle down.

I didn't want to be in contact with anyone who might connect me to that situation. I didn't want to be reminded.

Still, my client'd called me about a month ago.

We'd never spoken directly before. Only communicated through middlemen. It didn't bode well.

His voice sounded relatively calm. A clear Swedish accent.

He said, "The mission is over now."

"Of course the mission is over," I said. "I don't want to set foot in Sweden again for at least five years."

"I hope you won't need to."

I didn't want to have this kind of conversation. My assignments were business transactions. There was never any personal spice to them.

He went on anyway. "For me, personally, it feels finished. I know her now. I know that she's suffered in the same way that I've suffered."

I took a sip of my drink. "Was there anything in particular you wanted to say?"

"No, just that it's over now."

"But you've already said that."

"They murdered my sister eight years ago. You took care of the one who was responsible for that in the explosion. And his daughter took care of the other responsible party. And she will always sleep as poorly as I do."

"You're right. There's been enough killing. No more killing will be necessary. Now you never have to think about this ever again."

The man on the other end of the line seemed absorbed in thought.

I said, "It's over now. You can move on now."

"Maybe."

"I promise. It's over."

We ended the conversation.

I finished my drink.

Stood up, brought the newspaper with me, and went into the bungalow.

It was too hot outside.

A Note About the Author

Jens Lapidus is a criminal defense lawyer who represents some of Sweden's most notorious underworld criminals. He lives in Stockholm with his wife.

A Note About the Translator

Astri von Arbin Ahlander is a writer and translator from Stockholm. She cofounded the interview project The Days of Yore (www.thedaysofyore.com) and is the managing director of the literary agency Ahlander Agency. She previously translated the first two books in the Stockholm Noir Trilogy, *Easy Money* and *Never Screw Up*.